MW00512813

THE KING'S TEST

JUMPSTART DUCHY
BOOK 5

STEFON MEARS

Thousand
Faces
Publishing

Also by Stefon Mears

The Rise of Magic Series
Magician's Choice
Sleight of Mind
Lunar Alchemy
Three Fae Monte
The Sphinx Principle
Double Backed Magic
Mercury Fold (coming soon)

Cavan Oltblood Series
Half a Wizard
The Ice Dagger
Spells of Undeath

Power City Tales
Not Quite Bulletproof
No Money in Heroism

Standalones
Between the Cracks
Sects and the City
Prince of a Thousand Worlds
Devil's Night
Portal-Land, Oregon
Stealing from Pirates
Fade to Gold
With a Broken Sword
Twice Against the Dragon
The House on Cedar Street
Sudden Death
On the Edge of Faerie

Spells for Hire Series
Devil's Shoestring
Zombie Powder
Spirit Trap
Dragon's Blood

The Telepath Trilogy
Surviving Telepathy
Immoral Telepathy
Targeting Telepathy

Edge of Humanity Series
Caught Between Monsters
Hunting Monsters

Jumpstart Duchy Series
Into the Torn Kingdoms
The Dragon's Gold
The Gift Castle
The Deadly Feast
The King's Test
Triumph in the Torn Kingdoms

Short Story Collections
Spell Slingers
Twisted Timelines
Longhairs and Short Tales: A Collection of Cat Stories
Confronting Legends (Spells & Swords Vol. 1)
The Patreon Collection, Vol. 1-8 (Vol. 9, coming soon)

Nonfiction
The 30-Day Novel and Beyond!

Published by Thousand Faces Publishing, Portland, Oregon

http://1kfaces.com

Copyright © 2022 by Stefon Mears

Front cover image © Marin Iurii | Dreamstime.com (File ID: 193867781)

Hardback ISBN: 978-1-948490-47-4

Paperback ISBN: 978-1-948490-40-5

THE KING'S TEST

FOREWORD

The man known as Aefric Brightstaff was not born on Qorunn. He was born on the distant world of Earth, where he went by the name Keifer McShane.

On Earth, he knew the world of Qorunn only through *The Torn Kingdoms*, the setting of his favorite roleplaying game. His primary source of joy and solace, following the untimely death of his wife, Andi.

When a Jumpstart crowdfunding campaign for the next edition of *The Torn Kingdoms* offered him the chance to become a duke in the world he loved, Keifer pounced on it. Imagined they would send him a patent of nobility. Ask his opinion about the non-player character who'd bear his name and title. Perhaps even allow him to include Andi as his duchess, when the books went to print.

He couldn't wait to become a part of the world he loved so well.

But he mistook it all for make-believe.

Keifer didn't expect the great Mage of Marrisford himself, the one and only Kainemorton, to show up on his doorstep.

Keifer didn't expect to be transported to Qorunn, where he would start life anew as an orphan boy on the streets of the fabled city of Sartis. That shining beacon on the southern sea.

Now known as Aefric, he grew into a powerful adventurer. Widely believed to be a wizard, he is in fact the first of the dweomerblood. It is said that magic itself flows through his very veins.

As Aefric, he mastered the fabled Brightstaff. He fought in the Godswalk Wars, and saved countless lives at the Battle of Deepwater, in the kingdom of Armyr.

In gratitude, King Colm of Armyr named Aefric Duke of Deepwater. And no sooner had Aefric taken possession of his duchy than he prevented an invasion by Armyr's southern neighbor, Malimfar.

Since then, he has worked to unite his vassals. To heal his lands and his peoples from the damage done by the Godswalk Wars. To fight off assassins, slavers and smugglers. To deal with foreign intrigues and the influence of the pirate queen, Nelazzi.

All while being pressured to marry, and sire an heir who will one day inherit his duchy...

Keifer McShane. Aefric Brightstaff.

One man who has lived two lives.

This is book five of his story...

PROLOGUE

THE DUCAL STABLES AT WATER'S END WERE ABUZZ WITH LAST-MINUTE activity. Grooms and pages running every which way. Fastening this and attending to that. Shouting to each other in some kind of shorthand. Making sure that nothing was forgotten.

Aefric Brightstaff was getting used to the fact that travel now meant causing a great deal of fuss. But he was still adjusting to the sheer volume of bustle and noise involved.

He'd been in quieter taverns during harvest festivals, back in his adventuring days.

Of course, no tavern would be this busy at this hour. The early autumn skies were only just starting to lighten toward gray. And Aefric wondered a little if the grooms and pages kept up their wicked pace just to drive away the predawn chill.

He knew better, though. He had a schedule to keep, and everyone around him was just doing their best to help him keep it. To make sure that Ser Aefric Brightstaff, Duke of Deepwater and Baron of Netar, had all of his people and horses ready to board their ship with the morning tide.

All of his people and horses. This was a relatively small entourage for

him, these days. A half-dozen knights — his Knights of the Lake—
and the two dozen soldiers of his personal guard. Plus a modest
number of support staff...

...somewhere around here, anyway. Aefric didn't see their carts,
but he was sure that Ser Beornric Ol'Sandallas — his knight-adviser
and the captain of his personal guard — had it all under control.

Beornric had been a knight about as long as Aefric had been alive
— some twenty-five summers. And Beornric knew well enough how
to handle last-minute preparations for a ride that would take more
than an aett.

Eight days or so for Aefric to get to the royal capital at Armityr.
Then likely one night at Armityr, and on to Aefric's new barony.

Netar.

And it was Netar Aefric thought about that chill autumn morning. With the smell of hay and horses filling his nostrils.

King Colm could have given Aefric anything as a show of gratitude after Frozen Ridge. Ships. Money. Jewelry. Anything, really. But
he'd chosen to give Aefric another title. More land. A barony.

He'd given Aefric Netar.

Which begged the question. Why Netar?

It was of about average size, as baronies go. Some fifty miles long,
and bounded by the Maiden's Blood River on the west and the
kingdom of Rethneryl on the east. Major exports were iron and steel.
Very deep mines, from what his seneschal had told him.

His Keifer McShane memories of *Torn Kingdoms* sourcebooks and
adventures weren't much help here. Netar was hardly a footnote in
the sourcebooks. And the only adventure that featured it — was it *I17
From Beneath the Mines?* — was one of the few Keifer had never
played.

So what was it about this particular stretch of land? Why did the
king choose *this* barony for Aefric?

Because it was close to the capital, instead of a full aett's ride away,
like Water's End? Was he hoping to have Aefric closer at hand?

Was it the value of those iron mines? A gift of wealth for a duke
who, to be honest, already had a great deal?

Or was there something about Netar itself, that the king wanted Aefric to deal with personally? A problem, perhaps? Something brought up by the Godswalk Wars? Or some strange magic?

Or was there another reason entirely?

Why Netar?

1

When last Aefric Brightstaff had come to Armityr, he had found a city in pain.

The Godswalk Wars had used it hard. The walls that surrounded the city had doubtless looked impregnable in their day. Fully seventy feet high, twenty feet thick, and made from strong, white and gray stone.

But those walls had been broken through in at least four places.

Broken through. By might or by magic. Either way, a great deal of effort.

There must've been quite a siege.

And the invaders had not been kind, once they'd gotten inside. Whole sections of Armityr had been burnt away, or trampled, or simply sunk into the ground.

At least a third of the surviving populace had been reduced to living in tents and camps while working feverishly to rebuild what they could, of what they'd lost.

And the royal palace. Oh, that poor palace. The first truly great construction built entirely by human hands anywhere on Qorunn. It predated the kingdom of Armyr itself by *thousands* of years, and likely held at least one secret for each year.

That palace had been glorious, once upon a time. All that white and gray stone. Fitted together so tightly there'd been no need for mortar. The mighty keep. The battlements. The towers.

Aefric had never seen it that way. He's seen it with whole sections collapsed, to say nothing of its towers.

Aefric recalled —from his reading of *Torn Kingdoms* game books back on Earth as Keifer McShane — that the royal palace at Armityr once boasted as many as six tall towers, reaching more than two hundred feet into the sky.

True, smaller than Aefric's ducal castle, the Castle at Water's End. But what wasn't?

Still. Six tall towers.

Only two of those towers still stood this past spring, when Aefric had been named Duke of Deepwater by King Colm Stronghand.

And one of those towers had leaned badly. Like a staggered warrior, struggling to keep its feet in the heat of battle.

So much damage to such a famous castle. Not just one of Armyr's shining gems, either, but home to the royal family.

Nevertheless, King Colm had permitted only minimal work on the palace itself.

He'd insisted that restoring the city came first.

More than a season and a half had passed since then. They were now two aetts into autumn. The rains would soon be coming in earnest, making construction more difficult.

Aefric found himself caught between eagerness to see how well repairs were coming along, and reminding himself that, most likely, they still had a long way to go.

The eagerness was winning. Had been, since he'd crossed the borders of his duchy into the royal lands only a few days ago, riding the wide, smooth Kingsroad through rolling hills and farmland.

Now Aefric's pulse began to quicken. He and his entourage were nearing the end of this leg of his journey. The final waypoint, River-keep, now coming into view as the late afternoon sunlight at his back bled its way to orange.

Riverkeep. A squat, bulky gray stone keep. More than big enough to house a hundred soldiers, plus all their support staff and such.

Within Riverkeep's wide, hexagonal outer walls, that "support staff" had practically formed a small town. Smiths and wrights and other crafters, as well as a handful of farms and plenty of livestock. When Aefric had ridden through last spring, he'd even seen children inside those walls.

Anyone trying to lay siege to Riverkeep would have trouble waiting them out.

Trouble surviving that wait, too. Every hard point of Riverkeep's outer walls featured ballistae. And the keep itself maintained at least four impressive catapults on its roof.

A single keep, controlling access to both the Maiden's Blood River, and the Kingsroad. With walls extending into the wide river itself a good dozen feet. And between their ends hung chain nets could be raised to close the river. Chain nets thick and heavy enough to stop a warship.

And the Kingsroad, of course, passed right under the keep itself. Through a tunnel filled with portcullises and hundreds of murder holes, and across a drawbridge entirely inside those outer walls.

And yet, Riverkeep had been ignored during the Godswalk Wars. The borog armies spurred on by that fell god, Xazik the Flayer, had tunneled their way under the Maiden's Blood instead.

What a thing to contemplate. Tunneling their way under such a wide, deep river. Had that been easier or harder for them than breaking through Armityr's walls?

If it were harder, why go to so much effort instead of assaulting Riverkeep? If it were easier, why break down the walls at Armityr? Why not tunnel under them?

There was a point of strategy missing here somewhere.

Could it be that Armityr had been assaulted by something other than the Flayer's borog armies?

Aefric had never stopped to consider that before. Certainly he hadn't been anywhere nearby during the siege of Armityr.

In fact, he wasn't sure where he'd been at the time. He'd rushed about so much during the wars...

Riverkeep's gates stood wide open as Aefric and his entourage approached.

At last. He was almost there.

But between Aefric and those gates, a line. At least three long merchant caravans ahead of Aefric, and one of them looked to be hauling nothing but dark gray stone. No way their poor horses could get their loads moving quickly again, when the time came.

This would not be a short wait.

Frustration knotted muscles in Aefric's shoulders and jaw. He was so close to a true stopping point, only to be delayed here, while the sun was beginning to set behind him.

A *full aett's ride* to get this far, from Water's End.

A full aett. When he was adventuring, even ahorse he could have made this ride in six days. Four or five, it he rode his phantasmal *magaunt* instead of a mortal horse.

Of course, this trip would have been worse with a *full* entourage, instead of this relatively small traveling company of his Knights of the Lake — seven of those, if he included their captain, Ser Beornric — plus the twenty-four soldiers of his personal guard, and no more than another score or so of support personnel.

And all of them riding, either on horseback or in carts. So there'd been no slowing down for marchers.

Still. Eight days. And now, stalled. With Armityr so close that Aefric could just make out the shape of those white and gray walls in the distance, past the hexagonal gray stone of Riverkeep's walls.

He turned to grouse to Beornric about the wait — one advantage of having a knight-adviser was that Aefric had someone to complain to at moments like this — but Beornric wasn't there. Just an empty space between Aefric and his left-flank guard, Ser Vria Aldellac.

Vria was the smallest of Aefric's knights, with her fine-boned eldrani heritage. And woe betide any foe who mistook her beauty for weakness.

"Ser Beornric is still settling that matter between the cooks, your grace."

"Still?" Aefric asked. He knew that some people didn't travel well together, but this was the third time in the last four days Beornric had needed to settle some dispute between those two.

This time he'd been gone at least half an hour. Just how much trouble could there be?

As if hearing his cue, Beornric came riding up on his heavy black destrier. And he needed a big horse, for Beornric was a big man. Still heavily muscled, despite the sprinkling of gray among his black hair and bushy mustache.

"If I have to talk to those two again," Beornric growled, then trailed off as he seemed to realize that everyone else was standing still.

"Ah, Beornric," Aefric said, with a bitter smile. "I look forward to hearing all about this trouble between the cooks. We must have something to fill this wait."

"Wait?" Beornric said, frowning at Vria and then at heavily scarred Ser Wardius, who was riding guard on Aefric's right flank. "If this ever happens again, whistle the blockage."

He turned to Aefric. "I apologize for the delay, your grace. I'll just see about this *wait*."

Before Aefric could respond, Beornric had called one of the standard bearers to join him, and took off along the line, bound for the gates.

Aefric turned to Vria. "Whistle the blockage?"

"Standard military procedure, your grace," Vria said, looking a little chagrined. "Sometimes a force is moving and finds it way unexpectedly blocked. Such as when a bridge has been washed out, or a mountain pass destroyed by an avalanche. There's a whistle to send word back down the line so the commanders can adjust."

Beornric didn't need long to return. And he didn't return alone, but accompanied by six soldiers wearing the king's livery.

"As I thought," Beornric said, smiling in satisfaction and resuming his place beside Aefric, while Riverkeep's soldiers spread out around

Aefric's procession. "As his majesty is expecting your grace, Riverkeep had standing orders to keep us from waiting in line."

One of Riverkeep's soldiers whistled the ride, and Aefric's procession began to move again, just to one side of the line and straight for the gates.

Well, perhaps there were *some* advantages to traveling as a duke...

AEFRIC DIDN'T JUST GET TO SKIP THE LINE. SPACE WAS CLEARED FOR HIS entourage all the way through Riverkeep. With the king's soldiers guiding, they moved swiftly across the bridge, through the tunnel, and out the other side.

It all happened so rapidly that Aefric didn't have time to wonder what the soldiers had been searching for in those stalled caravans.

He was riding the Kingsroad again, with the sunlight dying at his back, and the shadows of Riverkeep stretching across a series of merchant encampments outside the gates of Armityr itself. The merchants and their workers were already lighting torches and lanterns — some of the wealthier among them bringing out enchanted lightstones — to chase away those shadows.

Those encampments were no haphazard collection of tents and pavilions, either. They looked like a temporary town unto themselves, stretching between Riverkeep and Armityr and split down the middle by the Kingsroad.

The smell of canvas and horses, of cook fires and ... was that blacksmith coke? Certainly it would explain the metal-on-metal ringing that underlay some of the hammering.

This temporary town was a busy place, and not just with work. Aefric could hear music and laughter as well.

The layout looked to be organized into two sections. The first bringing building supplies to Armityr — such as that dark gray stone Aefric had spotted among the caravans held up at Riverkeep — and the second supplying the first with whatever they needed in their camps.

Now that was odd. As though the merchants themselves weren't being allowed into Armityr...

Wait.

The city gates were closed.

The Kingsroad gates into Armityr, huge, heavy things of spell-hardened and iron-banded oak, sat closed and guarded by a score of soldiers in the king's livery. Each of them bearing pikes.

Looked as though all damage to the west side of those high, strong white and gray stone walls had been fully repaired. And soldiers patrolled them once more.

Clearly they were expecting some kind of problem. Still. Closing the city gates before full dark?

Aefric might've been troubled by this, but his guiding soldiers weren't. They just blew trumpets to clear traffic from the Kingsroad and led Aefric straight to the gates.

The pikemen held firm.

Aefric looked to Beornric, who usually spoke for Aefric in situations like these. Beornric nodded, and drew breath to bellow out a greeting.

Before he could, someone called down from the wall.

"By those banners, may I presume I have the honor of addressing his grace, the Duke of Deepwater?"

"You do," Beornric answered. "Who calls?"

"I am Ser Osvalt Ol'Nicnorra."

Aefric spotted the speaker then. An older knight, up on the wall, leaning with one hand on a crenellation.

"I must apologize," Ser Osvalt continued, "but by order of the king, the Kingsroad Gate is to be closed before sunset, and remain closed until morning. I have been instructed to ask your grace to proceed to the southern gate, where he will be admitted at once and escorted to their majesties' presence."

Aefric gave Beornric a nod.

"Very well," Beornric called back. "Thank you, Ser Osvalt."

Osvalt bowed to Aefric, but didn't seem to expect a response. The king's soldiers led Aefric and his company south around the city walls.

The city walls looked to be in good shape. Which made sense, if they intended to keep anyone out.

"Southern gate?" Beornric asked, as they rode. "Armityr didn't used to have a southern gate."

"It's one of the spots where the walls were broken through, during the wars," Aefric said. "It was being built when Faenella and I left after my installment ceremony. I had the impression it was added to ease bringing in wood from the forest to the south."

"It'll also give Malimfar and Caiperas an easier place to break through, if they invade."

"Almost verbatim what Faenella said," Aefric said, chuckling. Faenella Darkwalker was another former adventurer, raised up by King Colm to hold the county of Fyretti, in Aefric's duchy.

She was also of the Order of Blessed Knights. As devout as she was deadly.

"Not surprised," Beornric said. "By reputation she has a good military mind."

Sure enough, there were encampments around the southern gate as well. Smaller, though, and most of them looked to involve timber. And all lit up the growing twilight with torches, lanterns and lightstones.

No work being done down here. From the smells and sounds, most of the people were settling down to dinner.

The southern gate was smaller, only perhaps twenty feet across. Though also of spell-hardened, iron-banded oak.

The gate was opening as Aefric's party approached, but their way was barred by soldiers, with long spears pointed as though to hold against a charge. And Aefric spotted at least a half-dozen soldiers not quite aiming crossbows, up on the wall.

He sensed magic, too. There was a magic-user on the other side of all those spears. Someone of no minor talent.

All those weapons. Very nearly menacing. And the Brightstaff, sitting ready and waiting in its sling by Aefric's saddle.

Taking his signature weapon in hand would be all too easy.

But would it be the wrong move?

"What is the meaning of this?" Beornric bellowed. "His grace arrives at the invitation of his majesty, *your liege*."

"I am well aware of that, good Ser Beornric."

Aefric didn't know that voice. A woman's.

He spotted her easily enough, though, as she stepped through the line of spears. She looked youthful, no more than a decade older than Aefric. Not a wrinkle in her dark complexion, nor a gray hair in her long black curls. She wore robes of dark red and light gray, an interesting study in contrasts.

She carried an obsidian rod that looked more than a little like the strange rod that Aefric's court wizard and oldest friend — Karbin — often carried.

She didn't introduce herself. But then, many powerful wizards didn't, until asked.

Nevertheless, Aefric knew her. That rod. That aura of power. She could only be Nayoria, Royal Wizard of Armyr.

"May I approach, your grace?" she asked, her tone somewhere between humorous and respectful.

Apparently Beornric thought she erred too far on the side of humor. He frowned deeply, and with that mustache, it was quite a show.

Or was it the woman herself that made Beornric frown? He'd served more than two decades in service to the king. He had to have met — or at least seen — the royal wizard before.

Perhaps Aefric would remember to ask later. In the meantime, he answered her question.

"Please do approach," Aefric said. "Though I find myself unsure of the proper mode of address for a royal wizard. Shall I call you Lord Wizard?"

"I would prefer your grace call me Nayoria," she said, stepping smoothly past knights, soldiers and horses to stand between Aefric and Beornric.

"I shall then," Aefric said, and Beornric smiled. Likely pleased that Aefric hadn't permitted her a similar familiarity. "What's going on here, Nayoria?"

"I must ask your grace to bear with me for just a moment," she said, quietly. "Your identity is easy enough to confirm by the Brightstaff at your side, your grace. But would you do me the favor of speaking your name and titles for me? Softly, if your grace would be so kind."

Aefric frowned, and felt her casting a spell of detection, though she did little more than mutter.

"I am Ser Aefric Brightstaff, Duke of Deepwater and Baron of Netar."

She moved her obsidian rod sharply, as though catching Aefric's words.

Oh, he understood then. This was an identity test. And it wasn't for him.

Nayoria thrust her rod straight into the air while calling out the word *"Raikund!"*

A pulse of ultraviolet energy emanated from the tip of her rod, in all directions at once, striking every member of Aefric's entourage.

As her power touched them, each of his knights and soldiers straightened a little, but otherwise showed no reaction.

But from somewhere back down the line came two sharp cries.

"There!" Nayoria cried out.

Two youths — both wreathed in flickering, glowing orange light — leaped down from the kitchen carts and ran. One west, one east.

Neither got far. One was taken down by a crossbow bolt. The other was caught by rings of Nayoria's magic.

There was a good deal of shouting and crying out then. Weapons drawn. Accusations screamed.

Aefric called a halt to all of it by pulling the Brightstaff from its sling and causing it to sound a clap of thunder.

"What. Just. Happened?" he said into the silence that followed his thunderclap.

"Your grace recognized the spell?" Nayoria asked, smiling. Her magic conveyed the writhing former kitchen boy through the air. He no longer flickered orange, but was bound now. Ringed in strips of purple magic, including one around his mouth.

"Some sort of identity confirmation," Aefric said.

Nayoria frowned, one eyebrow high. "This is your grace's first encounter with the *raikund*?"

"Yes," Aefric said, "and I should warn you that I've had a very long ride."

"Forgive me, your grace," Nayoria said with a small bow. "I do not mean to try your grace's patience. Merely express respect for your grace's puissance with the Art. That he had never seen the *raikund* before, and was able to discern so much so quickly speaks well of your grace and his teachers."

"Thank you," Aefric said. "But that doesn't answer my question."

"The *raikund* tests allegiance, and identified two among your grace's entourage who owed their allegiance to someone other than your grace."

"Spies?" Aefric asked.

"Or assassins," Nayoria said. "Though they look a little young for that. We'll know the truth soon enough though."

Aefric's own soldiers brought the wounded youth up then. He'd taken a crossbow bolt through the thigh, but it could have been much worse.

"So," Aefric said, "I take it this means that the matter of those attempts on the royal family hasn't been resolved."

"That is a topic your grace should discuss with the king," Nayoria said. "I shall attend to the prisoners. Your grace and the remainder of his entourage are most welcome, and will be guided to their majesties at once."

"Indeed," Beornric muttered, as Nayoria left with the prisoners. "Welcome to Armityr, your grace."

"I feel welcome," Aefric said, just as softly. "Don't you?"

"Very much so. Shall I interview the cooking staff later and find out more?"

"Please do," Aefric said, as the procession began to move.

"Whether they're spies, assassins, or something else entirely, I want answers."

AEFRIC DIDN'T GET A GOOD LOOK AT THE STATE OF REPAIRS IN THE capital city as he and his entourage were guided quickly through the streets to the palace.

Dusk was rapidly giving way to night by then, and though the cobbled streets he rode were well lit, they were also a part of the city that ... well, it might have been restored, or it might never have been damaged.

If Aefric knew, he didn't recall. Either way, the buildings around him were all two and three stories tall, and all looked to be in good repair.

That was about all the attention he had for them. The day had grown long. And the delays first at Riverkeep, then at the two gates had made it feel interminable.

What Aefric really wanted — what he would expect under normal circumstances — was that he would be taken to his rooms and given the chance to rest and refresh himself before being brought to the royal presence.

But the tension in the air, the greeting at the gate and the discovery of two who were at least spies of some stripe — these things had left no doubt in Aefric's mind that his day would get much longer before he had a chance to rest.

At least, however, his horses would finally get *their* chance to rest. The king's soldiers guided Aefric first to the avener, where grooms would see to the horses while pages saw to the luggage.

Aefric's party was split at that point. Only his knights would be allowed to accompany him to meet their majesties.

When Aefric asked about that he was told — quickly, by a very nervous page — that the soldiers and others of Aefric's company were taken directly to their dinner, and would then be given lodging.

Aefric and his knights were then escorted into the palace by a side door, not the main entrance. And that nervous page — a coltish young woman with long, chestnut hair — hustled them up three flights of white and gray stone stairs just inside the walls.

They came out into a dark, narrow hallway, entirely paneled in dark hardwoods, and lit only by a single, thick pillar candle in a sconce.

The page picked up the candle, which cast scant light in the dark hallway.

Aefric didn't say anything. He just lit up the yellow diamond embedded in the top of the that six-foot length of white thunderwood that was the Brightstaff.

That yellow diamond was as big as the last joint of Aefric's thumb, which made it larger than the meager flame on that candle. And the light that diamond cast right now was enough to see clearly, but not enough to hurt anyone's eyes.

The page started to say something.

Aefric pulled a copy of that light from the tip of the Brightstaff and tossed it to the back where he was confident that one of his knights would catch it on a dagger.

The page worried at her lip.

"Were you told to bring us in darkness?" Aefric asked.

"No, your grace," she said, and every word sounded as though it had to be dragged out of her lips.

Why was this poor girl so nervous?

She needed one very deep breath before she could explain.

"It's a matter of both tradition and practicality, your grace," she said, lowering her voice now. "This passageway is secret, and too much light could alert the unwary."

"Do you usually escort eight people through this corridor?"

She frowned and blinked. Caught between puzzled and wary. "No, your grace."

"Then indulge me in preventing my knights from stumbling around in the dark."

She quickly bowed. "Of course, your grace. Please forgive me, your grace."

"There's nothing to forgive," Aefric said, smiling in what he hoped was a reassuring fashion.

Fortunately, the poor, nervous girl didn't have to escort Aefric much farther. They'd gone only perhaps a hundred feet down that corridor — passing at least four spyholes and two small doors that Aefric spotted — before she paused at a sliding door and knocked.

Knocked.

On a door that led out from a hidden corridor.

Aefric shook his head, but bit down what would have been intended as a humorous remark, but might've have been the last thing her nerves could take.

And he didn't need to make a page faint dead away right now.

He did extinguish his magical lights, though, leaving them in the light of her single candle, just as he heard a muffled voice say, "Come."

"A moment," Aefric said, and the page worried her lip again. "I should look proper to meet their majesties."

To Aefric, the spell he cast then was a little nothing. Something he'd puzzled out during his first apprenticeship, and now knew so well that casting it didn't even feel like effort. He could probably cast it while bound, gagged, and struggling against a double-dose of sleeping poison.

But to see the way the page's dark blue eyes widened as power shimmered down Aefric's body. To see the way her jaw dropped as the wake of that power left Aefric sparkling clean — from the tips of his long, sandy blonde hair, through his pale blue silk tunic and his dark brown riding leathers to the soles of his soft, high, calfskin boots.

Well, such a reaction was just a little reminder that even such simple magics as that one were not a part of most people's daily lives.

He smiled at her, though, and gave her a wink he hoped was reassuring. Just in case she held any fear of magic.

He knew from experience that some people liked magic in theory, or in little enchantments, but found actual spellwork ... disquieting.

She responded with a surprisingly bright smile as she slid the door open for him.

"This way, your grace," she said.

Beornric put a hand in front of Aefric, getting a frown from the page.

"If I may, your grace," Beornric said softly, "all this skulking about unsettles my stomach."

Aefric nodded, and Beornric entered first. Aefric noticed then that his knights all had hands on the hilts of their swords.

"Your grace?" the page asked, sounding nervous again.

"I'm sure it'll just be a moment," Aefric said.

In truth, it wasn't much more than that before Beornric leaned back through the doorway and said, "Safe, your grace."

Aefric entered the room.

This was a grand sitting room lit by a crystal chandelier, which hung down from a high ceiling. The south wall was mostly windowed, with views of part of the city.

The walls were plastered and painted a soft yellow. Decorated with paintings of the royal family, going back at least ten generations.

An array of couches that looked prettier than they likely were comfortable. White woods with cushions of powder blue. They spiraled across the pale hardwood flooring, leaving just enough space between them for comfortable passage and the occasional white table for drinks or the like.

Two ways out of this room besides the secret door. One was an arched set of double doors on the north wall, and the other, a single arched door in the east wall.

And standing in the middle of the spiral of couches was Ser Beatritz Ol'Teraak, captain of the Knights of the Crown.

Ser Beatritz was short, and thick with muscle. Clad in a tunic and leggings in the royal colors — forest green and gold — she wore her graying chestnut hair in a braid that hung next to the two-handed sword strapped to her back.

She had what looked like an arrow scar along the right side of her jaw, that also left her short an earlobe.

Standing with her were three ... squires, if Aefric had to guess. They all wore the king's livery, but with different sigils patched at their shoulders.

Beatritz and the squires bowed to Aefric, as his knights filed into the room behind him.

"Your grace," Beatritz said. "Ser Beornric. It is a pleasure to see you both in fine health. Especially after ... that incident at the Feast of Dereth Sehk."

The incident had involved assassins who'd come all too close to taking Aefric's life. He'd been luckier than he liked to think about.

But this was neither the time nor place to admit that.

"I don't die so easily as that," Aefric said, giving Beatritz a half-smile. "And it's good to see you too, Beatritz. May I ask what's going on?"

"A question that open-ended will have to be answered by his majesty, I'm afraid," Beatritz said. "But before I can escort your grace into the royal presence, I must first ask his knights for their weapons."

"Only my knights?" Aefric asked.

Beatritz smiled.

"His majesty wouldn't even consider parting your grace from the Brightstaff," she said. "But I believe it was her majesty who put it best. 'If Aefric wanted us dead, all he had to do was nothing when those assassins came. As far as I'm concerned he can carry a ballista into the royal presence if he can fit it through the doorway.'"

Aefric chuckled, a laugh which spread through the others and cut some of the tension in the room.

His knights surrendered their weapons, which were collected by the squires. Once that was done, Beatritz addressed the knights.

"I promise you all that your weapons will be treated with proper care and respect, and returned to your hands promptly when you leave the royal presence."

"A question," Vria asked, and continued after Beatritz nodded. "Wardius and I are on duty, guarding his grace."

"Ah," Beatritz said, before Vria went any further. "Then let me assure you that his majesty asserts the liege's privilege, and takes formal responsibility for his grace's safety while he is in the palace."

"Thank you," Vria and Wardius said, not quite in sync.

"And now, your grace, good knights, if you would follow me into the royal presence."

BEATRITZ LED AEFRIC AND COMPANY TO THE ARCHED DOOR ON THE EAST wall. She knocked on it three times, then opened the door without waiting for a response.

The room on the other side of that door was much smaller than Aefric expected. Square in shape and no more than five good strides across. Plastered ceiling and walls, with the former painted gold and the latter forest green, with the royal sigil — a golden oak tree — done large on the wall opposite the entrance.

And there was only the one easily visible entrance. The left-hand wall featured a tapestry of the Stronghand family tree, and the right-hand wall the Fyrenn family tree.

The former was expected, of course, but the latter? A concession to the king's second bride?

Near the door Aefric entered through, a hearth, where a fire kept the room comfortably warm.

In the center of the room, two couches faced each other. Both modeled after the same style as those of the great spiral in the room behind Aefric. Save for the color scheme. These two were done in gold leaf, with cushions of forest green.

On the couch under the royal sigil sat the king and queen of Armyr.

King Colm Stronghand, in a red samite shirt heavily embroidered with gold thread, and leggings of dark brown. He had more gray in his rich black hair and mustache now than he'd had only ... was it half a season ago that the king and queen had come to Water's End?

Clearly stress was taking its toll on the handsome man. Surprising, considering this was a man who'd led his troops into battle several times *before* the Godswalk Wars.

The king was somewhere about Beornric's age, and still looked ready to lead his troops to war again. Which he might just be planning to do. He certainly had been spending a good deal of time outside, for he hadn't lost much of his battlefield tan.

Queen Eppida Fyrenn wasn't much older than Aefric, and didn't look as though the stress of the current situation were getting to her at all.

Fashionably pale and strikingly beautiful was Queen Eppida. With her long, golden blonde curls and the Fyrenn sapphire blue eyes. Her slender form was sheathed in a surprisingly simple gown of burnt orange, cut just low enough to be daring. Or perhaps to emphasize the magical golden torc she wore.

Neither wore their crowns, even though they were receiving Aefric at Armityr for the first time since his installment as duke.

That was unexpected. Aefric's seneschal, Kentigern, had told Aefric no fewer than three times that they would want to greet him formally. Likely before the court. And certainly wearing their crowns.

And yet, this was clearly a private meeting, and about as informal as any meeting with them would likely get...

Both monarchs smiled when Aefric entered the room, though trouble lurked behind the king's smile.

"Aefric," King Colm said, more warmth in his smile now. "Come get the formalities out of the way and have a seat on the couch."

"Yes, your majesty," Aefric said, and approached. He bowed deeply and, following tradition, offered his liege his empty right hand.

Technically, if the king were displeased with Aefric, he would be within his rights to pull a dagger and cut Aefric's wrist. A cut for commensurate with the amount of displeasure. It could even be lethal, if such were merited.

Instead, King Colm gave Aefric's hand a kiss, to show that he was pleased with his vassal.

Traditionally, royal hand-kissing was done only by the reigning monarch of the pair. But as she had done with Aefric before, Queen Eppida made a point of kissing Aefric's hand as well.

Once Aefric was seated, with the Brightstaff standing tall beside him, King Colm nodded to Beatritz, who admitted Beornric.

He entered, bowed, and received the salute of a noble to a knight — King Colm made a fist with one hand, and grabbed that wrist with the other.

Queen Eppida, Aefric noted, left this to her husband.

Beornric then moved to stand behind Aefric, and just to his left.

There followed a procession of Aefric's Knights of the Lake. Each entered in turn, was permitted to bow and receive the salute, and then left the room again.

At Aefric's puzzled frown, Queen Eppida said softly, "Our words tonight are for no ears but yours and Beornric's."

Aefric nodded then, and waited until the last of his knights had departed. To his surprise, they were followed by Beatritz, but that page — the one who'd escorted him here — stood near the door, eyes forward and posture perfect.

At King Colm's gesture, she approached, visibly fighting her nervousness with each slow step.

"Did you introduce yourself?" the king asked her.

"No, your majesty," she said, still looking straight ahead. As though staring at some name on the Fyrenn family tree. "I didn't think it my place."

"Silly girl," the queen said. "You really must get these nerves of yours under control." She turned to Aefric. "She's been a wreck since she learned you were coming."

"Why?" Aefric asked.

Queen Eppida gave him a droll look, but the king answered.

"Aefric, I'd like you to meet Nesta Ol'Lamoric." He smiled. "One day she'll be ler of the Ol'Lamoric lands, which ... well. I won't spoil the surprise for you. Suffice to say, her family is important in Netar."

"And she's *usually* the model of poise," Queen Eppida added, tapping her chin with one finger. "If only I could imagine why she should be so nervous today..."

"Stop teasing the girl, Ep," King Colm said, gently. To Aefric he then added, "It's been a long day for you. Ishka?"

"Please," Aefric said.

"Four glasses with it then," the king said to Nesta, "and leave the bottle. We'll serve ourselves after the first round."

Nesta did seem more at ease now, given a task. She whisked through the door into the other room, and returned with a silver tray, a small, collapsible oak table, a cut crystal bottle, and four small glasses.

Most impressively, she carried all that with surprising ease.

She needed only one hand to set up the table, then set the laden tray on that table. She poured four glasses of the pale brown liquor, then served them in descending order of rank.

Once that was done, she bowed and asked, "Will there be anything else, your majesty?"

"Not now," King Colm said. "But do take care of those knights for me, while I speak with their duke."

"At once, your majesty," she said, and left the room.

Now, maybe Aefric would find out what was going on.

ONCE THE DOOR TO THE SMALL ROOM WAS CLOSED BEHIND NESTA, ONLY Aefric, King Colm, Queen Eppida, and Beornric remained. With Beornric the only one of them standing, but he seemed to expect that.

King Colm raised his small glass of ishka. "Armyr."

Aefric and the other three confirmed the toast, and drank. The brown liquor was strong, but surprisingly smooth, with a slight undercurrent of blackberry.

Unusual for ishka, which Aefric most often compared to scotch whisky, back on Earth.

King Colm himself refilled the glasses, then sat back and spoke with no further preamble.

"Caiperas was behind the assassination attempts," he said. "I've confirmed it now."

"Does that include the recent attempt on me at Asarchai?" Aefric asked.

Queen Eppida frowned and looked away. King Colm furrowed his brow at her, but turned back to Aefric and said, "That remains ... unconfirmed. But Caiperas seems the most likely perpetrator."

Aefric disagreed. He thought it far more likely that the pirate queen, Nelazzi, had moved against him in revenge for some of the troubles he'd caused her since becoming duke.

He had no proof of that just yet. But he trusted that his two best investigators, Karbin and Ser Deirdre Ol'Miri, would ferret out the truth.

"While I agree that no more likely candidate has presented itself," Queen Eppida said, "given the course of action you have in mind, Colm, I'd prefer we stick to those charges we *know* have proper basis. Other kingdoms will be watching."

"If I may, your majesty," Beornric said softly. He continued only after the king's nod. "His grace does have many enemies. Perhaps we'll learn more from those two kitchen boys."

"Yes," King Colm said, with a sigh. "I was all ready to apologize for the delays you faced at the gates, Aefric. Officially, of course, we're searching for Malimfari spies, not that we expected to find any. But Nayoria found *two* of your entourage who might be spies or assassins?"

"I'm not familiar with the spell she used," Aefric said slowly, "but she said it would find those who owed their loyalty to someone other than me. While I agree that makes them suspect, I don't think it guarantees that they're spies or assassins."

"They did flee, your grace," Beornric said softly.

"My justiciar is here at the palace," King Colm said. "We'll have the truth from them soon enough."

That actually helped Aefric relax. While being questioned by a holy justiciar of Taesark could be deeply unsettling, it guaranteed that there would be no torture. And if the lads didn't try to lie, perhaps even no discomfort. Or at least, not much...

"Well," King Colm said, "whatever we learn from those two, I must still act against Caiperas. The only question in my mind is whether to begin now, or wait until spring."

"Your majesty intends war then?" Aefric asked.

"I have confirmation that King Makarios himself was behind the plot to assassinate myself, my wife, my son and my daughter," King Colm said. "I will make Caiperas *bleed* for this. And I will send a *clear* message to all who think they can strike at us while hiding behind hired murderers."

"I say we wait," Queen Eppida said. "Hold this close to the chest and wait for spring."

"If we give them that long, we may find them ready for war," the king said, sounding as though they'd had this discussion before.

"They want us to move against Malimfar," Queen Eppida said, also sounding as though she were repeating a point she didn't like having to repeat. "They tried to make it seem that Malimfar was behind the attempts. So let them think we believe it."

"And risk starting a two-front war if Malimfar thinks we're coming for them."

"They're in no shape to fight after Frozen Ridge," Queen Eppida said patiently. "Ashling's scouts say they'll be a long time recovering."

"Your grace did me a great favor there," King Colm said with an almost feral smile. "Not just in decimating their forces with that fierce magical blizzard, either. The mercenaries they'd hired to pillage our lands wound up pillaging theirs instead."

"A fine bit of poetic justice, if I may say so," Beornric added.

Aefric said nothing. Stopping soldiers and mercenaries from invading had been one thing. He'd never intended to cause suffering among the *people* of Malimfar, much less the amount of suffering likely inflicted by those mercenaries.

"In fact," King Colm said, looking at the wand Garram, hanging at Aefric's belt. That wand had been a gift from the king, and it was that wand's magic that had allowed Aefric to summon that mighty blizzard. "If your grace could give me another Frozen Ridge, we could end this war as quickly as that one."

"Wouldn't work, your majesty," Aefric said. "Malimfar's armies were massed and ready to invade. Unless Caiperas was in a similar position, I couldn't even hope to do nearly so much damage."

Aefric frowned. "Not to mention that the last such effort nearly killed me."

"Well that's off the table then," Queen Eppida said firmly. "We did not just raise up a new duke only to throw his life away, did we, my love?"

"No," King Colm said quickly. "And I knew it hadn't been easy on you, Aefric, but it hadn't been made clear to me that you came close to death."

"I survived only through the grace of Kalinda. I wouldn't care to wager that the goddess of magic would save me twice."

"Understood," King Colm said with a nod. "So what do you think? Strike quickly now or wait for spring?"

"Wait for spring," he said. "You'll have more time to gather your forces. More time to prepare. And if the lie is sold well, you can catch Caiperas flat-footed."

"What do you have in mind?" Queen Eppida asked.

"Send a peer to treat with Caiperas. Can't be me. They've already made at least a formal overture toward marriage talks." Aefric shook his head. "Ashling would be best, but Wylyn would be almost as good. Have them negotiate a secret treaty to invade Malimfar with us. Us from the north, them from the east."

"Ashling should do it," Eppida said. "Wylyn may be good at deception, but my sister has forgotten more about trickery than even that old reprobate ever knew."

"Though there *is* one advantage to sending Wylyn," Aefric said. "He could claim that Ashling is already busy preparing to invade as soon as the winter snows melt."

"A good point," King Colm said, "but I agree with Eppida here. If I go this direction, the plan would benefit from Ashling's touch."

"Caiperas should assemble to invade from the southeast, if Ashling can arrange it. Then, while they're busy in Malimfar—"

"We strike deep into Caiperas before they can even mount a response. Brilliant."

"If it works," Aefric said.

"If anyone can sell them on it, Ashling can," Queen Eppida said, then turned to King Colm. "That will also give us almost two seasons before we begin. By then, we can resolidify our alliance with Rethneryl through Killian's marriage, and seal our new alliance with Varondam, through Maev's."

Oh. Good point. This *would* apply pressure for Maev to complete that alliance. Which most likely meant marriage for Maev to the king of Varondam.

Which was the last thing Aefric wanted.

Maev. Beautiful, fiery princess Maev. Was Aefric in love with her? Quite likely.

Such a strange thought, that. When he'd still been the man known as Keifer McShane, he'd thought he would never love again. Love had been murdered in the accidental death of his beloved Andi. Once college sweetheart, later wonderful wife.

When she died, he thought he'd never so much as touch a woman again. Let alone fall in love.

But then came the Jumpstart campaign for the sixth edition of *The Torn Kingdoms*, and suddenly, by the magic of the great Mage of Marrisford, Kainemorton, Keifer McShane became a street rat in Sartis known as Aefric.

He'd grown to adulthood again. Come to know women again, without the pall of Andi's memory casting them all into shadow.

Until that day in Kainemorton's tower. When the two lives merged. When the memories came flooding back. Then Andi's shadow loomed once more over all living women.

But so much time had passed for him. In some sense, at least. It had been two years since her death in some ways, but in others, more than two decades. Jumbled things together in his head. Left him confused and tentative.

Until an eager young serving woman named Octave offered him *leaba*, the pleasures of a bedmate, one night in the barony of Norra. And for the first time since his two lives had merged — the first time for the Keifer half of him, since Andi — he once more knew the intimate touch of a woman.

The healing of his heart began that night. But it took two women to truly make him feel ready to love again.

Byrhta Ol'Caran, who had inherited the legendary beauty of her eldrani grandmother. Quick, clever and caring, not that many ever saw past her looks to the woman underneath.

Princess Maev Stronghand. Beautiful in her own right and seemingly full of never-ending surprises. A princess who had trained as a true forester, as capable in the wilds as in politics. Who had worked as a lead scout during the wars. Who'd even gotten both the eldrani and the kindaren to share jealously guarded secrets with her.

Their two smiles were very different, but the mere thought of either set his heart racing.

If anything, he might be in love with both. Not that this was wise. He needed to marry. He owed it to his kingdom, and his people, to marry and produce an heir. Preferably more than one.

And given the life he led, sooner would be better.

But what was the point in allowing himself to love again, when likely he could not marry his love?

With each passing day it looked more and more likely that Princess Maev could only secure Armyr's alliance with Varondam through marriage.

And Byrhta was a wonderful woman, but as many had pointed out — often loudly — she didn't have the standing to marry a duke like Aefric. His heart might approve, but marrying the wrong woman might hurt his duchy.

Which brought others into the equation. Zoleen Fyrenn, perhaps.

Sister to both Queen Eppida and Duchess Ashling. Hers was the oldest family in Armyr, and one of the most powerful.

Sighild Ol'Masarkor. Likely more trustworthy than Zoleen, and with a family nearly as old and respected. Though not nearly as powerful.

And soon, a bevy of foreign princesses were due to descend on Water's End, each a potential marriage candidate for...

"Aefric," King Colm said, snapping his fingers. "Are you even listening?"

Oh, that's right. Aefric was still in that small sitting room, meeting with his king and queen to talk of plans for war.

"Please do forgive his grace, your majesties," Beornric said softly. "The road from Water's End has been long, and none of the days longer than today."

"Well," King Colm said, "I'll have his opinion on at least one more point before we conclude this discussion."

"I am yours to command, your majesty," Aefric said, trying to make up for letting his mind wander. And from the humor in the queen's eyes, he suspected she'd guessed where his mind had wandered to.

"I am only considering my strategies in the most general sense, at this point," King Colm said. "But I am thinking it may be worthwhile to have your armies combine with Ashling's in the south, giving the appearance of readiness to invade Malimfar. Meanwhile my forces and Wylyn's, along with whatever support we get from Rethneryl, mass not in Armyr, but in Rethneryl. That could give us an unexpected angle of attack."

"It could," Aefric said, "if the northern forces could gather without Caiperas knowing. If even one of their scouts or spies sees Armyrian troops in southern Rethneryl, though, the game's up. They'll guess the truth."

"I was hoping we could keep them so busy looking west that they don't look north," King Colm said, but not as though he believed it would work.

"If I may, your majesty," Beornric said. "A smaller version of that could work. A single strike team — perhaps the size of a company — could come down through Rethneryl and soften the way. Inhibit scouting. Sew chaos. Perhaps even slip into a key city and open a gate as your majesty's armies arrive."

Aefric chuckled. "Maev would kill to be part of that team."

"Maev will be too busy preparing to marry King Dalius," Queen Eppida said gently.

"Assuming she does," King Colm said offhandedly, while he considered Beornric's spin on his idea. "That we've had no news of an engagement yet—"

"Only proves we should remind her to stop dallying and *cement* this alliance. Hurting Caiperas will help Malimfar. We need a strong ally on their southern border."

"If you'll recall," King Colm said with one eyebrow high, "the alliance was my idea. I believe I know its value."

"Then you should help me persuade your daughter to *stop* playing games and get it *done*. She's had a more than a season now."

"And Varondam does *little* swiftly," King Colm said. "Besides, when we sent Maev down there I warned you, try to tell her how to accomplish her task and she'll find another way just to spite you."

"And he does mean to spite *me*," Queen Eppida said to Aefric, her tone now as arch as the king's. "His daughter has never given me a chance."

"That's not true," King Colm said. "It's just that you're both strong women. You're bound to butt heads from time to time, as I do with Killian."

"Killian knows his place," Queen Eppida said. "Does Maev?"

Behind Aefric, Beornric hissed in a breath.

"Are you suggesting," King Colm said in a voice both quiet and dangerous, "that I raised a daughter who will not do her duty for Armyr?"

"Are you suggesting," Queen Eppida replied in similar tones, "that I cannot tell the difference between a conflict of personalities and a conflict of people?"

"Your grace," King Colm said, without looking away from his wife,

"I think it's best we call this meeting here. Nesta will see you to your rooms and provide anything you require. There will be no formal dinner this evening."

"But—" Queen Eppida started.

"There will be no formal dinner this evening," King Colm said firmly.

She nodded, but looked ready to voice an objection the moment Aefric was out of the room.

"I am most grateful for your grace's advice this evening," King Colm said, still not looking away from Queen Eppida, who was staring daggers right back at him. "And we will speak again before your grace departs in the morning."

Aefric knew a dismissal when he heard one, and he was only too happy to get out of that particular room.

AEFRIC BARELY PAID ANY ATTENTION TO THE ROUTE NESTA LED HIM AND his knights on, once they left the royal presence. He did, at least, realize that he was still being escorted through dark, narrow, secret passages and up unoccupied stairways.

But what did all this secrecy mean?

Clearly some kind of formal dinner — likely an official welcome for the Duke of Deepwater — had been planned for that night. And canceled, by the king, apparently over some ongoing dispute between their majesties.

So was the cancellation something the king had decided on in advance? But only told the queen during that meeting?

That would explain why Aefric had been escorted to the palace not down a grand, wide street to its front doors, but along side streets to a more private entrance. Why he'd been greeted not by the whole court, but by their majesties alone — uncrowned — in what was clearly a private meeting room.

Certainly none of that was the expected way a monarch would receive one of the peers of the realm.

And yet, from the *way* the king made the announcement, the

cancellation seemed like something he only decided during the meeting. Certainly the queen hadn't been expecting it.

And if a formal dinner *had* been planned, that would explain why Aefric hadn't been offered food yet, despite the fact that he'd been riding all day. A fact not lost on his complaining stomach.

And why he was now being escorted to his rooms through hidden ways...

He was missing something here. Had to be.

In the meantime, at least Nesta seemed to have settled down. Her eyes still widened every time she looked at Aefric, but at least her smiles seemed less nervous. And her voice was steady when she finally slid open a panel door and said, "We've arrived at your rooms, your grace."

Beornric entered first, but quickly confirmed that the way was safe.

Not that Aefric had held any doubts, but given the strange turns the day had taken, he was happy to have a little reassurance.

His rooms were grand. Truly the finest appointments he'd been given anywhere outside one of his own castles.

Two sitting rooms, a dining room, a meeting room, a closet — already filled with clothes that had obviously been tailored with Aefric in mind — a bathroom with an excessively large black marble tub, and even a balcony, overlooking the lights of the city below.

All the furniture had been made from the finest greenwood or red calinwood. White oak floorboards, with plush, navy blue rugs covering much of the floors.

The plastered walls and ceilings had been painted Deepwater gray, and large tapestries featuring the Deepwater sigil — a sword emerging hilt-first from a lake — hung in the meeting room and the large sitting room.

Otherwise the paintings and tapestries on the walls were all landscapes of places in Deepwater. The great lake itself, of course, but also the Dragonscar, Water's End, the Forest of Souls, the Threepeaks Mountains, and more.

Fresh hibiscus flowers scented the rooms from strategically placed vases.

It was all quite a bit to take in.

"Is your grace satisfied with the state of the Deepwater apartments?" Nesta asked, and her smile told Aefric she could tell he was impressed.

"Each duchy has its own apartments?" Aefric asked.

"Yes, your grace," she said with a small bow. "And a guarantee of privacy while your grace is present."

Aefric looked about again. He probably shouldn't have been surprised to learn this. After all, he kept royal apartments ready for their majesties at both Water's End and Behal...

Beornric softly cleared his throat.

"Oh, excuse me," Aefric said to Nesta. "Yes. Most satisfied." He smiled. "I guess I should count myself lucky that they weren't damaged in the wars."

"But they were, your grace," Nesta said. "These rooms are part of the original keep which, like the towers, repairs itself by magic."

"It does?" Aefric asked. Odd that Aefric hadn't known that. Or, more precisely, that Keifer hadn't known that from his many, many readings of the *Torn Kingdoms* sourcebooks. Was this something new for the sixth edition, being added to the continuity retroactively?

Was that even possible? If so, what other changes could that mean?

Apart from the insertion of Aefric himself, of course...

Beornric cleared his throat softly.

"Excuse me," Aefric said with a smile. "The day has been long, and here I am thinking of magic when my knights must be starving. Please see them to their rooms and their dinners — in whichever order is more appropriate — then bring meals for Beornric and me when that's done."

"Of course, your grace," Nesta said with a bow.

"Thank you, Nesta."

The word of thanks — or perhaps it was hearing her own name

from Aefric's lips — seemed to throw Nesta off her rhythm. She got caught between a smile and a bow — and possibly a verbal reply.

She recovered herself, flushing brightly, and managed a not-entirely-awkward bow, before calling in servants to take care of the Knights of the Lake. Once that was done, she left to see about dinner for Aefric and Beornric.

The moment they were alone, Aefric raised a warning hand to Beornric. "Don't say it."

"Say what, your grace?"

Aefric raised an eyebrow.

Beornric started laughing. "Come now, your grace. Why would I suggest adding the name Nesta Ol'Lamoric to your growing list of potential wives? Just because she's a comely lass, of an old, well-established noble family, who's clearly smitten with the great Duke of Deepwater?"

"Got it out of your system yet?" Aefric asked.

"I think your grace will find—"

"She's a child."

"Hardly, your grace. In fact, I believe she's the same age as Vercy Ol'Karmak."

"Vercy's a child."

"Vercy is no more than a year from her majority and taking up the mantle of Baroness Riverbreak," Beornric said firmly. "These are both young women, and any other noble in Armyr would consider them of age to pursue at least the *promise* of marriage."

"I'm not any other noble," Aefric said. "And we have more important matters to discuss."

"I thought perhaps your grace wanted to wait for dinner for that conversation. I doubt Nesta will keep us waiting long."

"Fair enough," Aefric said, looking out the large windows near the balcony at the city down below.

Many of the streets and buildings were lit up for early evening activities. But there were large dark patches, where repairs were still a long way off. And from the pattern of torches, Aefric could see two large areas where people were still forced to camp within the walls of the city itself.

"I was hoping they'd be further along."

"A pity," Beornric said, stepping up beside Aefric. "But your grace should not avoid this topic."

Aefric sighed. "You have a point to make, I assume?"

"I know the Ol'Lamoric family. About as old and well-respected as the Ol'Masarkor family. And when one considers that the Ol'Masarkors have a barony and the Ol'Lamorics only a lerdom, that says something."

"What does it say?" Aefric said, more of his thoughts still down in those dark patches and worrying for those who might not have permanent shelter when the rains truly came.

"Aefric," Beornric said.

Surprise turned Aefric to face his knight-adviser. Beornric rarely used his name.

"We must discuss this."

Aefric sighed. "Oh, very well."

"If we exclude two obvious names," Beornric said softly, "then to this point your leading candidates have been Zoleen Fyrenn and Sighild Ol'Masarkor."

"I know, I know," Aefric said. "And Zoleen's a Fyrenn, and all that comes with that, while Sighild is vassal to one of my own vassals. Or will be, once she assumes her barony."

"Not what I was going to say," Beornric said.

Aefric frowned, but nodded for him to go ahead.

"It's obvious that while you *like* both Sighild and Zoleen to some extent or another, neither has stolen your heart. *More importantly*" — he said, before Aefric could interrupt — "it is fairly *well known* by now that neither has stolen your heart."

"You're planning something, I take it?"

"Princesses from Rethneryl, Shachan and Hatay are due at Water's End in only a few aetts. Once they arrive, pressure for you to choose a wife will increase dramatically."

"Especially a wife that could provide or solidify an alliance for

Armyr," Aefric said.

"Exactly." Beornric smiled. "So why not invite a few of your lesser choices to visit you first? Ler Idrina, from Felspark. Cyneswith, that future countess from Merrek. Nesta. Maybe if you gave them a little time and attention, really got to know them, one of them might win your heart."

"Of the names you just spoke, only Idrina has passed her majority."

"*Must* you insist on that?" Beornric asked, gnashing his teeth in frustration. "You're cutting yourself off from perfectly viable options. Options that might make you happy as both a man and a duke, if you'd only *give them a chance*."

"I was raised to believe that adult choices and responsibilities should not be forced on children, which includes anyone below the age of majority."

"And believe I'll be having words with Karbin about that, next I see him," Beornric said. "Maybe that's the way in the south, but it's just not how things are done here in Armyr."

It wasn't Karbin who'd taught Aefric that. In fact, he couldn't remember Karbin addressing the topic one way or another.

No, it was Keifer's life in the United States, back on Earth, where he'd been taught the dividing line between adulthood and childhood.

Aefric wasn't sure how to correct Beornric's impresson, though. Talking about Earth had never seemed a good idea...

"Elbar's Blood," Beornric swore. "You wouldn't have to *marry* or even *bed* any of them until they reached their majority, if you insisted on waiting. You wouldn't even be the first noble ever to insist on waiting that way. But you could still *spend time* with them. Give them a *chance*. And maybe choose a wife for yourself, free of excessive political pressure."

A knock at the door. Nesta, arriving with dinner.

"I believe we've taken this topic as far as we can, for now," Aefric said.

"Of course, your grace," Beornric said. And Aefric knew from his tone that they'd be revisiting this topic. Likely sooner than later.

But first, at least, he'd get to eat.

Roast pheasant with rosemary. Golden slices of potato and stalks of broccoli, both covered in molten cheddar. Served with a good, hearty dark beer, and honeyed oat bread.

Aefric and Beornric dined that night in the smallest sitting room — it turned out there was a third that Aefric had missed on his first time through his apartments in the royal palace.

Round and no more than three strides across, it had a round, burnished red calinwood table in the center and four matching chairs. Windows in three directions — glass, with Deepwater gray curtains drawn — and soft, magical light from a floating orb just below the center of the ceiling.

The door to the rest of the apartments stood open, with Nesta waiting just past the threshold. Handy for seconds — well, they'd had seconds, so thirds, if needed — refills, and, likely, dessert.

Aefric had originally intended to have her wait on the other side of a closed door. But once food was presented, he and Beornric had realized how hungry they were and gave their whole attention to their meal.

Even the mutual irritation of their last conversation seemed over-weighed by the pleasure of good food and drink with a trusted companion.

Aefric sat back in his chair, nibbling on a little bread to help clear the lingering grease from the roast pheasant. And perhaps from the cheese.

Good tastes, but sopping them up with bread seemed like the right thing to do.

"Your grace, ser knight," Nesta asked from the doorway, "are you ready for dessert?"

Aefric looked the question at Beornric, who nodded eagerly. "We are."

She gestured, and two nearby servants brought in a blackberry pie, still warm from the oven.

Beornric moaned in pleasure at the smell, which made Nesta smile. Aefric thought it might have also made her a little more generous with their slices. There didn't seem to be much left in the pan when she and the servants retreated.

"Would you get the door, please, Nesta?" Aefric asked. "I think it's time my knight-adviser and I had a private chat."

"Of course, your grace," Nesta said with a bow. "I shall wait on the other side of the next room, should your grace require anything else."

"Thank you," Aefric said, and Nesta closed the door behind her as she left.

Beornric practically whimpered, looking at the pie.

"Fine," Aefric said with a chuckle. "Have some pie before we talk."

"Your grace is a kind and generous man," Beornric said, tucking in, and moaning again at the taste of the pie.

Aefric almost joined him, as soon as he tasted that pie. The crust managed to be light and flaky, which still just a little crisp. And the filling was sweet and delicious, without being too sweet.

He'd eaten half his own slice before he realized it, then forced himself to have a sip of beer and slow down.

The rich beer went very well with the pie. Either that, or lunch had been *far* too long ago.

They finished their slices — Beornric making a point not to miss any crumbs — before Aefric said, "Where shall we begin?"

"With what's most important, I think," Beornric said, shifting to business mode. "You should be prepared. Her majesty will likely come to you tonight for the noble privilege."

The noble privilege. In all his wanderings, Aefric had never been anyplace that was as free with its sexuality as Armyr. Well, perhaps Goldenmoon. But Aefric had only visited Goldenmoon. He hadn't lived there.

Here in Armyr, though, nobles were considered free to pursue the bliss moment with whatever other nobles struck their fancy. Irrespective of rank, marriage or other entanglements, where there was mutual attraction, sex usually followed.

At least, so long as the would-be lovers were not related within three or four generations.

Armyrians referred to it as the noble privilege. It began as a means of avoiding dangerous jealousies and scandalous affairs, but had become a way of life among the nobility.

The idea of such sexual liberty had even spread to the common folk, in many of the cities and larger towns.

As far as Aefric could tell, there were only three real rules.

First, the nobles kept their dalliances among the nobility, and the common folk amongst the common folk (with the practice of *leaba* being the sole exception).

Second, the desire had to be mutual. No pressure was allowed. No gifts offered or expected. No obligation to assent, and no insult in refusal. Attraction was the guiding rule, not rank. Even the lowest noblewoman could refuse the king, if she didn't fancy him, and face no repercussions.

Third, one or both parties had to first drink nysta tea. A bitter brew, yes, but whether drunk by a man or a woman, it prevented conception until it cleared the system, at least a full day later.

Aefric often thought that it was the advent of nysta tea that had led to the spread of the noble privilege in the first place.

"I don't know," Aefric said. "It's true that the queen has come to me before, but only because her blood was heated by something I'd done. Like stopping that assassin on the road to Water's End."

"Believe it," Beornric said. "I've known their majesties longer than you have. And I'm confident that not only is her majesty coming to your rooms tonight, she's coming with an agenda beyond the bliss moment."

"You think she wants me to side with her in whatever conflict she's having with the king?" Aefric asked. "She'll be hard-pressed there. I don't want to get in the middle."

"I'm pretty sure you're already in the middle," Beornric said. "Which brings me to my second point. That canceled formal dinner."

"Yes," Aefric said. "Do you think the king planned to cancel it even before that meeting?"

"Yes," Beornric said. "And I think he kept that knowledge from her majesty so that he could un-cancel it, if he decided to."

"So the question is why."

"I don't think so," Beornric said. "I think the answer there is that she's likely been bringing in allies over the last several days, so you could hear her proposals from other mouths during the socializing around dinner."

"So they're fighting their own battle right now?"

"I believe so. Yes. I don't think they agree in how to go after Caiperas."

"She can't possibly be telling people his plans, though," Aefric said. "That would risk word getting out. So just what was she planning to do?"

"She's a Fyrenn," Beornric said firmly. "And she's every bit as clever and conniving as Ashling, don't let her persuade you differently. She could tell ten different stories to ten different allies, each of whom would bring you what they thought was their own interpretation of the right course of action. And each of them would be unknowingly setting the stage for her to tell you just the right thing to bring it all together."

"And leave me seeing things her way?"

Beornric nodded.

Aefric sipped his beer as he considered that. Beornric did the same.

"Do you think Zoleen's as scheming as her sisters?"

Beornric sighed. "I admit I'm tempted to say yes, because in my personal opinion she's not the best wife for you." He shook his head. "But I won't lie to you. She's not nearly as accomplished at manipulation as her sisters. Nowhere near it. Which is why I believe her when she says she's trying to free herself from the family reputation."

"Why do you think so?"

"Because Yrsa caught her," Beornric said with a snort. "Caught her manipulating those lers in Riverbreak to keep Byrhta Ol'Caran away from you. If it'd been either of her sisters, Yrsa would never have caught her."

"What if she wanted to get caught?" Aefric frowned. "Maybe as part of a deeper game."

"A deeper game that involved destroying your trust in her, just when you were really getting to like her?" Beornric shook his head. "No. She made a big mistake, as you have since taught her. I sincerely believe she won't do anything that foolish again. At least, where you're involved."

"What do you think about this war with Caiperas?"

"Hard to say," Beornric said, tugging on his mustaches. "With the king and queen enmeshed in their private feud, anything they present right now — especially privately — is as much of a move between the two of them as an actual plan for the future."

"So you think the war might not happen?"

"Too soon to say," Beornric said. "Colm can be daring on the battlefield, but he's generally cautious in his strategies."

"Wait," Aefric said. "He knows I have princesses coming for a visit soon."

"Yes?"

"So that means he can't be planning on having me start war preparations. Not with foreign royalty in my castle."

"True," Beornric said. "But he has you thinking about the marriage value of alliances, doesn't he?"

Aefric nodded, frowning.

"Which might've been the whole point."

"You mean..." Aefric shook his head. "You mean he might not actually be planning a war? That little presentation might've been to spur me into choosing the 'right' marriage, and doing it soon?"

"He's tricky man, Colm Stronghand," Beornric said. "There's a reason he's a good match for his new queen."

"But we can't assume he's *not* considering a war either," Aefric said, hearing the complaint in his voice now. "Because I can't be caught flat-footed if he calls on my armies."

"True," Beornric said. "But for tonight, let's focus on what matters." He leaned forward and pointed at Aefric. "Make the queen no promises. No matter how ... enticingly she asks."

Aefric heaved a deep sigh. The games royalty played sometimes made him miss the simple life of an adventurer. Yes, people had often been trying to kill him, but it had all been pretty straightforward, at least.

"Shall we finish that pie then?" Beornric asked, hopefully.

"Yes," Aefric said. "Let's."

LATER THAT NIGHT, AEFRIC SOAKED HIS TIRED MUSCLES IN THAT BLACK marble tub. A good tub full of hot water — in this case, scented with rose hips — did wonders after a long day's ride.

A rare, savored luxury for him, back in his adventuring days. But now, available anytime he wanted. One of the joys of his new life that he indulged frequently.

In fact, Aefric was amused to realize that this particular tub actually felt small. Even though it was more than big enough to accommodate two, or perhaps three people. Assuming they were sufficiently friendly.

Why, this tub was easily several times larger than those rare copper tubs he'd managed to squeeze into in inns, back in the old days.

And now, well, he'd been a duke less than half a year, and yet he was growing so accustomed to his new life that he could actually consider this sculpted masterpiece of black marble "small."

Truly, his enormously oversized tub back at Water's End was spoiling him. So large, it was, that Aefric often thought the old Soulfist dukes and duchesses must've favored bathing with six or eight of their closest friends.

One thing Aefric still wasn't used to though — people nearby while he bathed.

In this case, two servants. A man and a woman. Both ready to bring him towels and a dressing gown, the moment he decided he was done with his bath.

Speaking of which, it was likely time to get out. With no nearby

window, he couldn't gaze meditatively into the night. And his ponder-
ings of marriage and warfare weren't doing him any good.

"I believe I'm ready to get out," Aefric said.

"Oh, good," Queen Eppida said. "I'm just in time then."

Aefric turned. Queen Eppida stood in the doorway, clad in only a
sheer white dressing gown and a soft gray cloak, half-closed. Her
golden curls hung down loose just past her shoulders, and her smile
looked expectant.

The two servants glanced at one another.

"You," the queen said to the male servant, "leave us." She turned
to the female servant. "You, take towels and dry him well for me.
Make something of a show of it, while I watch."

"Providing the towels will be sufficient," Aefric said, arching an
eyebrow. "I can dry myself."

Queen Eppida arched an eyebrow right back at him.

"Is my duke countermanding an order from his queen?" she
asked.

"Not in the least," Aefric said. "I seem to recall that when your
majesty comes to me dressed for the noble privilege, I am to disre-
gard her rank and consider her only as Eppida."

"Well said, Aefric," Eppida said, chuckling. "You're beginning to
sound more like a noble than an adventurer playing dress-up. I
approve. In fact, I approve a great deal."

She walked slowly closer, her bare feet across the white oak. She
swung her hips just enough to make her cloak dance, teasing the
shapely body half-concealed by her thin dressing gown.

"Then you don't mind if I dry myself off?" Aefric asked, dragging
his eyes back to her face.

"I'm afraid I do," she said, close enough now to trail her fingers
along the marble rim, but not close enough to touch him. "As I've
arrived while you're already naked, I don't get to see you disrobe.
Thus, I'd like the pleasure of watching while a pair of interested
hands dries you for me."

"What if I'd rather have *your* interested hands do that? As
opposed to the hands of a servant, ordered to the task."

Eppida chuckled softly. "With your looks, your scars, and your lean muscles, do you really think drying you off is a task a woman must be *ordered* to do?"

She leaned closer with a small, teasing smile, and whispered, "I'm trying to do her a favor."

That sounded like assumption on Eppida's part. And even if it wasn't, Aefric still didn't like the idea of anyone being *ordered* to touch him. Even if that order fell on willing ears. So he struck a different tack.

"Maybe I've been anticipating your arrival," he said, voice low. "Maybe I've been looking forward to *your* touch, and don't wish more delays."

A mixture of truths in there. Beornric had warned him of her coming, after all, and Aefric had been preparing, mentally, in case she did try to maneuver him in her game against the king.

It was also true, though, that with her this close, he wanted her touch. He was only human after all, and the queen was a very beautiful woman.

"Well," Eppida said, her sapphire eyes smoldering with desire, "in that case."

She held out her hand, and the serving woman passed her a large, soft, fluffy gray towel.

The air was cold all across his skin, as Aefric emerged dripping from the tub and stepped onto the warmed stone drying surface.

Eppida began to dry him then. Slowly. Thoroughly. Lingering over his chest, shoulders, thighs and rump. When she finally reached the last place she had to dry, she lingered there too. Smiling as she got his heart pounding, and his breaths coming faster.

In fact, she lingered long enough that Aefric finally had to warn her, "Keep that up and I'll be finishing in your towel."

"Well we can't have that, can we?" Eppida said in a throaty voice. "I didn't drink that bitter tea just to waste your bliss."

She tossed the towel to the serving woman.

Huh. Aefric had forgotten she was there.

"Will there be—" the serving woman started to ask, but Eppida cut her off with a gesture.

"Leave us. At once."

"Yes, your majesty," she said and hurried from the room.

Eppida threw off her cloak, her breaths coming quick and heavy. Her pale cheeks and throat flushed with heat.

She spread her arms wide and closed her eyes.

"You know what I want! Do it!"

She could only mean the same thing she'd asked for the first time she invited him to her rooms.

Aefric brought his hands together, grasping the neck of her dressing gown not with his fingers, but with magic.

He yanked his arms apart, tearing the gown off her while the sound of ripping linen filled the room.

He flung the torn garment aside, leaving her wonderfully naked before him, arms still outstretched. Eyes still closed.

"Yes," she said. "Yes, Aefric. And now. And now..." She licked her lips, but Aefric didn't make her ask for what she wanted.

He lifted her off the floor with magic.

"Yes," she said, writhing with pleasure while he carried her that way into the other room and to the large featherbed, whose covers were already turned down and awaiting them.

In fact, a fire was already going in the hearth, and a bottle of sharabi, with two glasses, waited for them on a night table.

The magical light in here had been doused, and a handful of yellow pillar candles gave the room a soft glow.

He maneuvered Eppida under the Deepwater gray canopy and floated her two feet above the mattress.

He held her there a moment.

"Please, Aefric," she said, her sapphire eyes hungry, perhaps even needy, as she continued. "No more delays. Come to me *now*."

He dropped her on the bed and pounced on her. Savoring her citrus scent, her soft skin and her shapely curves. Her kisses were rough and passionate. Her nails dug into his flesh everywhere she clutched at him.

Their first time that night was frenzied. Wild. It didn't last long, but it didn't need to. If anything, Eppida beat Aefric to their culmination.

Afterwards, they lay entwined together, sweaty and satisfied — for the moment, at least.

"Much better," she said, licking a little sweat from his shoulder. "Gods, I'll have to dry Colm myself sometime. I had no idea how much fun it could be."

"I'm surprised you haven't."

"That's because you're an ennobled duke, not a hereditary duke," she said, patting his chest. "When you're raised to this life, you're accustomed to having servants handle such things. They do so from before you can walk."

She frowned at Aefric. "Do you really deny your servants that? Their chance to bathe and dry their duke? Even at Water's End?"

"As you say, I didn't grow up with it. To me it feels creepy to have someone else wash or dry me." He quirked a half-smile. "At least, unless I'm having sex with that person."

"If I'd known how appealing it would be," she said, "I'd've joined you for the bath, too."

"Perhaps next time," Aefric said.

"Perhaps," she said, then shook her head. "Of course, it wasn't supposed to be me in your bed tonight."

"No?" Aefric said, teasing his fingers down her side. "And who would you rather send to my arms?"

"Zoleen, of course," Eppida said, as though the answer should have been obvious. "Or would you rather I gave Nesta permission?"

Before Aefric could address either point, Eppida continued.

"She wanted to come to you tonight, you know," Eppida said. "Nesta I mean. Well, it's true of Zoleen as well, but let's discuss Nesta first."

"She's too young," Aefric said.

"She's not," Eppida said matter-of-factly, then tapped him on the nose. "And I can't imagine why you'd think she was. True, she's not finished blossoming, but she's certainly in bloom. It's not as though she's only just budded."

"But—"

"Yes, yes," she said, "I know. You're going to raise an objection regarding the age of majority. I *have* met you before. But let me ask you this, oh, wise one."

Aefric raised his eyebrows expectantly.

"How old were *you* when you first sought the bliss moment with a partner?"

"I don't see how that's relevant."

"Answer the question," she said, laughing. "At least tell me this much: were you older than Nesta? Or younger?"

"Younger," he admitted.

"Of course you were. As was I. As was Ashling. As was just about everyone you can name. In fact, I'd be willing to wager that Nesta has sought the bliss moment herself with a few of the more handsome pages we have running about the palace."

"Your point?"

"You don't object to the bliss moment," Eppida said. "*Obviously* you don't object to the noble privilege. So why make such a fuss over a year or so of life?"

"It just seems to me—"

"Wait," Eppida said, raising one hand. "This is going to be point where you tell me that she should be seeking the bliss moment with boys her own age, isn't it?"

Aefric frowned. "We can't have much of a debate if you keep raising my points for me."

"I'll do better than that," Eppida said with a smile. "I'll defeat this one too. You are no more than..." — she frowned, looking closely at Aefric's skin — "perhaps seven years into your majority. Am I correct?"

Aefric nodded, eyes narrowed suspiciously.

"And yet, I understand that this past spring you shared the noble privilege with Montess Ol'Nastath, while she was still Baroness of Riverbreak. And I happen to *know* that she was about a dozen years your senior."

"So?"

"So whether you wish to speak in terms of years of life, or percentage of life, the difference between your age and Nesta's is smaller than the difference between your age and Montess'."

"There is a difference," Aefric said. "I am an adult. Nesta is not yet. Not in the eyes of the law, and not in my eyes either. If she inherited her lands today, she would need a regent."

"She could not yet rule her lands because she has not yet finished her training to do so," Eppida said. "That her training will be completed around the time she reaches her majority is a matter of tradition. Not some innate statement of mental and emotional competence."

"Nevertheless."

"Furthermore," Eppida said, raising one eyebrow slightly. "Bliss is not nearly so complicated as rulership. And no Armyrian would mistake the noble privilege for anything more than it is. A night of shared pleasure."

"We could continue to debate this until dawn. Suffice to say we all have lines we will not cross. And when it comes to bliss, mine is the age of majority. You will not argue me past that."

"No?"

Aefric shook his head.

Eppida regarded him thoughtfully. "And when you decide something is a matter of principle, you will hold to it no matter what. Won't you?"

"It's who I am," he said, stroking her cheek.

"Well, then," she said, with more heat in her smile now. "More for me."

And she leaned in for the kind of kiss that could only start things up again.

———

THEIR SECOND TIME TOGETHER THAT NIGHT WAS SLOWER, AND certainly took much longer. Still, in many ways, it was no less frenzied.

Eppida was not a gentle lover. And she both had and favored a rough touch. Scratching, groping, biting and being bitten. Nothing that would leave marks, of course. At least, not where others would see them.

As she'd explained it once, in a moment of afterglow, she liked feeling reminders of a good night for the day or two to follow. And she liked leaving her mark on a man.

By the time they'd finished their second round, she'd left hickeys beside two of Aefric's chest scars, and he'd left a pair on her thighs. And he knew his back looked as though he'd lost a fight with a wildcat.

Which, one could argue that he had.

Nevertheless, they were both smiling as they rested, sitting side by side with pillows propped behind them, both of them damp with perspiration. They sipped sweet, strong, dark green sharabi from long-stemmed wine glasses.

Sharabi was a variant of wine popular throughout Armyr and the surrounding kingdoms. This variety tasted a lot like honeydew, a taste that went well with Eppida. He wondered if that was why she'd chosen this vintage...

"Now," Eppida said, with a deep breath that was more than a little distracting in her current naked and glistening state. "About Zoleen."

"She's here at Armityr?"

"Of course," Eppida said. "Because she hasn't seen you since you *banished* her from Water's End—"

"Not true," Aefric said, shaking his head just enough that he then had to wipe some of his long hair out of his eyes.

If they kept this up, he'd need another bath. Or at least, a spell. Of course, so would she...

"You most certainly did banish her from Water's End," Eppida said, pointing toward him with her glass. "Zoleen was quite clear on that point. You told her to leave and not return without invitation."

"Oh, I don't debate the banishment," Aefric said. "It's just not true that it was the last time I saw her. She met me in Kivash, only a few aetts ago."

"She didn't mention that," Eppida said, frowning.

"It didn't go well," Aefric said. "She pushed. Not the best course of action."

"Honestly," Eppida said with a sigh. "That girl really ought to learn to listen to at least *one* of her sisters. Very well, then. You've *barely* seen her since she left Water's End. True?"

"True," Aefric said. "And I admit I was pleased with the book she sent me at Asarchai, during the Feast of Dereth Sehk. And even more so with her letter."

"Good," Eppida said, smiling. "Very good." She stroked Aefric's shin with her foot. "Now. Zoleen had thought — and I agreed with her — that you might have been willing to speak with her privately at a neutral location like Armityr."

"I would have," Aefric said, then shook his head. "But there's no time now. I leave for Netar first thing in the morning, and then I'm going to be too busy for some time."

Eppida growled. "I knew it. I knew we needed that dinner. Oh, I could *kill* Colm for this."

At Aefric's shocked expression, she quickly added, "I'm speaking figuratively, of course, about the occasionally very frustrating man I'm usually quite pleased to call my husband. I'm not suggesting I would actually commit regicide."

"I didn't think you would," Aefric said in a reasonable tone. "It was still surprising to hear."

"Oh, believe it," she said. "He frustrates me sometimes as much as I frustrate him." She tossed her head thoughtfully. "Perhaps that's what makes our marriage work."

Aefric shrugged and sipped his sharabi.

"You wouldn't understand, of course," she said with a teasing smile. "Not yet being married."

Actually, he remembered being married to Andi quite well, on those times he chose to stop and think about it. But he didn't remember them frustrating each other often, much less counting on frustration as the key to a successful marriage.

Then again, Keifer and Andi McShane hadn't been nobility, let alone royalty.

Aefric considered that through a long sip of sharabi. Eppida sipped her drink as well, though Aefric couldn't guess what she was thinking.

"So. Zoleen," Eppida said then. "You're willing to give her another chance?"

"I'm willing to talk with her," Aefric said. "I can't promise anything beyond that, because I don't know how that conversation will go."

"But you aren't *against* giving her another chance."

"I'm better disposed towards her now than I have been in more than a season," Aefric said. "So now I consider it at least a possibility."

"But you would have sent her away, if she'd come to your rooms tonight?"

Aefric nodded. "Too soon for that. If I didn't know her, and it was just about chasing the bliss moment with a beautiful woman, that would be one thing. But the way matters stand between us right now, there would be expectations beyond the scope of the noble privilege. I wouldn't want to risk giving her the wrong impression."

Eppida frowned at Aefric. Toyed with her glass for a moment, then took another sip.

"What?" Aefric said.

"That's quite close to what Zoleen said you'd say." She shook her head. "I told her that a man will forgive a great many mistakes when confronted with naked and willing Fyrenn beauty. But she insisted that coming to you tonight would be a mistake. That you wouldn't trust it. You'd assume manipulation on her part."

Aefric nodded, wondering if Zoleen had finally understood what he'd been trying to tell her. Why going behind his back to distance a rival had so upset him.

"Suppose for a moment," Eppida said, "that Zollen had come to your rooms just to talk."

Aefric gave her a droll look. "Would you have believed that? If you were in my position?"

"No, I suppose not," Eppida admitted, shaking her head. "Well, Aefric, for what it's worth, she's willing to go to great lengths — great *distances* even — to prove herself trustworthy to you. If you'll give her the chance."

"You're not suggesting I take her to Netar."

"I said no such thing," Eppida said, smiling.

"I can't do it," Aefric said. "I don't know what's waiting for me in Netar. For all I know, the king gave me that barony so I'd have to fix some kind of problem for him. Politics, monsters, magic, could be anything."

"Does that sound like something Colm would do?"

"I don't know," Aefric said honestly. "I understand he's quite good at addressing multiple problems in a single movement, which suggests that I can't ignore the possibility."

Eppida sipped her sharabi thoughtfully.

Aefric nodded at her. "You know both the man and the situation better than I do. What do you think?"

Eppida opened her mouth to say something, then quickly closed it again with a pained expression.

"Damn it, Colm," she growled, then tossed down the rest of her sharabi. "He knew Netar would come up tonight, and he *forbade* me from speaking about it, even by implication."

Aefric didn't have time to consider what that might mean, though. Eppida was still ranting.

"Forbade! Me!" She hissed out a breath. "Between the two of us, he's the ruling monarch and I'm the consort. So he *has* the authority. But oh, I *hate* when he reminds me of that."

"I take it he doesn't do so often?"

"It has been two years, three seasons, six aetts and four days since the last time he forbade me anything. And no, I will not tell you what."

She slammed her glass down on the night table so hard the stem broke.

"No?" Aefric asked, giving her a small smile and fluttering his lashes. "Not even ... under duress?"

He grabbed her arms and legs with magic and pinned her to the bed.

"Oh, ho, ho," Eppida said with lust spreading through her smile. "You're a clever one, Aefric Brightstaff. And you know my weakness. But I beg you, before you give me the fierce *ravishing* I deserve, let me finish the point I'm *trying* to make?"

"Only if you do so quickly," Aefric said, tossing his sharabi glass over to shatter on the hearth, which made Eppida roll her eyes wildly. Her wrists and ankles strained fruitlessly against his power.

He didn't normally use magic this way, but oh, Eppida did make it appealing, enjoying it the way she did.

"Obviously ... since you don't know what..." — she whimpered — "to expect when you get there ... you won't let Zoleen ... accompany you ... to Netar."

"That's right," Aefric said, leaning down and kissing his way up her stomach.

"Bite," she said softly. "Never be afraid to bite me, Aefric. Never. Anywhere."

He bit down on the soft skin just below her ribs.

"Yes," she said softly. "Oh, yes." She shook her head, but seemed to gather herself. "Will you come again to Armityr on your way back to Water's End? Spend some time with Zoleen? Even just to talk?"

Aefric breathed hot air across her nipple, then flicked it with his tongue. Eppida groaned loudly, writhing even harder now.

"Answer me, you bastard!"

He almost said yes. It was a reasonable request, and the king would probably want Aefric to stop by again anyway.

But with Eppida pinned as she was. Needful. Almost desperate. Shifting her hips constantly. Her lips parted and panting. Her eyes dark with lust.

He couldn't resist teasing her just a little more.

"Maybe," he said, and then he took her nipple into his mouth and ended the conversation.

2

Dawn in Armityr came to Aefric through glass windows as curtains were opened by an older serving man that next morning.

Aefric lay alone among the tangle of sheets and blankets left by the previous night's festivities. He still tasted the dry remains of honeydew sharabi on his tongue. His skin stung in many places along his shoulders, back and buttocks. Likely wherever Eppida had gotten a little extra enthusiastic with her nails.

The queen was already gone from his bed, though. She'd left ... was it two hours before? Three? Something close to that.

He remembered her leaving. Apologizing for not staying the whole night. And she'd said...

What was it she'd said?

Oh, yes.

I won't see you again before you leave, but I'll see you when you come through on your way back to Water's End.

Had Aefric promised to return on his way back? He didn't remember doing so. But he might have.

Oh, where would be the harm, anyway? He was a peer of the realm. Surely he was *expected* to stop by the royal palace whenever he rode through the area.

Then again, if that were the case, why would she need to keep asking?

"Your grace." The old serving man had a slight quaver in his soft voice. Once Aefric was looking at him, he continued, "Breakfast for your grace and his knight-adviser has been prepared in your grace's smallest sitting room, in case he desires private discourse. Your grace's knights and retainers have begun preparations to leave for Netar."

"In other words," Aefric said with a yawn and a smile, "stop lolling about in bed and get moving?"

"Certainly I would not say such a thing when addressing the Duke of Deepwater." The old man winked. "But I might have, were I addressing my own son."

Aefric laughed and managed to extricate himself from the sheets and blankets.

"On the night table, your grace will find a small unguent that his majesty bid me deliver. He seemed to believe that your grace would know its purpose."

Aefric picked up the small silver bowl and smelled the familiar bitter herbal concoction. His majesty had given Aefric a jar of it after his first night with Eppida, as an excellent remedy for scratches and small bruises.

The relief that spread through Aefric as he applied it was sweet and most welcome.

"I've taken the liberty of laying out clothes for your grace in the colors of Netar," the old serving man said. "Will your grace consent to wear a bycocket? I've been told he does, on occasion."

"You sound like Dajen, one of my chief valets."

"My cousin," the old man said with a smile.

"Forgive me, I don't know your name," Aefric said, stopping and really looking at the man.

Well wrinkled and gray haired — definitely older than Dajen by at least a decade — but straight of posture and sure in his movements. And now that Aefric looked, he did see some similarities to Dajen, around the cheekbones and ears. Interesting.

"There's nothing to forgive, your grace," the old man said with a bow. "My name is Tashen, and I thank your grace for asking. I am pleased to serve your grace as valet whenever he visits Armityr, and to see to the care of his rooms, in his absence."

"Thank you, Tashen," Aefric said. "And a bycocket hat will be fine."

Aefric rubbed sleep out of his eyes as he cast once more that little spell of cleanliness. A bath would have been more enjoyable, but clearly he couldn't afford the time.

Netar's colors turned out to be the same as those of the royal family. Forest green and gold. The clothes laid out for Aefric included a samite tunic of forest green, heavily embroidered with golden thread, and riding leathers dyed forest green. The belt and boots were of brown leather, but both had gold buckles.

The bycocket hat was green, both pointed bill and turned-back brim, but the lush feather in the back was golden.

And it was a real feather.

Aefric thought about that as he dressed, while Tashen began stripping the bed of its soiled sheets.

"What bird gives a feather like this one?" he asked, holding up the hat.

"The royal peacocks, your grace," Tashen said, without looking up from his work. "When they're young, the males go through a phase where their feathers turn the most delightful shade of gold."

Aefric donned the hat then, and looked himself over in the mirror. Good enough. He called the Brightstaff to his hand, then, and went to join Beornric for breakfast.

This morning, the curtains in that small, round sitting room stood open. The three tall windows streamed in morning sunlight, and gave the view of a city already at work. Both in its repairs, and in what passed for its normal business these days.

On the table, the traditional Armyrian breakfast was waiting for them. Sliced meats, cheeses and fruits, served with honeyed oat bread. To drink, only water.

Beornric wore his armor today, which shined as though it had been polished overnight. Probably was. His graying black hair looked freshly brushed, as did his mustache.

He stood as Aefric entered. "Good morning, your grace." The moment the door closed behind Aefric, Beornric continued, softly, "What did she ask of you?"

"Not much, actually," Aefric said, taking a seat — allowing Beornric to do the same — and standing the Brightstaff beside him. The honeyed oat bread was still oven-hot, and the first bite tasted so good that Aefric forgot what he was saying.

"What constitutes 'not much?'" Beornric prompted with a sardonic grin, while he speared a slice of turkey on his fork.

"Mostly she seemed concerned that I give Zoleen another chance." Aefric sipped a little water. "Asked me to stop by Armityr on the way back to Water's End, so I could speak with her."

"And did you say yes?"

Aefric paused. Beornric made that question sound important.

"I don't recall doing so," Aefric said, frowning. "But she seemed to think I have. Why?"

"Because I don't think this is just about your giving Zoleen Fyrenn another chance to win your heart. Or if it is, then the king must have a different favorite. Someone he'd rather you chose."

"One of those incoming princesses?" Aefric asked, biting into a juicy slice of orange.

"No way to know just yet," Beornric said. "But—"

Someone knocked on the door.

"Yes?" Aefric asked.

The door opened and Tashen announced, "His majesty, the king."

Aefric almost knocked his chair over in his rush to stand. If Beornric had similar trouble with his chair, though, Aefric missed it.

"Good morning, Aefric, Beornric," King Colm said, stepping into the small room, while Tashen closed the door behind him.

This morning the king wore a simple white silk tunic over navy blue hose. His graying black hair was tied back in a ponytail.

In fact, the only sign of his office was the signet ring on the middle finger of his left hand, mirroring the position of his ornate wedding ring with its large diamond, on the right.

"Good," King Colm continued, before Aefric could offer his own greeting. "I see Tashen has prepared the Netar colors for you. Very good."

"I look forward to seeing what awaits me in my new barony," Aefric said.

"Yes," King Colm said, his lips curling in a small smile. "I imagine you do, just as I imagine you have many questions related to that barony."

"Your majesty is, of course, correct," Aefric said carefully.

"I will not address those questions here and now," King Colm said. "Doing so would delay you, and worse, might prejudice you. I wish to do neither."

"Prejudice me, your majesty?"

"Just so. For now, suffice to say that I look forward to discussing Netar with you at a later date."

"Then your majesty wishes me to stop by Armityr on my way back to Water's End?"

King Colm clapped Aefric on the shoulder and smiled as though Aefric had answered a question for him.

"That, my dear Aefric, remains to be seen." He reached down and took a strawberry from the breakfast table. "For now, see to Netar. The rest may just take care of itself."

He clapped Aefric on the shoulder again, smiling wider now, and said, "Good travels to you both. I'll be in touch."

"May I ask a question, your majesty?"

"Of course, my good duke," King Colm said, smiling. "Though royal prerogative may prevent me from answering it."

"I was wondering about the two spies or assassins from my entourage."

"Caiperan spies," King Colm said. "Planted at Water's End not long after the visit of Princess Xenia, though with the primary goal of finding out all they could about what *I'm* doing."

"I apologize for not catching them sooner, your majesty," Aefric said.

"Think nothing of it," the king said with a dismissive wave. "We all spy on one another constantly. The only time I make issue of it is when matters like war are at hand."

"What will become of the spies then?"

"Oh, I'll hold them for a time, pretending to try to prove they're from Malimfar. Then I'll let my justiciar confirm they're from Caiperas. Then they'll likely feed me a story about how they were placed to track your grace's progress on the marriage front, which will be true, if not the complete truth. I'll let on that I believe it and won't bother the justiciar with confirming it, because Caiperas is *supposed* to be an ally of sorts. Then I'll send them on their way."

"And they'll return to Caiperas even more convinced that we'll be going to war with Malimfar."

"Which may prove even more effective, if they're snatched by Malimfar on their way home." He nodded to Aefric. "Safe travels, Aefric, Beornric."

King Colm popped the strawberry into his mouth and left without even waiting for Aefric to say goodbye.

Aefric turned to Beornric. "Do you understand what just happened here?"

"About the spies, yes," Beornric said as they sat down again. "The rest of it, no."

"That's the part I'm most concerned about. Netar. The queen. Whatever game they're playing."

"I suspect we're happier not knowing."

"I disagree," Aefric said, taking a sip of water. "Let me tell you something I've learned in my travels, Beornric. When people withhold information 'for my own good,' the results are nearly always worse than if they'd just told me what was going on in the first place."

Beornric chuckled, picking up a piece of apple and cheese together. "And tell me, how many of these withholders have been kings and queens?"

"Three," Aefric said. "And each one almost got me killed."

Beornric frowned. "Perhaps things are different for adventurers." He shrugged. "I can tell you that many, many things have been withheld from me during my years of service to the king. And not once was I ever sorry about that later."

"Well," Aefric said, drawing a deep breath, "then let us hope that whatever's happening meshes more with *your* past experiences than *mine.*"

It was a lovely thought. But Aefric had trouble believing it.

AT LEAST THERE WERE NO MORE UNEXPECTED DELAYS OR MYSTERIOUS conversations before the time came to leave Armityr.

Horses were saddled. Carts were loaded. Knights and entourage, all ready to go. And Aefric noticed that the Deepwater banners had been joined by a second banner: the golden acorn on a field of forest green.

The impressively unaggressive sigil of Netar. Aefric wondered how many jokes they'd heard over the years about Netar's *potential.*

The morning was surprisingly warm, but storm clouds looked to be coming down from the north as Aefric and his party left Armityr along a road every bit as wide and smooth as the Kingsroad, heading due northeast.

"Are we heading into rain?" Aefric asked Beornric.

"I shouldn't think so, your grace," Beornric said. "The baronial seat of Netar is only a half-day's ride from the capital. We should be safely inside before the storm reaches us."

"I thought the Kingsroad ended at the capital," Ser Micham said, from Beornric's left.

As the son of Ajenmoor's mayor, Micham had grown up around ships, and had skin toughened by sea air. A fact that his father apparently never forgave him for.

Any more than he'd forgiven his son for choosing the knight's path in the first place. Let alone allowing a borog to mar his handsome features by taking half an ear with a spear. Micham never shied away from displaying the battle scar though, wearing his brown hair and beard fashionably trim.

Micham was one of the two assigned directly to guarding Aefric that day. The other, riding to his right, was Ser Arras.

Arras' pale beauty, hazel eyes, and aristocratic bearing, worked with the luster of her short, black hair to spur many rumors that she was the unclaimed bastard of Deepwater's late duchess, Arinda Soulfist.

Aefric had reason to believe those rumors were true. Regardless, she'd never shown any signs of dissatisfaction with her lot in life.

"The Kingsroad *does* end at the capital," Beornric said. "At the palace, to be precise." He nodded to the road they were taking through more farmland just outside Armityr. "This is the Netar Road."

The Netar Road led through farmland and hills for a time. Groves of trees here and there, never allowed to grow within arrow shot of the road. The Maiden's Blood River was off to their left, but never closer than a couple of miles away.

The groves became more common — beeches and birches, for the most part, but some oak and maple — as the farms and towns faded behind them.

For a couple of hours, it was as though they had the whole road to themselves...

"Where is everyone?" Aefric asked.

"I think we've passed the end of the king's farmland," Beornric said. "We aren't more than an hour or two from the border now."

"Fine, but why is there no traffic? No caravans? No merchants? No peddlers? No messengers? I don't think I've seen so much as a rider since we passed that last little town, and nothing at all coming from Netar."

"Could be the wrong day," Beornric said. "Maybe they only leave for the capital once or twice an aett."

But he didn't sound as though he believed it.

Old adventuring instincts flared. Tried to tell Aefric something was wrong. He found his muscles tensing, and his eyes darting about.

Catching the flight of every sparrow, crow, and rika. His ears alert for every rustle among the grass and trees. Every birdsong or bark of a fox...

Animals. He relaxed and chuckled to himself. If the animals were still going about their normal business, then there wasn't likely some monstrous threat lying in wait for him.

Whenever a monster moved into an area, the local fauna tended to flee or get eaten. Either way, they weren't around to rustle and sing and bark.

Around the time Aefric was starting to relax again, two things happened. First, he spied a town in the distance that had to be Netarritan. Second, his party was met by outriders on slender horses, likely chosen for speed over endurance.

All four outriders wore green leathers, with the acorn sigil of Netar embossed on the left shoulder. They carried swords at their sides and longbows in their hands.

Three of them had arrows nocked, but not pointed. A sight that sent a rustle of displeasure through Aefric's knights and soldiers.

Aefric found himself thinking about the bronze bracer worn on his left arm, under the sleeve of his tunic. It was enchanted to turn aside blades and arrows.

He hadn't enchanted it himself, but he *had* examined its magic. Seemed as though it should work. Though he hadn't tested it yet...

The outrider riding point — a slender woman with short blonde hair, and the only one who hadn't drawn an arrow — hailed them.

"Do I have the honor of addressing his grace, Ser Aefric Brightstaff, Duke of Deepwater and newly named Baron of Netar?"

"You do," Beornric said. "Although I believe it is against custom to address one's new liege with weapons drawn and ready."

"I quite understand," she said, "and I do apologize for the necessity. I am Ser Lachedea Ol'Valim, charged with safety of the road near Netarritan, which has proven ... uncertain at times. A truth that requires me, I'm afraid, to ask for confirmation of your grace's identity."

Beornric started to say something, but Aefric stilled him with a calming hand. He reached into his belt pouch for the Netar seal. He held up the seal, and floated it over to Lachedea.

She inspected it. Compared it to a scrap of parchment. Nodded.

"Identical," she said. "I hereby confirm the legitimacy of this seal."

The other outriders immediately put away their arrows and slung their bows over their shoulders.

She held up the seal, and Aefric called it back to his hand before putting it back in his belt pouch.

"Were you expecting an impostor?" Aefric asked.

"No, your lordship," Lachedea said, slinging her bow over one shoulder. "But one hundred fifty years ago, someone impersonated the new baron, and made off with a good number of valuables before he was caught. The test has become something of a tradition since then."

"Then you confirm," Beornric said, sounding irritated, "that you are addressing *your liege*?"

"I do," Lachedea said, then slipped down from her saddle and bowed low. "It is with great pleasure that I welcome your lordship to Netar."

As she did that, the other three outriders raised their right fists high in salute.

"Thank you, good ser knight," Aefric said, and as she rose from the bow, he gave her the salute of a noble to a knight. "But when did we cross the border into Netar? I didn't see a boundary marker."

"Properly speaking, your lordship has not yet entered Netar," she said. "My troop patrols into the king's lands with permission, thanks to a treaty even older than the tradition your lordship just endured. Netar begins at Netarritan."

With a quick movement, she swung back up into her saddle. "Would your lordship care to have us escort his party the rest of the way?"

"Is that tradition?" Aefric asked, one eyebrow high.

"Not specifically," Lachedea said. "But there is precedent, if your lordship is concerned."

"Well," Aefric said, "while such an escort would be my pleasure, I find I must refuse. I don't think it would behoove the new baron to take you from your post and leave the road unguarded."

"Even though the road has been quiet all day?" Lachedea asked.

"Turn a blind eye and you won't know what slips past you."

"As your lordship commands," Lachedea said with a smile and a bow. "I and mine shall resume our duties as soon as your lordship wills."

"Then be about your duties, good ser knight, and I shall see you later at Netarritan when I formally accept you into my service."

Lachedea and her outriders left the road then, and Aefric and his party began to ride.

"I think she approves of your choice," Beornric said. "Forgoing the escort and keeping them on watch, I mean."

"You think that was a test?" Aefric asked. "Seeing if I preferred pomp to security?"

"I might've tested your grace that way," Arras said from Aefric's right. "Were I in her place."

"Which brings me to another question. She gave my courtesy as 'lordship,' not 'grace,' and you didn't call her on it."

"She owes her service to his lordship, the Baron of Netar, not his grace, the Duke of Deepwater," Beornric said. "Everyone in Netar will address you the same way. And I expect they addressed the king himself as 'your lordship,' whenever he came to Netar. While his majesty held the barony, I mean."

"It's going to sound strange," Aefric said.

"Well, let us hope that is the strangest thing you have to deal with while we're here."

"Let's hope," Aefric agreed.

An arrow flew high into the sky and flared out into bright green flame. A signal arrow.

"I'd say the arrival of the new baron has just been announced to Netarritan," Beornric said.

"Well, then," Aefric said. "Let's not keep them waiting."

NETARRITAN WASN'T QUITE AS CLOSE AS IT HAD LOOKED, BECAUSE Aefric hadn't expected a town to have such impressive walls. Truly, Aefric had seen cities with walls that looked puny, compared to the mighty structure he approached under the high sun of midday.

These town walls had to be as tall as those of Armityr. And likely as thick. Not whitish stone, though, but a medium gray tone, which was interesting. Suggested they came from a different quarry, despite Netarritan's close proximity to the capital.

Even stranger, these walls also didn't look to have been scarred by the wars...

"Look at the *size* of those *blocks*," Micham said. And he had a point. The individual stones that made up the wall were rectangular in shape, but they had to be about five feet long, and maybe half as tall.

"Na'shek," Aefric said. "Only na'shek builders use blocks that size. I knew Netar was supposed to have a large population of na'shek, but I hadn't thought about what that would mean to construction. Bet that castle's going to be a treat."

The stone of the walls bridged the space above the iron gates, which stood some three times Aefric's height, and looked wide enough to accommodate six good-sized carts at a time.

Chainmail-clad soldiers on the walls all began to raise their right fists high in salute as they took sight of Aefric's approach.

Trumpeters played the baronial fanfare.

The iron gates swung slowly open.

Aefric had been wrong about one thing. Netarritan's walls weren't as thick as those of Armityr. They were thicker.

To enter, Aefric and his company had to ride through a tunnel some thirty feet long, under an impressive number of murder holes.

Assaulting this town would be no easy feat.

Aefric came through the tunnel onto tiled streets packed with people. A crowd so big and boisterous, Aefric thought of Asarchai, during the Feast of Dereth Sehk.

And not everyone among the cheering throngs was human. The

slate gray faces of na'shek were plentiful in the crowd, and here and there Aefric spotted the almost glowing beauty of the eldrani.

Of course, spotting na'shek was always easy, for they all stood two or more heads taller than even the tallest humans around them, and about twice as wide.

Much the same way, eldrani were easily spotted by their vivid hair colors. Not as many of them in the crowd as the humans or na'shek, but it still looked as though Netarritan had a larger eldrani population than most of Armyr.

That was interesting. And unexpected.

The na'shek, of course, would be drawn by the mines and smithing. But the eldrani rarely took interest in either. So what would draw them to Netar?

Aefric didn't spot any derekek, but that wasn't too surprising. They preferred places with easy sea access.

And as for kindaren, well, small as they were, they'd be hard to spot in a crowd like this.

In fact, so many people had come out to greet the new baron that Aefric found himself glad to have those lines of chainmail-clad soldiers, holding their spears horizontally and keeping the route clear for Aefric and his company.

If he'd had to ride *through* that crowd, they might not have reached the keep before midnight.

Plus ... there was something off in the cheering of the crowds. Something a touch shrill. Maybe even desperate. And the flowers they threw. Not roses, for love, or hibiscus, for health, but holly blossoms.

Holly. The plant Armyr associated with luck.

Even stable, calming Beornric had a concerned set to his face when he realized what the crowd was throwing.

Aefric tried to distract himself by paying more attention to his new town.

The buildings here in Netarritan were all stonework, whether they were as small as one-story houses and shops, or as large as the great domed temples, or the four- and five-story buildings that might've been homes, or guilds, or something else besides.

The road stayed wide and crowd thick all the way to the walls of the Iron Keep, the baronial castle of Netar. Walls that were taller still than those of the town itself.

Whoever'd built this place surely hadn't skimped on their defenses. Unless Aefric was mistaken, this inner wall even had a gatehouse. Hard to tell, from this vantage point.

The iron gates of those walls were closed, but that was to be expected. As were the red carpeting that had been spread out before the gates, and the more dignified crowd awaiting Aefric on that carpet.

These would be local knights and lers, and perhaps other important courtiers, with the castellan in charge. The knights all clad in full plate armor, and the lers and other courtiers in fine clothes. They stood in a semicircle, with the center of the arc being in front of the midpoint of the gates.

"One advantage of being a baron," Aefric muttered. "None of those long-form oaths of fealty to exchange with other titled nobles."

Beornric chuckled at that, though his eyes kept scanning the crowd.

Looking for threats? Was Beornric even more concerned about the tension in that crowd than Aefric was?

Aefric's knights and soldiers peeled to the sides as they reached the edge of the carpet, though four of his soldiers approached to take charge of the horses as Aefric, Beornric, Arras and Micham dismounted.

The castellan was easy to spot. First because he was in the center of the semicircle, and second because he was na'shek. And for a na'shek, he was tall. Aefric was considered fairly tall for a human, and Aefric judged that he only came up to this na'shek's chest. Somewhere around the sternum.

The castellan was broad, too. About as broad across the shoulders as Aefric and Beornric combined, with a little to spare.

His skin tone was on the darker side of slate gray, and his long, tight braids would likely have been the same shade as his skin, except that he'd colored them reddish. Likely using powdered sandstone.

He dressed in a toga made entirely of cloth-of-silver, befitting his rank and role, but his boots looked to be made from fine white doeskin. An affectation? Or an attempt to fit in with a largely human government?

He also wore an impressively large war axe, hanging from his belt as though it weighed no more than a rapier.

Aefric approached two strides onto the red carpeting, so that Beornric could stand comfortably at his side, with Micham and Arras at his back. This left him about four good strides from the castellan.

Beornric blew a whistle that Aefric had almost forgotten the knight carried.

The crowd settled down to a hush.

"Ser Aefric Brightstaff," Beornric called out in a ringing voice, "Duke of Deepwater, Hero of the Battle of Deepwater, Hero of the Battle of Frozen Ridge, and newly made Baron of Netar."

Some in the crowd cheered at that, but there on the red carpet, the locals all knelt. The lers and other courtiers on both knees, but the knights and soldiers — including the soldiers holding back the crowd, and those others up on the walls — on one knee, indicating that they were ready for action, if needed.

The castellan took one knee, which was no surprise. Aefric had yet to meet a castellan who wasn't a knight.

Aefric approached the castellan then. Beornric remained behind, but Arras and Micham continued to act as an honor guard.

Even kneeling, the castellan could have looked Aefric in the eye. At the moment, though, his eyes were respectfully downcast.

He pulled the war axe from his belt. Held it up lying flat across both his large palms. He spoke in a deep, rumbling voice.

"I am Ser Grond, Knight of Netar, and castellan of the Iron Keep. In token of the service I swear to you, I offer my axe."

There was a series of startled gasps when Aefric stood the Brightstaff to one side and picked up that axe. But he was expecting that. What he was doing was not strictly the way things were done, but it was what he'd done at Behal, and later at Water's End. He saw no reason to stop his personal tradition now.

Grond, for his part, gave no reaction at all.

The axe was every bit as heavy as it looked. And to say it was enchanted would have been misleading. The axe was magical, of that there was no doubt. But no spells had ever been cast on it.

The na'shek were not a people who could command arcane magic, as Aefric knew it. They did not feel its flow, nor cast spells. But their crafters understood some aspect of magic on a very deep level. And the best of them seemed to be able to imbue magic into every step of their forging.

The axe Aefric only just managed to hold without wavering could probably — in Grond's hands — cleave all the way through an armored knight in one swing.

"This is the finest axe I have ever held in my hands," Aefric said, not hiding the touch of strain in his voice. "Is it your work?"

"My father's," Grond said. "He made it for me when he learned that I had been knighted. It was the working of his life."

Aefric's eyes widened. That meant that not only had the smith poured magic into this weapon, but literally his own lifeforce.

Perhaps even his soul. Aefric was less clear on that point.

Either way, Grond's father had died in making this weapon.

"Then it is a sacred weapon, as well as a mighty one," Aefric said in Na'shese, which made Grond's eyes widen. Aefric switched back to the common tongue as he finished, "I am both pleased and proud that you now wield it for me."

Aefric handed the war axe back to Grond, then gave him the salute of a noble to a knight. "Arise, Ser Grond."

Grond escorted Aefric around the semicircle then, while Aefric completed the ceremony. With the Brightstaff trailing in his wake, Aefric took each knight's weapon and said a word or two, before accepting their service and saluting.

The lers offered their hands to be kissed, as Aefric accepted them, too, into his service. The first few stopped there, but then one pressed his forehead to Aefric's knuckles.

The movement caught Aefric by surprise. Pressing one's forehead to the knuckles of one's liege was part of the long-form oaths of fealty. When it was done on other occasions, it was usually to express gratitude or devotion.

As far as Aefric knew, he hadn't done anything in Netar that merited such a gesture. And yet, after one ler did that, the rest all followed suit.

The other petty nobles and courtiers needed nothing so formal, so they received only nods of acknowledgment.

Most of the knights and lers were human. But there were two na'shek and one eldrani among the knights, and one na'shek and one eldrani among the lers.

Finally, the soldiers needed only a quick, collective word of thanks for their service.

Once that was done, Grond bowed to Aefric and said, "Your lordship, Netar is yours. Welcome to your castle."

"Thank you, Grond," Aefric said gravely.

Grond turned to the soldiers atop the wall and called out, "Your baron has arrived!"

Fanfare blew again. The crowd cheered louder still. The gates creaked open.

Now, at last, Aefric could find out just what the king had given him.

SURE ENOUGH, THERE WAS A GATEHOUSE, SURROUNDING THE TUNNEL through the thick walls and into the area of the Iron Keep.

There were stables just inside the walls, from which Ser Grond called for his green-scaled rops.

Aefric had never seen a rops in the wild, only either working with the na'shek, or carrying them. They were clearly lizards of some sort, with their smooth skin. But they might be related to dragons or wyvern, given their scales, their four thick legs, their tails almost as thick as those legs, and their heavy, ponderous heads that were flat on top.

Rops — the word was both singular and plural — were nowhere near as fast or agile as even a decent horse. But they were furiously strong. And that flat, thick, bony head of theirs could knock down a small keep, given enough time and impetus.

Riding, Grond led Aefric's party — which now included the local knights, lers and courtiers, following behind — along the slated road, which curved around the hill up to the castle.

Which would mean that the Iron Keep just happened to be built on the only hill in the area.

"This isn't a natural hill, is it?" Aefric asked.

"Very good, your lordship," Grond said. "Most don't spot that. No, this hill was raised by the na'shek builders who constructed the castle."

"Did they build the hill after building the castle?"

Grond laughed a sound so deep that Aefric could feel it in his guts. In Na'shese, he said, *"I understand now why your lordship speaks our tongue. He is well acquainted with my people."*

"Traveled with a few, and fought alongside more during the wars," Aefric said in Na'shese, before switching back to the common tongue. "I take it that's a yes?"

"Yes, your lordship. That is our standard approach. Build first, then build up around."

"I know a little about the na'shek ways, but not everything. For example, I'm curious. Where did the gray stone come from? If Netar has a quarry, I don't know about it. And I'd think the white stone would be cheaper to bring in."

Grond laughed again. "Your lordship has only known us in war and human places then, never in the mines."

"Wait," Aefric said. "You mean all this stone came from the mines? *Netar's mines?*"

"Of course, your lordship. The na'shek do not waste stone. What we remove as we mine, we find other ways to use. Walls, castles, roads, houses. All of it came from Netar's mines."

"I knew the na'shek has ways of forging with magic. But I didn't know you mined with it as well."

"Not in the way your lordship uses the word," Grond said. "Your magic we would call *reke*. But the deeper secrets of the forge are *rekunt*. And the deeper secrets of the mine are *renkat*."

"I've heard *reke*, of course. But if I've heard *rekunt* or *renkat* before, I don't recall."

"Likely your lordship has not," Grond said. "They are not spoken of often, among non-na'shek. Not because doing so is forbidden. Only because we would not expect others to understand. But I think your lordship might."

"Perhaps," Aefric said, hesitant. "To a small degree."

Grond only nodded at that, as they continued up the hill.

As they rode, Aefric noticed more buildings down around the base of the hill, close to the castle walls. Barracks, from the look of them. And a couple of blacksmiths, tanners, wrights, and a few other buildings Aefric wasn't sure about.

Two loops around the hill, before they would finally reach the Iron Keep itself.

It wasn't made of iron, of course. More gray stone. From the mines, apparently. It looked to be a fairly low, flat keep. At least, compared to the likes of Water's End and Armityr. No more than perhaps four stories tall. With no towers stretching much higher. No peak in the center of the keep.

Octagonal, though, which was different. With rounded towers at each corner. Lots of arrow slits on the first three levels, and windows on the fourth.

Windows with...

"Are those iron shutters?" Aefric asked, pointing, as they completed the final circuit.

"Yes, your lordship," Grond said. "They slide into place, protecting the glass and those within, in the event of a siege."

"Have they ever been needed?"

"Not so far," Grond said. "But best to be safe."

When they reached the doors of the Iron Keep — these were iron, of course — Aefric noticed at least two score of grooms standing ready.

"No stables up here, your lordship," Grond said, as the grooms came to take charge of the horses. "But mounts can be brought up at a moment's notice. We have a system for signaling all the buildings below."

The doors were closed, and the portcullis down. But as soon as the horses stopped outside the doors, the baronial fanfare blew once more. The portcullis raised, and the doors swung open, revealing an antechamber.

"From here," Grond said, "your lordship could choose to retire to his rooms, host a formal reception for the knights and lers, or call a private meeting with his advisers."

"Let's start with the advisers," Aefric said. "We can see about formal receptions later, and a half-day's ride is hardly enough to require me to rest."

"Thank you, your lordship," Grond said, sounding relieved. "That would have been my request."

Grond immediately called for pages and dispatched them to gather the missing advisers.

The scale of the keep was unusual. It had been built for humans, but it was built by na'shek, who were much larger than humans.

The na'shek had clearly tried to make everything smaller than they would have for themselves, but they hadn't gotten it quite right.

As a result, all the doorways and hallways were taller and wider than Aefric was used to in his castles. That part was fine. But the stairs were *just* too big. By maybe a quarter.

In other words, they were big enough to *look* normal, which could lull you into not paying attention. Which would lead to tripping, falling, and generally embarrassing situations.

Fortunately, Aefric had been through his share of ancient ruins which were built for peoples other than humans. He reflexively noticed the difference in size and adjusted accordingly.

His knights, however, cursed and grumbled and occasionally stumbled as Grond led them up a side stairway.

"I do apologize about the stairs, your lordship," Grond said. "This keep is quite old, and the na'shek who built it had never worked with humans before. Your lordship will find that all more modern construction in Netar is ... better suited to human movement."

"I think we can adjust," Aefric said.

On the second, floor, Grond led the way along a hallway to their left.

"This floor is usually crowded," Grond said. "But with the timing of your lordship's arrival, the servants are busy below us, most of the soldiers are on the walls, and everyone else is — or was — out on the streets."

The hallway in question was of gray stone. No plaster here. No wood paneling on the floor. There were tapestries along the walls, most of which featured surprisingly lush landscapes. Were those places here in Netar?

The hallway kept going, even after it turned to the right, which meant they'd passed one corner of the octagon.

"Is the meeting room along the outside of the keep?" Aefric asked.

"Oh, do forgive me, your lordship," Grond said, bowing. "In my haste, I'd forgotten for a moment that your lordship has not been here before."

He took a right turn, which went about fifteen paces down a hallway with only one door on each side. The hallway ended in a large, glass window. On the second floor.

Grond gestured, and Aefric looked through the window.

Everything suddenly made sense.

There *was* no massive central structure to the keep. The walls *were* the keep. They were perhaps sixty feet wide, and surrounded a large, central courtyard. Easily large enough to host a tourney, or other event.

"Your lordship can just see the baronial apartments there," Grond said, pointing.

Off to the left, on the fourth floor, Aefric saw a large balcony, overlooking the central courtyard.

Wait. How could there be a central courtyard, if...

"Your builders built up the hill *after* building the keep," Aefric said. "Yes?"

"Well, most of the keep, your lordship. The octagonal portion."

"Then all of that..." Aefric pointed at the courtyard.

"Was built up later. Yes, your lordship."

"And now that's all solid dirt?"

"Not quite, your lordship. There is a rather extensive network of tunnels and rooms below. All quite solid and stable, of course."

"Of course," Aefric said, feeling almost numb as he contemplated the scale of what he'd just been told.

This hill. It had to be two hundred feet tall.

Just how big was this castle really? How extensive this network of tunnels? And what was it all used for?

Grond spoke into Aefric's silence.

"My people lived in tunnels, your lordship, before we came aboveground," Grond said. "It was only natural for us to build this castle as not merely a single structure, but a series of interconnected structures."

"I'll need a map," Aefric said.

"One awaits your lordship in his apartments," Grond said and, at Aefric's nod, resumed leading Aefric to the meeting room.

THE MEETING ROOM WAS ON THE FOURTH FLOOR, NEAR THE BARONIAL apartments, on the courtyard side. More gray stone. No floorboards. No plastering. Though at least rugs of woven rushes had been laid down. And from the sweet smell of their herbs, they were new-woven.

The ceiling was high enough that the oaken chandelier didn't make the room feel crowded. None of its candles were lit at the moment, because the many windows along the long outside wall supplied plenty of light.

A series of broad, pale oaken cabinets lined the wall beneath those windows.

The long inside wall was covered with maps. Maps of Netar, Armyr around Netar. The closest portions of Rethneryl, Malimfar and Caiperas. The trade routes through and near Netar, both by road and by river. And a couple of others besides.

One short wall held a door. Likely leading into the baronial apartments. Beside that door, a liquor cabinet, and on the other side of that, a series of well-used weapons hung on display. Swords and polearms mostly, but there was one large, wicked-looking spiked mace.

The other short wall held bookcases and more cabinets.

In the middle of the room, an octagonal oaken table, painted forest green, with the golden acorn of Netar done large in the center.

Each side of the octagon held a matching forest green chair. Three of those chairs were occupied at the moment, though those occupants were quick to stand when Aefric entered the room.

The first of these was a male eldrani with orange eyes and brilliantly yellow hair. Not blonde, like a human might have, but a true yellow. Like the petals of a sunflower. But what really drew attention was the scar marring the lightly tanned perfection of his eldrani beauty. A rough, jagged white line that started at his right temple, and curved down to his chin.

He wore full plate armor, enameled forest green and recently polished. At his belt hung a long sword on one side, and a short sword on the other.

This was one of the knights Aefric had briefly met, down by the gates. His name was ... Ser Keelastach. He hadn't given a family name, but eldrani often didn't. Not until they knew you well.

To Keelastach's right was, well, a fop. In fact, he reminded Aefric of Count Ferrin of Motte, and not in a good way. It wasn't that this man was slight of build, or that his black hair, pointed mustache and little goatee were all well-slicked. It wasn't even in his clothes. Ferrin tended towards loud, clashing colors, and this man wore a white silk tunic under a padded, pale blue doublet, with black hose, and a rapier at his hip.

No, there was something in the man's bearing that made Aefric think he would be trouble.

Across the table from the fop stood a female kindaren, only just tall enough for her head and shoulders to be seen over the table. She wore robes of muted brown and green, and carried an ironwood rod.

She was a magic-user, of course. Aefric would have known that from her appearance, even if he hadn't felt her soft thrum of power. Enough to mark her as competent, but far from overwhelming.

Specifically, she was a rare kind of magic-user that the kindaren called a *zulim*. A rune worker. She had three small pebbles, each marked with a softly glowing orange rune, floating in circles around her head, no more than two slender finger-widths from her short brown hair. In her right hand, her ironwood rod was graven with many dark red runes.

All three bowed to Aefric with words of greeting and welcome, while he stood the Brightstaff and sat in the chair that was unquestionably his.

Closest to the short wall with the door, this chair was the most ornate. Well engraved, with gold etching in the grooves, and the golden acorn of Netar done large on the center of the chair back.

Beornric sat at Aefric's right hand. Grond directly across. Keelastach sat to Aefric's left, and then the kindaren. To Beornric's right sat the fop.

Grond looked ready to say something, but Aefric turned to Keelastach. "You, I have met. Ser Keelastach. By your choice of chair, may I presume you are Netar's general?"

"Yes, your lordship," Keelastach said with a nod. "I have been pleased to serve his majesty in that role since before the gods came down to Qorunn, and I hope to continue in my post."

He looked pointedly at Beornric.

Aefric half-answered the unspoken question.

"I have no reason to replace the general who knows Netar's troops, defenses and terrain far better than I do. And I trust you will give me no reason to think otherwise."

Keelastach accepted the small compliment with a nod.

Aefric turned his attention to the kindaren.

"You I have not met, but I presume you have been serving as baronial court wizard."

"Your lordship presumes correctly," she answered in a high, clear voice. "I was honored to take up this post after the previous court wizard was killed during the wars. My name is Jenbarjen, and I suspect your lordship knows me for a *zulim*."

Aefric nodded. "In case there is any doubt, I have no plans to replace you either." He addressed them all then. "In fact, let me make clear that I do not intend to replace any of you, unless given cause."

Aefric turned an expectant look to the fop.

"Your lordship," the fop said with a slight bow, "I am Guimond Ol'Riel. And I have the pleasure of serving as Netar's historian."

"I'm sure you will serve me well," Aefric lied, then nodded to his right. "This is Ser Beornric Ol'Sandallas, my chief adviser, and captain of my Knights of the Lake, who are currently waiting on the other side of that door."

Aefric jerked his thumb to indicate the hallway.

"I note that two seats at this table remain empty," Aefric said.

"To my right," Grond said, "would normally sit the castle seneschal. But our last seneschal was dismissed by his majesty, and not replaced. I have taken up his duties in the interim, but would not be averse to finding a replacement."

"We'll see about that later," Aefric said, nodding, "and the other?"

"Our scoutmaster, who was already scheduled for patrol when word came that your lordship would be arriving today. She felt that ... she felt that maintaining our regular schedules was her more important duty."

"Is that what she said?" Aefric asked, one eyebrow high.

"No, your lordship, it is not," Grond said. "But if your lordship is curious about her precise wording, I would rather he ask our scoutmaster directly, when he meets her."

"Her name wouldn't be Lachedea, would it?" Beornric asked.

"It would," Grond said with a nod. "I take it she met you on the road?"

"She did," Aefric said, chuckling. "And I agree with her that our security is more important than the greeting ceremony. But as she has functionally absented herself from this meeting, she can't complain later if she doesn't like any decisions I make."

Aefric noted that his use of "I" and not "we" was not lost on any of them. Well, they had to expect that the new baron would do things his own way.

"Oh, she'll complain, your lordship," Keelastach said. "Possibly even if she *does* agree."

"Then I will deal with her when the time comes," Aefric said.

"If I might," Beornric said and, at Aefric's nod, continued. "Who normally occupies the chair I sit in?"

"That chair has always gone to the baron's chief adviser, whoever it might be. His majesty had many, over the years."

"Fascinating," Aefric said, "but I think it's time we cut straight to the heart of the matter. I noticed the lack of traffic on the road. Felt the tension of that crowd. Heard the desperation in their cheering. Just what momentous problem does Netar face?"

APPARENTLY, AEFRIC'S DIRECTLY ASKING HIS NEW ADVISERS ABOUT Netar's big problem threw them. Guimond's eyebrows tried to skip over his forehead and join his hair directly. Jenbarjen sat up so straight, with such a shocked expression that Aefric wondered if he'd offended her. Grond got an eager look to his eyes, but a suspicious set to his mouth.

Keelastach, though, thumped the octagonal table with a fist and said, "Finally."

Aefric exchanged wary looks with Beornric.

"I take it," Aefric said, "one of you is going to *tell* me about this problem? Or must I guess it?"

"Forgive us, your lordship," Grond rumbled. "It's just that we rather expected that his majesty had chosen his new baron specifically to deal with this problem."

"And it might be that he did," Aefric said. "His majesty certainly made clear that he didn't want to *prejudice* me in how I handled Netar's current situation. Which I found an interesting turn of phrase at the time. But I find it even *more* interesting now, given that *I am still waiting to find out what this problem is.*"

"Borogs, your lordship," Keelastach said. "And to be perfectly frank, I don't understand why they *remain* a problem."

"I must agree," Grond said. "We have more than enough troops to go in and deal with these borogs. Yes, it's likely that we'll lose some troops, but—"

Aefric waved him to silence.

"I asked about the *problem*," he said. "And what I am hearing are proposed solutions."

"The problem, your lordship, is that there are borogs in our mines," Keelastach said. "And the solution to this problem is both simple and time-tested."

"If I may," Guimond said, somewhere between raising his hand for permission and lifting an index finger to make a point.

Aefric nodded.

"It seems to me that his lordship wishes to know more of the details regarding the borog situation." He turned to Aefric. "Yes?"

Aefric nodded again, quicker this time, in hopes of someone getting to the point.

"Then I shall explain," Guimond said with a small bow.

"It was during the aett following the Midspring Festival this year that the first three miners were reported missing or dead. I can provide names, if your lordship requires them."

"That won't be necessary at this time. Do continue."

"These were followed by two more disappearances over the following two aetts. These incidents led to an investigation, which uncovered signs indicating the presence of borogs. This led to three inconclusive skirmishes, following which we pulled back and contacted his majesty — who was, at the time, Baron of Netar — for permission to conduct a proper assault."

All of this was coming from Guimond without his even checking a note. Perhaps there was a reason this man was court historian.

"As I understand the exchange of messages that followed, his lordship could not address the issue at the time, because as his majesty he was embroiled in trouble along Armyr's southern border."

"Yes," Aefric said. "The attempted invasion by Malimfar."

"Which, I understand," Guimond said, "we have your lordship to thank for stopping." He inclined his head to Aefric. "However, by law we could not proceed with our full assault without his lordship's permission."

"Which he continued to deny us," Keelastach growled.

"I was coming to that," Guimond said, actually chiding the general, which didn't strike Aefric as wise. "His lordship ordered us to take no further actions on the borog matter until instructed to do so."

Guimond affected a sigh. "This order ... did not go over well, among the members of this council."

Both Grond and Keelastach growled. Jenbarjen, though, simply frowned thoughtfully.

"The next information we had," Guimond continued, "was that your lordship was to be our new baron, and that your lordship would deal with the borog situation personally."

"Well," Aefric said with a sigh of his own, "the reason I didn't come here before now was that no one had *informed* me about the borog situation. I take it the stalemate has been bad for business?"

"Trade is down more than thirty percent, and our best mines and forges have slowed to a crawl," Grond said. "Worse, we have reason to suspect that the borogs have tapped into our veins."

"Unconscionable," Keelastach said. "Bad enough that the current delay could hurt Armyr if we were to go to war, but—"

"Hurt Armyr how?" Aefric asked.

"Netarritan is the primary supplier of weapons and armor for the royal army," Grond said, "and most of eastern Armyr."

A number of things clicked into place for Aefric.

"I take it there have been no diplomatic sallies from or to the borogs?" he asked.

"They're *borogs*, your lordship," Grond said, as though he thought Aefric didn't understand.

"That's a no, then," Beornric said, nodding. "No surprise."

"I don't understand what there would be to discuss," Keelastach said. "Surely we can't be expected to cede our mines to invaders."

"It's not that simple," Aefric said.

"Forgive me, your lordship," Grond said, "but it is *exactly* that simple. They are invading our lands as surely as they would be if they came across our border under sunlit skies. They are taking our resources, just as they would if they captured Lake Fist. We must treat them as all invaders have been treated since the dawn of time, and kill them."

"Tell me," Aefric said. "Do our mines and tunnels have boundary markers?"

"Excuse me, your lordship?" Grond said, narrowing his eyes suspiciously.

"Boundary markers. If a troop of hunters from Rethneryl tried to hunt in our lands, they would have to cross our boundary markers, warning them of the crime they were about to commit. Would the borogs have passed any such boundary markers down in the mines?"

"Well, I don't believe—"

"Guimond," Aefric said, "according to all reports and evidence, from which direction did the borogs come?"

"From deeper underground, your lordship."

"Then they came to our mines through *their* tunnels, not ours," Aefric said. "And since it sounds as though they would not have found any boundary markers in our tunnels, they had no reason to *know* that they'd entered our lands and were taking our ore."

Grond's slate skin, already a fairly dark tone, darkened further. Which, Aefric knew, meant Grond was getting angry.

Sadly, Aefric had expected that.

"Is your lordship taking their part in this?" Keelastach asked in disbelief.

"Not in the least," Aefric said. "I am merely trying to establish sufficient understanding of the facts of our situation, to ensure that I handle it properly."

"*What is there to understand?*" Grond thundered, standing. "They are *borogs*. They are dealt with like *this!*"

Grond pulled the huge war axe from his side and split the table in half.

Everyone but Aefric leapt to their feet. Beornric drew his sword and stood ready to defend. The other three backed away, watching. Perhaps uncertain what to do.

The hallway door slammed open and the Knights of the Lake came running in, weapons drawn. Micham and Arras in the lead.

Aefric stilled his knights with a raised hand, and stared calmly right back into Grond's furious glare.

"I have lived and fought alongside the na'shek many times in my life," Aefric said, voice quiet enough to make the others strain just a little to hear him. "Most recently leading more than a thousand against the borog forces of the Flayer at the Battle of Deepwater."

Aefric nodded once, slowly. "And so I understand the ancient hatred that lies between the na'shek and the borogs. For this reason and this reason alone I will not, in this one instance, execute you for the treason you just committed by baring your weapon and menacing your liege lord. Is that understood?"

Whatever Grond expected Aefric to say and do, it wasn't that. He stood there, bemused, weapon almost forgotten in his hands.

"*I asked you a question,*" Aefric snapped.

"Yes, your lordship." The answer seemed to come out of Grond without his thinking about it.

"Very good. You will now surrender your weapon to my knights." Grond hesitated.

"Don't be foolish," Beornric said softly.

Grond nodded. With one hand, he held the war axe out to the side. Micham sheathed his longsword and took Grond's weapon, while Arras kept both her swords out and ready. Just in case.

Aefric turned to Micham. "Have pages — as many as it takes —

see that weapon to my castellan's quarters. And make sure they take good care of it."

"And your safety, your grace?" Arras asked.

"I am in no danger here," Aefric said. "You are all to return to the hall. See to the axe, and close the door behind you."

Aefric and his new advisers were silent while his knights left them room. Once the door was closed again, he spoke.

"Ser Grond, as of now you are denied the power to bear arms in my presence."

"For how long, your lordship?" Guimond asked in a simple, business-like tone.

"Until I decide otherwise," Aefric said, then turned back to Grond. "Press me further, and I will have no choice but to remove you from your post. I do not wish to do that."

"That will not be necessary, your lordship," Grond said.

"I hope not." Aefric raised an eyebrow at his assembled advisers. "Well? Take your seats. We're not done here."

With the sundered table still between them, everyone sat once more.

"Now," Aefric said. "As I said, I am well aware of the ancient hatred between na'shek and borogs. And I have no intention of asking you — or them — to simply forget it. But the wars are over, and I have no wish to bring them back. Thus, I will have a *peaceful* solution to this, if I can find one that suits *our* needs, as well as theirs."

He held up a warning hand. "And yes, I will err on *our* side."

"I do not believe that a peaceful solution can be found," Keelastach said. "Not with borogs."

"You are only just meeting your new baron," Beornric said with a wolfish smile. "As someone who has known him some half a year now, let me tell you. He will surprise you."

"He already has," Keelastach said, and Aefric thought he heard at least a little respect in his general's voice.

"As this is Netar's primary concern," Aefric said, "I better see to it at once."

"At once?" Jenbarjen said. "Surely your lordship wishes to settle in."

"No," Aefric said. "Netar's businesses have been stymied for too long. I need to resolve this as quickly as possible."

"Well," Guimond said, "I believe I have a cousin who might be able to negotiate a—"

"No," Aefric said. "I'll go myself." He stood and took the Brightstaff in hand. "This meeting now stands adjourned. Oh, and Grond?"

"Yes, your lordship?" The poor na'shek still looked as though he'd taken a hammer blow to the forehead.

"I expect you to replace my table."

"Yes, your lordship."

"Come, Beornric," Aefric said, and left the room.

THE MOMENT AEFRIC AND BEORNRIC JOINED THE KNIGHTS OF THE LAKE in the gray stone hallway, Aefric closed the meeting room door with a gesture.

"Your grace," Beornric said urgently. "I'm not sure it's a good idea to leave those people alone right now. They feel ambushed. There's no telling how they'll react."

"I agree," Aefric said quickly. "Which is why you're not coming with me."

"*What?* But your grace—"

"But nothing," Aefric said. "My reputation will only go so far. Those are the best known and most respected leaders in this barony, and I need someone riding herd on them right now. Someone *they'll* respect, and who happens to have my complete trust. That's you."

"But you'll need me in those mines."

"I need you here even more," Aefric said. "Keep them busy. Get reports from each of them. Anything you can think of. Use the excuse that their new baron wants to know everything about Netar."

"Surely your grace isn't planning to go into those mines alone,"

Beornric said as though he thought Aefric might be planning exactly that.

"No," Aefric said with a smile. "That would be foolish for several reasons. I'll be taking the Knights of the Lake with me. But I'm leaving the soldiers of my personal guard here. Use them as you see fit."

Beornric grimaced, likely trying to find some way to argue for staying by Aefric's side and entering the mines.

"Is your command of Borog good enough for this?" he asked.

"Yrsa's been helping me expand my vocabulary since the Dragon-scar, but no," Aefric admitted. "I'll have to cheat."

"You told me once that you didn't know any language spells."

"And when I said that, I didn't. Not for spoken languages, anyway. Both Karbin and Kainemorton always insisted that a wizard should learn as many languages as he could. They only taught me spells to aid in *reading* languages, because misunderstanding ancient writings could be dangerous."

Of course, technically Aefric wasn't a wizard. He was the first of the dweomerblood. But this was no time to stress distinctions.

"Duchess Arinda often used a linguistic spell," Arras said.

"Exactly," Aefric said with a nod. "I found a good one in the Soul-fist grimoires, and practiced it just in case of, well, a situation like this one."

"What about food?" Beornric asked. "You haven't eaten since breakfast."

"And I'm not likely to until dinner. I'll be fine."

"I can't talk you out of this, can I?"

"No," Aefric said simply. "Now get back in there and make me proud."

Beornric steadied himself with a breath, turned, and went back into that meeting room.

Aefric turned to his Knights of the Lake. There were six in all, each in full plate armor and ready for action.

Heavily scarred Wardius, missing the tip of his nose and the smallfinger of his left hand, in addition to the two jagged scars on his cheeks, and the countless scars on his hands and arms.

Smallish Vria, with her orange hair and fine-boned beauty suggesting eldrani heritage.

Micham, with his handsome features roughened by years of sea winds and spray.

Aristocratic Arras, the likely bastard of Duchess Arinda, and the only Knight of the Lake to carry two swords.

Lean, shaven-headed Temat, with his dark skin and handsome features and that wicked scar across his throat.

And finally Leppina, with her strong build and deep tan. Her tight brown braid fell past her ribcage now. Aefric had heard that she only cut her hair until she was bested in single combat.

"All of you were with me at the Dragonscar," Aefric said. "All of you know Po'rek and Ge'rek, and so you know that borogs are just people. And they might be as good or bad as anyone else. So keep these things in mind, and keep your wits about you."

He turned then and led them back through those long halls and out through the keep entrance.

The blue skies of the early afternoon were beginning to darken, as storm clouds moved in from the north. And the winds were starting to pick up.

Nevertheless, the area outside the keep entrance was a surprisingly active place. It seemed that most of the knights, lers and others who'd gathered to formally greet Aefric had remained afterwards, chatting.

A cocktail party, without the cocktails.

At the sight of Aefric and his knights, striding with purpose, silence spread through the crowd.

Someone — one of the knights, Aefric thought — called out, "Shall we send for horses, your lordship?"

"No need," Aefric said, reaching into his pouch.

He pulled out a miniature enclosed carriage and set it on the ground. He whispered the right word of power, "*Arcoa,*" and stepped back.

It sprang into the air and assumed its full size. A grand ebony carriage, trimmed in gold leaf, and...

Aefric chuckled.

Normally, the doors and pennants displayed the Deepwater device. But that morning, it was the golden acorn of Netar on a background of forest green.

Of course. The carriage had been a gift from his majesty, a man of several titles. Apparently the magic of the carriage made sure that the devices it displayed would suit its owner's current needs.

The carriage was large enough to seat eight comfortably, so when a nearby page overcame his surprise and leapt forward to open the door for his baron, Aefric had all of his knights follow him inside.

Even more impressive, now, the magic of the carriage. The silk covers of the padded seats — in fact all of the interior — reflected the colors of Netar that morning, rather than Deepwater. And the device on the seatbacks an acorn, rather than a lake with a sword emerging from it hilt-first.

But the best feature of this carriage? Aefric didn't need to know exactly where he was going. He only needed to instruct the carriage to take him to the entrance of Netar's largest mine, and it began to roll.

Much faster, going down the hill in that carriage, than coming up had been, on horseback. Smoother, too.

As they approached the castle walls at the foot of the hill, Temat, who had been watching out the window, said, "Your grace, that knight scout returns, if you wish to accept her service now."

Temat sounded hopeful. One knight watching out for another. Aefric almost waved him off. He could accept the service of more knights later, if need be.

But then he remembered that the knight in question, Lachedea, also happened to be the scoutmaster of Netar.

With a gesture, he halted the carriage.

Temat opened the carriage door, and called out, "Ser Lachedea, wait!"

Aefric and his knights emerged from the carriage, just under the gatehouse.

Lachedea slid down from her slender horse, and her three compatriots did the same. They looked tired and ready to eat, but that couldn't be helped.

"Your lordship," Lachedea said with a bow. "Shall I take a knee?"

"Yes," Aefric said.

She did so, drawing her longsword and holding it across her palms. Her three companions also knelt on one knee, though they did not draw their weapons. Not knights, then.

But that was a detail that Aefric noted only out of the corner of his eye, for most of his attention was on Lachedea's sword.

It wasn't steel. Oh, the hilt was steel, with three pale yellow gemstones. But the blade had been forged by magic, and looked as though it had been created from a swift-flying white cloud.

"I am Ser Lachedea Ol'Valim, Knight of Netar. In token of the service I swear to you, I offer my sword."

Her eyes widened when Aefric picked up her sword. The blade was almost weightless. And the sensation of it on Aefric's hand was only a vague sense of pressure.

"This is an eldrani windsword," he said.

"It is, your lordship," Lachedea said carefully. "My dagger is a windblade as well."

"You must have done something very impressive for the eldrani to gift you such wonders. They tend to keep them in the hands of only their finest foresters and assassins."

Maev was an excellent forester herself, but even she didn't have a windblade...

"The tale ... will take some telling, your lordship."

"I don't need to hear it now," Aefric said, smiling. "I merely wished to make clear that I understand what it means that you carry such weapons."

Lachedea nodded, but she didn't relax until Aefric returned her sword a moment later.

"I am proud and grateful that you now wield such a blade in my service. Arise, Ser Lachedea."

As she did that, Aefric turned to her three companions and said a quick word of thanks for their service, allowing them to stand as well.

"You are the scoutmaster of Netar, yes?" Aefric asked, turning back to Lachedea.

"Yes, your lordship," she answered, sheathing her sword. "I apologize for missing your formal welcome, but—"

"No need," Aefric said, waving away the apology. "I agree with your choice. Although you *did* miss my first meeting with my new advisers, so let me bring you up to speed.

"In fact," he continued, smiling, "how would you like to do some scouting in the mines?"

"I'm not dressed for it," Lachedea said, indicating her green leathers. "But I can make do, if your lordship wishes."

"I do," Aefric said. "Come join me in the carriage and I'll tell you what's going on."

AEFRIC'S LARGE, MAGIC CARRIAGE WAS ACTUALLY FULL, FOR A CHANGE. With him sitting on one side, Lachedea facing him, and the six Knights of the Lake surrounding them.

The carriage rolled swiftly and smoothly through the streets of Netarritan on its way to the destination Aefric had given it — the largest of Netar's mines.

Along the way, Aefric told his new scoutmaster all about the meeting she'd missed. Including the ... excessive response of his new castellan, and how Aefric had handled it.

Through it all, Lachedea kept her own counsel. She gave no outward sign of either approval or disapproval about either Grond's actions, or Aefric's.

Aefric concluded with, "And now I'm on my way into the mines to get a look around. See what I can learn about these borogs."

"Is there anything specific your lordship hopes to learn?" she asked.

"Numbers would be good. Clan identity would be even better. Especially if more than one clan is involved."

"If that's the case, I haven't heard about it."

Aefric frowned. She'd just cut off his next question.

"*Heard* about it? Are you saying you haven't done any scouting in the mines yourself?"

"I wanted to, your lordship," she said carefully, "but I was overruled."

"By..."

"Both Grond and Keelastach," Lachedea said, and for the first time Aefric spotted a slightly bitter turn to her mouth as she said that. "They both agreed that sending scouts in was a waste of time. That what we needed to do was send soldiers in and simply clear out the borogs."

"Treating them like an infestation of rats?" Aefric asked.

"Just so, your lordship."

"And what do you think should be done?"

"That's not for me to say, your lordship. My role is simply to gather information."

"I find that the opinions of scouts often color the information they provide," Aefric said.

That got him a quirked half-smile. "And does your lordship then interview all his scouts for their opinions?"

"No," Aefric said. "But the opinions of a scoutmaster can color those of the scouts who work under her."

He arched an eyebrow.

"My views are both practical and direct," Lachedea said. "I desire Netar to prosper. My current understanding is that the borogs in our mines are preventing that. Thus, I would see those borogs removed from our mines. I have no special desire to see that accomplished through bloodshed, but I am not averse to that option."

"Fair enough," Aefric said. "Then I can count on your scouts to bring me information about anything that might threaten the prosperity of Netar?"

"That ... is a very open question, your lordship," Lachedea said, frowning. "I would amend it, in answering, to say that your lordship's scouts will bring him news about any and all *external* threats to Netar's prosperity."

Aefric chuckled. "I'm not asking you to spy on the citizens."

"Thank you, your lordship," Lachedea said, looking so relieved she must've considered that a possibility.

Then again, she didn't know Aefric any better than he knew her. So perhaps she had a point.

They rode in silence for a time, and Aefric was pleased to note that silence didn't bother Lachedea. Some people couldn't handle it. They'd start prattling about anything, just to make themselves comfortable.

Lachedea didn't have that problem. It spoke well of her, as a scout.

Besides, Aefric needed time to think through what he'd learned so far about his new lands, and more importantly, his new advisers.

The king had kept them in limbo for more than a season. Why? Why hadn't his majesty given them the permission they sought to "deal with" the borogs? His majesty certainly hadn't seem thrilled — a few aetts back — when he learned that Aefric had allowed more than a hundred borogs to live in the Dragonscar, mining gold.

Even though they considered Aefric their chief, and mined that gold for him.

Was it just that Netar was too small a concern, for a man who had all of Armyr to worry about? Or did the delay serve his majesty, politically? After all, surely the slowdown of Netar's productivity had to have been picked up by someone else.

Who? Who had profited from Netar's problems?

And why hadn't his majesty advised Aefric about the borog situation? Or at least suggested that an extant problem in Netar needed to be dealt with, not simply gotten around to whenever Aefric found the time?

The most the king had said was that he wanted Aefric to visit Netar before winter. But he'd hardly made it sound urgent.

"Have a look at your new barony, man," he'd said.

There had to be politics involved. Which might've been all the more reason to hand the barony — and its troubles — to Aefric.

Aefric was the newest member of the peerage, after all. But did that mean his majesty hoped Aefric would choose an adventurer's solution over a noble's? If so, what did his majesty expect an adventurer's solution would be?

Or was this a political move that meant — no matter what solution Aefric chose — King Colm could then shrug, smile, and say, "I had to give him *something* after Frozen Ridge, didn't I. Anyway, Netar's problem is solved, even if his solution wasn't what any of the rest of us would have chosen..."

And these advisers. Grond, Keelastach, Guimond, Jenbarjen and Lachedea. They'd been functionally ruling Netar for quite a while.

Was the king expecting Aefric to let them continue to do so? Or was he hoping Aefric would feel the need to move in and establish his own way of doing things? Which would also have the secondary effect of keeping Aefric close to Armityr...

Royalty. There was just no predicting it.

The carriage finally rolled to a stop. The door was opened by a very dirty and very puzzled looking soldier, clad in chainmail and half-helm, and carrying a spear.

"Your ... lordship?" the soldier asked, then got wide-eyed and quickly thrust his fist high in salute as Aefric got out of the carriage.

"That's me," Aefric said. And he had to say it loudly, because this was a noisy place.

A windy place, too. Aefric stood on a relatively narrow road along the side of the cliff, high above the valley that formed most of Netar. The winds were fiercer here, whipping his hair and biting his face with the first light hints of rain.

The view of the valley was lush and gorgeous, but he didn't have time to enjoy it. He turned back to the gray, rocky cliff face and the wide, rounded opening of the mine.

His first view was his knights, forming a line between Aefric and the company of some thirty soldiers, who all rushed to stand at attention. Spear butts on the ground and right fists held high in salute to their baron. They were all clad in chainmail and half-helms with nose guards.

A number of miners — even dirtier than the soldiers — grouped uncertainly near the mine entrance. Past them, the source of most of the noise. The harsh sounds of mining, as well as loud voices giving orders, reporting, or whatever else they might have been doing.

Aefric had been many things over the years, but he'd never been a miner.

He let them all wait a moment. Into that wailing wind he whispered, "*Arcoa*." With a pop he heard more in his mind than with his ears, the carriage resumed its miniature form.

Aefric then took his time, putting it back into his pouch, to give the soldiers and miners a moment to recover from any surprise they felt at the sight of sudden magic.

He turned and surveyed the soldiers, who held their salute. As he did this, Lachedea came over and stood beside him.

Aefric acknowledged the salutes with a nod, allowing them to put their fists back down.

"Who is your commander?" he asked, making sure his voice carried over the racket.

One of the soldiers stepped forward. Clearly a veteran. He had the grizzled look of a man who'd seen, well, likely as many campaigns as Beornric. He had the star of a sergeant at his left shoulder.

"I am, your lordship. Halvash is my name."

"Halvash, what news of the borogs?"

"No changes, your lordship. There's a no-man's land of about five hundred feet along three of the richest branches of this mine. They've been staying on one side, and we've got the other."

"Are they in other mines as well?"

"Not yet, your lordship. But it's just a matter of time, isn't it? I mean, breed like rats, they do."

"They say something similar about us, sergeant," Aefric said with a small smile.

"Will your lordship be giving the order to clear 'em out?"

"That remains to be seen. Pick a guide for me, sergeant. Someone who's been down to that no-man's land."

"Your lordship isn't thinking of going down there himself."

"I am," Aefric said, in a tone that brooked no debate.

"Well, then, I'm sure all my people would be as proud to escort your lordship down as I would my own self," he said with a smile. "Maybe even get to show your lordship what we can do."

"I don't require all of your troops, Sergeant Halvash," Aefric said. "For what I have in mind, a guide will suffice."

"Very well, your lordship. Dellim."

The soldier who stepped forward was so skinny he could have hidden behind his spear. But he had a steady look to his eyes, and a set to his jaw that suggested he'd seen action.

"Dellim here has spent more time down in the mines than the rest," Halvash said. "He'll get you down there and back, your lordship."

"Why have me along," Lachedea asked, only just loud enough for Aefric to hear, "if your lordship intended to bring a guide?"

"The guide is just to get us there," Aefric said. "Once we're down deep, I think you'll have plenty to do."

BACK IN HIS ADVENTURING DAYS, AEFRIC HAD DELVED INTO MANY AN abandoned mine. But he'd never had much cause to go into an *active* mine before.

It was a noisy, smelly, dirty experience.

Noisy because activity seemed to be everywhere. Clanging and hammering. Some of the miners sang as they went about their work. And all conversations and orders had to be shouted at volumes Aefric had mostly heard on battlefields.

But battlefields were open-air. Here in the confines of the mines, those shouts and clangs and more seemed louder still. Painfully loud in places.

And this was a mine large enough to accommodate both humans and na'shek. How much worse would it have been in a mine only large enough for humans?

A similar question could have been asked about the smells. Dirt and grease and human sweat and that dry, acerbic odor that came off of toiling na'shek. All of it underlain by the scent of burning oil from the many lanterns that hung from the buttressed supports.

The lanterns kept the mine lit, but dim and shadowy. Reminded Aefric of those times as an adventurer when torches and lanterns were preferable to magical light, because some creatures could sense spells. And those were creatures he didn't want to warn of his coming.

The sort of thought that got Aefric's heart pumping. Made him shake his muscles loose by reflex, in case quick action was needed.

The air even tasted almost right. Gritty, as it often tasted in old ruins and catacombs. But this air wasn't as stale.

And it was a touch ... oily.

Moving through the mines, even with a guide, wasn't a swift process. Yes, these mines were wide — five knights could have walked abreast with Aefric — and tall enough that even Grond could have swung that axe of his overhand without risking the ceiling.

So there would have been plenty of room. If those mines were empty. But they were far from empty.

Miners at work took up a fair amount of space. Especially the na'shek. Space for swinging their picks and hammers and other tools. Space for the rocks they chipped free, and space for the carts that stored the ore, as well as carried it to the surface.

And where the miners rested, they tended to flop about without much concern for impeding traffic. At least, until a cart full of ore rumbled through. Then everyone had to clear to the side, because those carts were big and heavy enough to require two rops each to push them up and out of the mines.

How far down he went that day, Aefric wasn't sure. The problem was that they were slowed so often to get around work that he

couldn't judge by his pace and he simply didn't understand the land-
marks the miners used to tell them how deep they were.

True, there was a spell he'd used for such purposes in his adventuring days. But he hadn't needed it for so long — well before the
Godswalk Wars — he wasn't quite sure he remembered it right. And
he didn't want to risk miscasting a spell in a public setting.

Made him quite grateful for Dellim, who read all the signs as
though he'd been born doing it.

Still, Aefric and the others had to have covered a good couple of
miles through those tunnels, at one angle or another, before they
finally reached an area where soldiers stood guard of the miners.

Or the mines. Or both. Aefric would have to remember later to
ask what their orders were, specifically. Just in case someone placed a
higher value on a cart of ore than on a miner's life.

The first soldiers they spotted were patrols of four. At the sight of
them, Dellim sped up.

Fewer miners down here meant less noise and apparently no
shouting. Aefric could almost hear himself think again. Allowed him
enough spare attention to pay more attention to what they were
passing.

Aefric saw what Grond had meant about richer veins now. Back
up farther in the mines, they'd passed places where the veins had
dried up, and others where it clearly took more work to get to the ore.

Here though, deeper in the mines, the ore glittered in thick veins
along the walls. Iron, and something more besides...

"Wait," Aefric called to Dellim.

"Yes, your lordship?"

Aefric pointed to the vein in question.

"No one said anything about gold veins. I thought iron was all you
mined down here."

"No, your lordship," Dellim said, nervously. "I mean, yes, your
lordship. I mean—"

"Calm down," Lachedea said to him. "His lordship isn't accusing
you of anything. He merely wants you to answer his question. What
do we mine down here?"

Dellim gave her a grateful nod, then bowed to Aefric.

"Most of what we mine is iron, your lordship. But there have been smaller, secondary veins in places. A good deal of tin in one of the other mines, as well as zinc. But sometimes we find small veins of something else. This is the only mine with a gold vein, that I've heard of."

"And you're not mining it now?" he asked, to clarify. Around him, workers were busy mining the iron, but didn't come near the gold.

Although it did look as though some of it had been mined, previously...

"I ... don't know, your lordship," Dellim said, nervous again. "But it looks as though we aren't?"

"That's all right," Aefric said. "I have an idea about what this means. Lead on."

The passage ended in a poorly lit cavern. Nothing more than a pair of lamps, hanging just inside it.

Aefric ignited the large yellow diamond embedded in the tip of the Brightstaff and lit up the cavern.

Not too big, compared to many he'd seen over the years, but not small either. Maybe ... fifty feet wide and sixty across. Shaped kind of like a kidney bean. Ceiling was about ... forty feet up. Wet, too. With stalactites that stretched down in more than a dozen places.

Bits of dried blood on the ground confirmed one of Aefric's suspicions — this was where at least one skirmish was fought. In fact, Aefric could even smell hints of old blood in the dusty air.

Three rough passages on the far wall of the cavern.

Nearly silent down here, with the mining sounds fewer and all of them behind him. If the borogs were mining somewhere down those three passages, Aefric couldn't hear them. Not that he really expected to.

"This is the limit of where we go, your lordship," Dellim said. "The cavern and those three passages constitute the no-man's land between us and the borogs."

"Very good. Thank you, Dellim. You'll remain with us for now, but if we begin to move, I want you at the back of the party." Aefric turned to Lachedea. "You wanted to know why I brought you down here?"

"I take it your lordship wishes me to investigate the three tunnels, establish whether or not the borogs have been obeying the terms of the cessation of hostilities—"

"No," Aefric said.

Lachedea's eyebrows raised, but only a fraction.

"There has been no attempt at diplomacy with the borogs," Aefric said. "So there has been no formal cessation of hostilities, much less any agreed-upon terms." He turned to Delim. "I take it soldiers check the area regularly, with orders to engage if any borogs are found in those passages?"

"Yes, your lordship."

"Borogs aren't stupid," Aefric said, turning back to Lachedea. "If they have to fight when they try to mine those passages, but don't when they stay back, they'll hang back, and watch those passages just like we do. If we moved into the passages to try to mine, they'd probably strike back."

"Yes, your lordship," Dellim said. "That's how we had the last fight. Got the better of us, the bastards. Till reinforcements arrived and we drove them back."

Aefric turned to Dellim. "When was this last fight?"

"Three aetts ago, your lordship. Had kind of an uneasy truce since then."

Lachedea nodded. "Your lordship already said he wants to know their numbers and their clan affiliations, if I can get them. What else does your lordship consider a priority?"

"Are they alone? Are we only dealing with borogs, or borogs and something else?" Aefric frowned. "And one more thing. But before I say it, I need to know something. What is your experience with borogs?"

"Fought them when they marched under the Flayer during the wars. That's about it."

"You worked as a scout?"

"I'm a forester, your lordship. Scouting makes the best use of my skills."

"Did you learn to read the mood of borogs?"

"No, your lordship. Under the Flayer's influence, there would be no point. What I would have learned would not be useful, once the Flayer returned to ... well, once the Flayer left Qorunn."

"Glad you recognized that," Aefric said. "Learn what you can, then. And if you can get a sense of their mood, I want to know it."

"Of course, your lordship."

Aefric nodded to her eldrani weapons. "I don't suppose the eldrani taught you any of their tricks."

"They never taught me the Cat's Eyes, if that's what your lordship is asking," she said, with a lopsided smile. "But with all the light your lordship is casting down here, my night vision should be more than enough to cover those passages."

She started forward. Aefric stayed her with a hand on the shoulder. When she looked back, he said, "Don't take any foolish risks. I'd rather have a little less information than have to replace my scoutmaster."

"Thank you, your lordship," she said, and moved off with impressively silent steps.

Now Aefric could only wait.

WAITING WAS NOT A SKILL AEFRIC EXCELLED AT. ESPECIALLY WHEN IT came to scouting. So many times, back in his adventuring days, he'd struggled to remain behind while someone else scouted an area ahead of him.

Those were the worst times. Fighting some fell foe or hideous monster, that was dangerous, but exciting. And ultimately, it was good for the people of Qorunn.

But waiting while someone else scouted. While someone else took the risks he couldn't take. While someone else entered the hazard, and could have been killed before Aefric could intervene...

That was the *worst*.

Most of the time, the scout came back just fine. Unseen, unheard, and unsmelt by the enemy. Reported their findings with a cocky grin.

But sometimes. Just sometimes. There'd be a cry for help and Aefric and others would have to go running full out. Not knowing what they were running into. Not knowing whether or not they would arrive in time to do anything but avenge the death of a fallen comrade.

Once, there wasn't even a cry for help. Just a loud, shrill scream, suddenly cut short.

That had been the end of Jobar. Cunning, funny little Jobar. With that smile that ticked to the left. And that way of juggling long daggers like they were apples.

Ripped open, he was, when they found him. Torn hip to shoulder. And nowhere around him, any sign of what had done it.

Aefric never did avenge Jobar. Never found the culprit.

He still heard that scream sometimes. In the worst of his dreams. And ever since Jobar, every time Aefric let someone go scouting, he listened for that scream. Mouthing silent prayers that it didn't come again.

The scream didn't come this time. But neither did Lachedea. And the longer he waited, the more uneasy Aefric got.

Twice, soldiers carrying lanterns came down the passage behind him for their routine check of the no-man's land. After the second time, Aefric asked one, "How often are these patrols?"

"Every hour, your lordship," came the reply.

"And the no-man's land is only five hundred feet long?"

"Or thereabouts, your lordship."

He dismissed the soldiers to return to their duties then, and once they were gone he turned to his knights. "Something's happened to her then. She should've been back by now."

Several of his knights nodded, but Vria frowned and said, "She may need more time, your grace. She could have found a hiding place that now risks exposure if she leaves it."

"Maybe," Aefric said, frowning.

"Should we go in after her?" Temat asked.

"No," Aefric said, shaking his head. "Too many things could go wrong. I'll just have to push on, and hope for the best."

He cast the Soulfist language spell then. It was disturbingly simple. Easier, in many ways, than the spell he knew that would let him read any language, because the Soulfist spell worked with the living, not dead words on a page.

The attempt on both sides to communicate was simply filtered through one of the ancient words of power, further shaped through a series of small gestures and bound to the caster's tongue and ears.

Simple enough that, once he'd cast it a few times, he might be able to forgo actually making the gestures and speaking the words aloud.

When he completed the spell, he strode into the center of the cavern, his knights following a few steps behind, and called out in a strong voice.

"Kaluuuuuuuuuuuuuu!"

"*Kaluu*" was a borog word that called one clan to come talk with another. It had no proper translation into the common tongue. Aefric pushed his breath to hold the final syllable as long as he could, because the borogs would judge him by it.

Aefric assumed a ready stance and waited.

Soon borogs emerged from all three tunnels at the same time.

Larger than humans, though smaller than na'shek, borogs reminded Aefric of the creatures Keifer had known as rhinos, back on Earth. Borogs were humanoid, but they had the same kind of skin, the same kind of heads, and the same kind of horns.

Five came from each tunnel. Fifteen in all. So they must've been at least *somewhat* impressed by how long he stretched the *kaluu*.

These borogs were kitted out in armor of beaten stone, and carried stone spears tipped in iron. If they displayed any clan affiliations, Aefric couldn't see them. Which was odd. Usually they were painted on bare limbs, or horns, or on their armor somewhere.

Then again ... there was something reddish on the left bicep of each borog. But if that was the affiliation mark, it wasn't one Aefric knew. They all had it though, so if it was, then they were all of the same clan.

When they saw the knights, the borogs kept to the tunnel entrances. Where they could fight five across without risking getting overwhelmed, if all the humans attacked any one grouping.

"Who calls old way?" one of the borogs asked. From the group on Aefric's right. This one stood a little smaller than most of the others. And the voice was pitched just high enough that this borog might've been female.

"Me calls," Aefric answered, in Borog. *"Aefric Brightstaff. Chief, Clan Thunder Stick."*

"Human. No borog. No can be chief."

"You challenge?" Aefric took one step forward. Thumped the butt end of the Brightstaff on the ground and let out a thunderclap loud enough to drop gravel from the ceiling and widen every eye around him.

The borog speaker hesitated.

Aefric spat toward her.

"You no chief. Fetch chief or die." He stomped his foot decisively.

A couple of Aefric's knights hissed in a breath, which meant their Borog was coming along well.

The borogs started snorting. And with the spell up, for the first time, Aefric *understood* their snorts.

When he'd had his first long conversation with Ge'rek and Po'rek in the Dragonscar, Aefric would have sworn that the borogs had a secondary language that consisted entirely of snorting.

And now, now he actually had some confirmation of this.

From among the groups of borogs came snorts of uncertainty, snorts of aggression, snorts of concern, snorts of worry, snorts of true bloodlust, snorts of curiosity and maybe one or two others he missed.

Aefric took advantage of the hesitation and caused white fire to play along the surface of the Brightstaff.

The speaker stomped her foot, and the snorting stopped.

"Chief come, maybe you die."

Aefric snorted, showing a complete lack of concern.

The speaker's eyes widened. She leaned over and butted the borog next to her with her horn. She snorted an order for that one to fetch the chief.

Aefric gave the speaker a derisive look while waiting for the chief's arrival. He let the flames die out along the Brightstaff, but he kept its yellow diamond lit.

The chief arrived in silence. Impressive, considering he was the size of Grond. But Aefric had noticed before, borogs didn't seem to make noise when they moved inside caves and tunnels.

The chief carried a heavy iron maul, and he carried it in one hand. His horn was brown with old blood, and where the others all had reddish marks on their arms, he had dried blood.

"*Me Lo'kroll,*" the chief said, stepping forward. "*Chief, Clan Blood Stone.*"

"*Me Aefric Brightstaff. Chief, Clan Thunder Stick.*"

Lo'kroll gave a small snort of understanding. Scraped one foot along the rocky ground.

"*Me hear of Thunder Stick. Far from clan, chief.*"

"*Clan is here,*" Aefric said, thumping his solar plexus. "*Clan is here.*" He stomped the ground. "*Clan is here.*" He smacked a bicep.

Lo'kroll scraped one foot along the ground. Gave a small stomp of approval at Aefric's answer.

"*Why come, Chief Thunder Stick?*"

"*You know why, Chief Blood Stone.*"

The next word Lo'kroll used didn't have a true translation. In the same way that Borog didn't bother with multiple pronouns for subjects and objects or to indicate possession, they didn't bother with gender in the third person. They used the word *ik* where the common tongue would use him or her or it, depending on context.

And for plurals, they simply connected two pronouns.

"*Ik and ik,*" — Lo'kroll nodded up the passage behind Aefric to indicate the miners — "*begged you come save from big bad borogs.*"

Aefric snorted his "no" and stomped his foot with a small scrape, before saying, "*Ik and ik begged me, let ik and ik kill borogs.*"

Lo'kroll snorted curiosity. "*You chief, Clan Ik and Ik?*"

Aefric heard that phrasing puzzle a couple of his knights, but with the spell up he knew with certainty that it was just a borog way of referring to an unknown clan.

Aefric gave a snort of assent and stomped his foot.

"Humanway ik and ik call me," — he switched to the common tongue — "Baron of Netar."

Lo'kroll snorted understanding. *"Ik and ik name you chief, then say all this you metal."*

Aefric nodded. *"Chief hands say, kill you and you. Take all metal."*

Lo'kroll snorted derision and nodded at Aefric's knights.

"Need more to kill Clan Blood Stone."

"What metal Clan Blood Stone dig here? Iron?"

"Iron. Sprite metal."

"Sprite metal" could mean either silver or copper, depending on context.

"Not god metal?" Aefric asked, meaning gold.

All of the borogs snorted in response to that, and all of those snorts said the same thing: no, but they could smell that gold was nearby.

"God metal there," Lo'kroll said, and pointed past Aefric with his horn. *"When ready, Clan Blood Stone take."*

Aefric snorted derisively. *"Hardly enough god metal for clan chief. You make whole clan watch you dig?"*

Lo'kroll snorted somewhere between derision and curiosity.

"You know where more god metal?"

"And the dark swallows all," Aefric said, which was a way of saying that a question's answer was too obvious to bother saying.

That brought a series of excited snorts from the assembled borogs that kept up until Lo'kroll stomped his foot.

"Where?"

"Far."

The previous speaker snorted irritation and said to her chief, *"Ik wants Clan Blood Stone to kill ik enemies. God metal here. We dig here."*

Lo'kroll responded with a warning snort that made the smaller borog back off.

Lo'kroll looked Aefric up and down. He snorted three times, each expressed suspicion.

"*Clan Thunder Stick digs much god metal,*" Lo'kroll said.

Aefric snorted agreement. "*Deep, deep veins.*"

"*You give some to Clan Blood Stone?*" Lo'kroll asked, still suspicious.

"*No. You want, dig god metal with Clan Thunder Stick, Clan Blood Stone become Clan Thunder Stick. Answer to me. Answer to me chief hand.*"

A great many snorts of complaint then. Loud ones, that continued until Lo'kroll stomped his foot.

"*If me say no?*"

Aefric snorted disappointment.

"*Overchief say all this metal belong to me,*" Aefric said. "*And overchief is overchief.*"

Lo'kroll snorted somewhere between acknowledgment and the understanding of what it was like to be middle management. He must've answered to an overchief before.

"*How long, me consider?*" Lo'kroll asked.

"*Sixteen generations,*" Aefric said.

As an underground dwelling people, borogs didn't track time by the movement of the sun. Instead, they tracked it by the life cycle of an insect they call *ulch*, which went through a generation in about an hour-and-a-half.

"*Meet here? Give answer?*" Lo'kroll asked.

Aefric snorted agreement.

Lo'kroll stomped his foot. Aefric followed suit.

Clan Blood Stone retreated into the no-man's land and beyond then.

"Your grace didn't ask about Lachedea," Temat said, softly.

"If they had her, Lo'kroll would've said so," Leppina said, then frowned. "I think. I didn't follow all of that."

"Well, you certainly got that much right," Aefric said. "Lo'kroll would've said something about catching a spy, if only to show me up."

"What happens if he says no?" Micham asked.

"We'll have to do the last thing I want to do," Aefric said simply. "We'll have to kill them all."

A SHORT TIME AFTER THE BOROGS DEPARTED FROM WHAT AEFRIC WAS coming to think of as the meeting cavern, Lachedea snuck back to the group.

Every inch of her, from her blonde hair through her tanned skin through her green leather armor had all been coated heavily with gray dust, undoubtedly to help her hide.

Did a good job. She was at least five steps out of the passage on Aefric's left before he spotted her.

"Thank you for distracting them, your lordship," she said, clapping dust from her hands as she approached, smiling. "I feared I might've been stuck in that hiding spot until the end of autumn. It was an excellent blind though. High enough for them to miss, but broad enough I could lie there comfortably."

"And pray," Aefric said, fighting not to show his relief at her return, "did you learn anything while rolling around in the dirt?"

"I can't believe so few borogs have given us this much trouble, your lordship," she said, shaking her head. "There aren't more than fifty in all. All part of the same clan, though some of them have singed spots on their necks, which makes me think that some of them were once part of a different clan."

"Refugees," Aefric said, shaking his head. "More people displaced by the wars and trying to figure out how to survive. Likely Blood Stone is a new clan formed of borogs who lost their previous clans, one way or another."

"They're digging iron and silver," Lachedea went on, "at least, I think they are. I mean, I could see where they've been mining, but I didn't see any of them doing it, and I didn't see any mining equipment. Not even so much as a pickaxe."

"They don't mine the way we do," Aefric said, dismissing the point.

"And they've cobbled together some pretty good makeshift forges."

"I thought the tips on those spears looked new," Leppina said.

"All right," Aefric said. "One more thing, and then we can head back."

Aefric cast a small spell that told him the time. Not much more than two hours had passed since sunset. That meant he would need to return the next day ... about an hour after sunset.

But then he looked at Lachedea, who was still trying to wipe and clap away all that gray dust and dirt.

"Well, two things, I suppose," Aefric said, then with a word and a gesture used his old cleaning spell to freshen both Lachedea and her armor.

She laughed, a sudden, delighted sound.

"*Thank* you, your lordship," she said, smiling brightly as she looked herself over. "This is the cleanest my armor has been in more than a season."

Aefric saw that his knights were looking at him hopefully. Their once-shining suits of full plate armor were now coated in grit, and their hands and faces and hair were as dirty as Aefric's own likely were, from moving through the mines.

He shook his head with a smile.

"The rest of us can clean up back at the castle," he said. "After all, none of *us* coated ourselves in dirt to sneak behind enemy lines today." He nodded back up the mines. "Let's go."

By all rights, the trip back up should've felt faster. They were going through known territory, after all, with a clear destination.

But it didn't. The trip back *dragged*.

Maybe it was because a lot of the return journey sloped upwards. Maybe it was because he marched once more through the nearly *overwhelming* racket of mining.

Or maybe it was just because he had more than a dozen things to do and couldn't do any of them while he was walking through a busy, crowded mine after a long, stressful day.

Whatever the reason, that hike back up from the meeting cavern felt eternal. Aefric almost worried that that whole sixteen-generation time period would pass before he tasted fresh air again.

As it was, all he tasted was grit with a touch of oil, on air rank with the efforts of humans and na'shek.

He was half-temped to pull out his carriage and let it carry him out of the mines. The tunnels were wide enough. But that would be too risky. One miner too slow to get out of the way, and the rush wouldn't be worth the price.

So Aefric marched as fast as he reasonably could, frequently checking with Dellim for updates about how much farther they had to go.

Poor Dellim. He looked desperately eager to give his new baron good news, but he must've felt badgered by Aefric's relentless questions about their progress.

Whereas his first answers were detailed about where they were, how far they'd come, and how much farther they had to go, Aefric's hectoring wore away at poor Dellim. His shoulders started slumping. His head hung forward. And he started to give the same answer every time Aefric asked. Always sounding as though he expected to be punished for not giving his baron better news.

The answer was, "Well, we've covered a decent distance, your lordship, but I fear we still have a good ways to go."

After the fourth time he got the same answer, Aefric realized what he was doing and stopped asking. He just kept up his march.

IT TURNED OUT AEFRIC DID DO ONE THING THAT SPED HIS PROGRESS back through the mines, even though he'd done it without thinking.

He kept the Brightstaff's yellow diamond lit.

Apparently having that much brightness with him persuaded the miners to clear a path without anyone saying a word.

Finally, after what felt like three aetts of marching through constant noise and grit up endless shafts, they neared the mine entrance at last.

Aefric noticed now that all of the soldiers who'd stood guard duty up above were now inside the mouth of the mine.

Aefric's eyes picked out Sergeant Halvash, towards the back of their crowd, talking with a couple of his troops.

"Sergeant," Aefric said, and waited until the sergeant was standing before him to continue. "First, let me say that Dellim was an excellent choice. He did everything I needed him to do, and he did it well. Second, are your barracks nearby?"

"Yes, your lordship. It's just, well, with the rains and us still being on duty—"

"I'm not questioning your presence," Aefric said. "How many in your barracks?"

"Fivescore, your lordship," Halvash said.

"Not enough," Aefric said, more to himself than anyone else. "Not right now." Louder, to the now concerned-looking sergeant, he said, "Send a runner to the barracks. By order of your baron, half your complement is now on duty at all times. I want twenty of you down guarding that cavern this side of the no-man's land, another ten patrolling the passage with the gold, and the rest close enough to answer if the hue and cry comes."

"Yes, your lordship," Halvash said, nodding in something close to satisfaction. "So it's finally time to deal with those borogs?"

"Right now I'm more concerned about the borogs trying to deal with us." Aefric raised an index finger. "Let me be clear. No hunting expeditions. No looking for trouble. I just want you down there guarding the ore and the miners, in case the borogs try anything. I'll be sending reinforcements."

"Your lordship," Halvash said, uncertainly, "if I might ask, what is the plan?"

"Don't worry," Aefric said with a smile. "I'll have all this resolved tomorrow, one way or another. But I *will* be here when it happens. I better not hear about anyone starting things without me."

"Yes, your lordship," Halvash said, excited enough now that he gave the battlefield salute (right fist raised, but the elbow bent sharply). At Aefric's nod, he turned and started giving orders to his men.

Aefric didn't wait. He led Lachedea and his knights out into the rain.

And what a rain. It was a downpour, with lighting flashing and thunder rolling across the valley below. They were standing in mud and drenched in mere seconds. But the air smelled and tasted clean — if wet.

Aefric laughed into the thunder.

"Well, my knights," he said with a smile, "at least your armor is getting a good wash."

At least a few of them grinned in reply.

Aefric quickly summoned his carriage, and got himself and his people inside, and the carriage rolling back for the castle. They were all shivering a bit now, but they could handle a little cold.

Next time, though, Aefric would have to remember to bring a cloak.

"If I may ask, your lordship," Lachedea said. At Aefric's nod, she continued. "Is the plan then to wipe out the borogs?"

"I hope not," he said, shaking his head. "I hope not. But I am worried they're going to try to snatch the gold overnight."

"They must know they're outnumbered," Wardius said.

"They do. But if Lo'kroll doesn't trust me, he'll see an early strike as his only shot at the gold."

"Your lordship," Lachedea said. "If we assume for a moment that — Lo'kroll is it? — trusts you, may I ask what the plan *is*?"

Aefric chuckled.

"Guess you weren't close enough to hear that part. By virtue of some events this past spring, I am now chieftain of a clan of borogs that live in an area of Deepwater known as the Dragonscar. I'm hoping to have these borogs join my clan. That would get them out of here, away from the na'shek, and living with other borogs in a place they can mine gold."

Lachedea stared at Aefric as though he'd sprouted fur and stared reciting dragon poetry.

Aefric laughed at her expression. He couldn't help it.

"Your lordship..." she said at last, "is *chieftain* ... of a clan of borogs?"

"Clan Thunder Stick. Yes."

"If it would not be a great imposition, your lordship, might I ask how this came to pass?"

Aefric laughed louder now, but stopped laughing as he told the story. Because though it seemed comical to him sometimes that he had managed to become chief of a borog clan, there was nothing funny about how it came to pass.

He told Lachedea how he'd freed a ship full of refugees from slavers, and found a pair of borogs among the rescued. How he'd stopped all talk of killing them but had been unsure of what he could do to help them find new lives.

He told her how he'd kept the pair with him as he and his knights explored the Dragonscar. How they'd fought fiercely to protect him from those enchanted stone men. And then how they'd smelled gold nearby.

He explained how that had been the answer. They wanted to dig the gold for him, and all he had to do was let them. And take a few steps to make sure no one went borog hunting in his Dragonscar.

Aefric even admitted that the forming of the clan itself had been quite accidental. On his part, at least. He told her how he'd learned a few aetts later that Ge'rek and Po'rek had reached out to other borog refugees, inviting them to come dig gold in the Dragonscar in Aefric's name.

Many had answered.

It was Ge'rek and Po'rek who'd named the clan Thunder Stick, after the Brightstaff. But Aefric agreed it was fitting.

"And at last count, Clan Thunder Stick numbered more than two hundred borogs," Aefric said as he finished the story. "So there should be room for another fifty or so. If they'll join us."

"If they don't?" Lachedea said.

"Unfortunately, if they don't, I won't have a lot of options," Aefric said. "Borogs acknowledge strength. We have something they want.

Gold. And gold is a metal they consider divine, in a way. Important enough to them that they'll fight to the death for the chance to mine it. Especially if they feel pressed. Which they undoubtedly do, if they're all refugees."

"There's no option for sharing?"

"Sadly, no," Aefric said with a sigh. "If I decided to cede part of the mines to the borogs, the king himself would likely overrule me. Netar's mining is too important to the Armyr's interests."

Especially if his majesty was considering going to war with Caiperas. But Aefric knew better than to mention that part.

"Then your lordship's hands are tied," Lachedea said, her expression neutral.

"How do you mean?" he asked.

"We are a long way from Deepwater and your lordship's clan. Between here and there are a lot of people who will kill borogs on sight. One way or another, your lordship and those borogs will have to fight."

"One thing at a time," Aefric said. "Let me get them out of the mines first. Then I can worry about how I'll get them all the way to Deepwater."

What he didn't say, though, was that once he let those borogs join his clan — assuming they were willing — he'd fight even the king's own troops to defend them.

And that, well, that could end very badly indeed.

THUNDER ROLLED OVER NETARRITAN. THE DARK SKIES LIT UP BRIGHT with each flash of lightning. And though Aefric needed only a moment to put away his carriage on returning to the Iron Keep, he, his Knights of the Lake, and Lachedea still got soaked to the bone by the downpour before they could get inside.

Drenched twice in one day. Surely the gods were having too much fun at his expense.

The castle's smallish antechamber was all gray stone, but it did have a fire roaring in the hearth and plenty of warm candlelight from a wooden chandelier.

Both servants and soldiers were waiting for Aefric in that antechamber. The two servants were baronial, with towels and fresh clothing for their lord. The two soldiers, though, wore the Deepwater tabards, and looked as though they had a message for their duke.

Aefric waved them all to wait. He turned to Lachedea.

"Good work today. Go get dry, and be ready with the dawn for an advisers meeting."

"Yes, your lordship," she said with a bow, then turned and left through the same side door Grond had taken Aefric through earlier.

He turned to his knights. "By Beornric's rotation, which of you should be on duty right now?"

Temat and Vria stepped forward.

"All right," Aefric said. "We're now officially back on rotation. The rest of you are dismissed for now."

He turned and spoke to the servant with the towels. A young man who looked stressed at having to wait to dry his baron.

"Send for a page to see my knights to their rooms. And to make sure they're fed."

"I ... yes, your lordship," he said, and handed his towels to the other servant — another man about his age, who looked as though he couldn't understand why his baron was waiting so long to change out of wet clothes — and left the room quickly.

Aefric turned to his two soldiers. He knew one of them by name. Tapenn. Easily spotted by his thick, bushy black mustache.

"You look like you have a message for me, Tapenn."

"Yes, your grace," Tapenn said with a small bow. "Ser Beornric suggested that, when your grace is ready, we should escort him to his office, where his knight-adviser stands waiting to update him on today's progress."

Aefric nodded. "A good plan."

The servant who had been carrying towels returned with a page. The page approached the knights, and the servant took his towels back from his fellow.

"Am I to change here in the antechamber?" Aefric asked them.

"No, your lordship," one said, eyes wide, while the other started to point, realized he might drop an article of clothing, and settled for shaking his head.

Aefric quirked a smile at them. "What are your names?"

"Olim, your lordship," the towel-holder said.

"Raen, your lordship," the clothes-carrier said.

"Well, Olim, Raen, I'm not sure what you've heard about me, but I have yet to kill a servant. Let alone one bringing me towels and fresh clothing when I'm wet."

They didn't seem to know how to react to that.

Aefric shook his head, and realized that most of his body was shaking with it.

"I just mean that you should both take a deep breath, relax, and tell me where can I change my clothes."

"Oh!" Raen said. "This way, your lordship."

That Temat and Vria came along didn't seem to surprise the servants.

One of the several doors out of this antechamber led to a small room that shared the other side of that roaring hearth. White pillar candles as long as Aefric's forearm stood on iron candlesticks that reached his waist, their flames working with the hearth to give the small room a yellow glow that matched the fire's warmth.

There was a large, well-cushioned forest green couch, under a painting of a maiden and a unicorn meeting in the woods.

In fact, this room held several paintings, all featuring maidens. Here at a lake. There, looking yearningly out to the sea at sunset. And others of a similar theme.

Aefric thought about that as he stood the Brightstaff beside him and stripped out of his wet clothes.

Olim rushed forward to dry Aefric, but Aefric took a soft, forest green towel from him. To the man's consternation.

"Every nobleman has his quirks," Aefric said gently as he started drying himself off. "Mine is that I prefer to wash and dry myself, unless a woman is offering me either *leaba* or the noble privilege."

Oddly, that seemed to relax Olim. He gave Aefric a knowing smile, and simply stood ready to take used towels and hand Aefric fresh ones.

The heat from the fire felt wonderful on skin Aefric only just realized had gotten cold and more than a little clammy in the wind and rain.

And getting dry again felt even better.

By the time Aefric was dry — and he made sure Temat and Vria dried themselves as well — he'd decided on the purpose of this room. One large, comfortable couch. Mood lighting. Paintings of maidens in romantic settings. And Aefric suspected that at least one of the two oaken cabinets in one corner held drinking vessels and alcohol.

This was an assignation room. Right inside the castle entrance. But the question was, did the designers intend this? Or did his majesty have it redecorated for this purpose?

He'd probably never know.

He was pleased to discover, though, that Raen learned quickly. He didn't try to dress Aefric, but simply handed over articles of clothing, once Aefric was dry.

A warm, woolen tunic of forest green, over brown woolen breeches. Fresh shoes of good leather, the same brown as the breeches, and a matching belt to replace the one Aefric had been wearing.

No hat to replace Aefric's bycocket, but once Aefric was dressed, Raen held up a pair of ivory combs and asked, "May I, your lordship?"

Aefric nodded, and let Raen detangle and organize the rats' nest his hair had become.

"Much better," Aefric said, when Raen was finished. "Thank you both."

"If I may ask, your lordship," Raen said, and waited for Aefric's nod before continuing. "Will your lordship insist on dressing himself each morning?"

Likely Raen had friends or relatives who worked in the baron's chambers, and was worried about their job security.

"I have learned the hard way that, in Armyr, nobles are expected to let others dress them," Aefric said with a nod of self-admonishment. "I am content to comply with this custom, most of the time."

He gave them a smile. "But when I'm cold and wet, I'll hurry into clothing myself, thank you."

Raen and Olim gave smiles that said they weren't sure they had permission to smile. Interesting.

"You're both dismissed," Aefric said, turning back to Temat and Vria. "All right. Let's go find out what Beornric's been up to."

AEFRIC'S BARONIAL OFFICE TURNED OUT TO BE DIRECTLY ACROSS THE hallway from his formal meeting room. Conveniently close to his apartments, he supposed, but in the moment it just meant another long walk around his hollowed-out octagon of a castle accompanied by Vria, Temat and two of his Deepwater soldiers.

He'd briefly considered flying across the courtyard, but he would have had to deal with complaints about leaving his guards behind again. Not to mention that the storm was still going strong, and he only just finally felt dry.

So he put up with one more long walk.

Grond had been right, though. That second-floor hall was busier this time. Servants and pages rushing back and forth. The occasional courtier bowing and wishing the new baron a good evening.

Wishes that were occasionally accompanied by come-hither looks from those who must've hoped to get invited to their new baron's rooms that night. Possibly to get a better read on what kind of person Aefric was. Possibly for the bragging rights of being the first local to bed the new baron.

Perhaps that was just the cynical part of Aefric, though, which seemed louder after a very long day. A day that wasn't over yet. Maybe some of these women actually found him attractive and were just looking for a good time.

Maybe.

But as Jobar used to say, "Bet on the ulterior motive every time."

Aefric acknowledged them all — every bow, every good wish, every shy smile and every sultry look — with a smile, a nod, and a quick word of greetings.

By the time he reached his office, that smile felt frozen onto his face, his grip on the Brightstaff white-knuckled, and his free hand kept clenching and unclenching.

It helped a bit that Beornric was standing outside said office, waiting with a relieved-looking smile. Beornric's first words helped even more.

"I told the cooks you'd want to take your dinner in your office, your grace. I hope that's all right."

"Beornric, I'd kiss you, but your mustache would itch."

"Your grace?" Beornric said, puzzled.

"Just an expression of gratitude." Aefric pointed to the two soldiers standing guard outside what he thought were the doors of his apartments, at the end of the hall. Each wore well-polished chain-mail under a Netar tabard, and carried a halberd. "They weren't here earlier, were they?"

"No, your grace," Beornric said, frowning at them for a moment, before turning back to Aefric. "Something about the official transfer of power, I think."

"Fine," Aefric said, reaching for the handle of his office door. "What do you bet that this is a custom that goes back to—"

Beornric cleared his throat. Aefric stayed his hand.

"Locked, I take it?" Aefric asked.

"I'm holding the set of keys that Grond had held in trust for you." Beornric took out a ring of some thirty or forty keys. "No lock in the keep is barred from the baron. You even have keys here that the castellan himself does not."

Aefric frowned as he thought about that. Nodded. "And I bet Grond didn't make copies of those, while he had them. What do you think?"

"That's my read on him as well," Beornric agreed, and held up the keys.

"You hold onto those for now," Aefric said, and gestured to the door.

"Thank you, your grace," Beornric said. He unlocked the door and swung it open, gesturing for Aefric to enter. "And welcome back to your castle."

As the door opened, it was lit by magic. Something on the ceiling. Felt like Jenbarjen's work. And he could sense a little more magic in the room, but it wasn't a ward, so he didn't worry about it yet as he looked around.

The light came from a small, convex bronze disc, affixed to the center of the ceiling. An orange rune glowed in the center, and the disc cast a warm yellow light.

Not bad, as offices went. Perhaps ten strides would take Aefric to the series of large, glass windows on the far wall. Not that there was much to see right now, save for the storm.

The far wall was the short wall, it turned out, though like the meeting room it had a series of cabinets under the windows.

The long wall on Aefric's right had eight good-sized bookshelves, all filled with books, surrounding a large painting of the king, holding a golden acorn among a forest of leafy oak trees.

Directly in front of the painting, a large, burnished-calinwood desk. A beautiful shade of dark red that practically glowed, but that was why calinwood was so popular among those who could afford it.

The desk wasn't rectangular. In fact, it looked as though someone had taken a longish rectangle and bent a soft curve into it. A matching calinwood chair — upholstered in padded forest green with a golden acorn on the chairback — waited for Aefric in the crook of the curve.

Four sturdy oaken chairs sat on the other side of the desk, two of them large enough to hold a na'shek.

At the far end of the bookcases on that wall, a door. Likely leading directly into the baronial apartments.

The long wall on Aefric's left held a series of tapestries surrounding a large stone hearth where a fire burned happily. One tapestry was a map of Netar. Another featured a spreading oak tree, with the names of past barons, likely going all the way back to the founding of Netar. The other two featured battle scenes that were likely important events Aefric would have to learn about at some point.

Near the cabinets, a pair of comfortable-looking couches faced each other across a low, oaken table. They weren't upholstered in forest green, for a change. A sort of dry, tomato-red color, instead. Worked well with the decor.

Aefric went straight to a bell pull near the bookshelf behind his desk, while gesturing for Beornric to sit on one of the couches.

"Your grace," Vria said from the doorway, and when Aefric looked up after pulling the cord, she continued. "Your grace's two soldiers wish to know their orders. And Temat and I wish to know if we should stand our guard out here or in there?"

Aefric sighed. "Too aggressive to have you in here, I'm afraid. You and Temat will have to stand outside. And as for the soldiers…"

He turned to Beornric, who was over by the cabinets. "Anything more you want with them?"

"No, your grace," Beornric said without looking back.

Aefric turned back to Vria. "Then they're dismissed for the night."

She bowed herself out of the room, closing the door behind her, and finally giving Aefric a chance to find out what had been happening while he was off in the mines.

Finally a moment without servants or guards or new nobles or anything urgently pressing on Aefric's attention.

He stood in his new office, with only Beornric for company. Which meant he could actually take a moment, yawn, stretch, and twist his body a little without anyone reading deep meaning into the movements.

There was the call of strange, new magic in the room, but it didn't feel threatening, so Aefric promised himself that exploring the new magic would be a treat he could enjoy when he finished the day's business.

Speaking of which.

Aefric took his seat facing Beornric, standing the Brightstaff beside him. A small silver cup of ishka sat on the table in front of him, and the rest of the bottle beside it. Beornric held a matching cup in his right hand.

"Good thought," Aefric said.

"To surviving our first day in Netar," Beornric said.

"Day isn't over yet," Aefric corrected him. "But I'll drink to our surviving the next few days."

Beornric's eyes widened, but he confirmed the toast and they drank.

This was an ishka blended with a touch of honey, stealing some of its bite and smoothing its way down Aefric's throat.

He made a sound of approval.

Beornric chuckled. "First cabinet on the right. First place I looked. Already had a taste, of course."

"You think someone might try to poison me?"

"Not any of your advisers, but they aren't the only ones in the castle."

That sounded like a good lead in to what Beornric had learned that day, but they were interrupted by a knock on the door.

Temat leaned in. "Your grace? Servants are here with dinner, and a page who says he was summoned."

"Send them in," Aefric said.

Four servants came in, carrying dishes and platters and more, but Aefric turned his attention to the page. Likely a new page. Aefric doubted this little girl had seen eleven summers.

Still, she gave a proper bow, and her voice shook only a little when she said, "How may I serve your lordship?"

Aefric was momentarily distracted by the wonderful smells of a savory dinner, but forced himself to focus before his rumbling stomach tried to guess what was in store for it.

"Do you know where to find my general, Ser Keelastach?"

"Yes, your lordship. General Keelastach takes his dinner with Ser Grond tonight."

"Well, I hate to interrupt them, but I need to see Ser Keelastach at once."

"Yes, your lordship. I shall bring him without delay."

Aefric nodded a dismissal and she hurried out of the room at something less than a run.

Which allowed Aefric to turn and see about the source of those wonderful, savory smells.

Oh, a juicy roast joint of beef, served with mashed potatoes and gravy, and a leek and lentil soup. Surprisingly, no honeyed oat bread. Instead, a basket of rolls of ... was that sourdough?

It was! Sourdough rolls, fresh from the oven.

Much as Aefric longed to ask about Beornric and the advisers — not to mention digging into that roast — he couldn't remember the last time he'd had sourdough.

That first bite was practically the bliss moment itself.

"A local specialty, I understand," Beornric said, ignoring the rolls for the roast on his own plate. "I'm sure the cook will be glad to hear you approve."

Aefric opened his eyes to see that the servants were gone. And that a tankard of a good dark beer sat beside his plate.

"A servant waits in the hall," Beornric said, "to answer calls for seconds or dessert, or to send for help taking away the dishes."

The roast was almost as good as the roll. Practically falling apart when his fork touched it, and so savory his mouth almost forgave him for all that dust and oil and grit earlier.

"What did you learn?" Aefric asked.

"I learned that all of your advisers are proud, accomplished people, who are worried that their new baron will treat them as an afterthought or, worse, treat Netar as a personal bank and pleasure pen."

Aefric frowned as he finished a sip of good, nutty dark beer that went very well indeed with the roast.

"They said that?" Aefric asked.

"Of course not," Beornric said with a wolfish smile. "But I've stared into the eyes of a lot of worried soldiers in my day, and I know the look."

A knock interrupted him. Temat opened the door enough to lean in. "General Keelastach to see you, your grace."

"Send him in."

A moment later, the general entered. He wore a dark yellow tunic over black hose, but still wore his longsword and short sword. His bright yellow hair was tied back in a tail, emphasizing his striking, eldrani features.

If Keelastach was at all irritated about being summoned from dinner, it didn't show in his face or his bow as he said, "Your lordship sent for me?"

"Yes," Aefric said, fighting the urge to stand. "I've taken the measure of the borog leader, and made plans for tomorrow. Most of those I'll share at our morning meeting. But right now I'm concerned about the possibility that their leader won't trust me."

"Your lordship expects a borog to *trust* him?"

"Yes, and for good reason. But if I'm wrong, the borogs may move tonight."

"My soldiers will be ready for them."

"I know they will, but I'd rather not spill blood if I don't have to. So. I've already given the order for fifty soldiers from the nearby barracks to be on duty down in the mines overnight, spelled by another fifty at the end of their shift. But I want more."

"Ah," Keelastach said, with an almost feral look in his eye. "Your lordship wants a large force on duty to act as a deterrent until he is ready to enact his plan."

"Exactly," Aefric said. "Borogs don't mind dying in battle. In fact, I sometimes think they prefer it. But they aren't suicidal. They won't start a fight they know they can't win."

"Will one hundred suffice?" Keelastach asked.

"Should," Aefric said. "As long as their numbers are easily discernible."

"I can ensure it," Keelastach said.

"One thing," Aefric said, raising one index finger. "No hunting expeditions. No assault of any kind until *I personally* give the order."

"Of course, your lordship," Keelastach said with a bow. "But what if the borogs attack?"

"Defend as a holding action. Keep them away from the gold vein, which will be their goal. But do not press and do not pursue."

"That's a hard thing to ask soldiers in the heat of battle."

"Are you telling me that discipline is a problem?"

Keelastach's chin snapped up defiantly.

"Not in the least, your lordship."

"Then I expect my orders to be followed to the letter, even if it means my general must spend the night ensuring my will."

"Your will be done, your lordship."

"Thank you, general. I'll look forward to your morning report."

Keelastach correctly took that as a dismissal, and left.

———

AEFRIC AND BEORNRIC ATE IN COMPANIONABLE SILENCE FOR A TIME. Enjoying the savory roast joint of beef, the mashed potatoes in a tangy gravy, the subtle, yet enticing leek and lentil soup. Perhaps most of all, for Aefric at least, those sourdough rolls.

And, of course, the nutty dark beer that went so well with the rest.

A warm fire. A surprisingly comfortable office. A trusted companion. Aefric finally found himself relaxing. Even the storm thundering outside was easier to enjoy, now that he was warm, dry, and had a full belly.

He sat back on the dark red couch, a sourdough roll in one hand and a fresh refill of beer in the other, and said, "So how are my advisers manifesting their worry that I'm going to strip-mine Netar of its resources?"

"What kind of mining?" Beornric asked with a quizzical expression.

Oh. Right. That was one of Keifer's phrases from Earth. Not a saying Aefric knew from Qorunn, which knew nothing of strip-mining.

Odd, the way Earth sayings came out of him sometimes when he least expected it.

"An old southern term," Aefric said. "Way of referring to stealing all of one place's resources for the benefit of another place."

"I don't understand," Beornric said. "How does it relate to mining? Or stripping? Like skinning? Or do they mean—"

"Keep this up and I'll think you didn't learn anything useful today," Aefric said.

Beornric sighed. "Excuse me, your grace."

"No excuse needed," Aefric said. "Just tell me about my advisers."

"I kept them busy with reports, as your grace suggested. I'm pretty sure they all knew you wanted me to keep them busy. Or, rather, that you had me keep them busy while I learned more about them. So they didn't fuss about going along with me. Or about answering all of my questions."

"Are you sure that wasn't pretense? Perhaps covering something else?"

"Fairly," Beornric said. "I also interviewed some soldiers and servants at various times, while waiting for one adviser or another. That helped me get a sense of who were dealing with, and largely confirmed what I was already figuring out."

"And your opinions?"

"I'll start with Ser Grond," Beornric said. "He's humiliated that you've denied him the power to bear arms in your presence, but I think he's even more upset about why you felt you had to do it."

"You mean he's upset with himself for that loss of control?"

"Yes," Beornric said. "I think he's ashamed. He considers himself an honorable, disciplined person. And I must say he has the respect of the castle's workers."

"Here's hoping they're right," Aefric said. "Pressure often reveals character flaws that most try to keep hidden. And my presence here is applying more than a little pressure to him. We'll see if today's behavior was an aberration or a warning sign."

"I suspect the former, to be honest," Beornric said. "I think the combination of the ancient na'shek hatred of borogs and the problems those particular borogs have been causing for the barony combined with a misunderstanding of your approach to simply push him too far."

"Fair," Aefric said, "but these might not be the last borogs we deal with. And if he's going to stay in his post, I need him to keep his temper no matter what he's dealing with. How are his organizational skills?"

"Impressive. I looked over the castle accounts and couldn't tell when his majesty had dismissed the last seneschal."

"Did you find out why he or she was dismissed?"

"No," Beornric said, grimacing. "I was more focused on the advisers who remain."

"Fair enough. Who's next?"

Beornric nodded to the door. "General Keelastach?"

"Yes," Aefric said with a deep breath. "In fact, I wish I'd gotten your report on him before he arrived."

"I doubt it would have changed the way your ... well, I hesitate to call it a conversation ... went."

"True, but let me know anyway. What do you think I'm dealing with in Keelastach?"

"He's a general who likes to fight," Beornric said. "He's eager for another war. But at least, if it comes, he'll lead his troops from the front, and he'd never ask them to do anything he wouldn't do himself."

"That's good, but still. A warmonger. Lovely," Aefric said. "And I just sent him down into the mines with an overwhelming force."

"And normally, that might be a problem," Beornric said with a broad smile. "But your grace questioned his discipline."

"Well, the discipline of his troops."

"In this case, it's the same thing," Beornric said. "He just had to promise you that discipline won't be a problem, and that his troops won't either start the fight, or pursue if the borogs attack but break against our defense. That means if his soldiers fail, he fails. A mark against his honor, against his skill as a general, and even grounds for dismissal, if you wanted an excuse."

"Well, good then," Aefric said, shaking his head. "Anything else I should know about him?"

"He knows your reputation, and I'm pretty sure he wants to impress you. But I think he also believes that when you talk about not spilling blood, that you plan on using magic instead of military might to deal with the borogs."

Aefric scoffed. "If I pull this off, it'll be a kind of magic. Just not the kind that uses arcane power."

"Does that mean I get to hear about the plan?"

"Yes, but not yet. Anything else I need to know about Keelastach? Or are we ready to move on?"

"On to Jenbarjen," Beornric said, and shook his head. "I'm not as good at reading magic-users, but I think she's worried about keeping her post."

"Did I or did I not say I wasn't looking to dismiss any of them?"

"You did," Beornric said. "But words alone might not be enough to allay her concerns. And frankly, she might have reason to worry."

"Oh, really?" Aefric said. "And why is that?"

"She showed me what I think was supposed to be a detailed accounting of all the magic users in Netar."

Aefric stopped with his tankard halfway to his lips. "There are enough to require a list?"

"It's a short list," Beornric said. "A dozen names. And the ink looked old, so I don't think it was very current. The book containing the list wasn't dusty, but I've certainly seen your grace clean with magic at a moment's notice."

"True," Aefric said with a smile. "But why is this a concern? I wasn't expecting her to track all magic use in Netar anyway."

"Well, apparently she's supposed to," Beornric said. "Because magic-users are to be licensed, if they want to practice their Art legally in Netar."

"Lovely," Aefric said. "So this is an actual job she has to do, and she hasn't been doing it?"

"No," Beornric said. "And I think she's worried about that, because the licenses are to be renewed annually, and the license fees are supposed to go into the baronial exchequer."

"And with the business slowdown, those fees are being missed?"

Beornric nodded. "Grond said something about a few small discrepancies he had to chase down."

"Think he was covering for her?"

"Yes."

"Think she pocketed the money?"

"No," Beornric said. "She seemed too embarrassed about having fallen behind."

"And just what *has* she been doing?" Aefric asked.

"Well, there hasn't been much call for her official work lately. She's focused on enchanting, you see."

"She's been taking side-jobs, hasn't she?"

"Right the first time," Beornric said with a nod. "She's been enchanting for many of the noble families."

"Let me make sure I understand this right," Aefric said darkly. "While collecting money from Netar to serve as baronial court wizard, she's been neglecting her duties and working magic for *other clients*?"

Beornric nodded.

"Has she at least been tithing any of her earnings to the barony?"

Beornric shook his head.

"All right. What reasons did she give to have me keep her on?"

"She's an enchanter," Beornric said with a shrug. "And she swears she's good at her work. That if you'll give her a chance, she'll prove herself."

"What do you think?"

"I think she's scared enough of being dismissed that she'll work very hard to prove herself."

"Fine," Aefric said. "I'll set her a task then. If she can accomplish it, she'll keep her job. If not, she'll be replaced."

"You have something in mind?"

Aefric smiled evilly.

"Don't tell me," Beornric said. "I think I'd rather find out with the rest."

"Anything more I should know about Jenbarjen?"

"I think we've covered her," Beornric said. "Ready to hear about Guimond?"

"I don't know," Aefric said with a sigh. "Am I?"

Beornric chuckled. "Heard it in my voice, didn't you?"

"I was expecting him to be trouble as soon as I saw him," Aefric said. "Reminds me of Ferrin."

Beornric tilted his head as he considered that. Considered it further through a sip of beer, then nodded.

"I could see it," he said. "Nothing overt, but something about their styles..."

"So," Aefric said, steeling himself for the answer, "what am I in for with Guimond?"

"Well, for one thing, he's probably the best historian you could ask for. His memory is flawless. Everything he's ever seen, heard, smelled or read. He actually had me test him. Ask him questions about Netar's history, and showed me reference books where I could check his answers."

"How'd he do?"

"Perfect. Every time. Even let me try to surprise him with odd lines of questioning, like the amount of trade drop-off during the Godswalk Wars."

"How bad was it?"

"The opposite," Beornric said. "Trade actually increased here because of the demand for weapons and armor. And siege weapons."

"Well, this sounds good so far. What's the bad side?"

"All that memory of his? It's not just for history. He knows every bit of gossip that he's ever come across, and that's plenty. Everyone who's doing something they shouldn't, everyone who slacked off at the wrong time. He knows it all. And he's willing to use that information. He's a political animal, as interested in furthering his family's interests as those of Netar."

"I can work with that," Aefric said, frowning.

"Really?" Beornric asked, straightening up. "Seems to me like the last sort of person you like to have around."

"In general, that's true. And in this case, it might be enough to take him off my council, even if I don't replace him. Depending on one thing. Is he honest?"

"That's a hard read to get right now," Beornric said. "I'm not sure."

"If he's honest," Aefric said, "I can work with him. Make him a resource instead of a problem. But if he's strictly out for himself and his family..."

Aefric sighed. "I'm going to have to figure out if I can trust him."

"Any idea how?"

"Only one, and I'm not thrilled with it," Aefric said. "When we're done here, go to the rookery and send a rika to the king. Ask him, on my behalf, for his impression of my historian, especially Guimond's honesty."

"Yes, your grace."

"That brings us to Lachedea," Aefric said, settling back on the couch. I saw her in action. She's good, and she's out for Netar first. She'll be a boon. Much like Grond and Keelastach will be, once they know they can trust me."

"Does that mean your grace will tell me about his day in the mines?"

"Of course," Aefric said. "But we'll need dessert."

He called in the servant, who brought them a wonderful blackberry pie. And as they ate, Aefric told Beornric all about how things went in the mines, about his conversation with Lo'kroll, and his hopes of getting Clan Blood Stone to join Clan Thunder Stick.

When he finished, Beornric shook his head and said, "I must say, Aefric. Working with you is never boring."

ONCE BEORNRIC LEFT, AEFRIC WAS FINALLY ALONE. TRUE, HE WAS IN HIS new office, not someplace he could sleep, but still. A rare moment to himself, without even a servant hovering in the background in case he needed anything.

A thought that made him start laughing, standing there in the middle of the room.

If his biggest worry in life was that too often he had someone watching over him *in case he needed anything*, he really had no right to complain.

Not like his old days as an adventurer, when getting out of a storm like the one still thundering outside meant paying for a room in an inn. A room he'd likely need to clean with spells to make sure it was pest-free. A room whose small bed had a straw mattress and, if he was lucky, one good wool blanket.

If he was very lucky, a wash basin and ewer of water. Because even small, copper tubs were too infrequent to count on.

Now look at him.

Two ranking titles. Four castles, plus a hunting lodge larger than the inns he used to sleep in.

He paused the counting for a moment. Netar likely had a baronial hunting lodge. His majesty was too fond of hunting not to have one built, if it didn't exist before.

The point was, yes, he had a lot of responsibilities these days. But the perks weren't bad either.

Such as the indulgence he finally got to allow himself right now.

There was magic in this room. Beyond what he carried, and the rune-graven bronze disc casting down light from the ceiling.

And now, Aefric got to find that magic.

He only needed a moment to determine that most of it was in the drawers of the baronial desk. But not all of it...

There. The central window along the wall. He walked over for a closer look, and now he noticed. Tiny runes graven along the bottom edge of the sill.

Aefric relaxed through a deep breath. Sent his attention outward into the flows of Qorunn's natural magical energies, and from there, along the edges of the enchantments on this window.

And they were plural. Two.

The first was scrying magic that could...

Aefric's eyes widened. It would show the rightful baron of Netar anyplace he desired, within his demesne.

The second was connected to another window, somewhere else. A form of two-way communication.

Impressive work, and fairly subtle.

He tested the scrying first.

"Show me my general," he said, with intention.

The view through the central window changed. Instead of showing the storm pounding Netarritan and the valley beyond, it now showed the mountainside. A rider in forest green full plate armor, a rack of antlers on his helm, at the head of a large company of soldiers on horseback, including about a dozen knights. All of them racing through the storm, almost to the mine entrance.

"Not bad, Keelastach," Aefric muttered. "Not bad. That should give the borogs some pause."

Aefric passed his hand over the window, and the scrying stopped. Once more he saw the storm outside his castle.

Aefric shifted his intention to communication.

"Connect the link," Aefric said.

The view shifted to swirling blue clouds.

Aefric had just begun to suspect that he'd done something wrong, when the clouds cleared and he saw King Colm, wearing a dressing gown, a robe and a big smile.

"Oh, good," his majesty said, pleasure evident in his tone. "I hoped you'd find that window on your first night. I used to use it to talk with Eppida while I was in Netar."

"I..." Aefric started, then frowned. "Well, then I suppose I shouldn't apologize for disturbing your majesty?"

"Not at all," King Colm said easily. "I was hoping to speak with you tonight. How did you find your first day in Netar?"

"Full of borogs and frustrated advisers, as I expect your majesty knew well."

King Colm had the audacity to laugh. "If I had any doubts that you could handle either, Aefric, I'd have kept the barony myself."

"I can handle them, your majesty. But a little warning would have been nice."

"No," King Colm said, suddenly serious. "It wouldn't. Though I can't explain why right now. Suffice to say that I need you to get Netar up and running at full capacity again as soon as possible. And you have my permission to use whatever means you see fit to do so."

Full capacity. Well, that precluded giving the borogs any of the mines. But Aefric had expected that.

"I take it your majesty doesn't want to hear what I have in mind?"

"No, I do not," King Colm said. "You work your magic, Aefric. Solve this problem for me."

"May I at least ask something about one of my advisers?"

"What would you like to know?"

"Guimond. Where are his loyalties? Is he trustworthy?"

"Ah, Guimond. The best and worst adviser you have," King Colm said with a sigh. "You can trust him to do what he thinks is best for Netar. But what he thinks best for Netar will see his family prospering, and won't always align with your wishes."

"So he'll work against me if he disagrees with me?"

"Possibly," his majesty said with a pensive frown. "I don't recall him working against me, but he might have in small ways."

"Will he tell me if he disagrees with me?"

"Only if you ask him. But if you ask for his opinion, he'll give it."

"Good enough for now, I guess. Thank you, your majesty."

"You're quite welcome, Aefric. Do enjoy Netar. It has a lot to offer you."

"I'll try, your majesty, but I can't stay long. And if my plan works—"

"*Don't finish that sentence,*" King Colm said quickly.

"Yes, your majesty. Suffice to say, then, that I'll do my best."

"That's all I ask. And as Eppida is waiting for me, I'll take my leave. But before I do, you should know that before midday tomorrow, Nayoria will dismantle the enchantment from this end. So you won't be able to reach me this way again."

"Of course, your majesty," Aefric said with a bow. "Thank you for allowing me this one use."

"A chance to surprise Aefric Brightstaff with magic?" King Colm said with a broad smile that made him look years younger. "I couldn't resist."

His smile picked up a mysterious quality as he added, "And I suspect you won't need to contact me for opinions again anyway."

"May I ask what your majesty means by that?"

"You may," King Colm said, clearly enjoying himself entirely too much. "But I decline to answer. Good night, Aefric."

Without another word, his majesty cut the communication from his end, and Aefric was staring at the rain once more. He wondered, for a moment, if Karbin could connect a window at Water's End to this enchantment...

He shook away the question. It could keep. First, there was the magic in his new desk.

In and *near* his new desk. One of the enchantments was on his desk chair, making it very comfortable indeed.

The desk had five drawers. Two on each side and a wide, shallow drawer in the center. Each of them carried an enchantment of permission. Only Netar's rightful baron could open them.

The contents of the drawers were sadly mundane. Old letters and writing materials. An amount of gold, silver and gems that would have impressed him once. Medals, to give those who performed great services for Netar. A collection of alcohols that were likely of high quality and more than a little rarity.

Better stuff than was in that cabinet Beornric had found, no doubt.

All very nice, yes. And doubtless quite useful. But Aefric had been hoping for something more magical. Something that...

What was this?

A small, slender folio, tucked away under the writing materials. Its cover was of forest green leather, with a golden acorn embossed in the center.

Aefric opened the folio to a random page and read someone's

impressively legible notes. Handwriting far too fine for a wizard, that was certain.

He read: *Ol'Nerrene family. Lands west of Lake Fist. Current Ler, Bara. Inherited six years ago, from her father Tindur. Given to drink and belligerence. Eldest daughter Drifa shows more promise. Encourage Bara to retire as soon as possible.*

Current location: Ler staying at Iron Keep, Netarritan, with eldest daughter and son Tinvald.

Aefric could feel a small, subtle pulse of magic from this little book, now that it was in his hands. Unlike the other enchantments in this room, it wasn't Jenbarjen's work. In fact, Aefric didn't know the signature.

And as he watched, the writing shifted...

...to match his own handwriting.

As it did, a line was added to the bottom of the Ol'Nerrene listing.

Opinions expressed above are those of previous Baron Netar, and will remain until new Baron forms opinions.

Wow. *This* was a piece of work.

Aefric began flipping through it. It looked as though every noble family in Netar was listed here.

This was tricky magic. Aefric couldn't have made something like this. And he doubted Karbin could have either. In fact, he wasn't sure he knew any...

Strike that. Kainemorton could make something like this. Aefric didn't doubt that. The great Mage of Marrisford could do damn near anything he set his mind to.

Yes, this little item, Aefric would keep. He suspected it would prove very useful indeed.

———

TEMPTED AS AEFRIC WAS TO ENTER HIS APARTMENTS THROUGH THE door by the windows of his office, he couldn't do it. Before Beornric had left for the evening, he'd mentioned that — by tradition — the new baron was expected to enter his apartments for the first time through the hallways doors.

Why this was a tradition, Aefric couldn't imagine. So he could be seen doing it? So the first time the baron went to bed, there'd be witnesses?

Honestly, it seemed needless. But then, a lot of traditions seemed that way, when you didn't grow up with them.

Heck, back on Earth, when Keifer McShane was a child, his extended family used to gather for one weekend every summer. And when they did, the gathering always included one "race."

The "race" involved getting nearly every member of the family — friends and lovers not included, unless they married into the family — to see who could hop a fifty-yard dash the fastest.

While their legs and feet were encased in sacks that — rumor had it — once held potatoes.

Potatoes.

Sure. Keifer had enjoyed those races. Looked forward to them, when he was a kid. But he'd grown up with it. If anyone had asked Aefric to stand in some kind of root sack and hop a fifty-yard race, he doubted it would sound like fun.

But if that were a tradition in Netar, then its new baron would sigh and step into that root sack.

And he would have to uphold this tradition as well.

So Aefric took up the Brightstaff and left his office by the hallway door. And when he did, the two halberd-carrying guards standing outside his apartments snapped to attention.

"I don't know if I'm supposed to say anything special," Aefric said, "but I'm ready to go into my apartments."

"No need to say anything special, your lordship," one said with a wink, and opened the doors for Aefric.

Finally. Floorboards. Aefric was getting a little tired of all this stone. Just the sight of cherrywood floorboards made something ease in his tight shoulders.

His rooms were beautifully appointed. Mostly in finely tooled greenwood. Two sitting rooms, one large, one small. A solarium, with views that were probably delightful when the skies weren't deluging Netar. Especially since its ceiling had been enchanted into transparency. Likely beautiful by sunlight.

A small library, two large closets — one for clothes and one for jewelry — bedroom, bath, and garderobe. A personal armory.

The décor was lovely. Paintings and tapestries. But Aefric didn't have much attention for these things at the moment. He was all for the bath.

A thought that made him realize that he didn't see any servants on duty. Just two pages. Young women, likely close to the end of their time as pages because they looked more like women than girls.

A line of thinking that showed how tired Aefric was. He stopped it before it picked up steam. He contented himself with noting that they had the pale skin favored by nobles, one with pale blonde hair and one with hair as black as that storm.

They were both watching him, clearly waiting for orders.

Aefric asked a question instead.

"No servants in the baronial chambers?"

"No, your lordship," the blonde said with a bow. "Our last baron was also the king. And by custom in Armyr, the king in his apartments is tended only by the nobility. That his majesty was here as baron didn't override that custom."

"His majesty's final orders," the brunette picked up, as though they'd rehearsed this speech, "were that we should continue this way, because our new baron was also a duke, and practically royalty himself."

That was an odd turn of phrase... "Those were the king's words?"

"Verbatim, your lordship," the brunette said, bowing.

The king was definitely playing some political game then. One that involved Aefric, but not in any way that Aefric could guess at.

At least, not now. Not after a day like he'd had.

"All right then," he said with a shrug. "If that is his majesty's will, far be it for me to override him. What are your names?"

"Aelgyth Ol'Raefaric at your service, your lordship," the blonde said, bowing.

"Eadwif Ol'Morabar at your service, your lordship," the brunette said, bowing.

"Pleasure to meet you both," Aefric said, with a nod. "Now. All I'll need this evening is a bath and my bed. And if anyone knocks, hoping for the noble privilege, send them away. I only want sleep tonight."

"Is your lordship certain of that?" Aelgyth asked.

"We are both of noble birth, your lordship," Eadwif said. "And when his majesty was baron, we were able to ease his mind, when the cares of office became too much."

Great. If the king himself enjoyed the noble privilege with these two, Aefric would have trouble explaining to them that he considered them too young to share the bliss moment with him.

The worst part was that they were both quite attractive. Aelgyth, with her soft hazel eyes and willowy frame. Eadwif with her fuller curves and wide, dark brown eyes.

In fact, if they hadn't been in their page uniforms, he might've believed they were of age.

But they weren't.

"I thank you," Aefric said. "And sincerely, you're both lovely and quite tempting. But all I want tonight is a bath and sleep."

"Of course, your lordship," Aelgyth said. "We'll see to both at once."

A good soak for sore, tired muscles. A good night's sleep. Honestly, these things would be a bliss unto themselves.

3

THE STORM PASSED OVERNIGHT. WHEN HE WAS AWAKENED, AEFRIC allowed the morning pages — apparently his majesty had favored being attended exclusively by attractive young women — dressed him in a dark red silk tunic over riding leathers, with good, thick leather boots.

If he was going back into a mine, he wanted proper attire. That also meant he refused all their attempts to put jewelry on him. He wouldn't risk losing any in the mines.

And though he wasn't *planning* to go into mines until later in the afternoon, he wanted to be ready if he needed to get there at speed.

He took his traditional Armyrian breakfast alone in his solarium. Seated on a low, well-padded armchair, with his selection of sliced meats, fruits and honeyed oat bread on a small table to his left, and a silver goblet of water on a small table to his right.

But not even enjoying the sight of the city by gray predawn could distract him from imagining ways that his next conversation with Lo'kroll could go very right, or very, very wrong.

Thus rested and refreshed, with the Brightstaff in his hand, the wand Garram at his belt, that defensive bracer worn on the skin of his left arm, Aefric stepped into his meeting room.

His advisers were already assembled. Beornric, Guimond, Grond, Lachedea, Jenbarjen and Keelastach. All of them in various combinations of a tunic and hose, with the exception of Jenbarjen, who wore robes in shades of dark red.

They all stood around a table. A *brand new* table. Proper large size. Proper octagonal shape. Proper green paint job, with the same size golden acorn in the middle.

Aefric made a show of looking over the table as he returned their greetings and took his seat, allowing them to sit as well.

"I must say, Grond, I'm impressed," Aefric said. "I thought you'd need at least two days to get an adequate replacement here, much less a table that is functionally identical."

"I was ... motivated, your lordship," Grond rumbled, but Aefric thought he sounded pleased at the praise.

"Good work," Aefric said, then took a deep breath. "All right. I know you're all eager to hear about the borogs and my plan, but first we must deal with the matter of Jenbarjen."

He saw her gird herself and pale slightly.

"Jenbarjen," Aefric said. "How many years have you served as baronial court wizard?"

"Four, your lordship, including this one."

"And in those four years, how many times have you taken a proper survey of the magic-users of Netar, and collected all due fees for new licenses and renewals."

"Once, your lordship," she said, looking down.

"Ser Grond," Aefric said, "do you confirm?"

"That is consistent with the records in our accounts, your lordship."

"Why was she not asked about this discrepancy before?"

"I do not know if the past seneschal asked her about the survey and license fees," Grond said. "After the seneschal was dismissed and I discovered the discrepancy, I confronted her. She made promises to bring the accounts current."

"And when was this?"

"This past winter, your lordship. I told her to bring the accounts current before the coming new year."

"I see," Aefric said, turning back to Jenbarjen. "I presume that if magic-users must be licensed in Netar, then there must be some sort of standard applied?"

"Yes, your lordship," she said. "Mostly, I have to be able to sense by their power that they've completed apprenticeship. But they are expected to cast a spell to demonstrate their command of the Art."

Ah, so this was as much about ensuring that Netar's magic-users were competent, and not frauds, as it was about collecting fees. That made some sense.

"And have you been administering these examinations without collecting the fees?"

"No, your lordship."

"So you pocketed the fees?"

"*No*, your lordship," she said quickly, her eyes widening larger than the runestones orbiting her head. "I ... I haven't administered any tests in three years."

"I see," Aefric said again. "And while you've been neglecting your duties to the barony, you've been profiting from your connection to Netar's nobility to sell them enchantments. Is this correct?"

Her mouth opened, and for a moment it looked as though she intended to deny it. But then she looked at Guimond and bowed her head.

"Yes, your lordship."

"Did you first receive baronial permission to solicit and perform outside work?"

"I asked our last baron, your lordship."

"Did he give you permission?"

"He ... didn't refuse me permission, your lordship."

"Do not play word games with me. If you can produce a written document in the hand of King Colm Stronghand and sealed with the baronial seal of Netar, then tell me and I can end this line of questioning right now."

Jenbarjen sighed sadly. She looked down and shook her head slowly.

"Guimond," Aefric said, "do you know how many such enchantments she's sold?"

"I believe so, your lordship," Guimond said easily. "Would your lordship prefer their number, the names of the families, or the cost of the enchantments?"

"A moment," Aefric said, turning back to Jenbarjen. "How many?"

She mumbled her response.

"Louder," Aefric said.

"Forty-two, your lordship." She sounded as though admitting this hurt her physically.

"Guimond, does this agree with what you know?"

"I only knew of thirty-six, your lordship."

"Very well," Aefric said. "Jenbarjen, you will provide Grond a complete list of these enchantments, including dates, the clients' names, the enchantments you provided, and the total amount you were paid. Do *not* deduct expenses. Am I understood?"

"Yes, your lordship," she said, carefully.

"Guimond, you will review this list with Grond, checking it against your own knowledge, and then checking a random selection of the totals with the clients to ensure accuracy."

"Of course, your lordship," Guimond said, at the same time Grond said, "Yes, your lordship. But may I ask why?"

"Because this was done without permission. And because this work was given priority over her position as court wizard. In other words, she did all of this at the barony's expense. Therefore, the barony should at least profit from it."

He turned to Jenbarjen. "As of right now, you owe the exchequer sixty percent of those fees."

"*Sixty?*" she cried, standing up on the seat of her chair.

"Sixty," Aefric said calmly, raising one eyebrow. "And be grateful that I'm not taking it all. You shouldn't have done this in the first place. But since you did, you should have tithed a reasonable percentage to the exchequer. As you did not, I will see to it that you do. With interest, and penalties. Thus, sixty."

He turned to Grond. "Oh, and tack on the missing license fees to what she owes."

He turned back to Jenbarjen. "How much of this can you pay now?"

"I ... I don't know, your lordship." She seemed embarrassed that she was still standing on her chair, and sat again.

"Grond, you will help her find the answer, and you will see to it that those funds are collected. And that she pays interest on anything she cannot pay now."

"Even if this beggars her, your lordship?" Grond asked quietly.

"She has been taking her pay, as well as living in the castle and eating our food. If I take every copper she has, she's hardly out begging in the street."

He turned back to Jenbarjen, who had tears in her eyes now.

"That is," he said, "assuming I let you keep your post."

"Please, your lordship," she begged. "I swear, I made some mistakes, but I'll never make them again. I'll serve you loyally. Just ... let me prove myself."

"All right," Aefric said softly. "I'll give you a chance to do that. First, obviously, you will take no more outside contracts until and unless the day comes that *I* agree to give you written permission. And do not expect that day to come anytime soon."

"I understand, your lordship."

"Second, you must pay what you owe. And I expect not to be kept waiting on this point. Third, I expect you to survey *all* of Netar for its magic-users, see to it that they're licensed, and collect this year's fees for the exchequer. And again, *do not* keep me waiting."

"Of course, your lordship," she said, penitently.

"I'm not finished," Aefric said. "I understand you think well of yourself as an enchanter. Well, let's see what you can do. First, I want you to produce something useful for me by sunset tomorrow."

"I can do that," she said softly.

"Second," he said, "I require a means of fast travel between here and Water's End." He shook his head. "I can't spend some ten days traveling every time I need to come here or go there."

"Ten days is not so long, your lordship," Grond said. "And there are benefits to taking the time. Seeing the lands. Visiting other nobles."

"Ten days can feel like eternity," Aefric said, "when matters are pressing. And I want at least the option of speed."

"Does your lordship have anything in mind?" Jenbarjen asked.

"I do, in fact," Aefric said, smiling. "My first thought is that you could make me a flying ship."

"A ... *flying* ... ship?"

"Yes," Aefric said. "As a noble I can't just take off on my own. That point has been driven in over and over again by my advisers. Thus, a flying ship would allow me to travel with speed and a degree of safety, even with my whole entourage."

"A ... *flying* ... ship," Jenbarjen said again.

"I suppose, if that's too much, a teleportation gateway connecting the Iron Keep and Water's End *might* suffice, but it would be an inferior solution. Faster, but nowhere near as flexible."

"I see," Jenbarjen said, looking pale. But then, teleportation was easily one of the trickiest forms of magic. Very few wizards could be said to have mastered it, and Aefric had barely begun to study it.

"I'm willing to consider other options," Aefric said. "As long as they include speed, the ability to transport many, and, ideally, flexibility of destination."

She swallowed audibly.

"I shall do my best, your lordship," she said, squaring her shoulders and holding her head high.

"I know you will," Aefric said, then gentled his voice as he continued. "You're off to a very bad start with me. But I *will* give you a chance. And if you prove yourself, I'll be willing to put the past behind us. But you *need* to prove that you're worth the effort."

Aefric glanced around the table as he finished.

"And believe me. Netar will benefit if I can get between here and Deepwater quickly."

"I understand, your lordship," Jenbarjen said.

"And now," Aefric said, "I think you have enough to be getting on with. You should get started."

"Now?" she asked, blinking.

"Now," Aefric said. "Someone can tell you later what we discussed here today."

"Yes, your lordship," she said, and left the room quickly.

WHEN JENBARJEN LEFT THE MEETING ROOM, A TENSE SILENCE descended on Aefric's advisers. He looked around the table at them.

Keelastach looked pensive, but there was something fierce in his orange eyes. Aefric suspected that the general agreed with his baron's decision.

Grond had schooled his na'shek features to impassivity. The stone wall behind him might've been easier to read.

Lachedea looked at Aefric with interest. As though studying the behavior of an animal she hoped to hunt or train.

Guimond's face displayed no emotion, but there was something excited about his aspect. Whether he agreed or not with what Aefric had decided, he seemed to be enjoying the process.

Or perhaps he took it as a good sign that his new baron was *including him* in the process.

Beornric, of course, was watching the others.

"All right," Aefric said. "Let's have it. You've all just seen your baron rule on a problem that you all likely knew about. Which means you all likely had your own opinions about how it should be handled."

"Your lordship has ruled," Grond said. "Certainly he does not expect one of us to gainsay him."

"You misunderstand," Aefric said. "What you say now will not change my ruling about Jenbarjen. But it might influence me going forward, if you raise a point worth hearing."

"Stern, but fair," Keelastach said. "Perhaps fairer than she deserved, but I suppose that remains to be seen." He folded his hands, steepling the index fingers and thumbs. "The only question I have is, what does your lordship intend to do if she packs and flees while we complete this meeting?"

Beornric laughed.

"You all know her better than I do," Aefric said. "Is she that stupid?"

"If I may," Lachedea said, and at Aefric's nod, continued. "If Jenbarjen did something so ... ill-advised, I believe his lordship would hunt her down himself."

"And kill her?" Keelastach asked, but he asked Lachedea.

"No," she said, tilting her head and narrowing her eyes slightly as she regarded Aefric. "I think he'd capture her and bring her back to stand trial."

"There is precedent," Guimond said softly, "for the execution of a baronial adviser who abandons their post when Netar stands under duress. The borog crisis certainly qualifies."

"Just as there is precedent for the arrest of a baronial adviser found guilty of gross dereliction of duty," Keelastach added.

"Well, that goes without saying," Guimond said, frowning. "And the punishment for that involves seizure of all lands, moneys and properties, prior to banishment."

"All right," Aefric said, tapping the table for attention. "I take it by this that none of you feel I overreached?"

"Well," Grond said, "I might suggest that the request for such a means of fast travel could be interpreted as ... excessive. Especially as it was implied that she must provide one if she intends to keep her post."

"Forty-two times she enchanted for other noble families, putting that work ahead of her duties," Beornric said. "I think his grace — or in this case, his lordship — is more than entitled to ask for an enchantment large enough to make up for forty-two smaller enchantments."

"They were certainly all much smaller than that," Guimond said. "At least the thirty-six I know about."

"Well," Aefric said, "if any flying ships had been sighted in this part of Armyr, I'm sure you'd all know about it."

"If I may ask," Grond said, not waiting for permission to continue, "what will your lordship do if she accomplishes every task set her today save for the fast travel?"

"I don't know yet," Aefric said. "We'll have to wait and see. But at the moment, we have more pressing matters. General?"

"At your lordship's order, I led a company of sixteen knights and one hundred soldiers down into the mines last night, with orders to act as a deterrent and, if necessary, fight a holding action without pursuing any advantages the borogs might yield."

"Did they attack?" Aefric asked.

"Your lordship, they did not," Keelastach said, sounding disappointed. "They seemed to keep busy enough on the other side of the no-man's land without involving us."

"How so?" Grond asked.

"I did not remain for the duration," Keelastach said, "because I gave my knights the task of carrying out my orders. Or rather, those of your lordship. But according to reports, a great deal of activity was heard last night coming from the other side of the no-man's land."

"'Activity' can mean a great many things," Lachedea said. "I hope you don't consider such a report complete."

"I was not finished," Keelastach said, arching an eyebrow aggressively.

Lachedea didn't look impressed.

"What kind of activity, general?" Aefric asked.

"Not the sounds of fighting, mining or smithing. There was a great deal of ... vocalizing."

"Vocalizing?" Beornric asked.

"Reports ... conflict on this point," Keelastach said, sounding a little embarrassed. "Some say they heard shouting. Others, chanting. One even claimed she heard singing, but as no one else said so, I'm inclined to discount that."

"Don't. They're all right," Aefric said, before Lachedea could interject. "Yesterday, as some of you know, I spoke with the borog leader. He is called Lo'kroll, and they are called Clan Blood Stone."

"I've never heard of a Clan Blood Stone," Keelastach said.

"I suspect it is a new clan, formed from those left clanless for one reason or another. I think it's likely the Godswalk Wars have created many new clans from the remains of many more broken clans."

"I understand that your lordship," Grond said, "in his capacity as Duke of Deepwater, has allowed a colony — or, rather, a clan — of borogs to live and mine in his lands."

Aefric could hear the anger underneath the na'shek's controlled tones.

"Yes," he said, looking straight into Grond's eyes. "More than two hundred live there now. They've formed a new clan, Clan Thunder Stick, and as you might guess from the name, they consider me their chief."

"And does your lordship plan to do something similar here?" Grond's tone was well-controlled, but he couldn't control the way anger darkened the slate of his skin tone.

"Expect borogs and na'shek to mine down there side-by-side in peace?" Aefric shook his head. "I may dream of a future where such a thing could happen, but I'm not foolish enough to think I live there now."

"What does your lordship plan then?" Keelastach asked.

"I have offered them the opportunity to join Clan Thunder Stick, which would let them come to the Dragonscar and mine gold, instead of iron."

"This is why your lordship believes they might trust him," Keelastach said suddenly. "Your lordship already has a respected position among them as a clan chieftain."

"Just so," Aefric said. "Those shouts your people heard last night? They were likely debate among the borog chief and his aides about my offer. The chanting would likely have been them seeking advice from their gods."

"*The Flayer?*" Grond said, trembling with rage.

"No," Aefric said calmly. "The Flayer is not their only god, nor even their most important. Xazik the Flayer is their ... punisher, if you will."

"Punishing those who aren't evil enough?" Grond asked.

"I know the na'shek and the borogs have their ancient enmity," Aefric said, "but do not mistake borogs for the dybbungstad. Borogs are not naturally any more good or evil than any of the rest of us."

"I respectfully disagree," Grond rumbled.

"Noted," Aefric said. "Now as I was saying, we of the other races know the Flayer as a god of chaos. But for borogs, the Flayer serves a role. His primary duty is to punish those who act against the clan. But the Flayer will also strike out at those who harm the clan. It was in that capacity that the borogs began following him during the wars. In the beginning, at least."

"What about the singing?" Lachedea asked.

"It means they reached a decision. One way or the other."

"And that they didn't attack last night," Keelastach said, "means your lordship thinks they'll take the offer and join his clan?"

"Likely," Aefric said. "Although it may mean they'll leave instead. They came here from somewhere, so they might turn around and go somewhere else. Either way, it should mean Netar's problem will be solved. At least, once we know."

"And your lordship must go down there himself?" Grond asked.

"I said I would meet Lo'kroll about an hour after sunset today," Aefric said, "and personally hear his decision."

"I should point out," Grond said, frowning, "that your lordship did not hold a feast last night to celebrate his arrival and taking up his post. A great many lers, knights, and other nobles have come a good distance..."

"All right," Aefric said with a sigh. "We'll have that feast tonight. But I still have to go into the mines, so it will have to be after that."

"Very well, your lordship," Grond said. "I'll see to the arrangements after the meeting. And today your lordship really ought to meet with delegates from local trade councils and guilds, as well as a handful of lers who have been waiting for the new baron to resolve disputes they have with their neighbors."

"Disputes the castellan couldn't resolve before now?" Aefric asked.

"Once the identity of our new baron was announced," Guimond said, "many such disputations were ... tabled, to await — and test — the new baron's justice."

"Wonderful," Aefric said. "Fine. I'll spend my day in meetings then."

"Thank you, your lordship," Grond said. "With that in mind, there is some other extant business that must be dealt with."

"Before we get to that," Lachedea said, "I have a question, if your lordship would be good enough to hear it."

"Go ahead," Aefric said.

"Supposing the borogs decide in favor of joining your lordship's clan. How does your lordship propose to get them all the way from the mines of Netar to ... where in Deepwater was it? ... the Dragonscar?"

"Well," Aefric said, "unless Jenbarjen has some brilliant revelation in the field of rapid transportation, I'll likely have to march them the whole way."

"We could probably sail across Lake Deepwater," Beornric said. "Save us a day or two."

Lachedea frowned and nodded thoughtfully. "And your lordship is aware of the king's bounty on borog heads?"

"No," Aefric said, wincing, "I am not."

"Nor should he be," Keelastach said. "That bounty was rescinded recently. Around the end of summer, I believe."

"And how widely known is that?" Lachedea asked. "Word went out, certainly. To all the titled nobility, as well as the mayors of cities and large towns. And how many of them simply 'forgot' to pass that word along?"

"'Forgot' to pass along a royal order?" Aefric asked. "Risky, isn't it?"

"Yes," Lachedea said. "But given the ill-feeling that yet runs rampant regarding borogs, how many will assume that the bounty was rescinded only officially?"

Beornric made a small frustrated sound.

"I take it you understand that?" Aefric asked.

"Bounties are common in times of war," Beornric said. "But officially rescinded once a peace treaty is signed."

"And yet," Lachedea said, "*un*officially, those bounties are often paid for quite some time. And the sort of people who go looking for bounties would expect this one to continue unofficially."

"We're talking about borogs traveling under my banner," Aefric said. "Surely that would discourage bounty hunters."

"By day, certainly," Lachedea said. "But by night? They might try to slip into your lordship's camp and claim the bounties. They might even expect your lordship's guards to turn a blind eye. We're talking about borogs, after all."

"Well," Aefric said with a sigh. "If Clan Blood Stone agrees, they'll be under my protection."

"Fighting the people of Armyr to protect borogs could do serious harm to your lordship's standing," Grond said.

"He's right," Beornric said softly.

"*Well, then by Elbar's Blood I'll have to think of something, won't I?*" Aefric snapped. "Now I imagine we have other business to deal with?"

AH, BUREAUCRACY.

If Aefric could have destroyed bureaucracy with a single spell — a bolt of lightning, perhaps — would he have made Qorunn a better place or a worse one?

Better. Surely better.

Yes, some kind of organization was needed to run any large area that played home to thousands of people. To keep them from hurting and killing and cheating each other. To make sure that everyone had work, and food, and a place to live, and a reasonable level of security. Or at least, access to these things.

But couldn't it be accomplished without locking Aefric behind closed doors for a whole day?

And it wasn't just that the morning advisers meeting dragged on. Though it did. Through midday. So many little things needed to be discussed with Aefric. Budgets. Candidates for seneschal. The state of trade, and what was being done to make up the shortfall in mining and forging. And more, more, more.

That meeting, at least, broke up for lunch and did not reconvene.

But there were other meetings.

So many meetings.

Guild masters and important merchants, all with questions and concerns that only the baron could assuage.

And then there were the nobles, with their grievances.

That little magic folio was helpful here. Gave Aefric context about the nobles who came before him, and a sense of what to expect from them.

But even the folio couldn't prepare him for what awaited him that day.

Grievances.

So. Many. Grievances.

From petty little complaints that should never have been brought before him in the first place — one ler was furious that his tailor had been hired away by another ler and somehow thought Aefric should intervene— to problems so big Aefric couldn't believe the grievers had waited for the new baron, instead of taking their problem to Grond and getting it resolved.

Biggest of those was over a series of three fields of grapes along a disputed border between two vintners who happened to be lers.

The Ol'Vashen family and the Ol'Limbaril family. Both identified by the folio as two of the most grasping noble houses in Netar.

Aefric had no trouble believing that. Both of them showed up in force: not just the lers and their spouses, but their children — four each — and a double-handful of siblings and close cousins. And they clearly tried to outdo each other in the way they decked out with fancy fabrics and jewels to meet with their simply dressed new baron.

In fact, they looked affronted that the baron was hearing their problem in his office, rather than in front of his whole court. And they were hardly mollified by the explanation that he refused to hold court until after he had *met* his court at the welcoming feast.

All of which just proved they knew a great deal less about their new baron than he knew about them. And that was saying something, considering that what Aefric knew about them fit into about six short paragraphs of that folio.

As for the dispute between them, it went beyond the mere question of ownership of those three fields. As if that wasn't enough. There was also the issue that the *entire year's yield* on those fields had been lost.

Of course, each family blamed the other for those lost crops. But the real cause was clear enough. They'd been too busy fighting about who owned the fields — while ostensibly waiting for a ruling — to properly tend them.

Each family wanted Aefric to make the other pay restitution for the lost crops, while acknowledging their claim to the fields.

Aefric did neither.

He told them they had two choices. They could share the fields — work them together and share the harvest — or bring their families together in marriage, and jointly give the newlyweds those plots as part of a wedding present.

Both families immediately started yelling objections.

Aefric calmly reminded them that they managed their lands *in his name*. If they couldn't do so peacefully, he would take back the disputed fields, creating a comfortable buffer of baronial lands between the two of them.

In which case, *they* could pay *him* restitution for the lost crops...

Of course, part of their frustration was that Aefric refused to even look at their claims. But he knew they had no merit. If either one had been legitimate — or, rather, more legitimate than the other — Guimond would have told him so.

Aefric had allowed Guimond and Grond to both sit in and advise during these long meetings. Gave him a chance to evaluate his new advisers, and gave them a chance to see their new baron in action. If what he was doing that afternoon could be construed as "action."

They were good at their jobs, at least. Grond acted as a familiar, stabilizing influence. Keeping the locals calm and collected — for the most part — while Aefric considered their complaints. Grond also soothed them — when necessary — as he escorted them out after each ruling.

Guimond sat close beside Aefric and whispered little details he knew about each case. And he knew at least one or two things about every single one. Always useful information.

Aefric spent his whole afternoon on meetings like those. Hard to say which were worse — the lers or the merchants and guildmasters.

Either way, when the last of those meetings was finally complete, he told his advisers two things.

To Grond, he said, "Good job today. I'm sure you disagreed with some of my rulings. I'd like you to write up a report about your disagreements, so we can talk about them later and develop a better working relationship. After all, when I'm not here, I'll need you running this place in a way I'll agree with."

To Guimond, he said, "Good work today. You were helpful, but not intrusive, and your information always timely and relevant. One thing, though, that I want you to know."

In this instance, he waited — all three of them standing there in the center of the gray stone hall — until he felt certain that he had Guimond's undivided attention.

"If I ever find out you're withholding relevant information from me, or slanting what you do tell me, in an attempt to sway my decisions to your liking, you better hope all I do is dismiss you. Am I understood?"

"Your lordship is as clear as the waters of the Risen Sea," Guimond said, though Aefric could tell he'd shaken the normally smooth man.

"Good. Now if you'll both excuse me, I have to get ready to meet with the borogs." He shook his head. "And at least I know *they* won't talk me to death."

WHEN AEFRIC WAS STILL ADVENTURING, HE NEVER FACED DEATH ON AN empty stomach if he could avoid it. But that late afternoon, as he returned to Netar's mines, he hadn't eaten since lunch.

He couldn't, after all. He was expected to attend a feast later — his own feast, in point of fact — and he would be expected to eat hungrily of the food put before him.

So eating before he met with Lo'kroll wasn't really an option.

Of course, Aefric wasn't expecting to face death in the mines that day. He considered it far more likely that the borogs would either accept his offer or decline in favor or retreating further into the mines.

They'd had more than enough time to realize just how many troops stood between them and that gold. That small vein of gold.

No. They wouldn't want to fight. Not when they had no chance of winning.

With that in mind, Aefric wasn't on his way to face death.

But he couldn't shake the feeling that something could go wrong. That someone would say the wrong thing, or misinterpret a small movement, and a battle would erupt all around him...

To try to avoid that, he took as many steps as he could.

He didn't go down there alone, but with Beornric, the Knights of the Lake, and Keelastach. All of them in their full plate armor.

Keelastach even wore that deer antler helm of his.

Aefric ordered all the miners out of the mines in advance of the meeting. That would ensure that no na'shek came close enough for their ancient hatred to cause problems. Keelastach had already been smart enough to send only human, eldrani, and kindaren soldiers down into the mines.

And Aefric had the soldiers of his personal guard "protecting" the miners. Which was as much about keeping the miners away from the borogs as it was about protecting the miners *from* the borogs.

The trip down seemed to take even longer than it had the day before.

Perhaps it was the silence. For without all the mining noises and the shouting and more of the miners, Aefric could almost feel as though he were adventuring again. Descending through questionable terrain towards some ancient ruin.

Had the right kind of smell. Dust and old sweat and hints of metal and oil.

As though the coming meeting itself weren't enough to get his blood pumping hard and all the good little readiness tension back in his limbs and fingers and toes.

Of course, this mine was in much better shape — and much better lit by hanging oil lamps — than any of the old, abandoned mines Aefric used to travel.

Perhaps it was the lack of conversation. Neither Aefric nor any of his knights felt the need for pointless chatter. So during the descent through the mines Aefric had plenty of attention to spare, imagining all the ways this might go wrong.

The wrong move by a knight could be misinterpreted, as could the wrong move by a borog.

Because they would all be there. Keelastach and the sixteen knights he'd brought down last night. Aefric's Knights of the Lake — seven, including Beornric.

Possibly all fifty of the borogs.

That's a lot of proud warriors. All of them on edge.

Worse, what if there was a flaw in the linguistic spell he'd gotten from the Soulfist grimoires?

What if Aefric tried to welcome the borogs into his clan and accidentally condemned them to death?

Sure, it wasn't *likely*. But the problem with that spell was that he couldn't check what he was hearing and saying against his own knowledge of the language. Or at least, he couldn't do so without the spell's interference.

If only he had someone with Yrsa's command of Borog here, to check him on what he said...

And what if he'd gotten his timing wrong? What if he got there late and the insulted borogs got belligerent? What if he got there far too early? What would that mean to the borogs? And how would he keep everyone steady while they waited for the borogs to show up?

So many ways this could all blow up in his face, and Aefric must have imagined all of them on that long descent into the mines.

Made him tense enough he had to keep rolling his shoulders so they didn't lock up on him.

After what felt like a whole nother aett's travel, though, they reached the soldiers on duty. Lining the walls of the mine. Easily a hundred fifty of them, looking fresh enough that they must've recently relieved the previous crew.

Aefric nodded approval at Keelastach, who widened his eyes as though he'd expected Aefric to miss that detail.

Soon after that, they passed the gold vein, with its honor guard of twenty soldiers, their spears held at the ready.

Finally, Aefric and his party arrived back in that kidney-shaped meeting cavern, with its dripping stalactites. This time the cavern was lit brightly by a ring of standing torches. The smell of pitch strong in the air.

No soldiers in here. No borogs yet either. Just Aefric and all those knights.

In fact, Aefric was currently the only one in that stone cavern *not* wearing full plate armor and carrying at least one sword. For that matter, several of the Netar knights also carried polearms. Halberds seemed to be in fashion among them.

Of course, Aefric had the Brightstaff and the wand Garram, in addition to his own spells. If it came to a fight, and he devoutly hoped it didn't.

If this ended in a slaughter, he was canceling the feast. Politics be damned. He couldn't wipe out a desperate people and then go eat and socialize as though nothing had happened.

Killing was one thing, when it was necessary. Wholesale slaughter, though, was something else altogether.

A difference he couldn't help thinking about as he waited. And cast the Soulfist linguistic spell, so he would be ready when they arrived.

Fortunately, the borogs didn't keep him waiting long.

AEFRIC HEARD THE BOROGS COMING BEFORE HE SAW THEM. WHICH, considering he was underground, was more than a little disturbing.

He'd known for years that borogs were especially stealthy underground. Pretty much every adventurer knew that. But back in the Dragonscar — first with Ge'rek and Po'rek, but also with several of their recruits — he came to understand just *how* stealthy.

There was something about being underground that stole the sound from borog movements. The same borogs whose footsteps he'd heard clearly on the rocky ground of the Dragonscar, under the clear skies of summer, had become impossible for him to discern once they entered a cave.

Even as he'd watched them enter that cave. Listening to their footsteps the whole way. As soon as they had stone surrounding them, the sound of their steps vanished.

At the time, Aefric had found that disturbing. But it was much less disturbing than what he was hearing now.

From all three passages of the no-man's land came the same sound. A sort of *clacking* that made tight echoes.

Rocks against rocks, maybe? If so, then they were banging a lot of rocks, because they weren't quite in sync. Even without considering the echoes.

"What is that?" Keelastach asked Aefric. "What does it mean?"

Aefric slowly shook his head, still watching the passages.

"I don't know," he admitted. Louder, he added, "Hold your lines. No menacing with weapons until we know there's a reason. I want swords in scabbards and halberd points *up*."

That got him some uneasy looks from the Netar knights, but they obeyed. Possibly because the Knights of the Lake obeyed without hesitation.

Then the clacking wasn't the only sound the borogs made. They began to chant in low voices.

"Live for clan. Fight for clan. Die for clan. All for clan."

That's what those voices were saying, over and over in hushed tones, more or less in rhythm with the clacking.

And it didn't sound like a good sign.

"Live for clan. Fight for clan. Die for clan. All for clan."

Borogs began emerging from the passages. Almost all of them carrying iron-tipped stone spears, and clacking the butts of those spears on the rocky ground as they walked and chanted. The few who didn't have spears had stone-handled iron axes, and clacked the butts of their handles on the passage walls as they entered the cavern.

They formed a long line along the opposite wall from Aefric and his knights. Spear-holders still clacking their spear butts against the floor. Axe holders now clacked their hafts against their horns instead.

And all of them still softly chanting.

"Live for clan. Fight for clan. Die for clan. All for clan."

If all the borogs were here — and Aefric didn't see Lo'kroll yet — Lachedea's estimate was close. He counted forty-seven.

Suddenly Lo'kroll's shout came from down the center passage.

"I come!"

Several of Aefric's knights started at the cry and moved for weapons.

"Steady," Aefric said. "Start a fight without my order and I'll kill you myself."

The borogs in the cavern stopped clacking their hafts, though they continued their chant.

"Live for clan. Fight for clan. Die for clan. All for clan."

A new sound emerged. Metal on stone, at the end of each chanted line. Likely the handle of Lo'kroll's large, entirely iron maul.

Sure enough, Lo'kroll emerged from the center passage — pushing through the line of borogs — smacking the butt of his haft against the stone of the cavern floor as he came.

Lo'kroll, clad in beaten stone armor, halted three steps in front of his reforming line and stomped one foot.

The chanting stopped.

"*Me, Lo'kroll. Chief, Clan Blood Stone. Me live for clan. Me fight for clan. Me die for clan. All ... all ... all for clan.*"

"FOR CLAN!" the other borogs shouted, waving their weapons in the air.

"Steady!" Aefric said to his knights.

Lo'kroll pointed at Aefric.

"*Ik say, 'Clan Thunder Stick greater than Blood Stone.*'"

The borogs behind him all snorted various degrees of derision while stomping their feet aggressively.

Lo'kroll thumped his chest. "*Me say, Chief Thunder Stick PROVE!*"

Lo'kroll assumed a ready stance, holding his maul in both hands.

Aefric stomped one booted foot, accepting the challenge. He snorted that he wasn't impressed.

That was a lie.

Dear gods, but this was a big borog. If Aefric stood on his toes, he'd stare Lo'kroll straight in the chest. And so broad. Aefric would need at least a dozen paces to walk all the way around him.

That wasn't all, either. Lo'kroll had two horns on his nose. That small one looked as big as a kindaren's helmet, and the big one was as long as Aefric's forearm, including his fist.

And so strong. That maul had to be immensely heavy. Its head probably weighed more than Aefric's. But Lo'kroll handled it the way Aefric handled the Brightstaff.

Quite a weapon. Enough to make Aefric wonder.

On Aefric's left bicep rode that bronze bracer enchanted to turn aside blades, arrows and the like. Would it turn away something as blunt as that maul? *Could* it turn away something so heavy?

Likely not. Such enchantments were meant to prevent assassination, not allow one to walk unhindered through a heated battle.

And Aefric could wear it without guilt, because he had no other armor. Not without casting a spell, which would have been cheating.

Lo'kroll, on the other hand, wore those plates of beaten stone. All of which looked thick enough to do serious harm to a sword's edge.

At least there were gaps between them, where they were held together by the sinews of some dead creature.

Of course, the hide beneath that armor was a lot thicker than human skin...

"Is this a challenge?" Keelastach asked. "Is he challenging you to a duel?"

"Me explain humanway to ik and ik," Aefric said, gesturing to the knights with his nose, as though it were a horn.

Lo'kroll snorted for him to hurry up.

Aefric set the Brightstaff to stand on its end, stepped in front of his knights, and turned to face them.

"It's a challenge, and I've accepted," Aefric said. "I have to prove I'm chief enough for Lo'kroll to follow, or cede Clan Thunder Stick to him."

"Then let him have your clan," Keelastach said. "They're borogs. They should have a borog leader anyway."

"They're borogs who are safe because I am their leader. And when I lead *these* borogs, they'll be safe too."

"Well," Beornric said, loosening his sword in its scabbard, "if it's a challenge you're entitled to a champion."

"This is Netar business, ser knight," Keelastach said pointedly, loosening his own sword in its scabbard. "And his lordship's champion should be of Netar."

"This is not that kind of duel," Aefric said. "Borogs would never accept a champion. I must fight for myself."

"But—" Beornric began, but Aefric cut him off.

"This is not open to debate. I will fight Lo'kroll myself."

"And if he kills you?" Keelastach asked.

"Then make excuses for me at the feast."

"Can your lordship at least use his spells?"

"No," Aefric said. "It must be melee. No thrown weapons. No bows. No spells."

"How can you be so sure?" Keelastach asked.

"Because I have a chief's hand named Ge'rek who had to fight off a challenger for his position. He filled me in on how such challenges work. Figure this one has to be at least as restrictive."

"Could you at least check?" Beornric asked.

"Ik and ik ask for clarity. Hand weapons and body only. Yes?"

"And the dark swallows all," Lo'kroll said with another impatient snort.

"Confirmed," Aefric said.

Keelastach drew his longsword and took a knee, offering the blade on both palms.

"Only yesterday I offered your lordship my sword," he said. "I imagined that I would be fighting his battles for him. But if he must fight this one himself, I hope he will do me the honor of wielding my blade."

Aefric paused a moment, touched by the sincerity in those orange eyes.

"I would be proud to," Aefric said, accepting the blade.

He gestured for Keelastach to stand, and leaned in close to his general and Beornric.

"If I win, they will follow me and obey me well. If I lose—" Aefric drew a deep breath — "let them mine that gold vein. It's all they're really after here. After they do, they'll leave in peace."

"But your lordship," Keelastach started.

"That is my command, general," Aefric said. "Obey it, or I'll find someone who will."

Keelastach frowned, but nodded.

And then it was time to fight.

AEFRIC HAD LONG SUSPECTED THAT HE WOULD DIE UNDERGROUND, doing something foolish. So at least, if he died there in that kidney-shaped cavern, he'd be living up to the expectations of his youth.

Of course, he'd never expected so many witnesses. He could even see Netar soldiers crowded around the mouth of the passage up, watching. Could hear them talking among themselves, but their voices just blended together until they sounded like the ocean heard in a seashell.

Well. He'd managed to survive his foolish decisions so far. He could only hope he'd survive this one too. If not for himself, then for those who would suffer in the aftermath.

Aefric began swinging Keelastach's longsword around in old training patterns — getting used to the feel and balance of the blade — as he turned to face that gigantic borog known as Lo'kroll.

Behind him, he heard some of his knights talking.

"Couldn't he use the Brightstaff?" Leppina asked.

"Might not be able to stop himself from casting a spell with it." That sounded like Vria.

"I hope his lordship knows what he's doing." That was Keelastach.

"He trained as a dweomerblade with the Iron Wands," Beornric's baritone said. "Knows how to use a sword better than you might think."

But would he be good enough? That was the question Aefric tried not to focus on as he ran through quick exercises with Keelastach's longsword.

His dweomerblade skills were his only chance. He couldn't cast spells, or wield the powers of the Brightstaff or the wand Garram against Lo'kroll. That would have been breaking the rules.

His dweomerblade training, though. *That* he could use. Kainemorton himself had said so, only this past spring.

Aefric had been sailing to Water's End for the first time, following his wild first few days as Duke of Deepwater, when his old mentor had appeared on the deck beside him to talk.

Before he left, Kainemorton had made a point of saying this: *The next time someone makes you fight a duel with a sword in your hand, for Kalinda's sake, use* all *your training. Your foe won't suppress any of his skills, and you shouldn't be expected to either.*

At the time, it sounded like admonition against the way Aefric had approached a duel with Ser Grud Ol'Garan. But Kainemorton never did one thing, when he could do two at the same time.

And that phrasing. Could it have been coincidence? Or had the great mage known Aefric would fight this duel? Nearly two seasons later and hundreds of miles away?

Aefric couldn't imagine how. But if any one person walking Qorunn could have known it, Kainemorton would be the way to bet...

"I thought our new baron was a wizard," Keelastach said.

"Honestly, I'm not sure *what* he is," Beornric said.

With good reason. None of them had ever met a dweomerblood before. Aefric knew for a fact that he was the first.

And if he died here that day, he might be the last.

He couldn't let that happen either.

He turned his full attention on Lo'kroll.

Lo'kroll snorted approval.

"Me speak humanway," he said. *"Hear you words. You true chief."*

"You give all for clan," Aefric said. *"You true chief."*

"Soon," Lo'kroll said, *"only one chief."*

Aefric snorted agreement.

Lo'kroll raised his maul high. Aefric did the same with his borrowed sword.

"For clan!" they shouted together, and all the borogs echoed them.

Not to be outdone, Aefric's knights roared their support.

Lo'kroll tested Aefric with a thrust of his maul.

Aefric stepped back, skipping to one side, and spun. From Lo'kroll's right now, he pointed the tip of his sword at the huge borog's eye.

Lo'kroll snorted amusement. *"Little sword break easy."*

"Come break it," Aefric taunted.

Lo'kroll thrust the maul head straight out again, fast as a punch. It was as though that maul weighed nothing to him.

But Aefric was ready for that thrust. Knew it for a test. That was one advantage of dweomerblade training. He'd learned to read the mind behind his foe's movements. Not as literally as a spell could, but there was a touch of magic to it.

So he sensed that the maul-thrust was a test, and dodged it the same way. A quick move just out of reach, then a skip and a spin to Lo'kroll's right.

The third time was no test.

The maul came faster. Aefric jumped back, but this time spun the opposite direction.

Just in time. The maul whipped through right where Aefric's chest would have been.

The move left Lo'kroll's back exposed, but Aefric was out of range.

He dove forward, rolling between those massive legs as Lo'kroll swung his maul around to guard himself.

On his way back to his feet, Aefric slashed inside the borog's leg. An area not protected by his beaten stone armor.

Lo'kroll's hide was thick all right. A slash that might've taken the leg off a human barely drew blood.

Next time — if there was a next time — Aefric would have to shunt even more magic into his blade.

Risky. Might lose track of Lo'kroll's intentions.

Still, the sight of that thick, brownish blood, got the borogs all stomping with excitement and the knights all cheering.

Lo'kroll snorted acknowledgment of the strike. Dipped his fingers in and tasted his own blood.

The borog chieftain would fight even harder now. But that was all right. Aefric was getting into the flow and movement of the fight.

He was starting to think he might live through this.

Problem was, he had to close the distance between them or he'd never make a meaningful strike. And that between-the-legs move wouldn't work a second time.

"*You quick,*" Lo'kroll said, and snorted to add, "*not quick enough.*"

Aefric snorted that he wasn't the one bleeding.

Lo'kroll shifted his grip. Spaced his hands on the long handle. Took two steps forward.

Only three more separated them now. And Aefric had nowhere backwards to move. The cavern wall, hardly two steps behind him.

Lo'kroll lowered his horn and charged. Held the maul ready to strike either direction.

Fortunately, Aefric's style as a dweomerblade focused on agility. So he timed his leap and went right over that lowered horn.

Unfortunately, Lo'kroll must've expected that.

Faster than anything that big should be able to move, Lo'kroll whipped his horn up at Aefric. Caught him in the belly and threw him.

Good thing the horn was so thick, or Aefric would have been impaled.

Small blessing. Still felt like he'd taken the full force of that maul to his guts.

Pain erupted all through his torso. He felt it all the way to his scalp. And breathing was just a memory.

Ironic, really, because he was flying wildly through the air — spinning haphazardly with no sense of direction — and yet not any part of all that air was willing to enter his lungs.

Thunderous noise all around him. Borogs cheering. His knights roaring. Somewhere was a crashing sound that made no sense at all. And none of it gave Aefric any sense of direction.

That was bad. Some part of him knew that.

Why though?

Oh, yeah. The ground would be arriving shortly. And violently.

Suddenly two voices raised in harmony and support, cutting through the thick noise. Four others joined them.

Aefric's senses snapped back into place. He knew his knights were to his right, the borogs were to his left, and the ground was—

He tucked and rolled just in time.

He staggered as he came to his feet. With one hand, he clutched his furious stomach, grateful that — however bad it felt — guts were not, in fact, spilling out through his fingers.

Well will you look at that? His other hand was still holding onto the longsword. Must've used the sticky-hilt technique without thinking. Good.

Across the cavern, Lo'kroll was staggered too.

Oh. That crash. Him and the wall, and he didn't have his horn in position to take the blow. That should make things about—

Oh, this was not *fair*.

Lo'kroll — who had been charging full out when he slammed into that wall — simply *shook off the impact.*

His step looked steady as he came for Aefric. Snorting derision. Readying his maul. Moving as though he might charge again.

Aefric's training told him that the crash had done *some* damage to the huge borog, but not nearly enough. Lo'kroll was in much better shape now than Aefric, and they both knew it.

Aefric put one palm to the blade of his sword. Drew on its strength. This wasn't healing. Not the way the priests of Nilasah healed. He couldn't repair the damage he'd suffered.

This was ... a way to stabilize himself, and let him keep fighting *despite* his injury. He wouldn't feel the pain. His muscles would work as though fully intact.

For a time, he would fight as though he hadn't been hurt at all.

But it wouldn't last long.

He put that hand back on his stomach. Continued to hunch forward and breath heavily.

Lo'kroll slowed his steps.

"Behold Chief Thunder Stick," he said. *"Lives for clan. Fights for clan. Dies for clan. All for clan."*

"All for clan," the borogs echoed.

Aefric winced at pain he didn't feel. Made his hand shake as he raised his sword to defend.

"Good fight, chief," Lo'kroll said, not quite in striking range. *"Lay down sword. Be chief hand."*

Aefric let his neck tremble as he shook his head. Spoke through gritted teeth. *"All. For. Clan."*

Lo'kroll snorted approval.

"You die as borog," he said. *"So me kill you quick."*

Lo'kroll raised the head of his maul high.

Moving at full speed now, Aefric struck. Channeling as much power as he'd ever managed using dweomerblade techniques.

Blade glowing blue with power, Aefric slashed across the unarmored spot at the backs of Lo'kroll's elbows.

Before the immense borog even finished howling in pain and

dropping his maul, Aefric spun and cut deeply across Lo'kroll's stomach, in the small gap between two plates of armor.

Aefric had heard falling trees make less noise than Lo'kroll did, hitting the ground. Even without taking into account his cry of pain.

Knights cheered. Borogs stomped their feet uncertainly.

Pain roared back into Aefric's system. He'd drawn too deeply on his skills in those strikes. Hadn't held back enough to control the pain, which was all the worse for his continuing to fight.

It was all he could do to stay standing, holding onto his blade.

"*Yield,*" he said. No pretense now in the shaky hand pointing his sword at Lo'kroll's eye. "*Live for clan. Live for Clan Thunder Stick! Chief say!*"

Lo'kroll blinked at Aefric.

Snorted submission.

AEFRIC'S MEMORY OF WHAT HAPPENED AFTER HIS DUEL WITH LO'KROLL was a little fuzzy.

He knew Lo'kroll surrendered. And when he did, Aefric dropped his borrowed sword and fell to the ground.

Managed not to hit his head. He knew that much. Mostly because tucking his head meant using stomach muscles that *really* didn't want to be used.

Honestly, it might've hurt him less to have let his head hit the rock.

He knew a healer had come up. The bright yellow robes and hand symbol of Nilasah are hard to mistake. Couldn't quite remember what that healer looked like...

Either way, Aefric knew he'd insisted that Lo'kroll be tended first. Lo'kroll was dying. Aefric only wished he was.

Well, he didn't *really* wish he was. It was just that death would have been a welcome relief from all the pain. He felt as though all of his insides had been beaten with sticks until they'd reached a fine pulp, then ground up with a mortar and pestle, and poured back in through his belly button.

Eventually, he knew the healer had tended to him, because that was when he lost consciousness.

He woke up back in his bed, in his apartments in the Iron Keep. Couldn't be mistaken for his bed at Water's End, after all. Even if he overlooked the Netar-themed décor, the bed itself was only maybe half the size of his ducal bed.

Of course, that still meant he could have been joined by three of his closest friends without any of them feeling crowded.

Beornric was standing over him. Aelgyth and Eadwif were over at the hearth, making sure the fire was sufficiently warm.

Surprisingly, no one else was in the room.

Although the Brightstaff, of course, was standing beside the bed. Waiting for him. Once more, it had followed him when he could not carry it.

"Ah, good," Beornric said with a smile that practically made his mustache touch his eyes. "Your grace is awake. Feeling better, I hope?"

He was, now that he thought about it. No pain? No pain. Aefric touched his stomach, which made him realize he was naked.

More important, though, was that his stomach was a little tender, but not even really sore.

Praise Nilasah.

Aefric cleared his throat, ready to say something to that effect, but it was still too dry for him to do anything more than croak.

Aelgyth leapt to bring him a silver goblet full of cool, clear water, smiling as she served it to him.

Water was a taste of paradise itself. Though Aefric's mouth and throat were so dry that half that goblet's cargo never made it to his stomach.

Finally, though, he was able to speak.

"I am," he said, nodding. "Thank you. And praise Nilasah. How did there come to be a healer down there?"

"Your general took you at your word about not wanting to spill blood. When he brought down the knights and soldiers, he brought down the baronial physician. Apparently he wanted to ensure that even in the case of mischance, the injuries and deaths were minimized."

"Speaking of deaths..."

"Lo'kroll survived," Beornric said, which was good enough news that Aefric eased back on the pillows as his knight-adviser continued. "The priest said he'll need three days before he can travel."

"How many has it been?"

"One. Your duel was last night. Well done, by the way."

"Thank you," Aefric said with a raised eyebrow. "And good job not mentioning that any of my Knights of the Lake could have done better. Or that Deirdre could have killed Lo'kroll in the first seconds of the fight."

"Didn't need to, did I?" Beornric said, eyes glittering with mirth.

"So it's the next evening," Aefric said, trying to sound casual. "How did the feast go?"

"You lived," Beornric said. "The feast was a celebration of the new baron's willingness to put all on the line for Netar. You've made yourself very popular."

"And doubtless made myself a few new enemies, even if they're hiding their feelings right now."

"Naturally," Beornric said with a smile.

"What about my new borogs?"

"They retreated farther into the mines, waiting for their new chief to take them to dig god metal."

"All right," Aefric said. "If the priest said Lo'kroll will need three days to heal, he'll insist he's ready to go tomorrow."

Beornric looked as though he wanted to argue, but decided against it.

"This means I really should be too."

"I knew you'd say that, and so did Grond," Beornric said, shaking his head in amusement. "He asked me to ask you to postpone at least one more day, so you can officially meet at least some of your nobles."

"Yes, yes, I know," Aefric said. "They came a long way to meet me, and I really owe it and on and on."

"That's about right. Not to mention that it would do good to make Lo'kroll wait a little. Make sure he knows who's in charge."

"Oh, he knows," Aefric said. "But fine. One more day. One. We leave the morning after."

ONE ADVANTAGE TO BEING WOUNDED IN BATTLE. AEFRIC HAD A LITTLE more peace and quiet that night.

Once Beornric was gone, he had time to himself to just rest and think. And no company to worry about, except for Aelgyth and Eadwif. And they were good about remaining in the background, only stepping forward when he wanted something.

With one exception.

Beornric had not been gone long when Eadwif went to fetch Aefric's dinner. And while she did, Aelgyth bowed and asked, "May I speak, your lordship?"

"You may," Aefric said.

"I wanted to let your lordship know that Eadwif and I will cease asking him to share the noble privilege with us. Ser Beornric, told us that where your lordship grew up, those beneath the age of majority were to be discouraged from pursuing the bliss moment with adults."

"He's right," Aefric said, half-tempted to add, *more right than even he knows.*

She bowed again.

"He told us that your lordship has adjusted well to our ways here in Armyr, but that this ... difference in our customs has proven a stopping point. Suffice to say that if your lordship should change his mind, we will not keep him wanting."

"Thank you," Aefric said, "but I don't expect my mind to change."

"In that case," she said with a playful smile, "I should like to inform your lordship that I come of age this winter, and that Eadwif does this coming spring."

"I'll keep that in mind," Aefric said, chuckling.

"Please do," she said. "For when I graduate from page training and return to my family's lands, I hope to do so knowing my baron a great deal better than I do now. And I'm quite sure Eadwif feels the same way."

"All right, all right," Aefric said. "If I am taken away by other business when you come of age, I shall visit each of you on your lands for expressed purpose of seeking the noble privilege with you. Good enough?"

"Your lordship is most kind and noble," Aelgyth said, sounding almost astonished.

Apparently Aefric's offer was a bigger deal than he realized. He really did need to remember that what he did, as a noble, was always a much bigger deal than it would have been when he was an adventurer.

Aefric's dinner arrived then, and he noticed that after his two evening pages had shared a hushed conversation, they were both far more attentive. And almost giddy.

Just how big a promise had he just made?

4

AEFRIC AROSE EARLY THE NEXT MORNING AND TOOK HIS TRADITIONAL Armyrian breakfast alone in his solarium. Watching the people of Netarritan awaken and begin to go about their business in the gray predawn.

After that, he dressed in a silk tunic of forest green over dark brown hose. His shoes and belt were a pale brown leather, both buckled with gold.

Sheathed, the wand Garram rode in its usual place, beside the pouch and noble's dagger on Aefric's belt.

The noble's dagger was one of Armyr's more interesting traditions. Every noble, even including pages on duty, wore a dagger at all times. Aefric's was a thing of beauty. A straight steel blade, with both its edges silvered, and its ebony handle carved in the likeness of a raven.

Finally, with the Brightstaff in hand, he entered his meeting room as the first rays of dawn came through the eastern windows.

His advisers were all waiting for him, standing beside their chairs.

Beornric, in a black doublet over a dark yellow tunic, with black hose, and his sword at his hip. More of a ... stark look than he usually chose. And he'd made some attempt to brush his mustaches.

Guimond, with his black hair, mustache and goatee all freshly slicked, adorned a white silk tunic over black hose. A pendant with a gold chain had been tucked inside his collar.

Lachedea's short blonde hair had been brushed thoroughly, which made Aefric realize she often didn't take the effort to do so. The green of her tunic was lighter than Aefric's, and suited her. She wore it with pale brown hose, and her windblades hanging at her hip.

Grond wore his cloth-of-silver toga today, with a matching torc around his neck.

Jenbarjen wore silk robes of jet black, trimmed in red, with small runes sewn in along the edges. Today she had three runestones orbiting her short brown hair, but she didn't carry her oaken rod.

Keelastach wore his bright yellow hair loose and wild. His tunic was a dark red, worn over dark orange hose, with his longsword and shortsword dangling from his belt.

They were all offering greetings when Aefric stopped and frowned. "Why do I feel as though you're all dressed up for something?"

It was Grond who answered.

"Ser Beornric was good enough to tell me last night that your lordship will be leaving us tomorrow. As I imagine your lordship will wish to make an early night of it, and as all of those who would attend are conveniently close at hand, I've arranged for a feast this afternoon, rather than this evening."

Aefric sighed. "And the reason *I* wasn't told this before I dressed?"

"The feast will wait for our baron," Guimond said, "but not for his advisers."

Grond frowned at Guimond answering for him, and added, "Your lordship's guests will expect him to make an entrance, so time to change will not be a problem."

"All the same," Aefric said, standing the Brightstaff beside his chair and taking a seat, "we should get started."

His advisers sat.

"Now, to begin the day," Aefric said, "I need to know the fallout from what I did in the mines. Beornric tells me my popularity is riding high, but you know the locals better than he does. Do you agree? What's the tone of my nobles and my people? And my soldiers, for that matter?"

Keelastach chuckled. "Word has spread about your lordship's courage and skill at arms, as witnessed by your lordship's knights and soldiers. Both would now follow him into any of the thirteen hells. Perhaps even all of them."

"The tale has grown with the telling, I presume?"

"It will over time," Beornric said. "Such things always do."

"But at the moment, the truth is still close to the tellings," Keelastach said. "And the truth is impressive enough."

"Even I'm not sure of the entire truth about that fight," Aefric said, shaking his head. "There was a moment after I got hit by Lo'kroll's horn. I was thrown through the air. No idea which way was up. Noise all around me."

Aefric frowned. "But then, it was like ... some kind of sweet singing gave me focus. I still don't know what happened there."

"Your lordship is human," Keelastach said, shrugging. "He should not be expected to recognize the eldrani song of awareness. But Ser Vria must have been taught it by her eldrani parent. She and I both recognized your lordship's ... condition in the same instant, and began to sing. Then four of your lordship's other knights — all eldrani, of course — joined in."

"Thank you," Aefric said. "And I'll need to thank the others. Your song saved my life."

"That is its purpose," Keelastach said, acknowledging the thanks with a nod. "To cut through battle fog and bring clarity to a warrior under duress."

Keelastach leaned a little further forward. "But offer no thanks beyond a quick word. It would be inappropriate."

"As you say," Aefric said with a nod. "What about the nobles? Where do I stand with them?"

"The nobles," Guimond said, "support your lordship openly, but privately some are divided. They whisper their concerns over your lordship's mercy to the borogs, who were so recently a mighty enemy of all."

"The Flayer was the enemy," Aefric corrected. "The borogs were swept up in divine power and will. And the wars are over."

"For some they will never end," Guimond said. "The whisperings I have heard do not speak of opposition. Not yet. Only of concern. They wait, and watch. They will judge your lordship by how Netar prospers."

"And by who benefits from the prospering," Beornric said.

"Is it ever otherwise?" Guimond asked. "For one to flourish, must not another languish?"

"Let's not get caught up in philosophy," Aefric said. "So the military stands behind me, but the nobles are unsure yet."

"Essentially correct," Guimond said, while Keelastach nodded.

"What about the common folk?"

"The common folk," Grond said, "celebrate their baron's courage and the return to work that is sure to follow his handling of the borogs."

"And their take on how I'm handling the borogs?"

"They rely more on rumors than the nobles," Grond said. "They know you defeated the borog chieftain in single combat, and that the borog problem in the mines is over. That's about all."

Guimond nodded agreement.

"Well," Aefric said with a deep breath, "that's probably for the best. At least, at this point. Though if they rely that much on rumors, the nobles could use them in a move against me."

"Won't happen," Guimond said. "At least not anytime soon. Your lordship has immense personal power and the king's obvious favor. Both will encourage nobles to find some way to work *with* your lordship, rather than against him."

"In other words," Beornric said, "they'll try to play up to you to win your favor."

"Isn't that what I said?" Guimond asked, one eyebrow high.

"All right," Aefric said. "Moving on. Who wants to start?"

"I will," Lachedea said, clearly beating Jenbarjen to the punch.

"The border is secure. Our neighbors are behaving themselves, and the summer problems with bandits appear to be at their end. But reports from the Rethneryl scouts say that Caiperas is gathering its forces. Reason unknown."

"We get reports from Rethneryl?" Aefric asked.

"We're on good terms with that kingdom," she answered. "So we have a longstanding unofficial policy of passing along word to them of anything that might affect them, and they do the same for us."

"Good policy," Aefric said. "I hope it continues."

"I should add though," Lachedea said, "that a number of bounty hunters have recently entered Netar. Likely drawn by the reports of borogs in the mines."

"Well, they can come, but they can't have the borogs," Aefric said. "Who's next?"

"I have something for your lordship," Jenbarjen said quickly.

At Aefric's nod, she pulled out a small pouch made from black velvet. Strongly magical. She floated it across the table to his hand.

"Your lordship asked me to produce something useful for him."

Aefric could have stretched his senses a bit and learned more about the magic of the pouch. But since she was obviously trying to prove herself, he restrained himself.

Instead, he opened the pouch. Saw four tiny orange runes, spread equidistant around the inside of the lip.

He reached inside. The pouch didn't look more than a few inches deep, but he quickly realized his whole hand was inside, and part of his wrist.

"Impressive," Aefric said. "How deep is it?"

"Your lordship is familiar with the large sacks used to tote root vegetables?"

Aefric chuckled, thinking about hopping races. "I am. Well done."

"There is more, your lordship," Jenbarjen said with a smile. "It will not gain in weight, no matter its contents. And if your lordship focuses his thoughts on anything he has put into the pouch, it will come to his hand."

"Really?" He turned to Beornric. "My keys, if you would."

Beornric handed over that ring of more than thirty keys to the various doors and locks in the Iron Keep.

Aefric dropped it into the pouch. Thought about the key ring and reached.

The ring of keys was waiting for his touch, at the lip of the pouch.

"Even more impressive."

"And there is a final point your lordship should know," she said. "Now that your lordship has recalled an object from within it, the pouch will open for no other."

"All right," Aefric said, nodding. "I admit. This is excellent work. I shall put it to good use."

"Thank you, your lordship," Jenbarjen said, getting a more determined look now. "And your lordship should know that I have already paid into the exchequer as much as I can at the moment, and I am taking steps to gather the rest. My debt *will* be cleared by the harvest festival."

Grond gave a subtle nod of confirmation.

"Tomorrow," she continued, "I begin surveying Netar for its magic-users, and when I find them I shall see them tested and licensed at once."

Aefric nodded. He was tempted to tell her he cared about results, not process, but it seemed important for her to let him know the steps she took.

And she wasn't done yet.

"Also, I have begun research towards a means of fast travel for your lordship, with a focus on the possibility of a flying ship."

"Very good," Aefric said. "I am pleased with your progress, and look forward to your results." He turned to the rest of his advisers. "Now. On to other business."

Because there was always other business.

THE MORNING MEETING LASTED UNTIL CLOSE TO MIDDAY ONCE AGAIN. The sun outside those large eastern windows dimmed now by oncoming rain clouds.

Aefric's stomach growled. At least the feast would, by definition, give him a chance to eat. He'd been shorting himself meals too often lately.

But before he could worry about the feast, he had one more matter to tend to.

He called for Beornric and Grond to stay behind while the other advisers filed out of the meeting room.

"Your lordship?" Grond asked with a bow.

"Did you have a chance to write up your points of disagreement with my rulings from the other day?" Aefric asked him. "I need to know where we stand with one another on the topic of justice."

"There's no need," Grond said. "Your lordship has a fair mind, which I approve of. He does take a stronger hand with his nobles than I might have in his name. But I don't know that this is a mistake. And if your lordship will support my doing so, I can try to match your lordship's ... firmness."

Aefric tapped the green table as he pondered that. "You're thinking of the vintners and their three disputed fields of grapes?"

Grond nodded. "Share the land, through work or through marriage, or give it back to the baron. Not even an option to split the fields."

"One field is always the most valuable, and another the least," Aefric said, rolling his eyes. "At least, in the minds of the owners, if not in their yield. No, splitting the fields might've solved the problem today, but they'd be back in a year or two with the same complaint."

"I'm not saying I disagree," Grond said. "But I am saying that the decision was ... more demanding than they likely expected."

"What do you think they expected?" Beornric asked.

"Likely," Grond said, "they expected his lordship to take a day or so to consider the problem. During that time, they would each try to play up to his lordship and win his ruling in their favor."

"That can't be how things are usually done," Beornric said. "His majesty wouldn't stand for it."

"His majesty played the game, when serving as baron," Grond said. And at Beornric's shocked expression, said, "Don't misunderstand me. I don't think any of the nobles ever won favor that his majesty hadn't already decided to give. But by playing the game, he let them believe they had influence over him. And by taking time to consider, he was able to find a reason to rule in favor of the noble he preferred."

"I don't have the patience for that," Aefric said.

"Obviously not, your lordship," Grond said, chuckling. "But your lordship might consider trying it. It has the advantage of playing the nobles against one another, which keeps them fighting for your lordship's favor, rather than fighting your lordship."

"He raises a good point," Beornric said softly.

"How about this," Grond said. "With your lordship's permission, I can make such weighty, but fair rulings in his name. The nobles will grow frustrated that the old ways aren't working. Then, when your lordship next visits, he can hear their complaints himself and *appear* to play the game, while continuing to rule as he chooses."

"I'll ... think about it," Aefric said.

"Precisely, your lordship," Grond said with a straight face.

Aefric blinked at the large na'shek. Narrowed his eyes. "Was that a joke?"

"If your lordship has to ask, obviously it was not," Grond said, still as stone-faced as only a na'shek can look.

Aefric shook his head. "Where do we stand on hiring a new seneschal?"

"I've narrowed the field to three candidates," Grond said.

"Who's the best of them and why?"

"I ... well..." Grond frowned. "I'm not sure I understand, your lordship."

"Yes, you do," Aefric said. "You have a favorite among these candidates, and a reason behind your choice. I want to hear it."

"All three would make good seneschals, your lordship. All three have the right training, and—"

"I don't doubt it," Aefric said. "But which is your favorite, and why?"

"He'll keep asking until you come clean," Beornric said softly.

"Drien Ol'Andebar," Grond said.

"Why?" Aefric asked.

"He is the son of Ser Layna Ol'Andebar," Grond said.

"And?" Aefric asked.

"Ser Layna shamed his family by fleeing battle, and beggared them with desperate business ventures, trying to restore the family name."

"Why does this make Drien a good choice?"

"Drien was a page here at the Iron Keep. I know his training, and more than that, I know the man. He burns to bring honor back to his family. He could do that as baronial seneschal, but only if his work was outstanding."

"So he's skilled," Aefric said, "and the most motivated of the lot."

"And likely the most loyal," Beornric said, "if he's given this chance."

"Agreed," Grond said.

"Settled then," Aefric said. "He's hired and to begin as soon as possible."

"Without even meeting you?" Grond asked.

"Tell him I'm trusting your judgment in this. That'll give him another reason to excel, so he doesn't make you look bad."

"I'll talk to him after the feast," Grond said. "And thank you, your lordship, for trusting me with this."

"Thank you for trusting *me*," Aefric said, "with how I'm handling the borogs."

"The fairness of your lordship has more than one edge," Grond said with a grimace. "If I would see those cut who deserve cutting, I cannot cry out unfairness if I find myself among them."

"I get cut by it myself sometimes," Aefric said, patting his tender belly, then girded himself through a deep breath. "Now I need to get ready for the feast."

A FEAST FOR THE NOBLES. OR AT LEAST, THE NOBLES WHO'D BEEN invited to attend.

Would that be all of them?

Aefric chided himself for not spending more time with the folio. Finding out more about the nobles he'd be dealing with every time he came to Netar.

Then again, there couldn't be all that many. Not really. This was a barony, not a duchy. Probably weren't more than a score of lers, and about as many landed knights.

There was only so much land to go around, and surely some of it was held directly by the baron.

So likely all the lers who could make it to Netarritan would attend the feast.

And this would be their first real look at their new baron. The impression he made now would be stronger and longer lasting than his arrival few days ago, in his riding outfit.

He needed to look right.

A bath would have been lovely. Not even for his muscles this time. Just because he wanted to be as clean as possible, considering how much time he'd spent recently in the grit and dirt of the mines.

Of course, his nobles might be willing to wait for him to change into appropriate clothing, but asking them to wait while he bathed first seemed a bit extreme.

Besides. He'd taken a bath before bed.

Still.

Alone in his bedroom, he stripped down to bare skin and used his old cleaning spell on himself.

Now, the clothing issue.

Strictly speaking, what he'd worn that morning would be fine. But back at Water's End, his two valets — Dajen and Ocheda — had emphasized over and over the importance of fresh clothes when it came to giving impressions.

Silk, they insisted, got a worn and wrinkled look after a few hours. He could clean that out with a spell. He knew that. But right now his day pages — Ganya Ol'Ispenn and Sendre Ol'Tanet — were busily comparing options in his closet.

They knew his nobles and their expectations better than he did. He'd benefit from letting them help choose his outfit.

And so, wearing only a thin, white linen dressing gown, he walked into his closet to see how they were doing.

Once upon a time, Aefric would have thought of this closet as big enough to get lost in. He'd rented smaller rooms — much smaller rooms — in inns, back when he was an adventurer.

And yet, he could see now that it was about a third smaller than his clothes closet at Behal and no more than half the size of the one at Water's End.

Still. It was well-stocked. Even included a number of swords that looked more ceremonial than functional, in case the baron wished a weapon at his side.

And as for clothes, a good many racks of all types and designs. So much cloth that sound was muffled in that closet, instead of echoing.

And all of that clothing would fit him, of course. That had been true at every castle and keep he'd stayed at since being made duke. He'd begun to speculate that the tailors of Armyr shared among themselves the measurements of every titled noble, in case they were needed.

Or perhaps tailors had their own kind of magic...

At the sight of their baron, the two pages immediately stopped going through options and bowed.

"We have just the thing, your lordship." That was Ganya, lithe and dark-skinned. Her hair a halo of tight dark curls, and her eyes almost amber in color.

"Should make just the right impression, your lordship." That was Sendre. A little taller than Ganya, and built about the same, but with hair the color of summer wheat, and skin so pale she might've been raised underground.

Ganya held up the tunic. Dark forest green samite, embroidered with gold right down to the acorn over the heart.

Sendre held up the hose. They gleamed like cloth-of-gold, but darker than usual for that material. More of a dark honey shade.

Still. They did gleam.

"The hose might be too much," Aefric said.

"This is just the kind of occasion for such hose," Sendre said, and Ganya nodded support.

"I was considering wearing some jewelry for this," Aefric said. "But with those pants..."

"A heavy gold chain, or gold bracelets would definitely be too much," Ganya said. "But among the jewelry your lordship brought with him, we found a ring that we both agree would be *perfect*. Capping the look, and requiring nothing more."

"Woven from sixteen shades of gold," Sendre said, sounding as though the mere thought of such a ring was almost too exciting to bear. "And anchored by that large, beautiful emerald. *Perfect*."

Aefric chuckled. "Queen Eppida herself gave me that ring."

Both nodded as though they either had known already, or had guessed. Which might've come as a surprise, except that they'd both served King Colm when he stood as baron. Which meant they'd had ample opportunity to study the queen's taste in jewelry.

"What about belt and shoes?"

"Dark brown leather," Ganya said, nodding to one side, where they sat waiting under a barrage of tunics.

"All right," Aefric said. "We'll see how it looks."

Then came the awkward part. He closed his eyes and focused on coming up with ways to get those borogs safely across hundreds of miles of Armyr, while two very attractive young women dressed him from the skin up.

When they finished, Sendre held a mirror for him, while Ganya took combs to his hair.

He had to admit. He looked good.

"Good choices, both of you," he said. "Thank you."

Both blushed at the praise.

He added his noble dagger and his usual pouch to his belt. Carrying the wand Garram might've been interpreted as aggressive. And he didn't want to wear Jenbarjen's pouch until he'd had a chance to study its spells.

He wanted to trust her. But if she were going to do something ill-advised, that pouch might be the way to do it. And she'd shown bad judgment before...

The Brightstaff, though, he took in hand. Surely by now everyone knew he carried it wherever he went. And if they didn't, well, then it was high time they learned.

THE GREAT HALL WASN'T QUITE DIRECTLY ACROSS THE OCTAGONAL KEEP from Aefric's apartments, but it was close. Three segments away, and those segments weren't short.

Still. The first-floor hallway looked to have been cleared. Or maybe it was just that all the servants were busy elsewhere, and the nobles were already at the feast. Waiting.

As usual for him these days, Aefric did not walk alone. He was escorted by two Knights of the Lake — Arras and Temat — and an honor guard of six Netar soldiers.

As they were on duty, Arras and Temat wore their full plate armor. Gleaming steel, and breastplates etched with the image of Lake Deepwater. The soldiers carried halberds and wore freshly polished chainmail under their tabards.

Very freshly polished. Aefric could still smell the oil.

For his approach, the stone floor of the hallway had been covered with rugs of forest green, freshly woven rushes.

The rugs did double duty. Lent the air a sweet smell, and kept all those marching boots from sounding too military.

The hallway in this part of the castle functioned as a museum of sorts. All along it, weapons and armor — obviously well-used, and in a few cases broken — were displayed, along with little cards that doubtless told of their historical importance.

The hallway ended in a wide, ornate double door, with the great hall on the other side. Both doors were closed when Aefric arrived. A nervous-looking young servant just outside those doors held up both her hands and said, "If your lordship would be so kind as to tarry a moment and allow me to fetch the herald?"

"Of course," Aefric said, with what he hoped was a soothing smile.

The servant vanished through the doorway like a mouse fleeing a cat.

Aefric had to hope that was nerves and not actual fear, on her part.

In fact, he had just enough time to start wondering if this was a topic he might need to address with Grond, when both doors were flung open. Two trumpeters played the baronial fanfare, and a herald called out in a loud, clear voice: "His lordship, Ser Aefric Brightstaff. Duke of Deepwater. Hero of the Battle of Deepwater. Hero of the Battle of Frozen Ridge. And *Baron of Netar.*"

Aefric stepped forward onto a landing at the top of a wide, gray stone staircase, with the nobility of Netar down at the bottom.

Oh, this design was *wild.*

The great hall included the first two floors of the keep. And since the outside wall had only arrow slits, it was covered with tapestries while the inside walls were mostly windows.

On a bright, sunny day it must've looked glorious. But the sky that day was filled with rain clouds again, coming down from the north.

On a platform almost immediately opposite Aefric was a balcony where sixteen musicians played a sweet tune of welcoming on a variety of stringed instruments.

And even though those musicians were technically on the castle's ground floor, what they stood on counted as a balcony because it looked as though it hung in midair.

The great hall itself continued below ground.

Down there, unconstrained by the main castle design, the lower part of the great hall had to be a hundred feet wide and twice as long. A rectangle of wooden chandeliers ensured there was more than enough light, despite the day's gloom.

As Aefric descended those stairs, he marveled at the size of the crowd. What had his estimate been? Perhaps forty lers and landed knights?

If that had been close, then they must've brought all the family they could. Because there were well more than two hundred guests in attendance. All decked out in finery. Even his other Knights of the Lake wore their best tunics and hose, save for Vria, who opted for a complex gown of blood orange.

Down below, off to his left and therefore in what there was of sunshine, Aefric saw the raised platform and long table he'd expected, but not arranged as he'd expected.

He'd expected that table to be his. For it to have his seat in the center, and a variety of the most important courtiers — likely selected by Grond, though doubtless with Guimond's involvement — getting their opportunity to speak with their baron while they ate.

But no. It was decked out not with place settings, but with food.

Food that could be eaten while standing and moving about...

Oh.

This wasn't a feast.

It was a buffet.

Sure enough. There were no tables set up in the middle of the room. Only along the edges, and none of them with place settings. And what chairs Aefric could see were not set at the tables, but had their backs to the walls. So that sitters could watch the room.

Aefric considered turning and leaving. He'd been ready for the level of socializing involved in a normal feast. But this. He'd be expected to talk to *everyone*, even if only a few words here and there. And with no tables in the middle of the room, there might be dancing as well.

A whole different level of conversation and politicking.

And the nobles were all watching him now. Already studying

him. Noting every little thing about the way he dressed, the way he moved. They'd analyze his every word and gesture...

This was too much.

As if knowing how Aefric would react, suddenly Beornric was at his side.

Impressive, the way so large a knight could seem to appear out of nowhere.

"This feast is critical, your grace," Beornric said softly. He looked ready to physically drag Aefric down the stairs, if needed. "With the recent attempt on your life, you have a standing excuse not to be drawn into alcoves or other privacy. But if you don't come down and socialize, you could jeopardize everything you want to accomplish here in Netar. You'd alienate—"

"All right," Aefric said, forcing a smile onto his face. "I'll do it. But between you and me—"

"You'd rather face Lo'kroll and his twin brother at the same time. I know."

The unexpected thought of Lo'kroll having a twin made Aefric laugh. And realize that he wouldn't have to do all this alone. He had support in this room. Beornric. His Knights of the Lake. Likely even his new advisers.

He could do this.

So with a deep breath to help bolster him, Aefric descended into the sea of waiting nobles.

THE NEXT SEVERAL HOURS WERE A BLUR.

He talked to everyone. He had to have. In fact, tired as his jaw felt later, Aefric was pretty sure he'd talked to everyone more than once. And each one of those conversations fell into the same four categories.

Some wanted to make sure the new baron understood how rich and important they were. How valuable their lands and their contribution to the economy and therefore, how important their opinions on everything that happened anywhere on Qorunn.

Well, that might've been an exaggeration, but not a great one. There were plainly some among the Netar nobility who were accustomed to thinking of themselves as the most important people around. And either they wanted Aefric to understand that, or they had hopes of placing themselves or their family members in key positions in the baron's court. Or both.

Oh, how unhappy they were to learn that Aefric not only wasn't replacing any of his top advisers, but had already found his new seneschal.

Most of them hid well their reaction to this news. Others got that sudden look as though they'd reached for a slice of lemon pie and gotten a slice of raw lemon instead.

Wouldn't do to insult the new baron's decisions, though. That might've endangered their futures. So, instead, they'd simply suggested that they'd be ready to help, when Aefric came to understand the limitations of his current castellan or seneschal or general or whichever other position they hoped to fill.

In the second category were those who wanted to impress the new baron with their own tales of battle, or claims to great skill, or how they *almost* became wizards, but how their family needed them for more mundane — yet crucial — pursuits.

That category included those who tried for reflected glory from the accomplishments — or reputed accomplishments — of ancestors or family members. Which great great uncle had saved a king's life during one war or another. Which cousin had done this great deed or won that battle in the Godswalk Wars.

Honestly, most of those second category conversations started to sound the same after a while. Largely because the speaker knew nothing — or perhaps next to nothing — about what it was really like to throw oneself into the hazard.

It didn't feel glorious. There were no moments of a single sunbeam breaking through the clouds or the world holding its breath while you did this amazing thing.

Real battles were mad scrambles of chaos that smelled of blood and death. Only skalds could make them sound romantic.

The knights were usually a lovely exception here. Most of them had fought in at least one battle. So they said no more than they had to, to make sure Aefric knew they were battle-tested and ready to fight for Netar, if need be.

For those knights, Aefric was even willing to answer questions about his own past battles and skirmishes.

The third category were the gossips, who were oh so eager to make sure Aefric knew about this petty grievance or that one. Who exaggerated their skill at arms or business, or who couldn't resist a wager, or who was living on borrowed money, and so on.

All of it put forth as though these people thought they made themselves sound better by making others sound worse.

Honestly, who could believe that worked?

All these people in the third category accomplished was clamming Aefric up, and ensuring he remembered not to trust them.

The fourth category were those who wanted to marry Aefric or bed him or both. Sometimes they spoke for themselves. Other times they had a family member speak for them first and make an introduction. But they were many, and some of them were quite forward in their intentions.

No matter what category they belonged to, though, all of the nobles, of course, had questions for their new baron. Sometimes about baronial policies — Aefric demurred those with the excuse that he was still settling in — but often about Aefric himself. His travels and adventures, or his take on Netar so far. Whether or not he agreed with the king on this policy or that one. If a duchy as remote as Deepwater could possibly compare to so wonderful a barony as Netar, which was practically part of the capital itself and on and on.

Given that some people managed to fit into more than one of those four categories — the fourth category in particular saw a lot of crossover — it was safe to say that Aefric had held the same six or seven conversations all day, in different configurations.

Honestly, the dancing was a welcome break. Even though it

tended to draw the fourth category, at least his dance partners mostly spent their time trying to impress Aefric with their poise and grace rather than talking his ear off about why they'd make a good wife or husband or lover.

There were exceptions of course. Some seemed to think he'd want to hear advance details about what they'd be like in bed, or as a spouse.

Fortunately, these exceptions were few. And the fact that those exceptions weren't asked to dance a second time might've contributed to keeping their number down.

Still. Aefric had finally found himself agreeing to an assignation for later that evening, just to try to cut down on all the come-ons.

Didn't work. If anything, saying yes to one woman seemed to encourage the others. The Armyrian way, in action.

All in all, the feast that day was at least as exhausting as trekking down into the mines and fighting a massive borog. If less physically harmful.

Even the food wasn't much of a relief.

Because all of the food had to be eaten standing up, there was no meal he could really dig into. Closest he came were the trenchers of beef and lamb, sometimes drizzled with melted cheddar.

Otherwise, it was sliced this or that. Vegetables and fruits and melons and meats. Very reminiscent of his breakfast.

Goblets of decent day beer helped.

Armyrian day beer was very much like what Keifer had known as India Pale Ale back on Earth, though with a low alcohol content. And sipping it gave Aefric a welcome excuse to delay answering one question or another, while he considered his options.

It also helped that servants trailed Aefric, carrying food and drink for him. Well, it helped make sure he got enough to eat and drink. Every so often, though, it might've been nice to use going to the buffet as an excuse to exit a conversation.

No such luck.

The feast lasted until sundown, when Aefric finally felt free to retreat to his apartments.

In Aefric's baronial apartments was a small sitting room that overlooked the courtyard. It would have been a perfect place for Aefric to sit with Beornric after the feast, decompress, and discuss what had just gone on.

Unfortunately, his majesty had decorated that little sitting room with seduction in mind. The only place to sit was a single couch that would have felt crowded with two, unless those two were very friendly.

Even if one of the two wasn't so large as Beornric.

So, instead, Aefric and Beornric sat in the medium sitting room, on lightly padded, but ornately carved calinwood couches, facing each other across an equally ornate calinwood table. At each end of the table, a matching armchair.

Aefric's view included the courtyard under clouds that threatened rain. Beornric's included a large tapestry commemorating the founding of Netar by Isembard Stronghand, youngest brother of Queen Celia Stronghand and King Colm's great, great, great grand-uncle — who was given the title and land as a wedding present.

In the hearth, a fire crackled merrily, chasing away the evening chill and lending a pleasant cherry scent to the air. From a disc on the ceiling, a warm yellow glow lit the room. Jenbarjen's work.

On the table between Aefric and Beornric, a bottle of ishka from the drawer in Aefric's office. A bottle that dated back to the founding of Netar. Beside that bottle, a second, lesser bottle of ishka.

Aefric picked up the bottle from his desk. It was still three-quarters full.

"Sure you want to crack open the good stuff?" Beornric asked. "Clearly it's intended for special occasions."

"And this counts," Aefric said, pouring each of them a measure into small silver cups. "I have met Netar's nobility and survived, and tomorrow I go back to Deepwater."

"With half a hundred borogs in tow," Beornric said.

"May we all arrive whole and healthy at the end of our journey."

Beornric lifted his cup in confirmation and they both drank.

Oh, but this was good ishka. Strong, but the years had smoothed its rough edges, and brought out its subtleties.

It tasted the way a good, hot bath felt at the end of an aett-long trudge through mud and rain. Soothing. Welcoming. Cleansing. And just a hint of divine good will.

Aefric's cup was empty before he knew it.

"Oh, dear gods," Beornric said, looking into his cup with clear disappointment that it was empty, "please tell me we have eighteen casks of that in the cellars."

"I don't know," Aefric said. "But I'm thinking of claiming all casks that still exist as rightful property of the baron."

"The nobles might fight you on that, but I'd support you."

They both chuckled.

Beornric glanced hopefully at the bottle.

Aefric shook his head.

"No," he said with a sigh. "That bottle goes back into my desk for next time."

"I've heard it said that mastery of magic requires a mighty will, but never before have I seen clearer evidence."

Aefric laughed again, and with a gesture moved the bottle out of Beornric's reach.

Beornric cocked an eyebrow. "Hardly necessary."

"Better safe than sorry."

"Fine," Beornric said, pouring them each a measure of the lesser, but still quite good, ishka from the other night.

"So give me the bad news," Aefric said. "How did I do?"

"I thought the feast went well," Beornric said. "You didn't commit yourself to anything. You kept the nobles guessing about what your plans are, and how they might win your favor."

"Oh, come on," Aefric said. "I'm sure there's bad news in there somewhere. Don't start holding back on me now."

"Honestly," Beornric said. "Everything I saw seemed to go fairly well." He frowned. "Well, there was one thing."

"If you make me ask..."

"The Knights of the Lake," Beornric said. "*I* was welcomed at the party because I'm known as your chief adviser. But I think the nobles were offended that the Knights of the Lake were invited to a party that they considered *theirs*. Probably didn't help that you danced with Vria and Leppina."

"I danced with everyone who wanted to. And besides, we're talking about *knights*. They're members of the nobility," Aefric said. "Why should visiting nobility have been excluded from the feast?"

"It's not that they're visiting nobles," Beornric said. "It's that they're widely known as the sworn guardians of the Duke of Deepwater. Having them at what was essentially your first party as baron — including two following you around in full plate armor and clearly on duty — made some think that either you didn't trust your new nobles, or that you consider Deepwater your more important holding."

Aefric gave Beornric a puzzled look. "They do realize that one is a duchy and the other a barony, don't they? Elbar's Blood, *Lake* Deepwater is larger than *all* of Netar. There's simply no comparison between the two, in terms of size, population, economy, status and so on."

"And which is closer to the capital, and therefore on the pulse of the latest fashions and so forth?"

"That was what..." Aefric sighed and slumped on his couch. "What they kept telling me. Over and over. Trying to get me to sound more impressed with Netar than I am with Deepwater."

"And how did you respond?"

"Noncommittally, for the most part," Aefric said. "Except when I pointed out that I'd hardly *seen* anything of Netar except the Iron Keep and one of the mines."

"Hardly the kind of answer that would satisfy them," Beornric said. "Thus, many will walk away uneasy about their new baron's level of commitment. And that you're leaving tomorrow won't help."

"Even though leaving means taking the borog problem with me? Getting the mines and forges back running at capacity, and getting Netar's economy moving again?"

"Doubtless making the citizenry very happy with their new baron," Beornric said. "But the nobles — even those who benefit from what you're doing — will feel slighted that their new baron didn't spend half an aett here before returning to Deepwater."

"I can't possibly make these people happy, can I?"

Aefric tossed down his cup of ishka.

"Oh," Beornric said, "they'll come around. Won't take long for them to see that you're not greedy and that your justice is even-handed. So most of them will come to support you. And the ones that don't, well—"

"I'd end up at crossed purposes with anyway."

"Just so," Beornric said, and sipped his ishka. "Although, since you brought up the borog situation..."

"Covered carts," Aefric said. "There's no other way to do it. Not without openly marching a company of borogs straight down the Kingsroad."

Beornric frowned. "I'd been thinking we might try something with hooded robes, but—"

"But no robe would hide their noses, let alone their horns." Aefric shook his head. "No. We'll need to cart them."

"Maybe six per cart," Beornric said, frowning. "That's nine carts. We'll look like a small caravan."

"A small caravan flying baronial and ducal pennants," Aefric said. "Should discourage any bandits."

"*Should,* being the operative word. Especially with what Lachedea said about bounty hunters."

"I've been thinking about that," Aefric said. "I'll need to warn all the nobles and mayors along the way that I won't be able to accept hospitality on this trip."

"*That'll* go over well," Beornric said with a grimace.

"It *will,*" Aefric said. "Because I intend to tell them I'm taking a company of borogs to the coast on royal business."

"*Royal* business?" Beornric asked in disbelief. "Are you sure that's wise?"

"The king himself told me I had his full support in handling this.

And can you think of anything people are less likely to question than royal business?"

"Still a gamble," Beornric said, pouring them both another cup of isha. "If his majesty disapproves, this could end badly."

"His majesty is playing some kind of political game and using me as a piece," Aefric said, picking up his cup. "If I have to have the responsibility, I might as well claim some of the authority."

Beornric chuckled and raised his cup. "Here's to having the nerve to do what needs to be done."

Aefric lifted his cup in confirmation and they both sipped.

"I'm hoping that the local nobles will be worried enough about the possibility of borogs 'escaping' to provide a military escort."

"Thus discouraging bounty hunters."

"That's the plan."

"Risky," Beornric said. "But it has to be better than marching fifty borogs straight down the Kingsroad."

"Glad you feel that way," Aefric said with a smile. "Because you get to send those rikas before you retire tonight."

"I never doubted it," Beornric said, and took another sip of ishka. "Am I informing Armityr as well?"

"Of course," Aefric said. "Her majesty must know I won't be able to stop over on my way back, as she'd wanted me to."

"Am I telling the capital that this is royal business?"

Aefric nodded as he sipped his ishka. "If it weren't, the queen would insist on my stopping anyway. This way, she can't."

Beornric whistled. "This may get you into trouble with her majesty."

"Might," Aefric said. "And honestly, I hate missing the chance to talk to Zoleen."

"You're ready to put ... this spring behind you?"

"I'm willing to talk with her, and hear what she has to say."

A light knock on the door was followed by Aelgyth leaning into the room.

"Your lordship? Mistress Verinne Ol'Obarrus has arrived."

"Earlier then I expected," Aefric said softly then, louder, added,

"Please see her to the small sitting room and make her comfortable. I'll be with her in a moment."

"Of course, your lordship," Aelgyth said, bowing as she left.

"Shall I see to the arrangements for tomorrow?" Beornric asked.

"Please," Aefric said, trying to recall which of the many women he'd met that day was Verinne Ol'Obarrus.

Well, he'd know soon enough.

———

THE SMALL SITTING ROOM IN AEFRIC'S BARONIAL APARTMENTS WAS ONE of the few that wasn't lit by Jenbarjen's glowing discs. Instead, behind the small, forest green couch sat a runner table, with a six-candle candelabra.

Only the two on the ends were lit. The other four trailed smoke, and the middle two wicks still glowed orange.

Apparently Verinne wanted mood lighting.

She was sitting on the couch, which had been turned away from the rainy view of the balcony and courtyard to face the hearth, where a warm fire lent the air a woodsy scent.

As Aefric entered the room, Verinne rose to her feet and turned to face him, wine cup in hand. The fire's light gave her skin a soft glow.

Now he remembered her. Her shy smile, but lively conversation. She'd managed to come across as friendly and interested without being pushy. She'd even apologized for the way her father had gone on and on about the family silver trade.

Yes. He'd agreed to share the noble privilege with Verinne because she seemed like good company.

Of course, it didn't hurt that she was about Aefric's own age, or that she was shapely and very pretty. With a heart-shaped face, large blue-gray eyes and long, wavy hair that managed at least three different shades of blonde.

But he liked even more that she was one of the few who hadn't overdone her outfit for the feast. She'd opted for a fairly simple gown of pale blue taffeta, its cut fashionable without being daring.

Her only jewelry, a whalebone cameo on a fine gold chain. Not some great family heirloom either. When Aefric had asked about it, she'd told how her sister had brought it back for her from a trading expedition. How she always wore it when her sister was away from Netarritan.

She wore it still in that small sitting room.

Verinne smiled as she stood and faced Aefric. She bowed, then lifted one eyebrow and said, "I promise I mean no threat. Though your lordship is welcome to search me for hidden weapons, if he likes."

"Have I a reputation for paranoia?" Aefric asked, puzzled.

"Not at all." Still smiling, she pointed at the Brightstaff in Aefric's hand. "I know it's said that your lordship carries his old weapon everywhere he goes, but I thought there were limits."

Aefric chuckled and set it to stand just inside the door.

"Watch this," he said.

He approached. Her eyes widened as she looked behind him, and he knew why. She was watching the Brightstaff follow him.

"It doesn't like being parted from me," he said, intending to sit then, but she surprised him by quickly offering her hand.

Technically, she had to right to offer her hand for him to kiss. She was a noble, and he was her superior. He just hadn't been expecting it.

As he kissed her hand, he wondered if she'd done this to show off the soft skin on the back of her hand, or the calluses on her fingers.

Odd that she had those calluses...

But he was distracted from that line of thought when she pressed her forehead to his knuckles.

Suddenly it all made sense.

Verbally thanking Aefric for inviting her to his rooms would have been gauche. But it had been clear at the feast that he had chosen her from a vast field of competitors. So she'd found a way to say thank-you, without actually saying it.

Subtle.

He sat and gestured for her to do the same.

"It has a mind then?" Verinne asked as she sat, looking again at the Brightstaff.

"I sometimes think it does," he said. "Admittedly, in this instance, I told it to follow me. But it does so on its own, if I'm rendered unconscious and moved."

"Could I touch it?" she asked.

"Yes," Aefric said hesitantly, "but never try to without checking with me first. And whatever you do, don't ever try to take it from me. Even in jest."

"I understand." She set her wine cup down on the small table between the couch and the fire.

Aefric took the Brightstaff in both hands and held it before her. She ran her fingers along the smooth white wood.

"What kind of wood is that?" she asked.

"Thunderwood. I've only ever seen it grow in one forest, near the eldrani city of *Ahlisklasach*."

She looked up at him. "What would happen if I touched the staff while you weren't touching it?"

"Pull back your hand," he said, "and I'll show you."

She frowned, hesitant, but withdrew her hand.

Aefric caused lightning to crackle along the Brightstaff's length, throwing harsh white light and smelling of ozone.

Verinne barely had time to gasp and draw back further before Aefric replaced the lightning with white fire.

"Your hands," she cried, and reached out as though to save him.

Aefric quickly extinguished the staff. "I'm safe. It's all right."

Verinne blinked against the room's sudden dimness. Her shaky hands seemed to be caught between reaching for him and pulling back.

Aefric set the Brightstaff to stand beside the couch. Took her hands in his. Hers were cold, and she gripped his tightly.

A tremor ran through her. "For a moment I thought—"

"The lightning and fire will not harm me because I am the staff's master," Aefric said gently. "But if anyone else touched it without my permission, or tried to seize it by force, they'd receive the full brunt of its powers. I wouldn't be able to save them."

"They'd ... I'd be incinerated," she said breathlessly.

"A tragedy I'd much prefer to avoid."

"I think I'd like a little more wine."

Aefric smiled, and released her hands. He poured for them both. As he did, Verinne seemed to recover herself.

"I bet your lordship met a few tonight whom he wouldn't mind incinerating."

"Oh, there were definitely a few who tempted me," he said with a conspiratory smile. "But I know they all have something to contribute to Netar's future."

"Your lordship surprises me," she said, taking a sip of wine. "I'd heard he was far more adventurer than noble."

"I've had to be more noble than adventurer of late."

He tried the wine then. Dark red, and a little too sweet. He wasn't used to wine that tasted so much of cherries.

"Not in the mines," Verinne said.

"Is that what they're saying?" Aefric asked, quirking a smile. "That I charged down there like an adventurer?"

"Well," Verinne said, playing with the rim of her cup, "I don't believe I heard anyone use the word 'charge.' But they do say that your lordship chose single combat with the borog chieftain over simply ordering his troops to slaughter the invaders."

"And would you have had me slaughter the borogs?"

"Father would say so. He would say that to do anything less invites more borogs — or worse — to invade. That they need to be stamped out."

"What do *you* say?"

She frowned into her cup. "I've had enough of killing."

Something in her tone...

"Did you fight in the wars?" he asked.

"I wasn't supposed to," she said softly. "It'll be my older sister who inherits, but my parents have no other children. Father didn't want to risk either of us, for fear of the Ol'Obarrus line ending. He sent me to stay with my uncle and his wife."

"But you didn't go."

"I couldn't," she said. "The war was everywhere. I couldn't *go hide* while everyone I know and love was in danger."

"What did you do?" Aefric asked softly.

"I cut my hair, stole armor and weapons from my uncle's guards, and ran off to join the royal army."

"Not even as a knight? As a soldier?"

"There are no knights in my family," she said. "We've never been warriors. I'm the first Ol'Obarrus in generations to even pick up a sword. But the king was taking everyone willing to raise arms."

"And you survived."

"Barely," she said with the ghost of a smile. "I have a scar I'd be delighted to show your lordship later." She touched her front, just beneath her sternum. "It runs from here" — she ran her fingers around to her back — "to here."

"I'll be sure to trace it with my tongue," he said with a smile. "How did you get it?"

"We were fighting the forces of the Flayer somewhere in the king's lands east of Deepwater. Not even borogs this time, but humans who served that foul god."

Aefric nodded. Sipped his wine.

"The sword went in through my belly, ran me through, and left me by way of my side. The pain was..." She stared into the fire for a moment. "The pain was beyond imagining."

"How did you survive?"

"Luck," she said, shaking her head. "There happened to be a cleric of Nilasah nearby when I fell. Crushed the swordsman's head with a morning star, then ... I still don't know how exactly he healed me."

"No one does," Aefric said. "No one but Nilasah's clerics. And I think even they don't understand all of their goddess' workings. Because I've watched them fail to heal people whose wounds were less than the one you describe."

"Then I don't know why She chose to save me."

"The gods have their own motivations," Aefric said. "And rarely do they bother sharing them with us."

"Your lordship sounds as though he too has been saved by a god."

"By a cleric of Nilasah?" He chuckled. "More times than I care to count. But by a god? Only once. And in my case, as with yours, a goddess."

Verinne leaned forward eagerly. "Surely your lordship won't be so cruel as to leave me wanting the tale."

He laughed softly.

"It was at what they now call the Battle of Frozen Ridge," Aefric said. "Everyone has heard how I summoned the blizzard that destroyed Malimfar's army."

"A feat worthy of legend, your lordship."

Aefric gave a soft snort.

"A feat beyond my power," he said. "I pushed myself too far. I was flying several hundred feet in the air at the time, and channeled everything I had through the ice powers of the wand Garram. The casting ... was too much for me. I lost consciousness. Fell straight to the ground below. By all rights there should have been nothing left of me but pulp."

"And yet your lordship survived," she said breathlessly.

"The last thing I saw before I lost consciousness," he said softly, looking into the fire as he remembered, "was a pair of silver eyes. The last thing I felt, a kiss on the forehead."

He shook his head and turned to Verinne. "I thought I'd imagined them. The eyes. That kiss. But when I was found later, I was unconscious and drained, but very much alive and unbroken."

"How?"

"The goddess of magic, Kalinda, is said to have silver eyes," Aefric said. "Perhaps She approved of what I did. Perhaps there's something more She wants me to do before I die. Either way, She saved me that day. She must've."

He reached out and stroked Verinne's cheek. "Just as Nilasah must've either approved of what you were doing, or had plans for you that meant you had to live."

"Your lordship," she said softly, setting down her cup, "I believe I've had enough wine this evening."

"As have I," he said, setting his own cup beside hers.

They came together then in a kiss. It was the wild, chaotic kiss of two survivors who didn't understand how they'd survived.

WITH THAT FIRST KISS, PASSIONS OVERWHELMED THEM. AEFRIC AND Verinne. Two people who should have died. Two people who'd been saved by gods they didn't understand. For reasons they couldn't begin to guess at.

That shared connection — that shared *incomprehension* — drove them to desperation as they sought the bliss moment together for the first time that night.

When Aefric thought back on it later, he wasn't sure if they tried to find solace in each other or understanding. Or whether they were just jointly expressing feelings that they could never put into words.

Either way, Aefric and Verinne's shared haste to lose themselves in each other led to some very expensive clothing getting torn off and cast aside, and the couch, table and wine all spilling to the white oak floorboards.

But then, that couch was always going to be too small for this sort of activity. Once passion overwhelmed decorum, their ending up on the floor was inevitable.

Still. They were looking into each other's eyes when the bliss moment came. And beyond the purely physical pleasure they shared was something greater.

Not love, nor infatuation, nor anything along those lines. But a kind of ... unification. In finding a way to express together what each had never been able to express alone, they had found a point of common ground that only the two of them could share.

With it came a kind of closeness and understanding that they might never feel with anyone else.

Afterwards, sweaty and breathless, they curled up together on the floor in front of the fire in that small sitting room. Peace had settled between them. And inside them.

Suddenly Verinne laughed. And there was something so pure about the laugh that Aefric found himself smiling, even though he didn't know what was funny.

He didn't need to ask, either. She smiled up at him.

"I was just thinking," she said. "Your lordship—"

"Aefric," he said. "At least when we're alone, I think you should call me Aefric."

"Thank you," she said, sounding more relieved than honored. As though she'd worried that the sense of connection had been entirely on her side.

Aefric nudged her shoulder with his chin. "You were thinking..."

"You were saying before about how you feel more a noble than an adventurer these days." She cocked an eyebrow and ran her fingers along his chin. "And yet, I find us not in your bed, but curled up before a fire. Isn't that where you adventurers find your bliss, while traveling?"

"Sometimes, yes," Aefric said. "But in my defense, what we just did felt more adventurous than noble."

"It did, didn't it?" Verinne smiled. "Do you think I could be an adventurer?"

"You ran away from home and took up arms for a cause," Aefric said. "You already are."

She lay her head down on his shoulder. "Then I guess my adventuring days are behind me too."

"They don't have to be," Aefric said.

"I have duties to my family," she said, fingering the cameo that had somehow survived the tumult. "Just as you have yours to Deepwater and Netar."

"But there is a middle ground," Aefric said. He extracted himself while she made sounds of protest.

Aefric stood, while she still frowned up at him from the floor. The firelight shone on her glistening skin.

"Kneel," he said.

"Already, Aefric?" she asked in a teasing tone as she got to her knees. "I'm happy to do it, you understand. Just impressed at your recovery time."

"That's not why." Though now he had to shake away that distracting option, and realized he was missing a key element to his plan. "And I'll be right back."

He turned and hurried naked through the door that led into his bedroom. He passed wide-eyed and curious Aelgyth and Eadwif on the way to his baronial closets.

He grabbed a ceremonial rapier. It had a gold hilt studded with emeralds. The colors of Netar, more or less. Seemed appropriate.

Scabbard in one hand, he drew the blade as he stalked back through his bedroom.

"Is everything all right, your lordship?" Aelgyth asked, hesitantly.

"Perfect," Aefric said, offering no further explanation as he stepped back into the small sitting room.

Verinne remained on her knees before the fire, looking up at him. She saw the naked steel in Aefric's hand, and her brow furrowed and mouth dropped open in confusion.

Aefric almost laughed at the sheer bemusement in her eyes. How could she not yet see what was going on? Was it really so far out of the realm of her expectations?

Aefric stood before her and raised the sword.

"Verinne," he said softly. "I would make you a knight of Netar."

"No," she breathed more than said. Louder, she continued, "Your lordship. Aefric. I ... I don't deserve—"

"You're as deserving as any, and more than many," he said, gently but firmly. "You defied your family to throw yourself into the hazard. Not for fame. Not for glory. Not for gold. But because it needed to be done. And you would have given all for Armyr, had not the merciful hand of Nilasah Herself reached down to preserve your life."

He had no doubts that every word she'd said of her experiences had been true. Something in how she'd told the story. And, of course, now he'd seen that long, harsh white scar tracing her left side, along with a number of other, smaller scars, and those calluses on her fingers and palms...

"But—"

"These are knightly deeds, Verinne," he said, maintaining that firm but gentle tone. "You should've been knighted for them before now. I seek only to correct that oversight."

"But Father..."

"This is not your father's choice to make," Aefric said. "It's mine, as Baron of Netar." He drew a deep breath. "But it is also yours, Verinne. I will not force it on you. Tell me no, and that will be the end of this. I'll put the sword away, and no one but the two of us need ever know of this moment."

Tears filled those wide, blue-gray eyes as she thought.

"Me?" she said in a small, shaky voice. "A knight?"

"If you truly wish to never kill again, you should say no," Aefric said softly. "Because every knight must be ready to take the life of an enemy, if needed."

"But what would it mean for me, Aefric?" she asked.

"It will mean training," Aefric said. "I suspect your skills have gotten a little rusty since the wars—"

"No," she said, almost absently. "I've continued to train with the guards. Father doesn't know, but I enjoy archery. And the way my muscles feel after a training bout with sword and shield."

"A knight needs more than a bow and a sword," Aefric said. "You'll need to learn to joust. And fight from horseback. And more."

"I could do that," she said softly.

"You would need to get ready and stay ready, in case the call to arms came."

"Could I be one of your guards then?" she asked, and Aefric heard a smile in her voice now. "Like Vria and Arras and Leppina?"

"They are Knights of the Lake," Aefric said. "A special order of the knights of Deepwater, sworn to the safety of their duke. You would be a knight of Netar."

"Then perhaps I could be the first Knight of the Acorn."

"Knight of the Acorn?" Aefric asked.

"Of course," she said. "Your baronial guardian knights. Surely you don't expect Netar to allow Deepwater to outdo us here?"

"Does that mean you wish to be made a knight?" Aefric asked. "Even if it means you might be commanded to take lives again?"

"Who would be able to command me?" she asked, serious now.

"Only myself, as your liege, and their majesties, as your overlords. Though you might also be expected to take orders from my castellan in my absence, and my general in my name."

She considered that for a moment. Nodded.

"I am willing to trust your judgment as I do their majesties." She nodded again. Drew a deep breath and let it out slowly. "I am willing to be knighted, if my liege thinks me deserving."

"Good," Aefric said, then focused himself through a deep breath. He reached out and gently tapped her shoulder blades with the flat of his rapier.

"Verinne Ol'Obarrus," he said. "In acknowledgment of your bravery in battle, I, Aefric Brightstaff, Baron of Netar, do hereby grant you the right to keep and bear arms as a knight of Netar. I further charge you to answer the call to battle, to protect the weak, to defend the innocent, and to take up arms in defense of the realm. Hereafter you shall be known as Ser Verinne Ol'Obarrus."

"Thank you," she said, and those tears trickled down her cheeks now.

She had to swear the oaths then, but did so solemnly, putting extra feeling into every word.

With the ritual complete, Aefric sheathed the sword and set it aside. But when he turned back, Verinne was still kneeling.

"As a knight now," he teased, "one knee is more appropriate than both. Shows your readiness to spring into battle. And anyway" — he extended one hand to her — "it's time to rise, Ser Verinne. My bed awaits."

"Let your bed wait a little longer, Aefric," she said, her voice lower and sultrier as she looked over his naked body in a way that caught his breath. "I believe there's something more I'd like to do while I'm down here..."

AEFRIC AND VERINNE DID MAKE IT TO BED A WHILE LATER. AND WHEN they did, he showed her that he was just as eager to give pleasure as receive.

After that, they sipped a dry white wine for a time. Then set the wine aside and explored each other's scars with fingers, lips and tongues while telling of how each scar was earned.

Aefric was just telling the story of the trapped tomb and the spike that had caught him through the muscle of his left calf, when Verinne quirked a smile and pounced on him.

He wasn't ready for the pounce, but he didn't fight it. She pinned him to the bed by his shoulders, gave him a quick kiss, then pulled back.

"Tell me," she insisted. "How many of your knights have you bedded? Am I the first or the fiftieth?"

"Third," he said.

"Really?" she asked. "Only two others? Shall I guess?"

"No need," he said. "Vria and Arras."

"Good choices," she said, which — no matter how many times he heard it — was still a strange sentiment for him to hear from a lover in bed. Her approval of his other lovers.

But that was the way in Armyr.

Verinne gave him a teasing look. "Not Leppina? Too many muscles for you?"

"While I admit that I don't like my women as muscular as Leppina, that's not the only reason. She has no taste for men."

"Like her duke then," Verinne said. "As I didn't hear Micham or Temat's names in there. And if you liked men at all, one or both would have bedded you by now."

"I note you didn't include Wardius," Aefric said.

"No," she said, sounding guilty. "I admit, most scars are sexy. But he has so *many*. And his poor nose. And—"

"No need to explain," Aefric said. "I assure you, his scars have many admirers."

"Good," she said, then crossed her hands on his chest and settled her chin on her hands. "Surprised there've been only two knights before me, though. Surely there are others you admire."

"There are," he said, thinking of that fiery redhaired dweomerblade known as Ser Deirdre Ol'Miri. "But in Deepwater there are so many lers and other nobles that—"

"Oh, I see," Verinne said, laughing. "So many women want to bed the duke that his knights are yielding their chances to the other nobles? Does his grace need someone to organize his sex life?"

"Hey," he said, tweaking her thigh. "In theory, I'm supposed to be finding a bride..."

Aefric found his mouth shutting at the look in Verinne's eye. It wasn't cunning, and it wasn't hopeful. But there was definitely something going on in there.

"Oh?" she asked softly, then nodded. "Yes, of course. The young duke — and now baron. All that land. All those subjects. You must have an heir. Preferably more than one. And while bastards can be acknowledged..."

She cocked an eyebrow. "In case you had any worries, Aefric, I was drinking that wine to drive out the bitter taste of my nysta tea."

"Good," Aefric said. "Because you arrived earlier than I expected. I hadn't had a chance to drink any."

"Wouldn't do to have my belly swell with your bastard," she said, still teasing. "After all, my armor wouldn't fit." She perked up. "I'll need proper armor, won't I?"

"Full plate is traditional," Aefric said. "And you'll need to learn to move and fight in it."

"Good," she said, nodding, then gave Aefric a more serious look. "And don't worry that I now imagine myself your bride. I would be a fit wife for a baron, it's true. But a duke needs a bride from a far grander family than mine."

"Being a duke's wife might interfere with your knightly duties anyway."

"You're teasing," she said. "But I do wonder how the training and such is going to work. I mean, normally, I know, I would have to squire for someone—"

"But knighthoods can be given in the battlefield without the normal squiring process," Aefric said. "I was never a squire, but I'm a knight."

"That's right," she said. "They always introduce you as Ser Aefric Brightstaff before they get to your titles and honors." She cocked her head. "Do you have a set of full plate hiding away somewhere?"

"Can't stand the stuff. And I think it might not go well for me to wear it when I'm playing with lightning."

She winced. "I imagine not."

"I do have a full set of leathers, back at Water's End. Relic of my time spent training as a dweomerblade with the Iron Wands."

"Can I come with you to Water's End?" Verinne asked suddenly.

"But Netar is your home."

"It is," she said. "But I do need training. Father will fight that if I stay here. He'll want to use my new title to gain political advantage, but he'll never agree to pay for my armor or weapons. And—"

"Slow down," Aefric said. "What if I speak to your father?"

"He'll say the right things while you're here, then do what he wants when you leave. He says forgiveness is easier to get than permission."

"And yet he wouldn't forgive you for being knighted?"

She shook her head. "He'll be furious."

"Well," Aefric said. "He spent enough time bragging about how wealthy the silver trade has made him. Clearly he can afford your weapons and armor. I'll have Grond commission them from the baronial smiths, and send the bill to your father."

A bark of laughter came out of Verinne that seemed to surprise even her.

"He'll be apoplectic."

"I'm not sure I'd be doing you a favor, though, taking you to Deepwater," Aefric said. "You might be better off undergoing your training here. I could assign you to Grond, or Keelastach, or Lachedea."

"Trying to get rid of me?"

"Trying to do what's best for you," Aefric said, giving her a soft kiss. "Better someone who knows you and knows your family handles your training."

"You're honestly not trying to get rid of me then?" Verinne asked softly. "I know what passed between us was intense, but..."

Aefric hushed her. "For me too. You're the first person I've met who ... who really understands."

And she did. He saw it in her eyes when she nodded and brushed a lock of hair away from his eyes. Aefric might never meet anyone else who truly understood the wonder and terror of experiencing divine intervention.

But Verinne understood.

"So no," he said then. "I'm not trying to get rid of you."

"Good," she said, and kissed him before settling on his chest again, her chin back on her hands.

"So," she said. "The one who trains me. It could even be Grond?"

"You like that idea?"

"I've seen him fight in tournaments," she said. "He's amazing. And his reputation for honor stands out even among the knights."

"He could oversee your training. He might hand the details off to..." Aefric frowned, thinking about the honorable na'shek. "Actually, I think he'd probably take it as a personal task, if I asked him to do it."

She nodded.

"But he'd be a stern taskmaster," Aefric said. "He won't look well on laziness."

Her turn to tweak Aefric. "Do I strike you as lazy?"

"Well," he said with a smile, "you *are* just lying about, at the moment."

She scoffed. "I *see*. And *which* of us got wrestled into their current position?"

"Let me think..." Aefric said, then made his move.

She was ready when he pulled her left. But she wasn't ready for the immediate shift back to the right. In moments their positions were reversed.

"You," he answered, and she laughed.

"All right," she said, still laughing. "You win. I submit. Come taste the fruits of your victory."

He kissed her then, and they left the jests and laughter behind for a time to seek other pleasures.

5

MUCH AS AEFRIC WOULD HAVE ENJOYED BREAKFASTING WITH VERINNE the next morning, he knew he couldn't. He had too many other matters to deal with before leaving for Water's End.

So he sent for a new dress for her — the one she'd worn last night was in no shape to be worn again — and while that was being arranged he had breakfast brought to her in his small sitting room, while he and Beornric met in his office.

Servants — or rather pages — had already straightened out the small sitting room, and cleaned up the wine. They'd even replaced the rapier in Aefric's closet, because he'd found it in there while he let the pages dress him that morning.

A dark green woolen tunic over dark brown riding leathers and heavy boots. A woolen cloak that matched the tunic, with a golden cloak pin in the shape of an acorn.

Well. Even if Aefric hadn't heard and smelled the rain that morning, he'd've known from the clothes that the weather was bad.

When Aefric entered his office, he found that Beornric was waiting for him, dressed in similar fabrics. Though his tunic was a dark red, and his cloak Deepwater gray.

Beornric looked longingly at the bottle of ishka on Aefric's desk.

"Long road ahead of us, your grace," he said hopefully. "Long, *cold* road."

"Forget it," Aefric said, putting the valuable bottle back in its proper drawer as he took his seat, standing the Brightstaff beside him. "And we'll need to summon Grond. He should know I've knighted Verinne."

"You *knighted* her? Just how good—"

"*Don't,*" Aefric said firmly. "Did you know that she defied her father and ran away to fight as a soldier in the Godwalk Wars? She's got a scar on her left side bigger than any of mine."

"Really?" Beornric said. "It's a wonder she survived it."

"It was the will of Nilasah," Aefric said. "Anyway, she clearly should've been knighted long ago, so I've taken care of the matter. But she'll need Grond to complete her training."

"I'll send for him at once," Beornric said. And as he did so, Ganya and Sendre brought in the traditional Armyrian breakfast.

Aefric started on a handful of strawberries while Beornric took his seat. "He'll be along in a minute, your grace, I'm sure."

"He won't keep me waiting. In the meantime..."

"I've sent the rikas and made the arrangements for the carts." Beornric shook his head as he picked up a roll of honeyed oat bread. "Don't care much for the weather."

"Can't be helped," Aefric said. "The longer we keep my new borogs waiting, the rougher the trip will be."

"Speaking of rough trips," Beornric said. "Can I at least persuade your grace to ride in his carriage? No reason for—"

"There's a very good reason," Aefric said. "I'm not making my knights and soldiers ride in the rain while I sit sheltered in a carriage."

"You're a duke," Beornric said. "They won't take it as a slight."

"I know they won't," Aefric said. "But how much better will they take it if I suffer in the wet alongside them."

"And if you get sick?"

"Is this your way of telling me you forgot to get some of that honeyed health concoction from the baronial physician?"

Nilasah's Warm Breath. Wonderful stuff. Just one mug was said to help a traveler stay healthy on his trip, no matter the prevailing conditions.

Beornric rolled his eyes. "Of course I didn't forget. And he already had enough brewed for all of us."

"Including the borogs?"

Beornric frowned. "Well, no. But I didn't think they'd drink it. They don't revere Nilasah."

"Get some more, then," Aefric said. "I'll want them drinking it too. One good draught each should get us all the way to Water's End, unless it's raining the whole way."

"You're evading the issue."

"No," Aefric said, wrapping a slice of turkey in a thin slice of cheddar. "Staying healthy is the issue, and I want the borogs included in it."

"The issue is you riding in the rain."

"That issue's resolved," Aefric said. "I will be."

"Aefric," Beornric said through gritted teeth, "don't make me tell you what you're acting like."

"This *is* acting like a duke," Aefric said. "My knights will be quicker to follow me if I don't put myself above them in situations like this one."

"Perhaps," Beornric said. "And by no means is that a certainty."

Aefric had a rejoinder ready, but Beornric spoke louder as he continued.

"*Even so,*" he said, "consider the perspective of those nobles whose soldiers we hope to have supporting us on this ride. What will *they* think, if the duke they meet looks like a drowned rat?"

"They'll think that rain falls on noble and commoner alike."

"Elbar's Blood, you can be stubborn!"

"Do you really think this is such a big deal?"

"I think you're already playing a dangerous game," Beornric said softly. "Telling everyone we're doing this on royal business, but not getting the king's sanction first."

"I have it already," Aefric said. "I spoke to the king just the other night."

He pointed to the window that had, until recently, been part of a two-way communication device with the royal chambers. Told the story of that conversation, and the implicit permission the king had given Aefric to use whatever extraordinary means he needed to get the job done.

"I doubt his majesty meant for you to use his name to smooth the way for taking borogs to the Dragonscar."

"His majesty didn't forbid it," Aefric countered. "And in telling me I had his permission to use whatever means I see fit, he made clear that he wants Netar up and running. He doesn't care how I do it, so long as I get results."

"Did you tell his majesty your plans?"

"No," Aefric said, smiling as he took a sip of water from his silver goblet. "In fact, his majesty specifically didn't want to know."

Beornric shook his head. "You're right. He *is* playing politics and using you as a piece."

"Exactly," Aefric said. "And more than that, I think he's using the Netar situation as some kind of test for me. So I need to succeed, and do so in a way he wouldn't expect. But a way he can use to his advantage, once I've done it."

"I hope you're right."

"Me too," Aefric said, taking a sip of water. For some reason, his mouth had gotten dry. He sipped a little more. "So you see, I've been given enough of a free hand that I can do this."

"Fine," Beornric said. "I agree. It sounds like you have the authority to pull this off. At least implicitly. But now *you* must agree to *look* the part. Maybe the Duke of Deepwater will ride through the rain to show camaraderie with his knights. But a *royal envoy* needs to look like a royal envoy at all times. And that means—"

"Not looking like a drowned rat," Aefric finished, and sighed. "All right. You win. I'll ride in my carriage."

"Thank you, your grace."

"And I think my chief adviser better ride in there with me."

Beornric shrugged. "If you think it's best. But I don't object to a little rain."

"Neither do I," Aefric said. "But you said appearances matter. And who handles all my introductions?"

"Good point," Beornric said. "I guess we're both trying to stay dry this time."

"Hope the others don't hold it against us."

"If they try to, Arras and Micham will straighten them out. They've got the best understanding of these things."

"We better—"

A knock at the door interrupted then.

"Your grace," Ser Wardius said, poking his head in, "your castellan is here to see you."

"Send him in," Aefric said, and a moment later, Grond entered, looking not quite right in a wool tunic and leggings, even though the dark blue worked well with his skin tone.

Na'sheks always looked the most natural in their togas.

Grond bowed, and said in that deep, deep voice of his, "You sent for me, your lordship?"

"Yes. Did you know that Verinne Ol'Obarrus fought in the Godswalk Wars?"

"Yes," Grond said. "Though her father discourages talk of that."

"Well, her father will likely hate me then," Aefric said. "Because I've seen the scar she got fighting for Armyr."

He traced it on himself, and told Grond how she got it.

"Praise Nilasah," Grond said, by way of answer.

"Praise Her indeed," Aefric said. "And praise the warrior who earned that scar. I've knighted her."

Grond's face grew inscrutable, but then he slowly nodded. "Earned, I agree. But her father will be furious."

"So I've heard," Aefric said. "Which is why you will see to it that the baronial smiths forge proper armor and weapons for her, and that the stables provide her a suitable horse and tack."

"Traditionally," Grond said slowly, "these things are paid for—"

"—by the knight's family, yes," Aefric said. "Which is why you will send the bill to her father and see that he pays it."

Grond nodded slowly. "It is just."

"And because I want to see her training handled by someone I can trust, I wish to charge you with that personally."

"Your lordship," Grond said, sounding touched. "I will consider it an honor, and instruct her to the best of my abilities."

"Then I know she'll become a great knight," Aefric said, nodding. "And when I've been impressed with your results, I'll restore to you the power to bear arms in my presence."

"Thank you, your lordship," Grond said with a bow. "I promise your lordship will be *most* pleased."

"I'm sure I will. You'll find her waiting in my small sitting room. Feel free to begin her training today."

"At once, your lordship," Grond said, smiling and bowing before he left.

"Think you've won him over," Beornric said.

"Guess we'll find out," Aefric said. "Now let's finish our breakfast. We've a long day ahead of us."

AEFRIC'S DEPARTURE FROM THE IRON KEEP WAS HANDLED WITH A GREAT deal less pomp and circumstance than his arrival. No red carpet. No assemblage of lers and other courtiers, hoping for a last glance or word with their baron before he literally carted away their borog problem.

Of course, it might have been a factor that the skies were pouring down rain as though they intended to fill the valley below Netarritan to the very brim of the mines.

There were, however, four groups waiting when Aefric and Beornric arrived by magic carriage at the bottom of the hill inside the Iron Keep's outer wall.

First, of course, were the Knights of the Lake. They all wore Deepwater tabards over their armor today, likely for a little extra warmth.

Even their heavy woolen cloaks might not provide enough after riding through the rain for a few hours. They also had care of Aefric's and Beornric's horses, for the trip.

Next were the two dozen soldiers of Aefric's personal guard, all as bundled up against the weather as they could be — over their chainmail — and still be able to move in a fight, if necessary.

Aefric was glad they'd be riding. For the extra speed, yes, but more because the only thing worse than riding through mud and rain, was *trudging* through mud and rain.

Third were the carts, with their draft horses and carters. Good carts for the trip. Wide and strong, with canvas tents stretched in an arch over the top, providing both room and shelter.

More of those carts than Aefric had expected. He'd been figuring on nine for the borogs, and likely three more for supplies. But there were fifteen.

Much as Aefric wanted to ask about the extra carts, though, his attention was drawn to the sight of the unexpected fourth group: two score soldiers, all mounted, led by General Keelastach himself, in his green full plate armor.

The general didn't even wear a cloak, presumably trusting to his antlered helmet to keep the rain off his head.

"General," Aefric called out the window of his carriage, "is there a problem?"

"No problem, your lordship," Keelastach said, nimbly guiding his destrier over so that he could be heard clearly over the downpour. "But I felt my baron and his ... cargo deserved a proper honor guard to see him safely at least as far as Armityr. And as much farther as your lordship will allow."

"Thank you, general," Aefric said. "Armityr will suffice. Netar will already be without its baron in residence for a time. I'll not deprive it of its general for any longer than I have to."

Keelastach smiled roguishly. "I rather suspected your lordship would say that. But the offer stands, if he changes his mind. Ultimately, his lordship is resolving Netar's problem. It's only right that Netar's soldiers aid him in this."

"He has a point," Beornric said.

"Yes, he does," Aefric said, nodding to the general. "But I've already reached out to the nobles along the way. If I now show up in force..."

"It could be misunderstood," Keelastach said. "A shame. Perhaps next time your lordship will take me into his confidence about such plans before enacting them?"

Aefric chuckled. "Fair enough, general. I'll do that."

"Thank you, your lordship."

They then made quick arrangements for when and where Netar's soldiers would join Aefric's party, and when and where they would depart again.

They couldn't join immediately, of course, because there was still the matter of getting the borogs into those carts.

With that in mind, Aefric ordered all of the soldiers —including those of his personal guard — to get in out of the rain for the time being.

With his knights and the carts then, he proceeded through town to the mines.

Along the way, Aefric listened to the steady drumming of the rain on the roof of his carriage. Made him feel guilty, knowing that just as much rain was pounding every one of his knights, but not their duke...

"I know I should feel guilty about this," Beornric said, looking around at the sumptuous carriage interior, currently decorated with Netar's colors. "But I don't. And neither should you."

Aefric looked the question at his knight-adviser.

"I've seen more campaigns than most of those knights have seen summers," Beornric said. "I've slogged through more mud and rain than all of them combined, even if it rains all the way from here to the coast on this trip. And the same is true of you. I know it. I know enough about the world to hear between the words when you talk of your adventures. How many nights did you spend wet and cold before his majesty created you Duke of Deepwater?"

"Nights?" Aefric said with a smile. "Few. I know a spell that creates a kind of small, weatherproof dome. Better than a tent, and dry enough for a fire. What's more, even those who might be looking for me wouldn't see that dome, much less me, inside it."

Beornric cocked an eyebrow and gave Aefric that *you're-evading-my-point-again* look.

How many times must Beornric have given Aefric that look, that he knew *exactly* what it meant?

"All right," Aefric said wearily. "You're right. I might've managed warm, dry camps, but that didn't help while marching or riding through storms and snows and such. Which I did a great deal of."

"Exactly," Beornric said. "You've more than paid your dues here, same as me. *Besides*," — he added quickly, seeing the objection rising in Aefric — "you have responsibilities and duties far beyond those of your knights. It's only right that you get the perks too. Like staying dry in weather like this."

"Fine," Aefric agreed. "I'll try to stop feeling guilty."

"Thank you."

"You're welcome. Now you can tell me why we're bringing so many carts."

"Oh, that?" Beornric said, sounding surprised. "That's right, your grace has never had to make arrangements for so many. I went with ten carts for the borogs, rather than nine. Figured the extra room would do them good. And we'll need the other five for extra food, clothing and pavilions, since we won't be staying in castles."

They discussed the logistics of the trip while the carriage carried them unerringly out of Netarritan, along the road, and finally down to the mines.

"The way has been cleared for us?" Aefric asked.

"The miners won't report until after we've left the area," Beornric confirmed. "And your soldiers have pulled back as well. We should have a quick trip down, even with the carts."

"Excellent," Aefric said. "Have the knights and supply carts wait just inside the mine with their horses, so they can all dry off, and tell the other carters to follow us down."

Beornric leaned out the window and relayed the orders, and then

Aefric got to enjoy riding this cart down through the long, mining tunnels.

Not at full speed, alas. That would have left the carters well behind, and defeated the purpose. But still, a lot faster than going down on foot.

A bit eerie, though, to ride through such silence. He'd grown used to thinking of the mine as a place of noise and chaos, but now there was only the sound of his carriage's wheels on stone.

Well, almost.

There was also *just* enough echo from those wheels to hint that the repetitive noise was hiding something more sinister.

The smell of oil lamps could have masked the approach of any number of monsters...

Aefric shook himself. He would probably never be able to venture underground again without old adventuring reflexes warning him of dangers he could conceivably face.

But probably wouldn't.

Finally they reached the kidney-shaped meeting cavern, and Aefric got out of the carriage. Beornric followed him, but Aefric gestured for the carters to remain in their seats.

He cast the Soulfist spell of languages, just to be safe. Wouldn't do to come this far and blow everything over a misunderstanding.

Aefric set the Brightstaff down and brought both hands up to cup around his mouth.

"Thunder Stick!" he called out in Borog.

"Thunder Stick!" came the distant response, in many voices.

Soon the borogs emerged from the three tunnel mouths, carrying their iron-tipped stone spears and axes. Forty-nine in all. All of them had marked themselves or their stone plate armor somewhere with the clan mark for Clan Thunder Stick.

Identical with Aefric's personal sigil, albeit less precise in its representation, the clan mark was the vertical image of a staff, with two bolts of lighting coming from the tip. One to the left, and one to the right.

Lo'kroll, still carrying his massive iron maul, organized the borogs into a line.

He turned to Aefric, stomped his foot, and snorted that all were present.

Aefric snorted acknowledgment.

"*Clan Thunder Stick split. Me and me here.*" Aefric stomped his foot. "*Me and me far away.*" He gestured with his nose in the vague direction of the Dragonscar.

He stomped his foot, and scraped it.

The borogs all scraped their feet in understanding. They were now part of a larger clan, but most of that clan was somewhere else.

"*Ik and ik*" — Aefric gestured to the carts with his nose "*carry me and me to me and me.*"

That got him some uncertain snorting. Borogs, in general, didn't ride in carts or have much use for horses.

Aefric stomped his foot decisively. Lo'kroll stomped his foot in support.

The other borogs all snorted submission.

"*Here to there, no fighting. Not with me and me. Not with ik and ik. None.*"

He stomped his foot again.

The borogs, Lo'kroll included, snorted displeasure, but scraped their feet to show obedience.

"*Chief hand, Lo'kroll, keep weapon,*" Aefric said. "*All others, on ground.*"

The borogs hesitated.

He understood why. They would feel vulnerable. But it couldn't be helped. Disarming them would cut down on the risks.

Aefric stomped his foot decisively.

Still they hesitated.

"*Who is chief?*" he asked, and all the borogs except Lo'kroll dropped their weapons to the rocky floor.

Good. Aefric had basically told them to obey or challenge, and he hadn't really wanted another fight.

"*Chief hand,*" Aefric said. "*Pick nine fingers. Each gets weapon.*"

Lo'kroll walked the line, and snorted his selections. The chosen borogs snorted pride and accomplishment, and stepped forward to pick up a weapon.

They all chose axes. Interesting.

"Five Thunder Stick each cart. No more. One finger or chief hand, each cart. Lo'kroll."

Lo'kroll quickly distributed the borogs and his lieutenants — the fingers — among the carts, taking responsibility for the lead cart himself.

Once they were all aboard their carts, Aefric said. *"Me and me ride by day. Sleep by night. Join me and me soon."*

The borogs all snorted their eagerness. They knew they were on their way to dig gold.

Aefric got back into his carriage, where Beornric nodded, looking impressed.

"Good job," he said. "I thought sure you'd have to kill at least one."

"We haven't reached the Dragonscar yet."

Beornric smiled, so Aefric pretended he'd been joking.

ONCE THEY WERE OUT OF THE MINES AND ON THE ROAD, THINGS GOT smoother. There was even a break in the rain around midmorning, which provided everyone a chance to stop and stretch their legs, and snack on an apple and some good sharp cheese.

But they were barely out of Netar at this point — still escorted by Keelastach and Netar's soldiers — and still quite a ways from the capital. So Aefric kept that rest short.

He got everyone back on their horses or in their carts, and back on the road.

From the sound of things, there was some traffic on the Netar Road that day, and all of it was being cleared for Aefric and his caravan.

On the one hand, he hoped that didn't cause ill-will. He hated exerting privilege that way. But on the other, he was glad not to deal with slowdowns. He wasn't sure how well the borogs would take to being cooped up for more than an aett of travel...

He and Beornric were discussing whether or not they could get as far as the Red Hand Inn before stopping for the day when he heard the halt being called from up ahead.

Frowning because someone else had called the halt for him, Aefric looked out the carriage window to see where they were.

Armityr. The capital. He could see the white palace itself as well as the walls of the city, and the tent cities outside them.

Beornric had just gotten as far as asking, "Shall I go see—" when Ser Micham rode up to the carriage window.

"Your grace," he said, "the king's soldiers are blocking the road. And the queen is with them."

Aefric glanced at Beornric. Said softly, "I knew she'd be unhappy that I wasn't stopping at Armityr."

"I beg your pardon, your grace," Beornric said, just as softly, "but I'd say you *have* stopped at Armityr."

"Good point." He turned to Micham. "Well, I suppose I'd better see what her majesty wants with me."

Micham reached down and opened the door. Beornric stepped out first, looking left and right as though checking for threats, then nodded to Aefric that it was safe.

Brightstaff in hand, Aefric got out of the carriage.

Interesting. Here the skies were blue and the midday sun bright. The winds that brought that storm down to Netar would apparently see it miss the capital.

Not entirely, though. The road was still tacky from recent rain.

He turned to see about this ... blockade...

Well. It seemed her majesty wished to make a statement.

More than two hundred soldiers blocked the Netar Road. All on foot. All in shining chainmail, and carrying halberds. And they weren't alone. Aefric could see a company of at least a dozen knights farther back along the line. Mounted, with lances in hand. They seemed to be surrounding something, but he couldn't see what. Likely the queen.

Beornric met his eyes. Both drew uneasy breaths, then Aefric began walking toward the front of his procession, Beornric one step behind.

They passed three of his knights — four, if he included Keelastach, which he knew he really ought to — and twenty of the Netar soldiers before reaching the royal soldiers.

A page stood waiting between the two forces. A handsome young man who couldn't be far from his majority. If he felt the tension in the air, he didn't show it.

"Your grace," the page said, bowing deeply to Aefric before turning to Beornric. "Ser knight," he said, with a lesser bow. "I am come to escort your grace and his adviser to the royal presence."

"Thank you," Aefric said. "Lead on."

Aefric expected the page to lead him around the assembled soldiers. He didn't. Instead, he led Aefric and Beornric straight through their ranks, with the soldiers clearing space, and reforming ranks behind them.

The process felt very military, and more than a little threatening. A glance at Beornric confirmed that he felt the same way.

Just how angry *was* her majesty?

When they reached the queen's ring of knights, the knights gave Aefric and Beornric disdainful looks before having their steeds make room.

Wait. Their armor. Aefric quickly glanced at all of the mounted knights he could see, confirming his initial suspicion.

Their breastplates weren't etched with the golden oak tree of Armyr.

These weren't Knights of the Crown.

What other knights would her majesty travel with? And where were the Knights of the Crown assigned to guard her today?

Just what exactly was going on?

Once the knights made room, Aefric saw a carriage that could have been twin to his own, save that the devices on the doors and pennants were the golden oak tree of Armyr.

The page led Aefric right to the door. Opened the door.

"Only your grace may enter," the page said. "I'm afraid, ser knight, that you must remain out here."

"Am I denied the Brightstaff as well?" Aefric asked.

"Of course not, Aefric," Queen Eppida's voice came from within the carriage. "I know you present no threat to me. Indeed, I know how you would throw yourself into the hazard to protect me, as you have before. You may keep your weapon. But do not keep me waiting."

"Yes, your majesty," Aefric said, trying to sound more contrite than confused as he got into the carriage.

The carriage door closed behind him with a sense of finality.

———

HER MAJESTY SAT ALONE ON THE GOLDEN SILK OF A BENCH SEAT. SHE wore a gown of sky blue, with her hair piled attractively atop her head, and would have looked devastatingly beautiful, if not for the cold distance in her expression.

Aefric offered her his hand. She took it. Toyed for a moment with her noble's dagger, but gave his hand a reluctant kiss.

"Be seated, Aefric, and tell me why you've disappointed me."

Aefric gathered himself as he took the offered seat.

"It was never my intention to disappoint your majesty," he said carefully. "I had hoped to stop for the night at Armityr on my way back to Deepwater, as we discussed. In fact, I had hoped to stop at many castles along the way—"

"Except that you're transporting carts full of borogs, yes," Queen Eppida said. "You are telling me what I know already. What I wish to hear is what I do *not* know."

"I'm not sure I understand, your majesty."

"*Why* are you transporting cartloads of borogs?" she said. "And *how* is this a royal assignment?"

"Well," Aefric said. "I am transporting them because they were causing problems—"

"In Netar's mines, *yes*," she said impatiently, leaning forward. "Again, what I know already."

She leaned back again. Arched one imperious eyebrow.

"Forgive me, your majesty," Aefric said. "But your majesty is so well-informed that she may already possess any information that *I* have."

"I think we both know that's not true," she said, still holding that eyebrow high.

Aefric frowned, not sure they were having the same conversation.

"Well, since your majesty knows the problem I am solving by transporting the borogs—"

"Why are you *transporting* borogs and not *killing* them?"

"There was no need to kill them, your majesty," Aefric said. "They didn't want to clog the mines or fight our people. They wanted to dig the gold vein that had been found. I happen to know where they could dig a great deal more gold, and benefit Armyr in the process."

"So it's true," she said softly. "There *are* borogs in the Dragonscar who call you chief. And they *do* dig gold for you. I thought surely Colm was joking about that."

"Not in the least, your majesty," Aefric said. "And I can assure you that their productivity is impressive. They're marvelous miners, and there truly is nothing that brings them more joy than mining gold. They consider the act of doing so a kind of connection with the divine. The Borog word for gold, *aur*, even translates to 'god metal.'"

"And you intend to personally escort some twoscore borogs *hundreds of miles* for this. You consider this a good use of the time and resources of a *peer of the realm*."

"I've already arranged for Netar's productivity to build back up to full, now that I've removed the problem," Aefric said. "I've also taken steps regarding certain shortcomings in the baronial coffers, and dealt with a few other relevant matters. Besides. I'll need to return to Deepwater soon anyway, because—"

"Because a number of princesses will be coming to visit you, yes,"

Queen Eppida said, looking at Aefric thoughtfully. "And you are willing to not only sleep out of doors, but risk your own life and the lives of your knights and troops — as well as those of any noble along the way willing to aid you in this ill-advised scheme — all to preserve the lives of twoscore *borogs*?"

"Forty-nine in all," Aefric said. "I counted them."

"I thought I understood you, Aefric Brightstaff," Queen Eppida said softly. "But I seem to have missed something."

Aefric didn't know what to say to that, so he bowed his head as though acknowledging a compliment.

The movement brought a smile to her majesty's lips, though it didn't last long.

"And now the other matter about which I still require enlightenment from you."

"Yes, your majesty?"

"*How* is this a royal assignment?"

"I'm afraid that on this matter," Aefric said carefully, "I must ask your majesty's pardon."

"Oh?" she asked, smiling. "Am I to understand then that my duke has overstepped his authority and claimed royal sanction that he does not possess?"

"No, your majesty," Aefric said, fighting down a pained expression. "I mean that I must ask your majesty's pardon for not answering this question."

She laughed softly. "You don't need to apologize for answering the other question first, Aefric. Just tell me now. *How* is this a royal assignment?"

She leaned forward again. An eager look in her eyes.

"But I *must* apologize, your majesty," Aefric said, looking straight into those sapphire blue eyes. "Because I cannot answer that question. It must be asked of his majesty, the king. Only he can answer it."

She sat back, blinking. Her lips parted for speech, then closed again. She frowned.

Aefric found himself wondering if he should just come clean.

Admit that he had implicit approval for any plan he made, but no specific orders from his majesty.

Then again, doing so might endanger the borogs. After all, she'd clearly rather see them dead than traveling with Aefric. And if she ordered them killed now, he'd have no excuse not to stop at Armityr...

"This is part of something bigger than Netar, isn't it?" she asked softly. "Colm has you doing this crazy stunt as part of something *else* he's doing." Aefric got the impression that she wasn't really talking to him as she continued. "You must be the distraction. Which means he wouldn't tell you...

"Where exactly does this journey take you, Aefric?" she asked quickly. "Tell me. And tell me your time frame."

"I—"

"That is a royal command, my duke," she said, with an intimidating smile. "And unless you wish to tell me that Colm has forbidden you from sharing these paltry details with me specifically, you have no cause not to answer in full detail."

"I take the Kingsroad to Behal," Aefric said. "From Behal I sail across Lake Deepwater to Lachedran. Then overland again to the Dragonscar. There these borogs will join the others."

"Yes, yes," she said, practically licking her chops. "And the timeline. When must you arrive at the Dragonscar?"

"As soon as possible." Which was true, because that was his plan. He needed to get this done.

"Depending on conditions, an aett," she muttered. "No more than ten days." Louder she said, "As soon as possible?"

"Yes, your majesty."

She nodded. "You'll try to make it within an aett then."

"If I can. Crossing the Deepwater by ship will help."

"All right," she said, smiling again and looking more relaxed. Possibly even triumphant. "*That* I can work with."

"I ... am pleased to have helped your majesty."

"Oh, Aefric," she said, and reached out and stroked his cheek. "Do not blame yourself when you get caught up in royal games. Obviously Colm and I are both fond of you."

Unsure what to say to that, he nodded again.

"It occurs to me," she said, not sounding at all as though what she was saying had just occurred to her, "that since you're already on *one* royal mission, what's another?"

"Your majesty?"

"Oh, don't worry, Aefric. This one will be far more pleasant, I'm sure. I merely wish you to transport someone for *me* as well. You won't even have to go out of your way."

"I ... well..."

"This is a royal command, my duke," she said gently.

"Of course, your majesty," Aefric said then. "Whom am I to transport?"

"Why, Aefric," she replied, smiling widely. "Couldn't you guess?" Louder, she said, "We're ready for you."

The carriage door opened, revealing Zoleen Fyrenn.

Zoleen Fyrenn.

There were three Fyrenn sisters of this generation. Ashling, the oldest, had inherited the duchy of Merrek. Eppida, the middle daughter, had married the widowed King.

Which left Zoleen. The baby of the three, barely into her majority.

Nevertheless, she had the Fyrenn beauty. There was no denying that. She had the soft, smooth skin, the striking features, the sapphire eyes. Her long, copper hair fell in waves well past her shoulders.

In fact, if anything, she was more curvaceous than the queen.

And she could also be fun to talk and laugh with...

She was dressed today for travel in questionable weather. A dark blue wool tunic over riding leathers, with a gray woolen cloak.

Wait. That tunic wasn't just dark blue. It was navy blue. And the cloak, Deepwater gray...

"I'd like to think your grace is undressing me with his eyes,"

Zoleen said with a small smile, "but unfortunately I suspect he's only noting the color of my tunic."

"I chose the colors," Queen Eppida said, reminding Aefric that he still sat in the royal carriage. He'd become distracted for some reason. "I think they look good on her." She turned to her sister. "Though I *had* asked you to wear a dress."

"If I wore a dress," Zoleen said softly, "his grace would feel obligated to offer me space in his carriage. By dressing to ride, I hope to make clear that I am content to sit my horse all the way to my ship, if he prefers."

Queen Eppida gave Aefric a look that clearly said she would more than *disapprove* of him making her sister ride her horse while he sat in his carriage.

"Of course you can ride in my carriage, Zoleen," Aefric said. "It's good to see you again."

Zoleen looked up at him so quickly that the eye contact was almost a physical pressure. "Is it, your grace?"

"Yes, it is," he said. "Though I should warn you that my carriage may not have room for all of your ladies, depending on your entourage."

"I have no entourage for this trip," Zoleen said, looking at her sister.

"You most certainly do," Queen Eppida said, smiling. "I've provided one. No less than the great duke Ser Aefric Brightstaff, himself. Along with his knights and soldiers."

"Are they ordered to accompany me all the way to Fyrcloch then?" Zoleen asked the queen in a tone that would have been impudent from anyone else.

"Of course not," Queen Eppida said, smiling even wider now. "They're on royal business for my husband, after all. But a handful of servants are joining his caravan even as we speak, with orders to attend your needs. And you'll have ladies and guards waiting for you on your ship. Did you really think I'd overlook a detail like that?"

"No, Eppy," Zoleen said with a sigh.

Her majesty cleared her throat.

"Excuse me," Zoleen said, not sounding apologetic. "No, your majesty."

"Better," Queen Eppida said. "Now, be off, both of you. You have a long way to travel and a short time to get there."

Aefric would have sworn that those last words meant more to the queen than they did to him. But he knew he'd be a fool to ask. So he stood. Bowed to the queen. Offered her his hand.

She didn't hesitate to kiss it this time.

He exited the carriage, and noticed that Beornric was watching the knights, who were all watching Zoleen. Many with clear longing in their eyes. Longing that turned to disdain, the moment they saw Aefric emerge from the carriage.

"Beornric," Aefric said, ignoring the daggers that several knights now stared at him, "Zoleen will be joining us as far as..." He turned to her. "I'm sorry. Her majesty neglected to tell me *where* your ship will be waiting."

"Behal, I'm afraid," she said, and her expression said that she wanted to say more, but that this wasn't the time and place.

"Behal is fine," Aefric said. "We'll be there in a few days. You'll be home in less than an aett."

"Thank you, your grace," she said carefully, with a small bow. She seemed even more aware of the attentions of those knights than Aefric was.

"We'd better be on our way," he said and, with Beornric, escorted Zoleen past the knights and back through the ranks of parting soldiers to Aefric's own waiting carriage.

When they reached it, Beornric cleared his throat and said, "Shall I mount up and see about getting us through or around this road-block, your grace?"

"Please," Aefric said, fighting down a smile. Leave it to Beornric to find a graceful way to give him an excuse to talk privately with Zoleen.

Keelastach rode up then. "Your lordship," he said with a small bow, then added, "Mistress Zoleen," with a nod.

"Zoleen, have you met Netar's general?"

She hadn't, so Aefric made quick introductions, then asked, "What is it, general?"

"We have reached the place where your lordship said that Netar's soldiers and I were to turn back."

He made a show of turning to the sight of so very many soldiers of the royal army, still blocking the road at the moment.

"In light of recent events," Keelastach continued, "I should like to repeat my assertion that your lordship would benefit from a continued escort of Netar soldiers."

Aefric quirked a half-smile. "I wouldn't see Netar's soldiers fighting the royal army."

"For which I am grateful," Keelastach said with a small bow. "But it would be right for them to do so, if your lordship were ... wrongly threatened."

"There was no threat here today," Aefric said firmly. "Only a point being made. And I don't think it was being made to me."

Keelastach frowned. "If I might ask—"

"I think it's better if you don't, this time," Aefric said softly.

"Of course, your lordship," Keelastach said with a nod. "Shall I lead our troops back then?"

"Please."

"Safe journeys, your lordship. Mistress Zoleen."

"And to you, general," Aefric said, turning then to his carriage.

One of the soldiers opened the carriage door, and Aefric lost a moment to cognitive dissonance.

He was a duke. A peer of the realm. He should enter the carriage first, unless the king or queen was present. That was the way of things. He knew that.

And yet, the Keifer part of him wanted to offer Zoleen the chance to enter first. She was a lady, and Keifer had been raised to be polite. Allowing ladies to enter first through doors was part of that...

Why did that surface now? And why did it come through strong enough to cause a conflict?

"Are you all right, Ae— your grace?" Zoleen asked.

Aefric shook himself. Forced a smile. "Sorry. Flashed on a memory. It's nothing."

He got into his carriage and sat before she could ask another question.

———————

SITTING ON THE PADDED SILK SEAT OF HIS CARRIAGE FELT EVEN BETTER than it should have. Something in the momentary conflict in his head had left him a little shaky.

Zoleen still looked concerned as she entered the carriage and took her seat, across from him. "Shall I send for something?"

"No, no need," he said, smiling a little more naturally now. Whatever was going on had passed. "Thank you for that book, by the way."

"You're quite welcome, your grace," Zoleen said, smiling. "It's only a starting point for a study of Dereth Sehk, and incomplete by nature, but it covers the essential points really quite well."

They fell to talking for a time about Dereth Sehk, and the great battle he led against the spreading forces of the derekek emperor, Orsk, back oh so very many centuries ago.

The discussion continued as the road was cleared and Aefric's caravan began moving once more. Zoleen knew her history quite well, and seemed more than happy to share her knowledge.

And yet, it was she who suddenly — in the middle of a point about how Dereth Sehk had managed to persuade even borogs and na'shek to fight as allies — stopped talking about history and said, "I need your grace to know something."

"I'd say I'm listening," Aefric said.

"I didn't ask for this."

"I'm not sure I follow."

"This," she said, gesturing at the carriage around them. "My being here. I didn't want to push my company on you. When word came that you wouldn't be stopping at Armityr, I told Eppy that I was fine just going back to Fyrcloch. To corresponding with by letter until you were willing to see me again."

"I—"

"Please, your grace," she said. "Let me finish."

Aefric nodded.

"It was Eppy who insisted that you escort me to my ship. I argued against it but, well, she's as stubborn as Ash, when she thinks she's right. But she doesn't know you as well as I do. She didn't listen when I told her that you'd only resent having my presence forced on you."

She glanced as Aefric, as though hoping he'd deny that. And he was tempted to do so, even though his feelings on the matter were mixed.

Instead, softly, he said, "You asked me to let you finish. Are you finished?"

"Not quite," she said, drawing a deep breath as though she needed to gird herself. "We've come far enough from the palace now that I'm pretty sure no one's watching us on her behalf. So, I want you to know that she never needs to find out what happens from here. Say the word, and I'll ride my horse all the way to my ship without a word of complaint. I'll be available if you want to talk, but I won't approach you without permission. Eppy may force me into your caravan, but I won't let her force me on *you*."

Aefric frowned. He'd seen such determination in a pair of sapphire eyes before. Ashling, when talking about the Malimfar threat at her border.

"You're serious, aren't you?" Aefric asked.

"Absolutely," Zoleen said firmly. "It was deception and manipulation that drove a wedge between us once. I will *never* make that mistake again, and I won't have *anyone* making it on my behalf. Not even if she can call herself 'queen' these days."

Something about Zoleen's tone in those last words made him laugh.

Unfortunately, she missed the humor. Looked at him with a mixture of hurt and confusion.

"Oh, no," he said quickly, all laughter gone now. "I'm sorry, Zoleen. I wasn't laughing at you. I was ... well ... it was just the *way* you said that. About the *queen of Armyr*."

"Oh, *that*," Zoleen said, with a small smile now. "Well, she may be the queen *now*, but she's still the big sister who used to steal my dolls and get me into trouble for things she'd done."

Aefric laughed again. "Which is what she did here today, isn't it? Tried to get you into trouble for something she'd done?"

"Of course," Zoleen said, laughing now. "She may be older, and the whole kingdom may jump when she raises her hand, but she's still just bratty little Eppy at heart."

They laughed about that for a moment, even sharing that laugh when their eyes met. It felt good. He'd missed laughing with her like that.

When the laughter passed, the silence that followed was more comfortable. Aefric almost hated to break it, but he had to.

"She's a better manipulator than that, though. And we both know it."

"Of course," Zoleen said, sounding sad to have to admit the truth. "You know why she wants me here. She wants us married. She wants me having your children. And really, she wants all that because she wants the Deepwater heir to carry the Fyrenn bloodline."

"Is that what you want?" Aefric asked.

"My oldest sister is a duchess in her own right," Zoleen said. "Shrewd. Clever. Powerful. Beautiful. All words that also apply to my second oldest sister, and our brother Mekel, as well. Though most would call him handsome, rather than beautiful."

She sighed. "Ash will marry whoever she damn well pleases. But make no mistake, it'll be a brilliant match. She'd die unmarried before she'd settle for anything less. And Eppy, well, she married the *king*, didn't she? Mek, he'll likely have his choice of princesses. So where does that leave little Zolly?"

"You mean the youngest Fyrenn sister?" Aefric asked. "The one who is as shrewd and clever as her sisters, but arguably even more beautiful? The one who has an even better sense of humor? I somehow doubt she lacks for suitors."

Zoleen smiled at the praise, but that smile gained a chagrined aspect before she spoke.

"You're right of course," she said with a sigh. "I have several. Including a king so old he must want me on his arm, because I can't believe he still desires company in his bed."

"Perhaps you underestimate your appeal."

"My appeal," she said with a snort. "Many want to bed me for my beauty. Much the same way I'm sure every noblewoman from Armityr to the coast must *salivate* at the thought of bedding *you*."

Aefric had a joke ready then, but Zoleen was picking up speed.

"But we're talking about more than the bliss moment. We're talking about marriage. And when it comes to marriage, they come to me because they want my family name, or my dowry, or access to my sister's trading fleet, or some other benefit. The usual things that nobility and royalty want from a marriage."

She looked away out the carriage window, at the farms they passed. Or perhaps the darkening skies.

"But the one man I want is the one man who doesn't care about any of that. The one ... the one who was coming to want me for me." Tears welled up in her eyes. "But I was too foolish to see how special he was. How rare. And I did something that any other noble would have seen as clever. But not him. He saw it for what it was. Saw *me* for what *I* was."

She hung her head sadly. "I was acting just like my sisters. Despite all my promises to myself, I was growing up to be just like them. He saw that. And he..."

She turned and looked at Aefric now. The pain he saw in her eyes was raw and very real.

"And *you*, you rejected me for it. And you were right to do so. I wasn't worth—"

"*Stop*," Aefric said, sharply enough that she startled into silence.

"Zoleen," he said, "it isn't a question of worth. It never was. I know how wonderful a woman you are. Which was why it hurt all the more to realize I couldn't trust you."

"But—"

"*But*," he said over her, "it's clear that you now understand what happened from my perspective."

"I do," she said. "Or at least I'm trying to."

"Which is all I really asked," he said. "Because I couldn't believe you wouldn't break my trust again. Not until I knew you understood *why* what you did upset me. But it's clear now that you do." He drew a deep breath and let it out. "So I think it's time we put past mistakes behind us."

"Truly?" she asked, looking as though she was afraid to hope.

"Truly," he said. "Now. Please. Tell me how Dereth Sehk managed to get *borogs and na'shek* to cooperate."

A quick, breathless laugh came out of her. She smiled, almost disbelieving, with unshed tears shining in her eyes.

Aefric smiled back, then looked out the window. Not really seeing anything. Just giving her the moment she needed to compose herself.

When Zoleen finally spoke, she said, "I only know what the histories say."

"It'll be a better place to start than I have right now."

"Then it would be my pleasure, your grace."

"Aefric," he said. "I think I'd like you to call me Aefric again."

The skies above might've been threatening rain, but inside that cabin Zoleen's smile was bright enough to banish every cloud for a thousand miles.

Unfortunately, as the histories recounted the great works of Dereth Sehk, he had a key advantage that Aefric lacked on the topic of na'shek and borog cooperation.

An invading force powerful enough to wipe out both the na'shek and the borogs — along with the humans and tarok — if they didn't all work together.

Apparently even the borogs and na'shek were willing to set aside their great hatred, in the face of getting wiped out of existence.

So it seemed that all Aefric needed was an equally...

Oh, that wasn't even a thought worth finishing.

Discussing the possibilities with Zoleen — who sat beside Aefric in his magic carriage now — was at least a pleasant way to pass the time.

Her vast reading of history might not have yielded easy answers for Aefric's borog-na'shek dilemma, but at least she helped eliminate many of the more obvious options.

Apparently he was far from the first to try to get the borogs and na'shek to cooperate. They were both such good miners that many before him had seen the benefits that could be reaped by getting them to ally with one another.

Unfortunately, repeated efforts over the years had made the problem clear: what they were best at was also what made them incompatible. Not only were their approaches to mining technique different, so were the divine connections and philosophies that they attached to mining.

The problem wasn't the ore itself. For borogs, extracting the ore from the stone was what mattered most. What became of the ore afterwards was less important. For na'shek, extracting the ore was less important than what was done with it afterwards.

Which was why the borogs were superior miners — though only a fool said so in front of the na'shek — but the na'shek were superior smiths.

So, many in the past had tried to get them to work together by having the borogs do the actual mining, and the na'shek handle the ore afterwards.

Didn't help. Because the real conflict turned out to be in the *stone*.

For the na'shek, the stone was equally as important as the ore. For the borogs, the stone was like bone, to be broken open so the marrow could be harvested.

A difference that inevitably led to spilled blood.

Beornric joined Aefric and Zoleen around mid-afternoon, because the rains had started again. Beornric raised his eyebrows when he noticed that Zoleen now sat beside his duke — close enough to imply at least a friendly intimacy — but said nothing more about it. Just joined in the conversation with his own thoughts about borogs and na'shek, and his take on some of the histories that Zoleen cited.

Beornric's views often differed from Zoleen's. Sometimes because he applied expertise based on field experiences she didn't have, but other times simply because he'd read different authors. Still, Aefric found the conflicting opinions useful, rather than distracting.

Unfortunately, even with multiple views and multiple intellects, by the time the halt came for the day's ride, no good ideas had been brought forth. Or at least, no ideas that hadn't been tried before. Often only to fail spectacularly.

Collapsed mines. Hundreds dead. An ending that kept recurring, when idealistic fools tried to make borogs and na'shek cooperate.

Was there really no way to do it?

When the halt came, they'd reached the fork in the Kingsroad, where the main thrust would continue on and eventually lead into Deepwater, but the northern branch would head for the duchy of Silverlake, and the southern branch, for Merrek.

Normally, Aefric and his entourage would have stayed at the nearby Red Hand Inn. But this time, even though the skies rumbled and threatened again, he and his company moved off the road on the south side.

While repairs were proceeding apace back at Armityr and environs, they weren't doing as well this far out. At least, not on the south side of the road.

Here, the lands still looked as though armies had recently fought their way across them. Or at least marched through, hurriedly.

The results, though, did leave a good deal of space for camping. Which was good. Because Aefric wanted as little crowding as possible. With his borogs in one pavilion, his knights in another, his soldiers in a third, and himself in the fourth.

It turned out that there was a fifth for Zoleen after all. That surprised both Zoleen and Aefric, who'd expected Queen Eppida to "forget" that in her efforts to bring them together.

Apparently that would have been too direct even for the queen.

Which was good, because while he was enjoying spending time with Zoleen again, he wasn't sure he was ready to share a tent with her yet.

More good news followed the discovery of the fifth pavilion. All of his people would get sleep that night. The local ler had provided a company of soldiers with torches and lanterns and specific orders to handle guard duty for him.

And with the Red Hand Inn so close by, they wouldn't have to cook, either. Aefric sent soldiers over to purchase hot, fresh food. So they dined that night on herb-roasted chicken, with a selection of savory root vegetables and honeyed oat bread, along with good, dark beer.

Aefric dined that night not with his knights or Zoleen, but with his borogs. He had the linguistic spell in place, and they shared stories of past fights while they ate.

All of those borogs had done more than their share of fighting. He had been right that they were all refugees. Left clanless by the wars, they'd fought in ones and twos, just to stay alive, until a band of dybbungstad captured and enslaved them.

But the dybbungstad hadn't counted on Lo'kroll. Or what the borogs could do with an able leader.

They rebelled against their "masters," and killed so many while escaping that even the dybbungstad opted not to pursue them.

After that, they wandered through tunnels. Mined where they could, ate where they could. Until finally one of them caught the scent of gold.

That was what led them into Netar's mines. And though they killed a few miners and more than a dozen soldiers, they lost nearly a third of their own number in the fighting.

Losses that led them to respect the no-man's land. But they couldn't bring themselves to leave, either. Not with gold so close they could almost taste it...

Aefric told them again about the mines in the Dragonscar. About all the gold they would be digging.

And he tried to warn them about all the soldiers between here and there. All those who would not see people, but enemies. And how they *must* refrain from fighting along the way.

"When ik and ik scared, ik and ik kill and kill and kill until the fear dies," he said. Which was as close as he could come, even with a good translation spell, to trying to explain the human need to kill whatever frightens them.

Some things just didn't translate.

TROUBLE CAME ON THE SECOND NIGHT.

The day itself had gone quite well. With Zoleen along, Aefric didn't feel as guilty about riding in his carriage — which had reverted to Deepwater colors and sigils now — while his knights and soldiers rode their horses. He was simply doing his duty as both duke and host.

Plus, there was less rain to feel guilty about. And the stories, jokes and general conversation shared by Aefric, Zoleen and Beornric seemed to make the hours fly by.

Again, that second night, the local landholder provided soldiers to stand guard while Aefric and his company slept. In this case they were in the barony of Redsoil, so it was Baroness Slishan who provided the assistance, along with hot food from her own cooks.

Apparently the baroness was doing better these days. When Aefric had stayed with her this past spring, the only time she stopped whining about her dire straits was then she tried pressing unwanted advances on Aefric and Beornric.

Not a pleasant experience. And perhaps she was trying to make up for some of that, because the roast lamb she sent was exquisite, and went quite well with a selection of roast carrots, potatoes and green beans. Instead of beer, she sent a dry red wine that complimented the juiciness of the lamb, and the spices of the vegetables.

With the baroness' guards in place — organized by their local commander, but their arrangements overseen by Beornric — everyone settled down for the night.

Alone in his pavilion, with his mind more settled that night by a good ride and good conversation, Aefric turned his attention to the pouch enchanted for him by Jenbarjen.

He knew of two primary ways to learn the secrets of a magic item.

The first was the method favored by adventurers, mostly because it was fast and reliable. Of course, it also required an expensive reagent, and had the drawback that it could miss the subtler nuances of the enchantment, should there be any.

With Aefric's reputation for leaning on his adventuring past, Jenbarjen might expect him to use that method, to verify the magic of her enchanted pouch.

All the more reason to use the second approach — deep, investigative meditation.

This method was slower, and the results varied with the amount of time and effort a magic-user was willing to invest in it. Not to mention the skill of the magic-user involved.

But Aefric had been drilled in this technique not only by Karbin, but by the great Kainemorton himself.

So sitting cross-legged on a carpet inside his pavilion, in the gentle light supplied from behind him by the Brightstaff, Aefric applied that second method.

He projected a small portion of his consciousness outward through the twists and flows of the magic inherent to Qorunn itself, and from there he focused down, down, down, into the pouch.

All about his awareness now, the web of Jenbarjen's spells. Stiff, harsh and angular. The clear runic work of a *zulim*.

Tonight, he would only survey the main structure of the enchantment. Look for the way the spells wove together, where they linked, whether or not there were easily spotted gaps or flaws.

The simplest part of the investigation, and the foundation of what he would do later. Likely the next night.

Even this low level of investigation, though, bore fruit. Rune magic *could* be subtle, but it seemed to work best when it was direct. And Aefric was able to quickly establish that the main enchantment involved spatial relations, connecting the physical pouch to a pocket dimension.

That was how such enchantments were usually done. But unless he was mistaken, this time Jenbarjen had—

A scream tore him from his deliberations.

It was a piercing scream. A sound he'd heard before. And each time he heard it, he prayed he would never hear it again.

It was the agonized sound of someone dying.

Aefric snapped out of his trance. Leapt to his feet. Grabbed his signature weapon. Hustled out of his pavilion, lighting up the night with the Brightstaff's yellow diamond.

Steel clashed with steel. Soldiers and knights rushed about. Shouts and chaos.

Temat and Wardius stood guard at the entrance of his pavilion, in full plate and with swords drawn.

"What's happening?" Aefric barked.

"We don't know, your grace," Wardius said. "Best you get—"

Aefric took off straight into the cold, misty air for a view of the scene. His soldiers were fighting the baroness' troops in a mad skirmish near the borogs' pavilion—

Which was shaking with combat.

This was a trap. Set to kill the borogs.

With a single mighty heave, Aefric's magic ripped the pavilion free of its stakes and cast it aside.

Inside was a bloodbath. Dead borogs. Dead humans.

The living borogs had the weight of numbers — easily three times as many as the remaining humans — and were using horns, fists and weapons to widen that margin.

Aefric burned to help them. To throw lightning. Obviously the baroness' soldiers had orders to kill the borogs. Orders that might even have come from the queen.

White lighting crackled along the Brightstaff and his hands...

No.

He couldn't just start killing soldiers of Armyr. Not even when *provoked*.

Instead Aefric reached for a spell that had saved his life many times, when he was a young magic-user and not up to fighting several enemies at once.

But could he use it here and now? Could he affect more than seventy with it? A lot to ask of that spell. It was good for a dozen, maybe, but not this many. Not unless he took longer to cast it. Drew power from...

No.

He didn't have time to get fancy, with incantations that tapped into this power source or that one. He needed to act *now*. Before still more people died.

So Aefric pulled from the power in his blood, and focused it through the Brightstaff, amplifying his magic. Pushed that spell far beyond anything it had ever done for him before.

Soft, thick yellow fog rushed down from the Brightstaff's diamond to cover all the combatants.

Dizziness assailed Aefric. The space between heartbeats stretched.

Lights flared all about him in the mist.

Which way was the ground?

Was he falling or flying?

―――――――

FALLING. AEFRIC WAS DEFINITELY FALLING THROUGH THE NIGHT SKY above his camp.

He gritted his teeth. Hard. Strained. Forced out one more little spell...

The air caught him. And as he floated gently toward the ground like a leaf on the breeze he realized that the clashes and thumps and grunts and shouts of battle had all grown still within his fog.

Not that he could see much in the dimness of irregular torchlight and lamplight. Wasn't it brighter before?

Aefric reached the ground, but his legs wouldn't hold him.

Caught himself with the Brightstaff. Not its magic. Just its physical support. His arms shook in protest.

Oh. The yellow diamond had gone out. Huh.

He tried to light it again, but didn't get much more than candlelight.

Suddenly Temat and Wardius were there. Each caught Aefric with one hand and steadied him, while their other hands still held ready swords.

Aefric's spell fog began to dissipate.

The combats were over. The combatants, all now unconscious on the ground. Asleep. His soldiers. The baroness' soldiers. The borogs. All of them. Fast asleep.

He loosed a breath he hadn't realized he was holding. It worked.

Aefric shook himself. Forced himself to stand without the help of his knights, though he did still have to lean on the Brightstaff.

The Knights of the Lake surrounded him, facing outward. All of them armed, but most wearing only the cotton tunics and leggings they normally wore under their armor.

Inside their circle, only Aefric, Beornric, and ... Zoleen?

Yes. Zoleen was there, gray cloak pulled tight over a dressing gown. She held a rapier with a comfort that said she knew well its use.

She looked good like that. With her long, copper hair loose and wild, sword in hand...

Wait. Sword? Where had she gotten a rapier? She certainly wasn't wearing a scabbard.

She and Beornric started talking at the same time.

"Aefric—"

"Your grace—"

Aefric held up a hand. Really, he was trying to stop the world from spinning on him, but only Zoleen and Beornric stopped. The world refused to obey.

"I'm ... all right..." he said.

"You're pale and shaking, Aefric," Zoleen said. "You need to sit down. You need to—"

"No," he said simply. "Not yet. Beornric?"

"Your grace?"

Good. No arguments from his knight-adviser. Or at least, not now. Though Aefric knew he'd hear about this later.

That was for later though. Right now, Aefric needed to focus.

"I want ... field medicine ... underway ... right now," he said to Beornric, gesturing with one hand so it was clear he was worried about the downed combatants, not himself. "And separate ... the groups. But don't ... bring them around ... yet."

As Beornric moved off to obey, Zoleen asked, "They're not dead? There was such a flash of red light. And that sound of thunder."

Light? Thunder? How had Aefric missed that?

Later for that.

"Sleeping," he answered her. "Arras?"

"Here, your grace." She didn't turn to face him, but he knew she was listening.

"You and Micham ... ride to Slishan. I want her physician ... right now ... no excuses."

"Shall we bring the baroness herself?"

"Her ... or her castellan," he said. Damn cold sweat getting in his eyes. "Whoever ... wants ... to answer for this."

Aefric stopped and reached inside himself. For the power he knew he was born to, but didn't really know how to use. He had no other dweomerbloods to teach him, and dweomerblade techniques helped only so much. They were good for combat and a few other things, but nothing like he needed now.

So he closed his eyes, and raised his empty hand in a halting gesture, to avoid interruptions.

He focused inward then, on his blood. Racing inside him with each rapid heartbeat.

Now on the magic that flowed *in* that blood. It was...

Oh.

Over the years, introspective meditation had taught Aefric what to expect when he reached within himself. Power. Blazing power.

But right now, that power was at an ebb. A trickle.

He must've pulled more for that spell than he'd intended.

Stupid. Could've been dangerous. And in the moment, it meant no relief was coming. He'd have to hold together through sheer force of will.

Well, it wouldn't be the first time.

The Knights of the Lake were adjusting to close the gap left by Arras and Micham, but Aefric pushed through and forced them to follow him. Zoleen stayed at his side, watching him carefully.

Leaning on his staff, he made his way to a group of baronial soldiers who huddled together near the edge of camp. They looked confused, but had ready pikes in hand.

And they were still conscious. Must not've entered the fight.

Aefric drew deep breaths and made those soldiers wait until he had enough air to talk.

Hey. The world stopped spinning. Good. But his knees were still weak, and he could feel his hands shaking. And the cold sweat on his forehead was getting clammy.

"All right," he said, his voice low and dangerous. "Who will speak for you?"

"I will, your grace," said a man who didn't look any older than Aefric. And he didn't have any officer's designation on his armor or tabard either.

"Why you?"

"Sergeant's over there," he said, pointing to the sleepers. "Are you going to kill us too, your grace?"

"Remains to be seen," Aefric said. "Did you have orders to kill us all? Or just whoever stood between you and the borogs?"

"No, ser. I mean no, your grace," the soldier said quickly. "We were sent here to guard. But it was a human scream that came from those *things'* tent. And while we didn't have orders to kill 'em, your grace, we didn't have orders to let them kill us either."

"So you're suggesting ... the borogs began this conflict?"

"Yes, your grace."

"Temat, Leppina," Aefric said, and when those knights stepped up, he addressed them. "Disarm these troops. See them seated and under guard while I sort this out."

"Yes, your grace," they said, almost in sync.

Aefric checked on his sleeping soldiers next. It looked as though only about six had gotten into a fight with eight of the baroness' troops. And the only wounded there were on her side.

Aefric had Vria and Wardius shake his soldiers awake. It took much more effort than it should have.

"What happened?" he asked Arda, the most senior of the soldiers in this group.

"There was a commotion in the borogs' tent, your grace," she said in hushed tones. "Then the scream came, and that lot" — she gestured to the sleeping baronial soldiers — "said they wouldn't stand by while the borogs started killing."

"And what did you do?"

"Well, we know your grace wants us all getting to Deepwater alive, including the borogs. So we got in the way and, well, things got heated."

"Good work," Aefric said. "Disarm the sleepers, then wake them and keep them under guard while I sort this out."

"Yes, your grace," she said, and as she did that, Aefric walked over to the mess of borogs and humans. They were all sleeping. Even the ones receiving field medicine on their open wounds.

Just how much power had he *put* into that spell?

Beornric stepped up to Aefric.

"How many dead?" Aefric asked, in hushed tones.

"Currently, a dozen humans," Beornric said, matching his quiet. "Though another five might not live to see morning. Among the borogs, six. And four of them look to have been killed in their sleep."

"Someone's going to pay for this," Aefric said.

"I agree," Beornric said. "But these aren't the baroness' men. And I don't just say that because they're not wearing tabards. They're a rougher sort, and mismatched."

"Bounty hunters?"

"That's my bet."

"All right. Disarm them and hold them under guard away from the others. Might be better to keep them asleep as long as you can."

"What about the borogs?"

"I'll handle them myself," Aefric said, ignoring Zoleen's frown. "And that'll have to do for now. We can't do much else until the baroness or her representative arrives."

As Aefric turned to see about the borogs, Zoleen called to her servants for a cloak and forced it on him.

"You're shaking and sweating, Aefric," she said. "You need rest. And tea. You don't need to deal with borogs right now."

"Yes, I..." He frowned. "Where did your rapier go?"

Zoleen's firm expression broke into exasperated laughter.

"You're worried about that now?"

"Well, you had it moments ago. Can't have you dropping weapons—"

Zoleen held up her noble's dagger. Her eyes focused for a moment, and it became a rapier. Another moment's focus, and it was a dagger again.

"Nice work," Aefric said. "Subtle."

"I'll tell Sirondfar you approve," she said, smiling as she referred to Ashling's ducal wizard. "He made one each for Ash, Eppy and me. Probably for Mek, too." She cocked her head to the side. "Would you consent to sit and drink tea if I menaced you with my vicious blade?"

"No," Aefric said. "I have work to do."

He didn't wait for a response. He cast the Soulfist linguistic spell — which took more effort than he liked — then turned and walked among the borogs until he came to Lo'kroll.

Right in the front, of course. And even under Aefric's sleeping spell, the huge borog clutched his heavy iron maul.

Of all the times not to be wearing jewelry...

Aefric cast a small illusion, so that the sleeping borog would smell gold ore. Lots and lots of gold ore. All of it ready to be mined...

Lo'kroll's eyes fluttered open. He leapt to his feet, looking around for the gold, but was still too groggy for that. He overbalanced, and had to catch himself with his maul.

He thumped the side of his head several times with one fist, and that actually seemed to help wake him up.

"*Chief hand,*" Aefric snapped. "*What happened?*"

"*Me and me sleep,*" Lo'kroll said. "*Where chief say me and me safe.*" He snorted disgust. "*Not safe. Ik and ik kill. Tarokway.*"

Huh. Apparently the borogs associated the tarok with stealthy, murderous activities. Good thing Aefric had used that translation spell or he would've missed that completely...

"*Na'kel wake. Kill ik with horn punch.*" Lo'kroll pointed with his own horn at a borog corpse. Presumably Na'kel. "*Dying human scream. All wake. Scrap.*"

Lo'kroll gestured toward the unconscious, likely bounty hunters. "*Chief kill?*"

"*Chief stop.*"

Lo'kroll snorted approval. "*Kill now?*"

"*Not yet. First me speak with chief, clan ik and ik. Ik land.*"

"*Ik and ik kill clan,*" Lo'kroll objected. "*Now clan kill ik and ik.*" When Aefric hesitated to answer, Lo'kroll added, "*And the dark swallows all.*"

Aefric snorted aggressively. "*Who is chief?*"

Lo'kroll's nostrils flared as though he considered challenging, but finally scraped his feet submissively on the ground.

"*Chief handle,*" Aefric said. "*Gather me and me there.*" Aefric pointed with his nose toward the pavilion he'd thrown earlier. "*Wait for chief word.*"

Aefric turned and walked away towards the center of camp. Zoleen joined him quickly. Apparently she hadn't wanted to approach the borogs herself either.

Then again, that might just have been respecting the size and fierceness of Lo'kroll...

"Will you rest now?" she asked.

"I'll sit for a moment," he said. "Until Arras and Micham return with aid."

One of her servants brought a mug of hot tea, and Zoleen pressed it into Aefric's hands.

Oh, but that was tasty stuff. Blackberry ... and something else. Something that spread warmth inside him. And not the fake warmth that alcohol gave either. This, this had to be some kind of herbal remedy.

Yes. He had to wait anyway. Better to sit a moment, and drink this excellent tea.

———

THE NIGHT AIR WAS COLD, AND SMELLED OF SPILLED BLOOD. AEFRIC could feel the tension. Among his soldiers and knights. Among his borogs.

Even among the baroness' soldiers — all of whom were now under guard — but he was less concerned about them.

In fact, he hoped to project calm strength as he sat in his camp chair, drinking that marvelous blackberry herbal tea.

It spread a restorative warmth inside him. Probably not bringing back any of the power he'd recklessly overspent, but easing his own tensions and helping him focus for what lay ahead.

Aefric was just finishing that mug of tea — which pleased Zoleen immensely, by the look in her eye — when Arras and Micham returned.

They weren't alone, either. They rode with twenty more of the baroness' soldiers, along with a fit but elderly man, and a solid, young woman who wore the bright yellow robes of a cleric of Nilasah.

"Here first," Zoleen called to the healer, gesturing to Aefric.

"No," Aefric said. "I'm unharmed. See to the wounded. And let me know if you need help getting cooperation from the borogs."

The way things had been going, Aefric half-expected her to object to being told to heal borogs. But she didn't.

Good.

"Your grace," the elderly man said, dismounting. He bowed. Despite the late evening hour, he was dressed in a dark blue silk tunic under a dark gray doublet, and brown riding leathers. He had a longsword at his side.

"I am Ser Pamund Ol'Masoric, castellan for her lordship, Baroness Slishan," he said. "Might I ask what has happened? Your knights showed no patience for anything but demands."

Ah, the noble technique of managing to sound both respectful and disdainful at the same time.

How Aefric loathed it.

He stood, Brightstaff in hand and the yellow diamond shining out brightly now.

Well. That really *was* good tea.

"When the lives of Armyrian citizens hang in the balance," Aefric said, "I firmly believe that healing comes before explanations."

"I quite agree, your grace. But now that the physician is here, perhaps an explanation will be forthcoming before the dawn?"

"I was hoping for the same thing," Aefric said, with a smile that lacked any humor at all. "We can start with who is responsible for this betrayal? Was it you and the baroness? Or one of your soldiers?"

"You *dare* accuse me of betrayal?" Pamund said, drawing himself fully erect and putting one hand on the hilt of his longsword.

All twenty of his nearby soldiers — still mounted — did the same.

Aefric's own soldiers and knights readied weapons in turn.

"I recommend against hasty action, ser knight," Beornric said darkly. "It would not go well for you."

"I will *not* be accused—"

"*I am the wronged party here,*" Aefric said, and for a moment the Brightstaff's diamond flared brighter still. "I trusted to your soldiers to guard my camp. And yet, members of *my* entourage were *murdered in their sleep.* And the only hue and cry from *your* soldiers led to them fighting with *mine.*"

Pamund narrowed his eyes. Eased his hand away from the hilt of his sword. "Would your grace be so kind as to tell the whole story?"

"There is little more to add," Aefric said. "While your soldiers *pretended* to stand guard, killers managed to slip past their perimeter *unchallenged*. Armed and armored killers. How many, Beornric?"

"Twenty, your grace."

"*Twenty*," Aefric said. "Armored in leathers. Some of it studded. All with swords and daggers. And they made it through the perimeter and into the borogs' tent *without challenge*."

Pamund frowned as he considered that. "Your grace said something about the hue and cry?"

"Yes," Aefric said. "When one of the murderers failed to assassinate his sleeping target, that borog awoke and killed his would-be killer. That led to a scream."

Aefric pointed with his thumb to the group of baronial soldiers who'd been fighting his troops.

"I was told your soldiers then assumed that the borogs had simply started killing for no reason."

"Well, they *are* borogs, your grace," Pamund said, as though the answer was obvious.

"On the strength of such *inane logic*," Aefric said, "your soldiers moved in to ally with the murderers. *All* of the borogs would have been slaughtered, were it not for the intervention of myself and my troops."

"Would that really have been so great a loss, your grace?" Pamund asked softly. "It is known that his majesty only has you transporting them so that their blood need not be spilled where goodly people walk—"

"Are you the king, then?" Aefric growled.

"I ... your grace?" Pamund said, drawing back from Aefric.

Aefric closed the gap. "You claim to speak the king's motivations. So you *must* be the king. Is that right?"

"Of course I am not the king, your grace."

"Then you are on the king's council, are you? You have the king's confidence, such that he shares all his plans and ideas with you?"

"No, your grace," Pamund said, looking around now for assistance, and finding none.

"Then how *dare* you, ser knight, interpret my *royal mission* for me?"

"I ... I..." Pamund dropped to one knee, head bowed. "Please forgive me, your grace. I am not a young man, and my memory failed me. I forgot that your grace was on—"

"Don't hide behind your age," Aefric said. "I know knights and lers who are both older *and* more competent than you are."

"Fine then, your grace. Please do accept—"

"It *was* you who gave the order, wasn't it?" Aefric said. "*You* who arranged for those murderers to come into my camp tonight."

"I—"

"In fact, you made *all* the arrangements, didn't you? Chose the soldiers who came to guard. Made sure they all had reason to hate borogs. And you made sure to hand-pick a group who would turn a blind eye when asked. And now that it failed, you're trying to make excuses."

"But—"

"Tell me, *ser knight*. Did you do this for profit? Or will you share in the—"

"*They are borogs,*" Pamund yelled. "Same as killed my children and grandchildren! They *all* deserve death!"

Pamund drew his sword. So did the soldiers he brought.

Beornric jumped in front of Aefric, sword in hand.

Aefric's other knights and soldiers drew weapons...

"*Pamund!*" Aefric knew that voice, but he'd never heard it express command before.

Baroness Slishan rode up, flanked by four knights.

The baroness was an older woman, with a matronly air. But unlike when Aefric had seen her this past spring, she wasn't clad in in frippery and affecting youth.

Her graying hair had been tied back. She wore chainmail and wool in somber colors.

Chainmail? This was a woman whose whole life had been about humor and parties, until the death of her sister and her sister's child had forced the barony on her.

Apparently she'd finally come to terms with her new station in life, and developed the decisiveness she'd been lacking.

Slishan jumped down from her horse with more agility than Aefric would have credited her with, and stalked up, while her knights took charge of the troops Pamund had brought with him.

"Pamund," she said, holding out her hand.

Pamund hesitated.

"Make me ask and it will go worse for you," she said.

Pamund bowed his head and handed her his sword.

Beornric lowered his blade and stepped back to Aefric's side.

Slishan turned to Aefric. Bowed. "Your grace. I must offer my deepest and most humble apologies. You must believe me. I had no idea what my castellan was doing in my name."

"It's—" Pamund started, but Slishan spoke over him.

"*Silence,*" she said. "You have done enough damage for one night." She turned back to Aefric. "When I heard word that you'd sent for my physician, I couldn't imagine why. Then I saw that one of the soldiers *I'd* assigned to guard you tonight was instead on duty in the main hall. From there, the rest was easy to deduce."

She shook her head. "I know he hates borogs, your grace. But I never thought he would try something like this."

"These are your lands, your lordship," Aefric said. "Justice here lies with you."

"My castellan has interfered with a royal envoy on a mission for the crown," she said, and Pamund cried out as though struck. "That is treason. He dies by hanging. Those who followed his orders and attacked your grace's entourage had no reason to know they were committing treason. They will serve a sentence in my dungeons, and pay a fine to your grace's coffers. Does your grace find this acceptable?"

"What about the bounty hunters?" Aefric asked.

"They are hunting an illegal bounty," she said in a harsh tone. "They know the penalty."

Death, by the king's decree. The royal attempt to avoid situations much like this one.

Aefric nodded.

"Beyond that," she said, "I wish to make reparations as a sign of good faith. My castellan's lands and properties are now forfeited to your grace. And I wish to go further, to make good what was done in my lands."

"How?"

"I and my knights and soldiers will personally escort your grace as far as he must go on the king's orders."

"I trust you will forgive me if I feel some hesitation at accepting that, given tonight's events."

"Of course," she said, with a brusque nod, and put the edge of Pamund's longsword to her thumb. She drew a small bead of blood. "By the blood I now spill, I swear that I and mine shall faithfully follow the orders of your grace, and his knight-captain Ser Beornric Ol'Sandallas, until such time as our task is complete. And should we fail, may Ulna the Traveler spill the rest of my blood to ease your grace's path for the rest of his days."

She leaned down and sealed the oath by pressing her bloody hand to the dirt.

WHILE BEORNRIC AND SLISHAN HANDLED THE SECURITY ARRANGEMENTS that night, Aefric crossed the camp again to talk with his borogs.

This time, Zoleen didn't try to talk him out of it. She followed along in curious silence, but hung back a bit when he reached the borogs themselves.

Lo'kroll had them well-organized. They stood in a circle, facing inward but irregularly looking around, to ensure their own safety.

Aefric was pleased to see that the baronial physician was among them, doing Nilasah's work. Though few of the living borogs seemed to need much help, and the dead ones were beyond her care.

Their six dead had been arranged in a circle, inside the group of living borogs.

"*Chief hand,*" Aefric said in Borog.

Lo'kroll stepped out of the circle and approached Aefric.

"*Clan kill ik and ik now?*" Lo'kroll asked.

Aefric snorted a negative. "*Clan Ik and Ik land. Chief, Clan Ik and Ik do killing.*"

Lo'kroll snorted displeasure. "*Ik and ik not killed.*"

"*Chief hand, ik and ik gone rogue. Clan Ik and Ik lose status. Kill ik and ik to regain some. Guard me and me now, to regain more.*"

Lo'kroll snorted grudging agreement, and stamped his foot. But then he snorted curiosity.

"*Clan Thunder Stick greater. Clan Thunder Stick take land?*"

"*Some,*" Aefric said, snorting agreement. "*Me arrange with Chief, Clan Ik and Ik.*"

Normally, by now, Aefric knew he and Lo'kroll would be referring to Baroness Slishan and her lands and retainers by a more accurate term. Likely some invented clan name based on her baronial device, which was a red hill on a background of canary yellow. So something like Clan Red Hill.

But they maintained calling them only *Clan Ik and Ik* as an insult. As a way of saying their clan weren't worth remembering.

"*God metal?*" Lo'kroll asked.

Aefric snorted satisfaction that was not quite perfect because it lacked a single element. "*Yes. But already dug. No more here to dig.*"

Lo'kroll snorted the same sound.

"*Blood, land and god metal,*" Lo'kroll said with a snort of approval. "*You good chief.*"

Aefric gestured toward the dead with his nose. "*Not good enough.*"

Lo'kroll snorted disagreement. "*Borogs live. Borogs die. And the dark swallows all. But good chief uses deaths. Make clan stronger.*" He thumped Aefric on the chest in approval. "*Good chief.*"

"If I may," the healer said, in the common tongue, as she stepped up to Aefric and Lo'kroll. In Borog, she continued, "*Dead Clan Thunder Stick ready.*"

Lo'kroll and Aefric snorted thanks.

To Lo'kroll, Aefric said, "*Organize sleep.*"

Lo'kroll moved off to do that, and the healer said to Aefric, "Your Borog is flawless. I wish mine were as good."

"It's not normally this good," Aefric said. "It's spell-aided right now."

"Wise," she said. "I've ensured the bodies won't decay for two aetts." She looked up sharply at Aefric. "Is it true what they tell me? You're taking them to more of their clan?"

"Yes," Aefric said.

"Clan *Thunder Stick?*" she asked, while looking directly at the Brightstaff.

"That's right," Aefric said.

She lowered her voice. "You're the chieftain of a borog clan?"

Zoleen cleared her throat and raised an eyebrow as she stepped up.

"Excuse me," the healer said. "*Your grace* is the chieftain of a borog clan?"

"Obviously you already know this," Aefric said. "But I don't know your name."

"Tajie, your grace," the healer said with a small bow.

"Well, Tajie, does any of this present a problem for you?"

"No, your grace," she said, smiling. "I don't understand how this can be, but I believe it means the borogs are right to trust in you. Which means I didn't just heal people on their way to the executioner's block."

"Not among the borogs," Aefric said, then nodded over at the bounty hunters. "Among the humans, I can't promise you that."

"Punishment for crimes committed is one thing," Tajie said. "Punishment for one's nature is another."

"On that, we agree," Aefric said.

"If I may, Aefric," Zoleen said, and when he nodded, continued. "The fighting has been resolved. The guilty have been uncovered, and justice is underway. The wounded have been healed or are healing, and the dead prepared for travel. Have I missed anything?"

"Those are the essentials," Aefric said, "though Slishan and

Beornric might need my assistance, organizing this new guard of ours."

Zoleen raised both eyebrows high. "And does Beornric often need his duke's assistance organizing such things?"

Aefric chuckled. "I'm pretty sure you know he doesn't."

"If I'm no longer needed here." Tajie started, but trailed off when Zoleen raised a halting hand.

But Zoleen's eyes were still on Aefric as she spoke.

"Then you've taken care of everything you need to take care of *right now*. Yes?"

"Yes."

"Good." She turned to the healer. "Tajie, is it?"

"That's right, Mistress Zoleen. How may I be of assistance?"

"You may tend this patient right here," Zoleen answered, patting Aefric on the shoulder. "He's just admitted that he has the time."

Aefric laughed, but had to admit that he was still leaning pretty heavily on his staff.

"All right," he said wearily. "You win, Zoleen. Tajie, I am unin-jured, but I did overstretch my magic a bit. I'm more exhausted than I should be."

"His camp chair is right over there," Zoleen said helpfully, "by the fire."

Aefric led the way there, while Tajie checked something in the yellow bag she wore, draped across one shoulder. Like her robes, it was sealed with the Hand of Nilasah.

"You're enjoying this," Aefric said to Zoleen, as he eased down into his chair.

Zoleen didn't answer. But at least she had the good grace not to deny it.

6

AEFRIC SLEPT HEAVILY THAT NIGHT. LIKELY BECAUSE OF WHATEVER exactly it was the healer had done to him before he turned in.

She'd burned some kind of incense that smelled vaguely of orange and cinnamon, and waved it around him while offering prayers. And then...

Well, that was all he really remembered.

But it must've been strong, whatever she did, because all that shouting and hammering going on outside his pavilion — not to mention hoofbeats and more — really should've woken him up.

Aefric dressed quickly in a silk tunic of navy blue over his brown riding leathers, with darker brown for his leather belt and high, riding boots. A Deepwater gray cloak completed the look, and he stepped out of his pavilion.

Into the wrong camp?

It was only just dawn, and a bit chilly still, but even so there was enough gray light for Aefric to see the strangeness all around him.

The camp he knew — the camp he *expected* — included seven knights, twenty-four soldiers, forty-three borogs, and one noble-woman. Maybe seventy-six living people, himself included.

The camp around him now had more than doubled in size overnight.

Vria and Wardius, at least, were right at hand in their full plate. They offered quick greetings.

"Have we been invaded?" Aefric asked.

"In a manner of speaking, your grace," Wardius said, with a quirked smile that could have been mistaken for one his many scars. "By the good intentions of her lordship. Apparently our escort is to include twenty of her own knights, and more than a hundred of her own soldiers."

"We'll have to slow to a march," Aefric said.

"No, your grace," Vria said. "They're all mounted. And they brought carts of their own supplies. And extra, in case we have need."

Well. Apparently Baroness Slishan intended to make a statement with her escort.

Aefric found the baroness talking with Beornric and Zoleen.

After the usual greetings, Beornric said, "Her lordship has already sent outriders ahead, to ensure the Kingsroad will be cleared for us."

"And rikas," Slishan said. "To make sure all the nobles along the way know I'm handling security for your grace. They are welcome to provide food, if they wish, but we'll have no need for additional soldiers. More importantly, no need for unknown armed men in your grace's camp."

"I'm surprised you're allowing food," Beornric said, in a joking tone.

"We'll be testing any food they provide," Slishan said in a serious tone. "Though I didn't think it politic to point that out."

"Fair enough," Beornric said.

Aefric looked around, at the work being done to tear down the camp and pack for the day's travel. He also noted the pennants...

"I see my device," Aefric said to the baroness. "But not your red hill."

"No, your grace," Slishan said. "I allow my knights their own devices on their persons, as is there right. As I wear my own. But this is your grace's mission, and your grace's caravan. I'll not have anyone mistaking that."

Ah. She didn't want to be seen as horning in on Aefric's royal mission, and thus stealing part of the "glory."

Aefric wondered what she'd say if she knew the truth about what his mission was. And what it wasn't.

Better not to find out.

So Aefric left Beornric and Slishan to see to the details, and took his traditional Armyrian breakfast with Zoleen by the fire. By the time they were done, the camp was packed, the horses mounted, and the carts readied.

Aefric summoned his carriage and they took to the road.

Despite the increase in numbers, travel was smoother with Slishan's escort. Perhaps because of those outriders. Certainly there were no slowdowns on the Kingsroad.

Late that day they crossed the border from the king's lands into the Kerrik Forest, at the eastern edge of the duchy of Deepwater. They camped that night in Kerrik, and took to the road again before dawn the next day.

For two more days they traveled the Kingsroad in peace. Between the barony of Norra to the south, and the county of Motte to the north. Then past the barony of Felspark to the south and along the border of the barony of Riverbreak, all while passing the county of Goldenfall to the north.

From what Aefric could see as he glanced out of his carriage every so often, the lands of his vassals were recovering well from the Godswalk Wars. Doubtless due to the aid of those clerics of the Green Lord that Baron Osmaer Greenhand had provided.

By day, Aefric rode in his carriage with Zoleen. With Beornric as well, when the rains came through. And by night, Aefric had enough time and space to himself, in his pavilion, that he investigated Jenbarjen's pouch thoroughly, and proved that it did exactly — and only — what she'd said it did.

From that day forward, it became the pouch he wore at his belt every day.

But toward the end of the fifth day of travel, somewhere on the Kingsroad between Riverbreak and Goldenfall, Aefric heard cries of alarm from somewhere back along the caravan.

Ser Temat, who had been riding guard to the left side of Aefric's carriage, called in, "Your grace! The borogs!"

Zoleen got maybe as far as "Aefric, maybe you should—" before Aefric was out the carriage door and flying back along the caravan, Brightstaff in hand.

The borogs still had ten covered carts, though the last one carried only their dead.

Their second-to-last cart in had tipped over on its side — right there in the middle of the wide, smooth Kingsroad — and was shaking so badly it wouldn't hold together much longer.

Aefric heard snorts mixed in with heavy thumps and snarls in Borog that he was pretty sure were all threats and swearing.

He quickly cast that Soulfist linguistic spell.

Yes. He now knew with full certainty that the snorts and other verbalization were all challenges and insults. The kind they threw around when fighting.

The caravan had stopped now, and borogs were hustling out of the other carts. Likely to watch the show, judging by their eager snorts and foot-scrapes.

Aefric quickly landed. He grabbed the tipped cart by magic. Didn't just try to right it, though. He lifted it into the air — no more than five feet off the ground — and started shaking it.

"*Chief! Chief! Chief!*" the borogs surrounding him started chanting.

"Do you need assistance, your grace?" That shout came from Baroness Slishan, currently behind her knights, who all had lances raised as though ready to charge when the signal was given.

"Stand down, your lordship," Aefric said, not looking though, because he needed all his focus on the cart. "Leave this to me."

Aefric shook the cart harder and harder.

Borogs began falling out, only to land heavily on the ground.

When the fifth hit the ground, Aefric set the cart down on its wheels. He walked up to the downed borogs. A bruised, bloody mess, all of them. One had even been slashed by an axe near the left shoulder, and was bleeding profusely.

"Your grace." Tajie's voice, from somewhere behind and to his right. "I'm here and ready to help."

Aefric raised a halting hand to keep her back.

Aefric snorted anger and stepped up to the borogs who were still disoriented, but trying to hit each other.

Aefric began smacking arms with the Brightstaff. And he wasn't gentle about it. He continued hitting them until they stopped trying to hit each other.

"*Up,*" he said, in Borog.

They started moving to stand, but not quickly.

"*Up,*" he said, sharply this time, and jabbed each of them with the Brightstaff's butt, to prompt them.

Once they were finally standing, Aefric stepped in front of the one holding the iron-bladed axe.

He struck that borog's weapon hand soundly.

The borog dropped the axe.

"*Did chief say fight?*" Aefric asked.

All five of the guilty borogs started talking at once. Giving the same lame excuses humans would have given in their position. Each trying to justify his actions by blaming another.

Some things, it seemed, translated all too well.

Aefric stomped his foot, and they fell silent.

"*Did chief say fight?*" he asked again.

They all snorted guiltily that he hadn't.

He struck each of them on the head with the Brightstaff then, letting off a small thunderclap with each strike, and hitting hard enough to knock even those big, strong borogs to the ground.

"Tajie," Aefric said, then switched to Borog as he pointed at the one who'd been axe-cut. "*Heal this cut. No scar. No other healing.*"

"*Chief!*" the wounded borog pleaded, but Aefric stamped his foot.

"*Chief hand,*" Aefric called out, while Tajie hurried forward to apply her art.

"*Chief,*" Lo'kroll said, stepping forward.

Aefric pointed with his nose to the borog who'd held the axe. *"This finger is broken. No weapon for ik. Choose another."*

Lo'kroll snorted assent. Stepped up and punched that borog across the snout, knocking him to the ground.

"Clan Thunder Stick, back in carts," Aefric said. *"Many miles to go."*

"Your grace," Tajie said, in the common tongue. When she had Aefric's attention, she added, "No scar? But don't scars have meaning for them?"

"It's a punishment they'll understand," Aefric said. "And serve a lesson to the others that when their chief says not to fight, he means it."

She nodded. "Which is why you don't want me to treat the other minor injuries?"

"That's right," Aefric said, and turned and walked back towards his carriage.

At least he'd stopped them before anyone died.

ZOLEEN'S COMPANY HAD DEFINITELY BEEN ONE OF THE HIGHLIGHTS OF the trip, for Aefric. She was an excellent traveling companion, and they spent their days talking easily. About themselves, about history, about magic.

Aefric stayed away from anything that verged on current politics, and she seemed to respect that choice. Until, on the sixth day of travel, late in the morning, as they approached Behal, where her ship was waiting, she disrupted a conversation about the history of the county of Fyretti to ask:

"Aefric, do you think the queen sent me to spy on you?"

Aefric frowned and sighed. "The thought had crossed my mind."

"Let me phrase that differently then." She cocked her head slightly. "Do you think I'm spying for the queen? Or for Ash, for that matter?"

"Deliberately? No," Aefric said. "I'm pretty sure you know that if you were and I found out about it, that would be the end of any friendship between us."

"Oh, I know it," she said. "And I think it's safe to say that Ash and Eppy know it too."

"Yes," Aefric said. "But subtle as those two can be—"

"Aefric," Zoleen said, urgently taking his hand in both of hers. Her hands were soft and warm, and he was suddenly aware of how closely they sat, side by side. And this time, she was wearing a dress of pale green chiffon that made her look so good she might've walked out of some poor artist's fever dream, to taunt him with his inability to capture her beauty on canvas.

"I'm not spying for anyone," Zoleen said. "I know Eppy's worried about your mission for the king, but have I asked about it even once?"

"No," Aefric admitted.

"No," she said. "And I don't want you to tell me about it. Not now. Maybe when it's all over, I'll get to hear the story. Just like the story of how you came to be a chieftain for borogs. And I can tell you, I'm *dying* to ask that one."

Aefric felt his jaw slacken with realization. "You don't know that story?"

"A few rumors," Zoleen said. "Nothing more. And likely not close to the truth." She leaned a little closer. "But Eppy is worried about you and borogs. So I haven't asked. Do you understand what I'm saying?"

"You've been avoiding topics you think she wants to know about."

"Mostly the topics I *know* she wants to know about," Zoleen said, a determined look in her eyes. "But the ones I *think* she wants to know about too. Just to be safe."

"Do you know what the queen's up to?"

She cocked an eyebrow and gave him a lopsided smile. "I'm not spying on *her* for *you* either, Aefric."

"You're right," Aefric said, chuckling. "Excuse me."

He tried to raise his hands in surrender, but she still held one of his hands in both of hers. And she didn't let it go.

"I asked you first if you thought Eppy sent me to spy on you," she said softly. "I think she did. Because I think she and the king are quarreling about something. Something to do with you. But I don't know what. I mostly wanted to make sure you knew, I'm not her spy. And I'm not Ash's, either."

"Thank you," Aefric said.

"But that brings me to another point," she said, voice still soft. "We *are* friends again, aren't we, Aefric?"

"We are," he said. "In fact, I know you have to return to Fyrcloch. But I hope you'll be able to visit me soon at Water's End."

"There's a second question answered," she said with a small, but very sincere smile. "And I'd be more than happy to. Preferably before that gaggle of princesses descends on you."

"Gaggle?" Aefric said, smiling. "Is that really the proper term?"

Zoleen shrugged, but kept looking Aefric in the eye and smiling. "Murder seemed a little judgmental. Unkindness wasn't strong enough. Flock was too general. Thus, gaggle."

"Fair enough."

"But when I visit you," she said, "do you think I might be invited to your rooms again one night?"

"Are you kidding?" Aefric asked. "I've been struggling not to invite you to my pavilion these last couple of nights on the road. I just thought it felt ... inappropriate."

"I confess. In a camp pavilion surrounded by your knights, soldiers and borogs is not my first choice for how I might come to your arms again," Zoleen said, smiling. "But I will say I would've considered it."

"My knights obviously don't feel any compunction against it. I'm pretty sure I heard the sounds of at least of few of them having fun by night."

"They're knights," Zoleen said, shrugging one shoulder again. "If they didn't find their pleasure while in the field, they might go long stretches without. And I don't think I'd wish that on anyone."

"True enough."

"Which brings me to my last question," Zoleen said, more serious now. "I know that the candidates for your hand are many, and formidable. Several princesses — including Armyr's own, if she has her way. That incomparable beauty, Byrhta Ol'Caran. My own cousin, Sighild. And even, I believe, my sister Ashling?"

"I don't think Ashling's serious," Aefric said. "She just enjoys teasing me."

"Oh, she wouldn't tease about marriage," Zoleen said. "If she offers, she means it. I know she favors women, but the two of you would make a match good enough for her to overlook that little detail."

"She does like to rhapsodize about the women we could share together."

"Just so," Zoleen said, shaking her head. "Leave it to Ash to make my life more difficult even in this."

Before Aefric could respond to that, Zoleen continued, "And I'm fairly certain there are a bevy of lesser-born candidates as well, yes? Lers and other minor nobles?"

"There are," Aefric said. "Beornric talks of inviting some of them to Water's End."

"Before the princesses arrive," Zoleen said. "Clever. The royal families would have to bargain harder if someone else wins your heart." She squeezed his hand. "What about me, Aefric? Am I out of the running? Or do I still have a shot?"

Only a few days ago, Aefric would have said she was out of the running. That they could never have repaired the damage between them enough for him to consider her seriously as a bride.

But now...

"I make no promises here and now," he warned.

"I'm not asking for any," she said.

"But yes, Zoleen, you still have a shot."

"Then I shall have to do my best to make sure my arrow finds a truer mark than any of my foes," she said, determined once more.

Aefric didn't know what to say to that. But Zoleen did.

"With that in mind, Aefric," she said, "may I ask one small boon?"

"What?"

"One kiss, to send me on my way?" She quickly added, "Here and now, between only us, not out on the docks where others will be watching. A kiss. Not a statement. A—"

Aefric brought one hand to her smooth cheek and guided her mouth to his.

Zoleen's lips tasted of the sweet wine they'd shared with lunch.

The kiss deepened. With a small sound of pleasure, she released his hand and put one arm around his waist while her other hand buried itself in his hair.

He slid his free hand around to rest on the small of her back.

How long that kiss went on, Aefric wasn't sure. But it ended only because Vria knocked on his carriage door and said, "Your grace, we've reached the docks of Behal."

When she pulled back, Zoleen was smiling the way she had that time he'd seen her beat his seneschal, Kentigern, at chess. Aefric hadn't thought she'd "won" anything there in the carriage, per se, but it *had* been a marvelous kiss.

Nevertheless, she departed, saying nothing more than, "See you soon, Aefric."

And Aefric knew, as he sat there a moment before leaving his own carriage, that he would still thinking about that kiss for the rest of the day.

Maev. Byrhta. Sighild. Zoleen.

Why, oh why, would Beornric want to bring yet more candidates for his hand to Water's End?

He was having a hard enough time choosing as it was.

THERE WERE THREE TRUE CITIES IN THE DUCAL LANDS OF DEEPWATER. One, of course, was Water's End. The ducal seat. Another was Ajenmoor, the port city at the mouth of the Searun River which, as the name might suggest, ran from Lake Deepwater to the Risen Sea.

The third was Behal. Near the southern tip of massive Lake Deepwater. It was said to hold the first ducal castle built in these lands, and was a major source of trade both along the Kingsroad as well as the Haven, Tainfyr, Golden and Fyrsa Rivers.

Its main docks, inside great Lake Deepwater itself, were always busy. But Aefric and his caravan weren't at the main docks. They were at the small, secondary docks, down where the high arching Kingsroad Bridge crossed the Haven.

These secondary docks weren't intended for large ships. They mostly handled small fishing and pleasure craft that sailed the Haven and Tainfyr.

But Behal knew that the duke was coming. And Behal's castellan, Ser Grey, had arranged with the local mayor to have the secondary docks cleared of their usual traffic by late morning, to allow two larger ships to dock there.

The first — and, honestly a ship small enough not to need special arrangements — was Zoleen's. A two-masted sloop amusingly called the *Duchess' Errand Boy*. Zoleen's ladies were on deck, resplendent in their finery, and her guards stood beside them. Two knights in shining full plate armor, and at least a dozen soldiers.

The second ship was Aefric's, and the real reason the secondary docks had to be cleared. This ship was large enough to carry the whole of his party without anyone feeling pressed for space.

In fact, this was one of the two massive warships that patrolled Lake Deepwater. Not that they could have left the lake. They were too big to sail under the Kingsroad Bridge, and had too deep a drag for the Searun River.

This ship was the *Calming Influence*.

Aefric escorted Zoleen onto the wooden dock and right up to the gangplank of her ship.

"It's been a pleasure traveling with you," Aefric said. "I hope the rest of your voyage is swift and safe."

"Thank you, Aefric," she said. "And I hope the same for you."

She reached up and stroked his cheek, while giving him a private smile.

So much for not wanting to put on a show. Aefric knew well that all of her ladies were watching Zoleen give Aefric an intimate touch, while calling him by name.

"I'll see you soon, dear Aefric," she said, and Aefric made himself turn away, so no one could say he watched her walk all the way up the gangplank.

Though he had to admit. It was tempting.

When he returned to his caravan on the cobbled streets beside the dock itself, he saw Beornric and Slishan quarreling in hushed tones.

"Good," Slishan said, turning as Aefric approached. "Your grace, perhaps you can settle this for me."

"He'll tell you the same thing I did," Beornric said, sounding frustrated.

"What seems to be at issue?" Aefric asked.

"Your good knight-adviser seems to think that I and mine should turn about here and leave you unguarded the rest of the way."

"I agree with him," Aefric said. "I am and have been most grateful for your escort. But from here, it is no longer necessary."

"But I had heard your grace was to see these borogs all the way to the coast," the baroness objected. "That's at least another fifty or sixty miles. More than that if you make for Ajenmoor."

"By land, yes," Aefric said, calmly. "But we take to water, now. On this great beast."

He gestured to the *Calming Influence*, with its three masts and multiple decks, its pairs of aft catapults and forward ballistae.

"And if I find it insufficient," Aefric said, "I can summon its twin, the *Lake Monster*. What protection could I really need beyond that?"

Slishan frowned. "I do not question the value of your grace's warships—"

"Slishan," Aefric said, "honor has been more than satisfied by this portion of the arrangements we spoke of. Trust me. We need escort no farther. Redsoil needs you more than I do. Not to mention that without his baroness *or* his castellan, your seneschal is likely at his wits end by now."

Slishan somehow managed to frown and smile at the same time.

"In friendship," Aefric said, "I tell you it is time to turn back."

"Your grace is certain?"

"I am," he said. "And I shall inform his majesty of the aid you provided after the unforeseeable betrayal of your castellan."

Slishan's nostrils flared in a deep breath. She nodded brusquely.

"Your grace is most kind." She bowed. "Then I and mine shall take our leave. May the winds favor you, your grace."

"And may the rains make a hole for you," Aefric said, and they parted ways.

Once she was out of earshot, and under cover of the noise of Aefric's knights, soldiers, carts and borogs all boarding the *Calming Influence*, Beornric spoke.

"Even if our destination wasn't the Dragonscar, I wouldn't have wanted her along now. We'd need a second ship. She's slow us down."

"So you do think speed still matters?"

"Don't you?"

Aefric nodded, and spoke quietly. "I'm not sure what game the king and queen are playing, but the queen seemed intent on whether or not we'd complete our journey within an aett. The less time we take, I think, the better."

Beornric made a show of looking off at the departing *Duchess' Errand Boy*. "What do you think she learned from us?"

"The queen?"

Beornric nodded.

"Nothing. Not from Zoleen."

"You sound sure."

"Zoleen was quite clear on this point," Aefric said. "And she knows the consequences, if she goes behind my back again."

"She's back on the list, isn't she?" Beornric asked with a grin. "I saw the way she stroked your cheek."

"Oh, Beornric, do we *have* to talk about that again?"

"I think it'll be a fine topic to discuss over lunch."

"What if I say no?"

Beornric chuckled. "No good. I saw the satisfied way she walked up that gangplank. That was the walk of a woman who accomplished a mission. And since that mission wasn't for the queen, I can think of only one goal she might have accomplished. Redeeming herself in your eyes."

"Fine," Aefric said with a sigh. "You're right. She's back on the list of bridal candidates."

"Excellent. The only question now is whether she deserves a higher place on that list than Sighild Ol'Masarkor or lower. I suspect lower, because I doubt you want to be bound so closely to the queen and Duchess Ashling. Though that may depend on how much those two would want to make of Sighild's Fyrenn blood, should you marry her..."

Beornric was going on already, and lunch hadn't even been served yet.

***

Lake Deepwater. The first time Aefric glimpsed its eastern shores, during the chaos of a great battle, he'd mistaken it for the Risen Sea.

An understandable mistake, under the circumstances. Especially considering that the lake was more than seventy-five miles long, and nearly forty miles across at its widest point.

Yes, there was a reason the duchy was named after this lake. There were none that could compare within at least three aetts travel.

Today, the winds weren't *against* Aefric, but they weren't helping either. They came from the west, and while he had confidence that the captain could tack to the wind for at least a little speed, it wouldn't be nearly enough.

Not when their destination port was Lachedran, at the northern-most tip of the lake.

And so, cutting short his lunch of shredded roast beef with cheese — as well as his unwanted conversation about bridal candidates — Aefric mounted the high afterdeck and cast for a spell he learned from Sirondfar, Ashling's ducal wizard.

Sirondfar was a *ventavis*, a master of the magic of weather and birds, and he knew well the spells that would make the wind serve him. Aefric himself knew little of weather magic. But Sirondfar's wind spells had come in handy for him more than once.

He'd even had enough practice with them now that maintaining them for a few hours wouldn't steal *his* wind.

With strong winds now filling the *Calming Influence's* sails, it soared across the waters. The cool spray kissing Aefric's sun-warmed face made him smile, as he remained on the afterdeck, maintaining that spell through the afternoon.

And he cast his spells well. Instead of arriving at Lachedran well into the evening, the sun was only just setting when the *Calming Influence* put into port.

As Aefric's caravan disembarked onto the westernmost pier of the pale, beechwood docks, he noted not only the complete lack of pomp and circumstance, but the lack of any formal greeting at all.

That would be strange for most towns. But for Lachedran, it was *very* strange indeed. Especially given that the local mayor, Brangton Couglas, seemed to *love* Aefric's attention.

Hard to believe Couglas wasn't here, making a speech, and ensuring that all the local citizens knew that he, personally, knew the duke.

Aefric pondered that as he pulled his cloak a little tighter against the chill breeze of oncoming evening.

In fact, now that he took a moment to look around, it seemed that there wasn't even the usual work being done near this pier.

Further down the docks, Aefric could see the usual business going on. Dockworkers loading ships that planned to sail on the morning tide. Sailors disembarking at the end of their shifts, ready to hit the taverns and inns.

But the three nearest piers were all empty of ships and business. Not even the town watch, coming to check out the new arrival...

"Ah," Beornric said, stepping up beside Aefric. "You've noticed the peace and quiet. Nice, isn't it?"

"Would be," Aefric said, checking the nearby streets for any parades that might by lying in ambush. "If I thought I could trust it."

"You can," Beornric said. "I made arrangements with Grey this morning at Behal for her to contact Mayor Brangton. So he's been told that we're to come through in secret, on a royal mission. Looks as though he's upholding his end of things."

"Oh, he must be *biting through his tongue.*"

"Likely," Beornric said, smiling. "But you should know. I had to promise that we'd spend two nights here on our way back to Water's End. One so he can show you off, and another so you can meet with his wife about your 'lost lers' project."

Ah, yes. The mayor's wife. Karaleca Ol'Nara. She and her brother Morgard were both the children of a ler, displaced by the Godswalk Wars. She was leading an effort on Aefric's behalf, to find other citizens of Deepwater similarly displaced.

Aefric wanted *all* such refugees found and helped, but the nobles would be easiest to find, in most cases.

"I'm sure Leca has made good progress."

"I agree. She's a sharp one."

"Wait," Aefric said, turning to Beornric. "You made these arrangements with Grey? This morning?"

"Yes," Beornric said, practically radiating amusement. "We spoke on the docks. For several minutes."

"She was down there herself?"

"She was."

"How did I miss this?"

"*Well,*" Beornric said, all but laughing now, "you *were* a bit distracted by a certain young noblewoman..."

"If you bring up the list again right now, I'll throw you into the lake."

"Wouldn't dream of it," Beornric said. "After all. *Someone's* got to organize this mess."

Aefric was pretty sure that Beornric was chuckling into his mustaches as he moved off then, to organize the caravan.

They had to get out of Lachedran as soon as possible. Even with an agreement in place, he didn't trust Mayor Brangton not to find Aefric's presence too tempting to ignore.

With Zoleen gone and the rains a good hour to the east, Aefric didn't summon his carriage. Instead, he and Beornric rode with the knights. First by the dying sun, and then by the light of his own spells, cast on swords and pikes along the line.

They rode north out of Lachedran until they passed the last of the outlying farms, hewing east, close to the edge of the rolling foothills between them and the mighty Threepeaks Mountains.

After days of traveling with so large an escort, their camp that night seemed small and quiet. But in a comfortable way. As though the guests had gone, and only family remained.

They rose early the next morning, and pushed to cover more ground. Not so much by increasing speed, which would've been hard on the draft horses with their carts. Instead, they took the fewest, and shortest, breaks they could afford, while not stressing the horses or themselves too badly.

Good land up here, for overland travel. Fields that would make good farmland at some point, along with occasional hills and small groves of trees, mostly oaks and maples.

Nevertheless, Aefric was pleased that the old scout trails were getting turned into something like a real road. One of the benefits of bringing down gold from the Dragonscar.

Here and now, it was helping them make better time. By spring, the way would likely be wide and smooth.

Following that developing road, they stayed west of Lake Dragonskull and the Elquill River, which ran down out of the mountains to feed the lake.

The sun was just starting to set as they approached a clearing on the east side of the road. It looked to have been used as a camp many times, and even had stacks of ready firewood, and a dug-out ring of stone, for a large campfire.

The caravan was making for the clearing, when Aefric called out, "Ho! Steady on! We do not stop here!"

His orders were carried up and down the line, and the caravan began to pick up speed again.

Once they were riding once more at traveling pace, Beornric said,

"I'm not sure that covering a few more miles is worth forsaking such a good campsite."

"We're not covering only a few miles," Aefric said. "We're making for the ridge above the Dragonscar."

Beornric frowned. "Either way, we get there tomorrow. That's the eighth day. Why push through the night now?"

"Because this way we arrive at the *start* of the eighth day," Aefric said. "I should have time to ensure that the borogs are settled with their clan before sunset. If we wait…"

"If we wait, we arrive late afternoon, assuming we make good time," Beornric said. "Is there some borog concern about sunset that I don't know about?"

"No, but there might be a royal concern," Aefric said, frowning. "This way, the task of getting the borogs settled in the Dragonscar is *completed* by sunset on the eighth day. Just under one full aett. If not, then I miss that deadline."

"A deadline you set, on a task you chose," Beornric said softly.

"Yes and no," Aefric said. "I've suspected for some time now that part of the conflict between their majesties involves both me and the borogs."

"It seems likely," Beornric said.

"Well, then part of the issue might be how well I handle the borogs. Given that the queen fixated on whether or not I completed bringing the two groups together within an aett, I want to make sure I do."

"Didn't you say that the timing might have to do more with something else? That she thought the king might be using this as a smokescreen?"

"Yes," Aefric said with a sigh. "But when do either of them do only one thing, when they can accomplish two at the same time?"

Beornric laughed. "I do believe you're coming to understand what it means to deal with royalty."

Aefric frowned deeply. Beornric's words had triggered a question. But it was a question he didn't want to ask, because he knew what would follow.

Unfortunately, Beornric had been coming to know his duke too well.

The big knight grinned.

"Why yes, your grace," he said in teasing tones. "That *does* mean that marrying a princess will likely enmesh you in more games like this one."

"I'm sure I don't know what you mean," Aefric grumbled, trying to think of a subject change, when all he could really think about was that Beornric's words were true about Maev, as well as any other princesses he might consider marrying.

If anything, those words were *truer* about Maev. Because it was *her* father, King Colm, who'd put Aefric in this position in the first place...

"Well," Beornric said. "Then let me enlighten you. You see, of all the bridal candidates you have so far — and at the moment I'm speaking of only the major candidates — only Byrhta Ol'Caran and Sighild Ol'Masarkor come without a direct connection to the royal family. Although, to be sure, Queen Eppida would play up their kinship, should Sighild become your bride..."

This was an important conversation. Aefric knew it. Beornric always managed to slip real, useful information into these discussions about Aefric's bridal options.

But did Beornric have to *enjoy* it so much?

THE MOON WAS GONE NOW, HIDING SOMEWHERE BEHIND THE CLOUDS above the Threepeaks Mountains. But dawn was still an hour or two away when Aefric and his caravan arrived at the makeshift camp up on the southern ridge above the Dragonscar.

The camp had once been nothing more than a tiny, hidden spot where scouts slept. While they kept an eye on the borogs in the Dragonscar, yes, but also while they watched the duchy of Silverlake. Because the northern ridge above that great chasm that was the

Dragonscar was the end of Aefric's lands and the beginning of Duke Wylyn's.

That tiny camp had expanded over the season-plus since Clan Thunder Stick had begun digging gold for Aefric. Every two or three aetts, a small, heavily guarded caravan came up from Lachedran to collect that gold, before taking it south to Water's End.

The camp reflected that. Enough of the grassland had been cleared of spare trees to accommodate about forty people, accompanied by horses, carts and mules. Stone rings for three small campfires, rather than one large one, to reduce what Silverlake's scouts could see from the northern ridge.

Three scouts were in residence at the moment, and at the sight of Aefric's spell-lights on the poles that carried his banner, those scouts leapt to attention.

The caravan immediately began to make camp.

Aefric wondered if he had enough time for something to eat. He was still tasting that jerked boar he'd eaten a handful of hours ago. And even three good apples hadn't chased away that salty, gamy flavor...

One of the scouts approached. A tanned, weathered woman who'd seen at least five summers more than Aefric.

"Your grace," she said with a bow. "We were not told of your coming."

"What is your name, soldier?" Aefric asked.

"Delari, your grace," she said with a bow. "Senior scout at this camp."

"Well, Delari," Aefric said, dismounting and pulling the Brightstaff from its sling, "there's a reason you weren't told. This is the final stage of a royal mission."

She bowed again. "How may we aid your grace?"

"Talk with Ser Beornric," Aefric said, knowing there was no need to point him out. He was known to everyone in the military, here in Deepwater, even if he hadn't been obviously in charge of setting up camp.

"At once, your grace," she said, and moved off.

Aefric walked toward the back of the caravan, where the borogs from Netar were only just getting out of their carts. Along the way, he cast the Soulfist linguistic spell, mentally reminding himself to practice his Borog, so he wouldn't need the spell for long.

"*Chief!*" Lo'kroll said, as soon as he saw Aefric approaching. He quickly organized the borogs into two ranks.

Aefric looked them over. No unexpected bruises. No new injuries. Good. He snorted approval.

"*Gather the dead,*" he said. "*Me and me come together now.*"

The cheer the borogs gave then wasn't a verbal shout, the way humans did. Rather it was a combination of stomping and scraping their feet, the way they would have before going into battle. A means of expressing excitement and anticipation.

Beornric hustled over to Aefric.

"Your grace, you aren't doing what I think you are."

"We're here," Aefric said. "Of course I am."

"You need sleep. It'll keep until morning."

Aefric did need sleep. He could feel that slight soreness to his eyes and that stretched ache in his arms and legs. That touch of heaviness to his movements.

He'd slept well on this trip, when compared to how he used to sleep as an adventurer. Actual padding beneath his bedroll. Regular, hot food, and so on.

But compared to the way he'd been living since being made duke, conditions had been positively barbaric. And the difference was proving harder on him than expected.

Apparently the soft life of a duke wasn't ideal for maintaining field readiness. Who knew?

Oh. Right. *Everybody.*

"Doesn't matter," Aefric said. "We're here. I'd like to get this done."

"It'll keep till morning," Beornric said firmly. "Get some rest. A few hours, anyway."

"No," Aefric said, shaking his head. "The borogs down in the Dragonscar will figure out that more borogs are up here on the ridge.

I think they could smell them. And I can't exactly send a runner down to Ge'rek to tell him that everything's fine."

"You *knew* you were going to do this tonight," Beornric accused.

"Yes," Aefric said. "Just as I knew you'd try to talk me out of it."

"You're taking your knights along, at least."

"Not as guards," Aefric said, "no. All of these borogs are part of my own clan. They'll all fight to protect me."

"And if there's something more than borogs down there?"

"Delari!" Aefric called.

"Here, your grace," she said, running over and bowing quickly.

"How are things in the Dragonscar? Any threats I should know about?"

"Only the borogs near here, your grace," she said. "And I believe we're not supposed to count them a threat."

"That's right," Aefric said, turning back to Beornric. "Next question?"

Beornric tugged his mustaches, but that didn't help the sour look on his face.

"None," he said. "But I wish to make clear that I believe even your grace does his best thinking when well-rested. And that this course of action might be ill-advised."

"Noted," Aefric said. "But you know why the timing of this is important. If I can complete it before dawn of the eighth day, so much the better."

"Very well, your grace," Beornric said. "I shall see to the camp then. But Micham and Leppina *will* come along. Just in case of *unknown* threats."

"Very well," Aefric said.

Micham and Leppina were quick to join Aefric, as he gathered his borogs and made for the Dragonscar itself.

THE DRAGONSCAR.

The story went that, thousands and thousands of years ago, when the Risen Sea was still a vast valley, one of the great dragons of yore died while flying.

This dragon was said to have crashed into solid rock. But the dragon was so big and powerful, that even in its death throes it tore its way through more than a hundred fifty miles of rock before finally reaching its end.

A fantastic story.

But Aefric wondered if the truth might be even more fantastic. Because he'd ridden to the end of the Dragonscar. He'd seen the massive skeleton left behind by that ancient dragon.

Was it large enough to have caused the Dragonscar? Yes.

But...

That skeleton, it wasn't facing into the rock. It was facing *outward*, toward the sea. And the *shape* of the Dragonscar. It could have matched the pattern of the damage done by a dragon's breath. If that dragon had first put its jaw on the ground. Perhaps, as it lay dying in its cave, deep inside the rock.

But could any dragon — even one the size of that great skeleton — have created that chasm with a single dying breath?

A scary thing to contemplate.

And yet, Aefric could never enter the Dragonscar without thinking about it. Even now. Scant hours before dawn, after a long, hard ride through the night.

Fortunately, what had been a tricky descent of more than a hundred feet this spring had been eased by engineers and stonemasons. Turned into a true, proper pass, that led an easy, wide descent, with several switchbacks, from the ridge down into the Dragonscar itself.

A beautiful place, seen in the light of the Brightstaff's yellow diamond. If stark in its beauty. Solid rock in browns and reds, but with occasional patches that could even be called beige.

Once the chasm walls had been jagged. But centuries — or perhaps millennia — of winds and rains had worn their edges round.

Winds that never really seemed to stop coming in from the Risen Sea. Even here, more than a hundred miles from the coast, Aefric could feel the ghost of their bite. And possibly, unless his tired mind played tricks on him, smell hints of their salt air.

Aefric led the descent. Lo'kroll followed, two paces back, flanked by Micham and Leppina.

Lo'kroll had his maul in hand, of course, but the knights kept their weapons sheathed, for now.

The rest of the borogs followed, in an order chosen by Lo'kroll, based on their current standing. With those most deserving at the back right now, as honor guard for those who carried the dead.

The party had barely reached the chasm floor when Lo'kroll sniffed the air and said, *"God metal."*

Excited snorts and stamps came from back along the line of borogs.

No surprise that they could smell it already. Not far ahead of them now as they moved deeper into the Dragonscar, were three caves on the south side, and two on the north. Two of the three caves on the south side held gold veins, as did one cave on the north side. Though the south side veins were far, far richer.

Aefric had to push his tired legs a little faster now. The borogs were eager, and it wouldn't do for them to feel constrained by the pace of their chief.

When they reached the place of those five caves, Aefric turned to the south side and thumped the butt of the Brightstaff onto the rocky ground, letting out a thunderclap.

"Thunder Stick!" came the call from inside the two closest caves.

"Thunder Stick!" the borogs behind him called out as well.

Already Aefric thought he could hear snorts of puzzlement coming from those caves, but he must've imagined them. There was no way he could have heard them yet.

But soon those snorts were audible enough, as borogs began to file out of those two caves. All of them carrying iron weapons, and falling into ranks in front of their caves of god metal.

More than two hundred borogs came out of those caves. Two-hundred-fifteen, by Aefric's count. And the two last borogs to emerge were Ge'rek and Po'rek.

Aefric was embarrassed to admit that when he'd first met Ge'rek and Po'rek, he'd thought of them as "the larger borog" and "the smaller borog," respectively.

Since then, he'd noticed little details. A slightly darker shade to Ge'rek's hide, and a slightly wider space to his eyes. And Po'rek had a fairly narrow horn for a borog, and a way of standing that made him look heavier than he was.

They were the only two to come out of the caves not carrying weapons. Instead, each carried a heavy stone basket filled with gold ore. Perfectly clean gold ore, without a speck of dirt.

"*God metal for chief!*" Ge'rek said, as he and Po'rek put down the baskets.

"*God metal for chief!*" the other borogs called out. The ones behind Aefric, as well as the ones in front of him.

Aefric snorted a grateful acknowledgment of the gold, which got an impressed snort from Ge'rek and a foot-scrape of disbelief from Po'rek.

But then Ge'rek snorted fury. "*Lo'kroll!*"

"*Ge'rek!*" Lo'kroll said, stamping one foot and stepping forward.

"*Did chief say fight?*" Aefric asked.

Both Ge'rek and Lo'kroll snorted hesitant agreement than he hadn't.

"*But, chief,*" Po'rek said. "*Blood spills between them.*"

That meant that each blamed the other for at least one death. The idea was that blood would not stop spilling until one of them was dead.

But there had to be a way around this.

"*One clan now,*" Aefric said. "*Thunder Stick.*"

"*Thunder Stick!*" the borogs cried.

"*Old crimes die with old clans.*"

Lo'kroll and Ge'rek both looked ready to kill one another. And much as Aefric liked Ge'rek, he didn't like his chances in a fight between the two of them. Lo'kroll was a full head taller, and perhaps a quarter again as wide.

"*But, chief,*" Po'rek said. "*Ik and ik always same clan.*"

"Old clan is dead," Aefric said. *"Old wound is dead."*

"Blood spills," Lo'kroll said.

"And the dark swallows all," Ge'rek agreed.

"Even chief cannot stop blood," Po'rek said with a regretful snort.

No way around it then. Damn. Well, if Aefric couldn't stop it, he could at least control it.

"Lo'kroll. There." Aefric pointed.

Lo'kroll went to stand in the indicated spot, some twenty paces away.

"Ge'rek. There."

Aefric pointed to an equidistant spot. Now the two stood forty paces away.

"Where blood spills, blood spills," Aefric said. *"But now and after, one clan."* He thumped his chest. *"Me."*

Aefric went and stood with the Dragonscar borogs. He stomped the ground *"Me."*

The borogs before him all stomped the ground with impressive synchronicity. The sound echoed up and down the chasm.

Aefric went to stand with the borogs from Netar. He stomped the ground. *"Me."*

Those borogs all stomped the ground, trying to match the volume of the other group. They had no prayer of doing so, but it was a valiant effort.

Aefric walked up to Ge'rek. Stomped his foot on the rocky ground. *"Me."*

Ge'rek stomped agreement.

Finally, Aefric walked up to Lo'kroll. Stomped his foot one more time. *"Me."*

Lo'kroll stomped his foot.

"One clan," Aefric said. *"Thunder Stick."*

"Thunder Stick!" the borogs all shouted, and began stomping their feet.

Aefric turned to Po'rek. *"Weapons?"*

"They choose," Po'rek said.

Lo'kroll hefted his maul.

Ge'rek called for a longsword. Three borogs raced to be the one to provide it. Ge'rek chose the sword he liked best, and its provider stomped his pride.

"*Ge'rek and Lo'kroll say blood spills,*" Aefric said. "*Chief say, spill all.*"

That was what came out when he intended to tell them to start their fight.

Ge'rek and Lo'kroll trotted closer, horns lowered, until they were only five or six paces distant from each other.

Aefric's jaw slackened with realization.

There was a slight hitch in Lo'kroll's gait. When Aefric had fought the huge borog only a few days ago, his movements had been smooth as any great warrior's.

But here and now, he was favoring his right side. Just a little, but enough to say he wasn't fully healed.

Surely the cleric of Nilasah had left him something to...

Oh. He hadn't trusted the healer's brew, without the healer around to blame if something went wrong.

Borogs didn't worship Nilasah. And without Aefric ordering him to follow the healer's instructions, Lo'kroll hadn't done so.

Ge'rek spotted the weakness. Started circling to Lo'kroll's right. Lo'kroll moved left, holding the circle.

Ge'rek snorted insults at Lo'kroll. Demeaning the bigger borog's capabilities in battle. Lo'kroll snorted insults right back, deriding Ge'rek's size and muscles.

Ge'rek lowered his head. Started a charge.

Lo'kroll lowered his head. Raised his maul to intercept.

Ge'rek pulled up short and slashed at Lo'kroll's arms. Perhaps aiming for the scar Aefric had left in their fight.

Lo'kroll yanked his maul up, so his arms were out of range.

But the cut had been a feint. Ge'rek lowered his head and charged.

Lo'kroll couldn't get the heavy maul back down in time.

Ge'rek's horn tore into Lo'kroll's right side.

Lo'kroll trumpeted pain. Tried to bring his maul down to intercept.

Ge'rek's sword was faster. It bit deep into the freshly opened wound. Blood and worse gushed in its wake.

Lo'kroll finally managed to bring the heavy iron head of his maul into Ge'rek's side, but there wasn't much behind the blow.

Ge'rek stepped back.

Lo'kroll fell to the rocky ground and died.

Aefric started to say something, but Po'rek snorted softly that Aefric should wait.

Ge'rek stood there, watching Lo'kroll's life bleed away, until the blood stopped flowing.

"Blood spilled," Ge'rek called out and stomped one foot. *"Ge'rek stopped the flow."*

"Ge'rek!" the borogs all shouted, stomping their feet to acknowledge his victory.

Feeling as though he had no choice, Aefric stomped his feet too. He was sorry that Lo'kroll came all this way only to die. But if he had to choose between Lo'kroll and Ge'rek, that was no choice at all.

THERE WAS NO BIG CEREMONY OR RITUAL TO INCORPORATE THE NEW borogs into Clan Thunder Stick.

Apparently, by defeating a rival chief in single combat — Lo'kroll, in Netar's mines — Aefric had simply won the right to take worthy members of the losing clan to join his.

It was unusual to claim the *whole* of the losing chief's clan, but there was precedent.

So after the fight between Ge'rek and Lo'kroll, there was only the matter of adding Lo'kroll's body to those that had died at the hands of the bounty hunters, and then a small service for them.

Po'rek led the service. It seemed that he'd been named the clan's Godspeaker. A position below chief, but about equal with chief's hand, and an important adviser.

Po'rek told the tale of the great god Keduk, who first taught borogs to form clans. It was Keduk who judged the dead. Those who lived and died for clan and blood above all would be welcomed to join His clan in death.

Those who were not chosen were sent to the Flayer for punishment. That they might learn to put clan before all else.

Po'rek then, in the chilly gray light of predawn, went from corpse to corpse, reciting one or two deeds each had done for clan, and how each had died. Recommending each of the dead to Keduk with prayers and blessings.

Finally, the pyre. But not a funeral pyre as humans knew it. The borogs would work the flames so that the bodies took as long to burn as possible. It was said that the greater they'd been in life, the longer their bodies would take to burn, and the farther their smoke could be smelled.

Aefric did not have to stay for that (Ge'rek and Po'rek both made that clear). He ignited the fire by hand, there in the center of the rocky floor of the Dragonscar, but he left the clan to tend the flames and handle the bodies.

Dawn was only peeking over the horizon when he, Micham and Leppina reached the camp atop the southern ridge.

The camp had been arranged in a pattern that had grown familiar to Aefric now. He knew without looking which pavilions were where. Where the carts and horses were kept. Where the guards were patrolling.

The familiarity of it brought a smile to his tired lips. These were good men and women, who served him. If any of them had uttered a word of complaint about this strange mission, Aefric hadn't heard it.

His soldiers and knights looked to just be starting their day. The campfires burned merrily, tended by one of the scouts, and Aefric could smell that they were preparing leftovers from last night's roast lamb.

His stomach rumbled and his mouth watered, but food was a secondary consideration just then.

"Beornric," Aefric called, fighting a yawn as he walked into camp, heading straight for his pavilion. "I believe I'm ready for a few hours sleep before we start our journey back to Water's End."

"I've little doubt," Beornric said, approaching from his left. Doubtless close to the best vantage point for watching down into the Dragonscar. "But unfortunately, sleep must be delayed."

Aefric turned to complain, and realized that his knight-adviser wasn't approaching alone.

Nayoria, the royal wizard, walked beside him. Her dark complexion and tight, black curls as fresh as though she'd slept a full night. Which meant that either she had mastered teleportation or she'd cleaned up with a spell while Aefric ascended the pass.

A spell, he decided. No way her robes — dark red and light gray — would be so spotless otherwise. She wore three wands at her belt, as well as her obsidian rod.

"Nayoria," Aefric said, leaning only a little on the Brightstaff. "A pleasure to see you. Though I must admit, an unexpected one."

"Not an official visit, your grace," she said with a smile. "I happened to be passing through on my way to Ajenmoor, and wished to stop in and offer greetings."

"You have business in Ajenmoor?"

"A ship awaits to carry me across the Risen Sea."

"Anything I can help with?"

"Your grace is most kind to offer, but I travel on personal business." She met Aefric's eye as she continued. "Though I would appreciate a brief chat in private."

"My pavilion is right over here," Aefric said, pointing. Though it likely didn't need to be pointed out, given that it featured the Deepwater sigil, and was the only pavilion with guards standing outside the entrance.

"Ser Beornric," she said, "you're welcome to hear my words as well."

"Certainly, lord wizard," Beornric said, and together the three entered Aefric's pavilion.

With a word, Aefric lit the small, strategically placed stones whose glow now made the interior cheerfully bright.

The three of them sat on camp chairs, around a chest.

"There's food and drink in the chest," Aefric said, "if you would like either."

"No, thank you, your grace," she said. "I wish only a moment of your time."

She lowered her voice.

"As a policy, I do not deliver messages for the king. But in this case, I am doing his majesty a personal favor. And I truly am bound across the Risen Sea on a personal matter, so I did not have to go out of my way."

"I understand," Aefric said.

It was true that magic could speed communications beyond any other current means. But it was also true that this would require wizards and other magic-users to become little more than glorified messengers.

So far, that was a line that no one was willing to be seen crossing. The main exception was the occasional delivery, couched as a personal favor.

"What word, then, from his majesty?" Beornric asked softly.

"I must first ask that your grace confirm for me what I believe my eyes saw. Did your grace truly integrate the borogs from Netar with his clan in the Dragonscar? The one known, I believe, as Thunder Stick?"

"I did," Aefric said. "And before dawn broke on the eighth day after I left Netar."

"Then this is the message his majesty bid me deliver."

Aefric sat forward as she pulled a vellum scroll from her pouch, sealed in green wax with the oak tree of Armyr.

Aefric reached for the scroll.

Nayoria pulled it out of reach.

"Before I hand this over, I wish to be clear about something," she said, now holding the scroll in both hands. "I do not know what this scroll contains. I do not know what matter it pertains to. But whatever it says, I am not a part of it. This is between his majesty and your grace. Am I understood?"

"Of course," Aefric said. "Why would I expect otherwise?"

"Because intrigue is afoot," she said simply. "And here I come to you at dawn, well away from your castle, delivering a secret message from his majesty."

"You know more about this than you're saying," Beornric said, but not as an accusation.

"I am a wizard," she said with a smile. "I always know more than I say." She turned back to Aefric. "But in my time as royal wizard, I have managed to stay out of the castle intrigues." She held up the scroll. "And this is no exception. Whatever this is, I deliver it only as a favor for a man I have come to call friend, while I am about business of my own."

"I understand," Aefric said. "And in case it becomes important later, thank you for your clarity now."

She nodded, and handed over the scroll. She stood.

"May I speak frankly for a moment, your grace?"

"Please do," Aefric said.

"I ... have reason to suspect that your grace may become more involved in the royal court than he has been. Should this prove to be the case, I would offer the following advice."

She pointed at the scroll.

"There are times when intrigue suffuses the very air at Armityr. When anything you do, whether it is delivering a message for a friend or delivering a number of borogs from an untimely death, may be used by someone else for their own purposes. Learn to recognize those times, your grace. And when they come, breathe carefully."

She left then, and Aefric looked at Beornric.

"Did you find that as disturbing as I did?" he asked.

"Probably not, your grace," Beornric said. "But then, I lived at Armityr for a number of years. What concerns me more is why she thinks you might become more involved with the royal court."

"His majesty gave me Netar," Aefric said. "Perhaps he hopes I'll choose to live closer to the capital?"

"Perhaps," Beornric said. "Or perhaps he plans to name you to his council."

Aefric looked at the scroll in his hands, suddenly less eager to open it.

"He wouldn't," Aefric said. "He needs me out here, ruling his largest duchy. Protecting his largest stretch of coastline. Making sure recovery from the wars continues at the pace I've set."

"Only one way to find out," Beornric said, nodding at the scroll.

Aefric opened it and began to read.

My Dear Duke of Deepwater,

Well done, Aefric! I knew I was right to put my faith in you. You have done me a great favor by handling Netar the way you did. And an even greater favor by joining those borogs to your others in the Dragonscar both successfully, and within an aett.

An aett!

Many here at Armityr believed that you would be endlessly slowed down by the borogs fighting among themselves. That you would be lucky to reach the Dragonscar within twelve days, let alone ten.

And yet, even with bounty hunters and the queen herself delaying you, still you managed it within but an aett.

Unquestionably, this proves that the borogs show you obedience as true as any knight's. How you continue to produce such miracles, I do not know. But you must know that you are becoming invaluable to me.

I cannot reward you overtly for this. Too many would take it as gloating on my part. But I will reward you all the same. Look for it to come soon.

A great many things are in motion right now. Make ready for war come springtime, and be ready yourself if I need you in the interim.

Magnificently done, my duke.

By the hand of His Majesty,
Colm Stronghand
King of Armyr

WHEN AEFRIC FINISHED READING THE LETTER, HE GAVE IT TO BEORNRIC to read while he pondered its contents.

He dug among the food and drink in the chest to pull out a waterskin and two silver goblets. He poured, then set one goblet on the chest in front of Beornric. Sat back in his camp chair and sipped from his own.

"Well," Beornric said as he set the letter down and picked up his goblet. "It seems we don't need to worry about the king disavowing your mission. If anything, he seems to have claimed credit for it."

"That doesn't surprise me," Aefric said, frowning. He wished he'd gotten some sleep. His brain felt a little fuzzy, and most of his muscles were pointing out loudly that his bedroll lay only a few paces away. "I'm more worried about the implications. 'Many things are in motion. Be ready if I need you.' Why might he need me? What else is going on?"

"That's not all," Beornric said, shaking his head.

"I knew I was missing something," Aefric said. "What?"

"Nayoria didn't hand over this scroll until she confirmed what you'd done, and by when."

"You think she had a second scroll?"

Beornric nodded. Sipped his water.

"Why should that matter, though?" Aefric asked. "The other might only have been condolences for failure, or even lesser congratulations for accomplishing the task, albeit not within the timeline."

"The task you set yourself," Beornric said, "on the timeline you set."

"But the king claimed credit for," Aefric said.

"Because he put his faith in you," Beornric said. "He gambled on you. And he won."

"Gambled with whom, though?" Aefric said. "Surely the queen wouldn't bet against me."

"Perhaps, perhaps not."

"You think this is a Fyrenn matter?" Aefric said. "The king always said that when Fyrenn interests were involved, the queen became tenacious as a werewolf."

"Just the queen?" Beornric asked, one eyebrow high.

"No," Aefric said. "He was warning me that all Fyrenn women shared this trait. Implying Zoleen. Though I don't know. She…"

Aefric shook his head, but his brain still felt fuzzy. "We're getting off track."

"There's no real way for us to know the answer here," Beornric said. "Any more than we can guess what might or might not've been in that second letter."

"So I guess the only real concern here is my own curiosity."

"And *that* is exactly what Nayoria was warning you about," Beornric said, setting down his goblet. "You can't avoid having one action or another become part of someone else's intrigues. But you *can* avoid becoming *involved* in them yourself. All you have to say is *no*, to your own curiosity."

Aefric slumped in his chair. He was too tired for this conversation.

"My own curiosity? How am I supposed to say no to that? Curiosity is critical for a magic-user. It's a wonder that *Nayoria* contains herself."

"She fights the same urge you feel," Beornric said. "And she wins. So can you."

"Maybe," Aefric said. "But I'm not at Armityr now anyway. Out here, I'm free to be curious."

"'Be ready if I need you,'" Beornric said. "The king's own words. You might get called to the capital at any time."

"Fine," Aefric said. "But he won't call on me this morning. Let me get some sleep."

"Fair enough," Beornric said, getting to his feet and starting for the tent flap.

Just before he reached it, Aefric called to him.

"Beornric," he said. "You served the king for years. What's your best guess about what the king might've written in that second letter?"

Beornric tugged at his mustaches.

"My best guess isn't about the contents of the letter," he said. "So much as about the king's purpose behind all of this."

"The intrigue, you mean?"

"No," Beornric said. "Intrigues and power plays come and go. They might even have been incidental in this case." He shook his head and sighed. "I think his majesty has something in mind for you. But he needed to test you first."

"The borogs, you mean?"

"I mean Netar, the borogs, all of it. One big test."

"And you think I passed?"

"Oh, I'm sure you passed. The only question is, what does it *mean* that you passed?"

"Great," Aefric said, chuckling humorlessly.

"What?" Beornric asked.

"We might as well pack up camp and get moving," Aefric said, standing up and stretching. "If you think I can sleep after that, you're mistaken."

"Sorry," Beornric said with a wistful smile.

"That's all right," Aefric said. "No sense in making everyone sit around waiting while I sleep anyway."

Beornric started to say something. Aefric stopped him with a raised hand.

"I know they would," he said. "But now there's no reason to make them. Let's go home."

SIGN UP FOR STEFON'S NEWSLETTER

Stefon loves to keep in touch with his readers, and loves to keep you reading. The best way for him to do both is for you to sign up for his newsletter.

Sign up at http://www.stefonmears.com/join

If you sign up for Stefon's newsletter, you get...

- Monthly updates about his publishing and travel schedules
- His latest news, in brief, and answers to reader questions
- A free short story for signing up
- List-only offers and occasional specials
- Plus a free short story every month!

ABOUT THE AUTHOR

Stefon Mears has would love a ship like the one Aefric wants. Stefon has more than thirty books to his credit, and he never stops writing. He earned his M.F.A. in Creative Writing from N.I.L.A., and his B.A. in Religious Studies (double emphasis in Ritual and Mythology) from U.C. Berkeley. He's a lifelong gamer and fantasy fan. Stefon lives in Portland, Oregon, with his wife and three cats.

Look for Stefon online:
www.stefonmears.com
himself@stefonmears.com

CPSIA information can be obtained
at www.ICGtesting.com
Printed in the USA
LVHW111502161222
735294LV00005B/11/J